Live Me

A *Pieces of Broken* Novel

CELESTE GRANDE

Cover Design by:
Sommer Stein of Perfect Pear Creative Covers

Cover Photography by:
Perrywinkle Photography

Interior Design and Formatting by:
Christine Borgford, Type A Formatting

Dedication

To my husband, Fred who will stand by my side no matter what for the rest of my life, my baby boy, Christian who has made me realize a love I never knew possible, and (by the time you're reading this) my new baby girl, Cienna who I have yet to meet, but can feel rolling through my belly and my soul already. I **live** you guys. A world where there's no you means there's no me.

"To plant a garden is to believe in tomorrow."
~ *Audrey Hepburn*

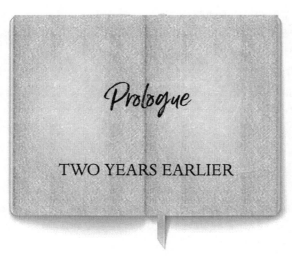

Prologue

TWO YEARS EARLIER

HE'S HERE.

My body stilled. Erratic breaths sputtered through my lips as my eyes darted around for a sign someone was home.

We were alone.

Very alone.

Lounging against the kitchen counter, one foot resting in front of the other, his hands were propped behind him, curling around the edges. With just his eyes, he looked up at me, calm and relaxed as though he was waiting. The corner of his mouth turned up in a cocky grin and he raised a menacing eyebrow. "Hey there, beautiful. I was hoping to catch you here."

My subconscious spit at his casual tone. That word, beautiful, scampered like a thousand tiny bug legs along my skin. Venom and bile pooled in my mouth as I tried to push past my unresponsive senses. "W-Where's Abby?"

Cool and assured, the corner of his lip quirked and I fought to contain the sourness it created in my belly. He pushed off the counter and prowled toward me, his eyes never leaving mine. "I wanted her to relax a little so I sent her for an afternoon at the spa. I told her I'd stay here, get some work done and see her when she got back from her day of pampering. But we both know that was just an excuse."

My legs were numb, forgetting how to work. I wanted to back up. I wanted to run. I wanted to scream . . .

But no one would hear me.

At the very least, I wanted to say no, but every fiber of my being was failing me. I was at his mercy.

And he knew it.

"I've missed you, beautiful. I've been waiting patiently for you to walk through that door. My mouth is watering already. I can actually taste you." Cocking his head to the side, he licked his lips to accentuate his point and my stomach rolled. "Would you like to taste me?"

Please, not again. "No . . ." His chest met mine, cutting off my choked whisper with a sharp intake of breath.

Reaching up, he slid his thumb into my mouth, his eyes concentrating on my lips. A lone tear trailed down my cheek as I braced for the inevitable.

Numbness, please give me numbness.

His body shivered and that sideways grin was back as he pulled his thumb out of my mouth, lowered his head, and began to kiss me.

Mary had a little lamb, little lamb, little lamb . . .

Innocence stolen
A life lost.
Trust broken.
Pieces of me scattered about like a dusting of shattered glass.
Dismembered
Crumbled
A constant beat down A never-ending cycle of torture.
An ache in your brain reminding you of poor decisions.
How one thing—one tiny little thing can change the course of your life.
TAKE. Your Life.
Own it.
Dismantle it.
Wreck it beyond recognition
Stolen
My life was stolen.
Maimed
Destroyed
Distorted to the point it was unrecognizable.
I stumbled about like an incoherent mess through the fog, unsure of what tomorrow would bring.
Truth? More torture? Absolution?
It was anyone's guess. Most of all mine.

Chapter 1

PRESENT DAY

WE'RE ALMOST THERE.

It was nearing dusk, and the heat from the day was being sucked out by a comfortable, cooler breeze. Excitement buzzed through the air and with each step forward, the sounds emanating from an overbearing bass intensified. I wished I could enjoy it the way everyone else seemed to be, the way a typical college-goer would. Instead, I was envious of my friends, looking on at them with longing as they laughed and joked together. They kept a fast pace, anxious to get to the party. None of them noticed I'd been trailing behind them for the last five minutes.

Jostled to the side, I flinched as I grabbed my shoulder. "Hey!"

A guy dressed in only a pair of cargo shorts, his toned body glistening with a sheen of sweat, looked back at me. In a backward jog, he bounced from foot to foot, balancing a sloshing red cup. "Sorry." He tossed me a chaste wink before turning to scurry to the other edge of the lawn.

I scowled, trying to think of something witty to throw at him, but he was gone before one came. *Why the hell am I here? I can't do this.*

Hand still clutching the sore spot, I was about to turn around and go home when Jessie spun to face me, her blonde ringlets whirling in a blur. She slapped her thighs in frustration and jogged back to where I stood. "Come on, Eva!"

"I'm not going." I frowned, still babying my arm.

Jace and Sandra approached, flanking a dissatisfied Jessie, who planted her hands on her curvy hips. "Why are you being so difficult? It'll be
fun. Think of all the hot guys who'll be there."

I thumbed toward the jerk's retreating figure. "You mean the imma-
ture boys like the one who just ran me over?"

Jessie waved her hand. "Po-*tay*-toe Po-*tah*-toe. Just—let's go."

I sighed. "It's a frat party, initiation thingy. Remind me again how
this concerns me?"

"Because it's fun! F-U-N. Fun! Tell her, guys," she prompted.

My brow rose as I turned to Jace, my oldest and dearest friend. I'd
met Jessie and Sandra when I arrived on campus last week, but Jace was
another story. He'd handed me a tissue when a boy made me cry in kin-
dergarten, and we'd been friends ever since. He knew me inside and out;
knew my background and my idiosyncrasies.

I'd forced him to enroll at Columbia with me because I couldn't do
this without him. He was far from the studious type, so I'd pretty much
taken his placement test for him, swapping papers back and forth every
time the proctor looked away. I'd even written his essay. Now I just had
to hope he could keep up with the classes my scores had gotten him into.
He was supposed to be my ace in the hole in situations such as these, but
right now he was failing miserably.

"Jace, a little help here." Impatience coated my voice.

He placed a hand on his chest, a mischievous glint in his eye. "I'm
personally hoping to see some men forced to wear leotards, honey. I'm
with Jessie on this one."

I gritted my teeth. *I'm going to kill you.* I knew he could read my
mind, but he was choosing that moment to play dumb. "I hate you guys."

"Shut your face," Jace threw back. "You need to get the full freshman experience. You'll thank me later." He nearly yanked my arm out of
its socket as he pulled, sending my legs flailing behind me as he dragged
me toward the booming crowd.

Stopping just before the chaos, he gave my hand a sharp squeeze,
acknowledging for the first time how hard this would be for me. I raised
the corner of my mouth in a half smile, then filled my lungs with an exorbitant amount of air to fortify the strength I'd need to get through this.

Truth was, one would never truly know what went on in the mind of Evangelina Ricci. On the outside, I had everything put together, perfectly gift wrapped with a tight little red bow. While inside, I was shattered shards of glass. But, if you lined those pieces up *just* right, when the light hit them, you had a beautiful prism shining a magnificent rainbow for the world to see, love, and appreciate.

That was me. The perfect optical illusion. A master of disguise.

"You ready, baby girl?" Jace asked.

"As ready as I'm gonna be. And don't think I'm not chewing your ass out later for this." I looked at him from the corner of my eye.

He squeezed my finger between his. "Don't worry, I won't be far. If I think it's too much for you, we're out of here."

I nodded, trusting him enough to know he had my best interests at heart. "How do I look?" I flashed a toothy, well-rehearsed smile, batting my green, feline-shaped eyes.

He rolled his eyes. "You know you're heart stopping. Now let's go." He smacked my ass and, like the crack of gunfire at a race, left me in his dust as he jogged into the festivities.

I stood there for a moment, letting my protective gates come crashing down to a locked position as I secured one of my many faces in place.

The imaginary clapperboard snapped.

Let's do this.

Chapter 2

CAUGHT UP WITH JESSIE and Sandra, determined to show them a different Eva. "All right, ladies. You wanted me here, now try and keep up." I tugged one of Sandra's ginger curls in a backward jog.

The girls looped their arms with mine.

"Thank God you're back. I thought we'd lost you for a second there. Where'd you go?" Jessie asked, scooping up the front chunk of her hair and tossing it to the other side.

Uh oh. I was slipping. Time for a Band-Aid. "I'm just tired, and my boyfriend doesn't like me going to these things. Sorry I was being a party pooper," I lied.

"Tell us again why we haven't met this boyfriend?" Sandra inquired.

Because he doesn't exist. I expelled a dramatic huff. "I told you, he goes away to school. Maybe one weekend he'll come here, but I usually go there to see him."

I'd been using that excuse for so long I was sick of it, but it served its purpose. Short weekend trips by myself always helped keep up the façade, strengthening my resolve to be alone and do everything on my own. I was used to solitude, even though I was also used to being crowded—a walking contradiction.

Looking around, I tried to redirect their attention. "Okay, ladies, enough talk. Scope out the keg. I hope you brought your big girl panties. You're gonna need 'em." My mouth slid into a sly grin.

Out of necessity, I'd learned a long time ago how to divert people's attention. It was crucial when they pried a little too deep. The bat of an eyelash and a simple look seemed to enamor them, and I needed it that way. I had it down to a science. I only wished I could see myself through the same eyes they did. I was one big mirage—a house of mirrors. I could keep you running in circles, seeing a million different faces of myself, but none of them were the real, flesh and blood, true-to-life me. They were all different reflections of the pretty face I was forced to look at every day, never revealing the ugliness that lay beneath it.

Dirt billowed up in dusty clouds as we approached the rowdy crowd. *Fun times.* I waved my hands in front of my face to disperse the dirty smoke, taking an inventory of my surroundings. Sweaty guys showing off six-packs they had—or *didn't* have. Cackling girls trying to one-up each other to get noticed. People participating in games in random quadrants of the park while others huddled around a cluster of kegs nestled beside a set of trees.

Bullseye!

I draped my hair over one shoulder and picked at the dirty-blonde ends, zeroing in on the mind-numbing liquid. Beside the keg, a small group of girls was circled around one guy. They stared starry-eyed, taking turns hanging from his sculpted bicep and vying for his attention. I rolled my eyes. They could have him. I just needed a drink to take the edge off and help me blend. I was familiar with guys like him—gorgeous, suave, and toting that cocky, I-can-have-any-girl-I-want attitude.

Normal, I reminded myself. *This is normal. Act fucking normal!*

His eyes lifted from the girls and settled on me as he tried to hold their conversation. I recognized that I'm-coming-to-get-you look. It turned my palms slimy. Taking a deep breath, I flipped an internal switch, turning off my inhibitions.

His mint-green eyes flicked to my fingers as I grabbed the nozzle at the top of the silver cylinder. I pumped the top as fast as I could, trying to pour my drink and get out of there.

I was too slow.

Not more than two-seconds later, cocky Mr. Perfect stepped away from the girls as one of them was mid-sentence, and ambled to my side. His hand was just about to cover mine—to do the honors of pouring—when I slipped in my haste, sending the liquid down the outside of the cup and over my jittery fingers. I shook off my hand, expelling an exasperated sigh.

"Didn't mean to make you nervous." He flashed a dazzling smile that probably got him laid most nights a week.

I didn't want to seem like a freak, and the last thing I wanted was to give away my weakness, so I did the first thing that came to mind. "You don't make me nervous, but now you owe me one." I wrapped my fingers around his red solo cup, pulling it from his grasp. I curled my lips and took a sip.

His tongue flicked out to wet his lower lip before he bit down, his pupils dilating a fraction. It sent a warm flutter to my already nervous belly, and I jutted my eyes away, feeling self-conscious. The looks on our bystanders' faces were enough to make my heart race. I didn't want to be on this guy's radar, but now it looked like I'd just placed myself in the dead center of it.

"I would've poured you your own." My gaze flickered back to his widened stare.

"Maybe you should've let *me* pour my own." I bit back through an obviously phony smile.

His eyes danced with excitement. "An independent girl. I like that. What's your name, Little Miss Forward?"

I ignored the prickles that crawled up my spine and looked at him over the rim of the cup. "Evangelina." *God, get me out of here.*

He leaned on a tree trunk and crossed one leg over the other, getting comfortable. "I'm Eric. Do you make a habit of taking what doesn't belong to you, Evangelina?"

I shrugged nonchalantly as if I wasn't trembling inside. "I was thirsty. You had a drink. Opportunity knocked."

Eric's smile broadened, a gleam radiating as he studied me. "You're new," he stated matter-of-factly.

"I am." I scanned the crowd for my friends. I had to bail, and quick. My eyes found Eric's one last time.

A confident smile spread across his handsome, yet boyish face. "Well, then you're in luck. I'm an old dog here. It would be my honor to show you the ropes." He straightened and slipped a heavy arm around my shoulders in an I'll-be-in-your-pants-by-sundown gesture.

Last straw.

I jerked forward, completing a combination duck-sidestep, and separated myself from him. Tipping my head back, I emptied the remnants of the cup down my throat. "Thanks for the drink, Eric, but you're really not my type. Maybe I'll see ya around."

I placed the barren plastic back into his limp hand, and I knew, by the rosy hue that tainted his cheeks, I'd bruised his ego. I walked off, leaving him scratching his head as his waiting fan club looped their arms through each of his.

Still moving at a clipped pace, I approached the traitorous, open-mouthed duo who looked at me as though they were in the presence of royalty. "I thought you guys were right behind me." I cranked my head from left to right, loosening my neck and rolling my shoulders, trying to pull myself from the bad place my mind was headed. I stopped when they didn't respond. "What?"

"You realize that was Eric Matthews, right?" Jessie's eyes were wide.

"Does that mean something?" I pulled my hair over my shoulder and peeked back at him.

The girls looked back and forth at each other. Sandra clarified. "You just left him speechless. That doesn't happen."

"You know him?" I asked.

"Um, everyone knows him. Do you live under a rock?" Jessie's voice squeaked.

"Maybe." I shrugged, shaking out my hands at my sides, attempting to still them before someone noticed. "I just rattled him a little bit. It's no big deal."

Sandra shook her bright red head in wonderment. "Whatevs, man. You're a goddess. You're going to have to teach me how to do that."

"Do what?"

"I don't know. You're just so confident. People notice you no matter where you are and you're not fazed by it. I'd probably be a stuttering mess and trip and fall or something."

My subconscious scoffed at her assessment of me. But, I couldn't blame her. She could only see what I *allowed* her to see.

Everyone *knew* me, but no one knew *me*. No one knew what I thought or how I felt or what was really inside, bottled up and waiting to explode like a shaken up can of soda. And I preferred it that way. Let no one in—*ever*.

Standing at five foot, one inch, I didn't don the most dominating appearance, but when I walked into a room with my head held high, I gave off the vibe I was strong-willed and couldn't be messed with.

If they only knew how weak I really was . . .

"People smell fear, San. They're animals by nature. You just have to douse yourself with enough perfume to make them sniff you and walk away. Confuse them. There's nothing to it." I shrugged. "Now, come on. These bitches are drinking my beer."

AN HOUR LATER, I WAS toast. Well, not completely toast, but I closely resembled the jelly smear. I felt good. Numb. Turned off. Relaxed.

First mistake.

"Jace, can you feel your teeth?"

He sucked on his pearly whites. "Sure can. My legs though, not so much."

"Attention! Attention!"

My head whipped around in the direction of a strong voice shouting through a bullhorn. I groaned inwardly at the familiar face. Eric's lips grazed the plastic mouthpiece as he spoke. "Time to get the real party started. We're gonna have us a bit of a game, boys and girls." Short pieces of rope dangled from his hand, and my breathing hiccupped in my throat.

"I know you've all been trying to get closer to the opposite sex all day, so now's your chance." A smile lit his face as he relayed the rules of the grown up version of a three-legged race. "You'll be tied at the thigh and have to make it around those cones for three laps. Every time you reach a marker, you'll have to do a shot. Losers chug. There's only one rule—no same-sex pairings . . . Unless you like that sort of thing." He winked and the crowd electrified, hooting and hollering, grabbing at each other's hands, claiming partners.

Jace licked his lips. "Please, someone tie me to that boy."

I set my drink down and started to walk away. "That's my cue, Jace. I'm outta here."

He did a double-take, and then grabbed me by my elbow, forcing me back. "We've been over this. It'll be fun. You need to do these things if you want your life back, Eva."

"And get tied to some random guy? Not happening." I tried to leave again, but he held me firm.

Rubbing a smooth cheek, he clucked his tongue ring at me. "I'll be your partner, bitch. I don't wanna be tied to some messy slut anyway. Don't make a big deal."

"Fine," I relented.

We approached Eric, hand-in-hand in an unbreakable bond, and asked to be tied to one another.

"Didn't you guys come here together?" Eric asked, holding the rope tight to his chest.

I squared my shoulders. "Yeah, so?"

"So maybe I wasn't clear enough with my instructions. You have to be tied to someone of the opposite sex . . . who you *don't* know."

My breathing caught, and the hair on my arms bristled. I shook it off and stood up straighter. "I have a boyfriend."

A broad smile spread across Eric's face. "Thems the rules, sweetheart."

I waved my arms. "Forget it. I'm out."

Jace grabbed me yet again and, for the second time today, I wanted to cause him bodily harm. He was really testing the limits of our friendship. My eyes popped out as far as they could go as I stared him down.

"Let's just do it," he coaxed.

"Jace!" He couldn't be serious. He knew me better than this.

"Come on, Eva." Jace pulled the pouty-lip trick he knew I couldn't refuse. "I don't want to leave yet. It'll be fun. What do you think is going to happen on a big open field with a million people around?" My eyes followed the swing of his arm, pointing out our company. "Besides, this is why we're here. Normalcy. This is normal, darling." His eyes were soft, though his tone urging.

He was right. It should be easy enough to fake this, and I wouldn't be alone. But still, the thought of being pressed up against someone made me nauseous. It made me think of *him*.

I bit back my trepidation. "Whatever. What do I have to do?" I turned back to Eric and was met with a wry smile. *What does this guy have up his sleeve?*

"I'm so happy you asked. Evangelina, I'd like you to meet your new partner." Eric gestured to his left in a sweeping motion. "Big Jim."

I gasped, stumbling backward as I looked at the burly man meant to be tied to me. *I think I'm going to be sick.* "You can't be serious."

"Oh, I'm serious, sweet stuff. Get acquainted."

Great. Of all the people to piss off, I had to pick the ringleader. *Good job, Eva.*

I didn't want Eric to think he'd gotten the better of me, so I popped my hip and shot my hand toward him, my best dirty scowl in place. Eric only chuckled in my face, fueling my rage. I ripped the rope from his hand, nearly pulling off one of his fingers in the process.

"Take it easy, sweetheart." He rubbed his palms together.

"This *is* me taking it easy," I growled. "And I'm not your sweetheart."

He laughed outright as I stalked off to Big Jim, who was bigger than huge, and more than eager to be tied to the cute little blonde. *Awesome.*

"Hey, Big Jim. I'm Little Eva, so be gentle with me. Deal?"

"Sure thing, little lady." His tone was friendly, despite his overbearing size. "Here, give me that. I can tie it." He went to grab the rope, but I snatched my hand back before he could get a good grip.

"No, that's fine. I've got it." No way was this guy getting a free feel.

My fingers moved like lightning over the rough twine. I thought I could do this. But the second his leg pressed against mine, pin pricks traveled over my skin like swift little insect bites. My stomach rolled in nauseous waves, and sweat beaded on my forehead. *God, please, not now.* If I had an attack here, tied to this guy where I couldn't get away, I was done for. There'd be no hiding it.

I pulled on the ends of the rope harder than I intended to, making the knot tighter than necessary. Big Jim flinched, and I winced looking up at him. "Sorry."

He rubbed his meaty leg. "That's okay. I just hope I don't need an amputation after this." He flashed a lust-filled grin. "Although, being tied to you, I'm not so sure it wouldn't be worth it."

I rolled my eyes and clamped my jaw shut to stop from telling Big

Jim where he could shove it.

At the starting line, I glanced around at all the couples, unfamiliar with each other, talking a mile a minute. They flirted and laughed, and I realized how out of place we must have looked as we stood mute side by side.

Jessie hobbled next to me, tied to a pint-sized, doofy-looking kid, her face screwed in a pout. I guessed she didn't get the better end of the get-to-know-you, tie-together. I scanned the crowd one more time and took note of where Sandra and Jace were, each of them tied to their respective partners. Then I forced myself to relax. There was no reason to panic.

What's the holdup? I wanted to get this over with and detach myself from this less than desirable ogre. Leaning forward, I craned my neck to yell at Eric to hurry when my words became trapped somewhere between the bulge in my throat and my tonsils.

On the far edge of the long line of pairings, Eric wore an animated grin. He was laughing as he leaned into some other guy's ear, a finger pointed directly at me as he spoke, not trying to hide the fact he was talking about me.

But what halted my words—stopped me cold, wasn't the fact that he was trying to embarrass me. It was . . .

Him.

The guy.

The one he was talking to.

He wasn't laughing along with Eric. His full lips were pursed together, his body stoic as he stood with his hands rooted deep in the pockets of his faded jeans. Even from this distance, I could see the intensity in his eyes, and they were locked and loaded—on me.

With his chin dipped forward slightly and his head tipped marginally toward Eric's words, he gave the impression he was listening while his gaze ate me alive, penetrating every morsel of my body, unblinking and unwavering.

I suddenly felt weak, limp even. And, for a moment, I was thankful for Big Jim's stability.

Eric continued rapping his mouth while this guy, this beautiful stranger, stared at me as though it pained him to not come rip off the annoying piece of rope and carry me off somewhere. Eric caught me staring and flitted his fingers in the air, waving at me. Embarrassed, I shook my head, breaking myself from the mystery man's stare, and planted my focus on the open field.

But I still felt his eyes on me.

More words resounded through the bullhorn. "All right, everyone. At the sound of the whistle, I wanna see you hobble. People are waiting at the cones with your shots. Drop 'em back and keep it moving. Ready? On your mark . . . Get set . . ." The whistle shrilled.

I was too preoccupied, wondering if the stranger was still looking and why it even mattered to me, that I didn't move right away. But I didn't have long to think about it.

Big Jim took off like a bullet.

I lurched forward, my feet tripping over themselves. Not wasting time, he grabbed me around the waist, supporting my weight as he continued to run. My body turned rigid as it banged against his side. His fingers wrapped around the edge of my belly, and my core tightened, wanting to throw him off me. He forced his grip deeper into my flesh and hoisted me higher until my toes were dragging on the ground.

I screeched, punching him in the chest out of instinct.

He merely laughed and pulled me tighter. "Come on, beautiful. You're making this harder than it needs to be."

And that was it.

My body stopped its fight. My field of vision closed in tighter and tighter, until it was merely a pin-hole in front of my eyes. I went down in slow motion, and then the world disappeared.

"Come on, beautiful. You're making this harder than it needs to be."

I'm pinned against the wall, his body pressing into mine so tightly it's hard to breathe. His mouth clamps down over mine, his tongue probing between my tight lips, trying to gain entry.

In his sweet, coaxing tone, he threatens. "The harder you make this for me, the harder I'll make it for you in the long run. Do you want everyone to know our little secret?"

I shake my head violently.

His hand snakes up my throat and grabs my chin. "I didn't think so." He scrapes his thumb along my mouth. "Now open those rosy little lips for me, beautiful. I can't wait another second to have you."

There's no use.

Relaxing my lips, I tighten my eyelids so I don't have to watch. His tongue enters my mouth, mingled with a wet saltiness, and he moans. The rise and fall of my chest slows as I give myself over—go somewhere else. It's just a body. My soul can go anywhere.

His hand trails down my side. He's not being rough, but every touch feels sharp, like nails being raked across my skin. It comes to rest on my thigh, at the end of my shorts, and he skims his finger along the perimeter before tugging sharply at the edge.

My hand flew down to claw at his fingers.

Voices.

"Dude, can't you see she's freaking out? Give me a hand, fucker!"

Warm breath touched my ear. "I'll get this untied, sweetheart. Just hold still."

Blinking, I turned my head in the direction of the friendly voice and found myself staring into the bluest pair of eyes I'd ever seen. Worry and compassion seeped from them as he placed a hand to my cheek and spoke again. "You're okay. I'll have you free in a second."

It was him. The guy Eric was talking to. And up close he was even more mesmerizing. Calm washed over me until I registered the weight bearing down on the lower half of my body. Big Jim was laughing uncontrollably, in drunken hysterics.

My body shot up, knocking him to the side. "Get off me!" I screamed at the oversized oaf as I tried to tear at the rope that still bound us together.

Beautiful stranger trained his eyes on Big Jim. "Dude, I'm telling you right now. If you don't stop and let me get this off her, I'll cut your leg off to get her out." He looked just as bothered as I was for some odd reason.

"All right. All right. Jeez, what's wrong with you guys?" Big Jim rolled to his side and folded his hands on his chest, waiting to be cut loose.

My fingers fumbled haphazardly with the beautiful stranger's, both of us struggling to set me free. He stilled my hands with his, his voice low and gentle. "I'll do it. Just hold still a sec. Can you do that for me?"

Nodding, I sucked my cheeks in, holding back tears.

Jace ran up to us, huffing and puffing. He put his hands on his knees and bent forward, trying to catch his breath just as this unnamed man finished untying the last knot.

I looked up at my best friend, silently pleading for his rescue.

"What happened? Heat got to you again?" Shaking his head with a chuckle, Jace played off my mishap. "I can't take you anywhere." He tugged me to my feet, then tucked me under his arm. "Thanks, guy. I got her now."

Turning me around, he urged me forward, speaking discreetly. "Hold it together, baby girl. We'll be home in a minute. I'm sorry. I'm so, so sorry, love."

I peeked back between our shoulders. The mystery man remained motionless, one hand on the dirt, the other on his leg as he kneeled beside Big Jim, watching each step of my retreat. I couldn't shake the numbingly breathless effect of having those eyes directed at me. A regular girl probably would have introduced herself, said thank you. But I wasn't a regular girl. I was me.

Looking forward, I buried my face in Jace's neck, feeling the familiar burn invade my throat.

Chapter 3

I exist on a scattered plane. A place where lightness and darkness meet somewhere in between. Uneven slats I maneuver around and hop across, trying to maintain stability. Some shedding enough light to shine and others enough darkness to hide behind. I live in the gray area. The bubble in the middle, never sure which direction to go.

TAP, TAP, TAP.

My pen bounced off the page.

I'd dreamed of this day for so long. My world centering around this very moment for hours on end, thinking it would all be different once I got here; that I'd take back control and make something of myself.

So why didn't I feel relieved? And why did my insides still feel so dirty?

I sucked in a ragged breath, expelling the air slowly to tame my erratic heartbeat.

Free. I was finally free.

Lies.

I could tell myself that all I wanted, but I never would be, would I?

Didn't deserve to be. I'd brought all this upon myself, and asked for every bit of torture that came after the night I handed over my soul, sealing the deal with the devil himself. Now, I was his little fucking puppet—a marionette dangling from his strings.

"Evangelina Ricci." My name pulled me out of my distracted haze.

Great. Minute five, day one, and I'm already fucking this up. I shook my head like an Etch-A-Sketch, attempting a clean pallet, and sat up straighter in my chair, focusing on the balding man at the front of the room.

Time to turn on the charm.

"Yes, Professor Klein," I answered in the sweetest voice I could muster.

His frown deepened as he peered over the top of his glasses, scanning the crowd, then softened just a bit when he zeroed in on me. "A simple present would suffice. Try to stay with us would you please, Miss Ricci?"

Really? Roll call in college? "Yes, of course. Sorry, sir."

"Thank you." He continued on. "Ryan Stevens . . . Seymour Townsend . . ."

I knotted my sweaty hands together and wedged them between my bouncing thighs, looking around the class at my peers. Curling my back, I slid lower in the hard plastic chair. After the scene I'd caused this weekend, I wondered if I could pull this off at all, or if I'd be forced to slink back home with my tail between my legs.

Fuck that.

I wasn't going back there. Not until I was ready.

Coming here was nothing more than the coward's way out, disguised as plans for a bright future. I tucked my demons away behind goals and ambitions; swallowed them down and buried them deep within myself; imbedding them further into my soul.

The plan had always been the same. Do well in school, make lots of money, establish a great career, and make a name for myself. I needed to ensure I could run wherever—whenever I wanted, and be independent on my own. It was such a lonely existence, but it got me through.

Except my brain was never still. It was such an effort to weed through the ramblings in my head and make sense of them that I found myself perpetually exhausted. Another punishment of mine.

No peace.

You're not going to do this right now. Focus!

I straightened my spine and managed to get through the rest of class taking notes and going through the motions, keeping any negative thoughts at bay. I even answered a few redeeming questions before hightailing it out of there.

I could do this.

THE HALL HAD THAT FIRST day feel. A bunch of people with nervous smiles and wandering eyes shimmying about. The anxiety in the air was thick—girls toting giant backpacks, guys trying to act laid back, but the doubt in their eyes giving them away.

A high-pitch screech shrilled in my ears. "Eva!"

I stopped walking and sighed inwardly, just needing a few minutes alone. I'd left New Jersey as one of the most popular girls in the town, and it seemed to have followed me to Manhattan.

Cue cheesy, overly friendly smile. "Hey, Jessie. What's up?" I didn't want her to think I didn't like her. We'd met when she bumped into me while buying school books. She kept apologizing and insisting I let her buy me a coffee to make it up to me. Ever since, we were becoming fast friends.

She jogged to meet me. "You feeling better? I was worried the other night when you left the frat party, and you haven't answered your phone."

I immediately felt sorry for brushing her off. She was sweet, and she meant well. "Yeah, I'm fine. I guess the heat got to me. Sorry if I made you worry." I used Jace's lame excuse, even though in reality it was a little chilly that night.

"As long as you're okay." She relaxed. "You have plans later? My last class is at three, and I'm dying for a mani/pedi. Wanna come?" She really was a cute girl. Tight blonde curls, big amber eyes, and this almost childlike personality. Kind of like an overgrown Shirley Temple.

I smiled. "Sure. I could use some girly unwind time. Meet me at my apartment at four-thirty."

Jessie gave a few short claps of her hands, bouncing up and down.

Her smile was so broad that I swore she was going to wind up with a mouthful of hair one of these days. "Yay! Okay, see ya then. I can't wait!" She popped a kiss on my cheek and hurried off to her next class.

I watched her retreating figure, looking on with wonder at how she could be so genuinely happy. Then I remembered once upon a time *I* was happy like that, too.

I'm three, my sister five, and we're sitting, legs dangling off the swing on our front porch. Chocolate ice cream runs down our arms, dripping from cones and onto our flowered, cotton jumpers. We giggle over our chocolate-coated chins.

Mommy comes out, and we give her sly little grins. "Look at you two! Did you even eat any of it?" She's pretending to be mad, but her smirk gives her away.

We bat our eyelashes and sing in a chorus we've mastered, "Sowwwyyyy, Mommmyyyyyy."

"It's okay," she says, giving up the charade. "Come and get washed up, you two."

The glider flies behind us as we hop off, leaving brown, sticky footprints in our wake as we scurry around to the side of the house to use the hose and wash away the evidence, giggling all the while. With an evil laugh, Mommy turns on the water and sprays us, and we run in circles, screaming and laughing, trying to escape.

The giggles faded, and I was left in a hall, surrounded by strangers. My smile slowly receded at the corners as I hung my head, tucked my hair behind my ear, and quickly walked away before anyone could see the tear forming in the corner of my eye.

I swiped at my cheeks and kept my head bowed, raising my eyes sporadically so I didn't bump into anyone. Still unsure of the geography of the building, I chanced a glance up, elongating my body to peer around and find an exit, when my feet stopped moving.

The guy who had helped me the other night stood in front of me, leaning against a wall with his knee bent. He was laughing as he spoke excitedly with Eric. Motionless, I stared, blinking away the tears I was struggling to keep at bay.

He looked so different when he smiled. Different from the guy whose intense gaze stayed focused on me. Different from the one who helped me with concern etched into his features. He looked carefree and alive, how a typical, college-aged person *should* look.

I took a long, deep swallow, watching the hair that loosely brushed his forehead. His Adam's apple vibrated in his throat with each hearty chuckle, and he had the cutest dimple I'd ever seen. I didn't get to see that the other day.

I studied his movements, cataloging each of them into compartments in my brain so I could call upon them whenever I liked. I envied him. And even stranger was I felt myself *wanting* to know him.

Just as that thought brushed my subconscious, Eric nodded his head in my direction, a snide smirk on his lips. The stranger looked over then, and his smile faltered, his dimple slowly disappearing. Recognition flashed in his eyes, and he dropped his foot from the wall and started toward me.

Crap!

Turning, I shrunk myself as small as possible and squeezed through the throng of students, desperate to find a way out. In the near distance, I saw it—the double doors I entered this morning. *Finally!* I slammed my palms on the metal and shoved through the doors, ducking to the side. After a few moments had passed, I chanced a look through the glass cut-out.

In the midst of the crowd, his eyes darted from left to right, studying everyone. He completed a slow spin, scanning faces. Not finding what he was looking for, the tension in his shoulders slackened. He laced his fingers at his nape and looked up, working the bones in his square jaw. Then he slapped his palm on the wall, hung his head, and turned to walk in the opposite direction.

Disappointment washed over me from the outside in. I wanted to open the door and call to him, but I refrained. Instead, I blew out the giant lump of air I was holding, then ran down the steps and away from him.

Hiding in a corner on the great lawn, my body crumpled. I curled up, tucking my knees under my chin. That was twice I had faltered, twice I'd almost showed how weak I was—how broken. I couldn't allow that to happen again. I needed to try harder. Shut off certain parts of my brain while still allowing the other parts to function.

Visions of those blue eyes flashed before me, but I pushed them aside. I didn't know why he was invading my thoughts the way he was. Or why I even cared at all. But the look on his face as he tried to get to me, desperate and determined. He looked so genuine. So good. So . . . not for someone like me.

I laughed inwardly for being stupid enough to even think about that guy. I was losing it. Shaking my head, I pushed to my feet and rushed off to my class so I could put this first day—the day that was supposed to be the best day, behind me.

FORTY-FIVE MINUTES AFTER ARRIVING AT the salon, Jessie and me were donning pretty, pink, semi-sticky fingers and toes. I felt totally refreshed and wore a contented smile. I didn't get those often and had to remember to thank Jessie for that one day.

Clasping my hand in both of hers, she tugged and did a backward walk. "Come on, we're meeting Sandra and Jace at the pizzeria." She smiled her famous *Jessie* smile.

I didn't argue. I was a sucker for New York pizza. The smell of cheese, basil, and garlic wafting through the air grabbed me from blocks away.

Sandra and Jace saw me and huge grins split their faces. "You came!" Sandra hooked an arm around my neck and squeezed.

"Of course, I came. I heard you guys would be here, and I couldn't resist."

We decided to split a Margherita pie and chose a table outside before the chill inevitably kicked in. There were probably only a couple weeks of warmth left, but for now it was still summer, and we were holding onto it for dear life.

I tipped my nose up to the dry, crisp air. The sun was just beginning to set, creating an orange hue so bright it was almost hard to look at. White, wispy clouds lined a clear sky. A refreshing breeze slid under my hair and softly blew it to the side as I sat in one of the metal chairs lining the sidewalk.

Jessie and Sandra took seats across from each other, and Jace sat across from me. He swung his legs onto my lap and leaned back, stretching his arms above his dark brown head, streaked with swipes of blonde.

"What a long day." He inhaled, and then huffed out a large breath of air. "Ugh, and it's only day one. I'm gonna need me a sugar daddy to help pass the time if I'm getting through this." He turned his hand over and examined his nails, accentuating boredom.

We all laughed.

"What? I'm serious. And don't you bitches be getting in my way either. They don't call me the corrupter for nothing."

"You're terrible!" Sandra chortled, slapping his arm.

"Oh no, honey. I'm so, so good. Trust." He raised one wicked eyebrow at her before coolly slipping a pair of sunglasses over his honey colored eyes, and scoping out his surroundings with a puckered lip, reminding me why I loved him. "What was I thinking, agreeing to this?" And here came his bitching.

"That you love me of course." I batted my eyelashes at him.

"Yeah, yeah." He rolled his eyes, dramatic as usual.

"Hey, Eva, those guys are staring over here." Jessie's gaze was focused on the table in the corner, and she wiggled her eyebrows up and down. "Hubba hubba."

"Hubba hubba? What are you, five?" I laughed, then egged her on. "Go say hi. Your curls are extra bouncy today."

Her delicate nose scrunched up. For once, not the smile. "Um, I don't think they'd have much interest in me. They're foaming at the mouth, staring at *you.*"

I chanced a sideways glance, pretending to care. "That one with the sandy hair and bulging biceps is kind of hot."

That was all she needed to get her going. "Go! Go!" She shoved my arm.

"I can't go." I chuckled, shooing her hand away. "I have a boyfriend, remember?" Just as I finished the sentence, Mr. Bulging Biceps made his way over. He looked like he was walking the runway as he weaved in and out of tables. I glanced over at Jace, who was already eyeing me, and then back to the runway model.

Here I go. I was well trained in this dance.

Runway model stopped directly in front of me and scanned every inch of me in under three-seconds.

My subconscious rolled her eyes.

"Hey." He ran a hand through his sandy blond hair, giving me a coy little smile and exuding confidence.

"Hi." I smiled politely.

"I'm Drew."

"Hi, Drew. I'm Evangelina." I kept him at arm's length. If you got my full name, you were getting brushed off.

"Nice to meet you, Evangelina. Is this your boyfriend?" He nodded his head at Jace but kept his focus on me.

Jace lowered his sunglasses to the tip of his nose. "Seriously, hot stuff? That's your segue? I know you can't be that naïve. Get on with it." He flicked his wrist twice in our direction.

"Down boy. Don't be jealous." I kissed my hand and blew the air at Jace, then fixed my gaze back on Drew. "This is my faithful sidekick, Jace, and he's happy to make your acquaintance. Aren't you, love?" I cocked an eyebrow at Jace.

Jace blew him a kiss and licked his lips. I think my new suitor might have almost just fainted.

Swallowing hard, he tried to save the moment. "Okay . . . well, since you're boyfriendless—"

"Well, now, I didn't say that," I interrupted.

"Oh." He shook his head and blinked, clearly rattled.

From the corner of my eye, I noticed Sandra and Jessie do almost the same thing. This was their first experience with the Eva/Jace show as well. Jace and I made a good team. We didn't even have to speak. We were in each other's heads and knew exactly what we needed from the other. He was my Will, and I his Grace.

Staring down at his feet, Drew's hands fell to his sides. "So, you *are* taken? I should've known someone as gorgeous as you would have a boyfriend." It worked. He had that deflated look I'd come to know so well.

No, I'm damaged. "Yes, I do. But I *am* flattered. Who knows, Drew, maybe sometime down the road . . ." I let the insinuation linger there. I didn't like to hurt their egos too badly, but I couldn't let them find out how tainted I was. At least this was one aspect of my life I knew I could control.

Looking into my eyes, he was hopeful again. "Now that's one road I'm going to try my best to find. I'll be seeing you, Evangelina."

"I look forward to it, Drew," I said through a plastic smile.

He returned, a little less confident, to his table of friends who were clearly laughing at his expense.

"Aw. He was such a cutie, Eva!" Sandra whined.

Jessie chimed in. "Seriously, girl. You made him look like a fallen warrior. This must be one hot guy you keep refusing people for."

Jace spoke up, doing his thing. "Don't you worry those pretty little ringlets. Her man is one sweet piece of candy." He took his legs down, came over to my side of the table, and sat on my lap. Wrapping his arms around my neck, he kissed me on the temple.

I looked up at him. "Love you."

"Love you more, munchkin."

We continued to sit there, joking and going over our days of syllabi after syllabi. The sun had now completely set and I'd started to get a chill when Jace politely informed me I needed some beauty rest.

"Gee thanks." I screwed my face in a pout.

"I only speak the truth." He pulled me up by my hand, and we started in the direction of our apartment building, leaving the girls to make their way to the dorms.

"Thanks for having my back, love." I rested my head on Jace's shoulder as we walked, intertwining our hands.

"You know I always do." He kissed the top of my head. "But, you need to rub some shit on your face or something and make my job a little easier."

We laughed in unison as we walked up the steps to our apartments.

"Love," he recited our standard parting endearment.

"Love," I replied.

I gave him a kiss on the lips, and he was gone. Time for my much needed beauty rest.

Yeah, right. I should be so lucky.

Chapter 4

D AY TWO.

Sunlight peeked through my window, flooding the room with scattered rays. A small smile formed on my face. My mood usually mirrored the weather, so days like this made me want to take extra care with my appearance.

I rubbed my eyes and gave a good stretch. Swinging my legs off the side of the bed, I caught sight of my pretty little toes. Wiggling them, I made a mental note to get them done more often. I needed things to feel good about.

After shooting my mom the quick, weekly email I'd promised, I went straight for my go-to jeans that hugged all the right curves and had holes in all the right places. I probably should have retired them years ago, but they were my favorite, so I planned on keeping them until they were nothing but threads. I opted for a fitted white tee and, since I'd gone to the trouble of doing my toes, I decided to show them off a little and chose a pair of brown strappy sandals.

Back in the bathroom, I went to work on my mane, pulling the top half into four intricate knots. They lined the top of my head, each bunch falling loose over the rest of my hair. All of the different shades of blonde melded together like woven gold. Carefully, I applied mascara strand by strand. My eyes were my own personal arsenal, and I needed those babies at attention.

When I caught a glimpse of the alarm clock on my bedside table,

I started to panic. *Shit.* I had to hurry. I sprinted to the living room and hung my satchel over my shoulder, then popped the collar of my leather jacket, and ran out the door. Hopefully the gods would be kind and get me there on time.

BREATHE, EVA. YOU'RE GOOD.

I made it with a few minutes to spare. Ugh, but this was Global Economics. No matter how hard I tried, I hated the stuff. I had a difficult enough time focusing on the classes I *did* like. The only thing that was going to get me through this one was having Jessie and Sandra with me.

I was studiously taking notes while Jessie sat behind me, twirling a strand of my hair laying on her desk. It was comforting, actually. My sister used to play with my hair all the time.

That thought made me fidget.

"Sorry, was I bothering you?"

"No, don't be silly," I whispered over my shoulder. "It just tickled for a second."

"It just looked so soft and shiny. Shiny things distract me." That caused a round of giggles and a glare from Professor Collins. Jessie winced. "Let's meet up later so you can clue me in on what Professor Stiff Pants has been babbling about up there. Apparently, I was too engrossed in your luscious locks to pay attention."

"We'll do dinner at my place." I looked to my right. "Sandra, you come too in case there's anything I missed."

She tapped her pen to her chin and looked up toward the ceiling for a moment. "How about spaghetti and a special salad?"

"Oh right, I forgot you're the aspiring chef. Score." We all laughed, and the professor made an overzealous clearing of his throat.

Oops, did it again.

I whispered this time. "No more, girls. We'll catch up later."

AFTER TRYING MY BEST TO stay focused and retain something all morning, the cafeteria was a welcomed break. Needing to sort out my head and be by myself for a rare moment, I grabbed a small salad, and meandered through the crowd to find an out of the way table by the window, still wanting to make the most of the weather.

My phone chirped, alerting me to a text message.

My sister.

> *Hey, girl, hope your first day went well. I can't believe you didn't call to fill me in. Just because I didn't go away to school doesn't mean I don't want to hear all about it. I miss you. Call me. XO*

I sent out a quick reply so she wouldn't worry.

> *Me: Hi, it was good. Just really overwhelmed. I'll call you as soon as I can. XO*

I lowered the phone, and my heart sank. I knew she didn't understand why I'd been so distant the last few years. We were best friends, always labeling ourselves: BFFL.

Beautiful

Funny

Flippin'

Loud

Don't ask where that came from. Kids come up with funny things. She acted like she didn't notice my detachment, but I knew it had to be bothering her. It was bothering *me*. She was the one person I always ran to with anything, and she wouldn't judge or ask twice. She'd always defended me and protected me. But I couldn't chance her finding out, and I knew how hard she could push, so I'd distanced myself, when that was the last thing I wanted to do.

I missed her so much I—

"So the lady *does* stay still," a smooth voice said as a large form slipped into the chair beside me.

With a huff, I turned, preparing for battle. "This seat's ta—" When I saw who it was, my mouth clamped shut, and I lost my words.

"You gonna eat that?" He nodded toward my untouched meal.

Blue. All I could register was the color blue.

He cocked his head, waiting for my reply.

Voice, find your voice! "Excuse me?" Shaky as shit. I sounded like an imbecile.

"I was just wondering if you were actually going to eat any of that food or perhaps you'd rather I give you some salt for the fingers you're chewing so unmercifully. You gotta let up, girl, before you wind up with nubs instead of those pretty little manicured nails." He tapped the edge of my fingertips and electricity bolted through me, hitting my toes and shooting straight back up to my chest. "There are starving children in Cambodia, ya know." His face split into a grin.

I'm sorry—what? I can't hear you. Your dimple is in the way.

I tried to compose myself, but my ears were ringing from the blood that managed to pump straight from my heart into their canal. *Well, this is something new.*

It was him—the beautiful stranger with captivating eyes that had some weird hold on me. And he was just as heart stopping as I'd thought. I'd convinced myself I'd made him out to be more perfect than he really was. That it was the heat, or the beer, or temporary vision loss. But it was . . . none of those. His features were striking. Sharp, but friendly and somewhat overpowering. He carried a clean crispness that I wondered what smelled like and I struggled with the beauty of him. It was as if each of his features were fighting to be the most dominate in a battle none of them could win against the others. Each time my eyes fell on a different one, they'd declared it the victor. High cheekbones, soft dark hair, and God that dimple, they all had me fascinated.

At my lack of words, he continued, "You're a hard one to tie down, aren't you?" His eyes were friendly and inviting as he peeked up at me with his chin dipped low.

"I'm sorry." With nothing more intelligent to offer, I lowered my gaze.

"Are you?"

My head snapped up at his surprising response. I narrowed my eyes. "Should I be?"

"Well, yeah. A guy could get a complex." He relaxed back in his chair and the front of his dark hair brushed the corners of his electric blue eyes. Though he tried to keep a straight face, a teasing grin played on his lips.

The corner of my mouth twitched. This guy was painfully adorable. "I'm sorry, I didn't catch your name the other day."

The edges of his mouth rose, forming the most amazing smile I'd ever seen. Rosy lips that were neither too thin nor too plump framed a set of straight, white teeth. But the best part was his eyes smiled along with them. Those eyes—they were a color I'd never seen before. Icy blue crystallized sapphires that literally sparkled. Like, literally.

And they were moving closer to me.

Back up!

He extended his hand in the short distance that remained between us. "Blake. Nice to meet you . . ." He hung there, his eyebrows raised.

That's your cue, dummy!

"Evangelina," I blurted out the way you would if you'd just remembered the key answer on a test.

That is my name, right?

I cleared my throat and repeated a bit slower, "Evangelina. But my friends call me—"

"Angel," he interrupted, matter-of-factly.

"What?" I frowned.

"Your name. It's Angel." He said it as a statement, like I didn't have a name all along and he was there to do the honors.

"That's one version, yes, but no one calls me that." *Was I just about to tell him to call me by my nickname?*

"You're saying I'm no one?" His eyes turned sad, and he pouted, making a show of looking like I'd hurt his feelings.

"What? No, of course not," I stumbled out. "That's not what I meant. I mean . . ." His saddened expression bothered me more than I cared to admit. I blew out a puff of air in defeat. "It's fine. Call me whatever you want."

"Angel." My supposed name rolled off his tongue as though he'd actually tasted it, and I thought maybe he had. He considered it another moment before his gaze slipped down to my lips. "I like that."

Flutters ran rampant in my heart, sending warmth to my cheeks. My belly was a mess of knots, forcing an unexplained heat to swell in its pit. One I'd never felt before. Fire knots. There were fire knots in my belly.

"Um, thanks." I glanced down at my lap, my white knuckles gripping the edge of the seat, needing something to keep me grounded.

Geez, what's happening to me? I was Evangelina Ricci—heartbreak extraordinaire. I never let anyone get this close.

Get away from him, Eva! Do your thing and make him go away!

"So, Angel . . ." He propped his hand under his perfectly squared off chin. "Since we're properly acquainted now, why don't you tell me why you keep running away from me? I promise I shower. Sometimes twice a day." There was that sexy ass grin again.

And why did he have to mention the shower? My mind immediately flashed to his wet muscular form, beads of water dripping from the tips of his hair, rolling down the curves of his back—

I need out now!

"I haven't been running from you." Flushed, I pressed the button on the side of my cell phone and glanced at the screen before stuffing it into my bag. "But would you look at the time. I have an English class to get to." I pushed back from the table and swung my satchel over my shoulder.

That's it, girl. Move your ass!

In one swift motion, Blake was on his feet, beside me. "Oh, really? Me, too. I'll walk over with you."

Sure you will. This boy doesn't miss a beat.

"Who's your professor?" I asked, hopeful I could end the madness and reclaim the use of my lungs. And my legs.

"Sorrenson."

No such luck.

"Well, what a coincidence." I looked up at him out of the corner of my eye, raising a brow.

His smile widened as he realized he had me for the next hour and fifty minutes.

Figuring I better buckle in for the ride, I slowed my pace. Mr. Tall, Dark and Delicious wasn't going anywhere any time soon. He just got exactly what he wanted.

"Wonderfuckingful," I muttered under my breath.

"What?" His eyebrows pulled together.

"Huh? Oh . . . um, weather's beautiful." *Way to go, Eva. Who ARE you right now?*

We headed out of the cafeteria, and the unusually warm air

enveloped my goose bumped skin. I stopped and tipped my head to the sun, inhaling a deep cleansing breath in an attempt to regain my composure. Soaking in some vitamin D, I searched for my equilibrium.

Feeling him watching me, I opened one squinting eye. Blake raked a shaky hand through his carefully styled, raven hair.

"Sorry, you caught me." He shoved his hands in his pockets and looked down at the ground, rocking back on his heels.

I threw him a bone to lighten the mood. "Caught you what?"

He looked up and I sent a quick wink his way.

Oh god, there's that dimple again. Put that thing away!

Standing side by side for the first time, I now realized the contrast in our size. He had to be at least a foot taller than me. His broad shoulders and muscular build were so dominating it made me feel even smaller than I already was.

As if he could read my mind, Blake said, "You're a tiny little thing, aren't you?"

I rolled my eyes. "The only thing tiny about me is my height."

His eyes fluttered quickly to my chest, and I realized how bad that sounded. I sucked in a sharp breath. "Um, I mean . . . I was talking about . . . Oh, just forget it. I don't know what's gotten into me today!" *My personality. I meant my personality!* I hung my head in shame.

He smirked. Thankfully, he threw me back my bone. "Shall we?" Blake extended one hand in front of us, touching the small of my back with the other to inch me along.

Heat rippled up my spine, that small bit of contact making it seem like September had just turned into July. And there were those fire knots again. I clutched my belly, willing them away.

"You okay?" Blake took my upper arms in his hands and studied my face. After the other night, he probably thought I was a fainting spell waiting to happen.

"Me? Oh, yeah, I'm fine." I waved him off. "Cafeteria food. Bleh."

His shoulders relaxed. "Yeah, that stuff'll kill ya." Grin. Dimple.

I forced my eyes down and focused on the burgundy stones lining the walk. He drifted a little closer than I was comfortable with and, although something in me liked it, I nonchalantly took a small side-step to the left. From my periphery, I saw him glance at me out of the corner of his eye. He'd taken note, but didn't say anything. His hands returned to his pockets, his biceps flexed as if he was using them for restraint.

"So I don't know how I've never noticed you before. You're a junior? Did you just transfer in?" He looked confused.

"Nope, I'm a freshman. Just got here. And don't you make fun, either." I nudged his arm.

"A freshman?" He raised his eyebrows. "How'd you wind up in such an advanced English class?"

"Yeah, I'm a bit of an English buff. It's kind of my thing. It's not my major, but I have a passion for it."

Blake's eyes lit up. "Really? I'm impressed. You'll have to show me your work one day." He pulled open the door to the building and gestured inside. "After you, madam."

"Why, thank you, sir." I followed his direction, conscious with every step that he was behind me.

We walked a short hall and came upon the classroom that would house my discomfort. All sets of eyes were immediately on us, but I wasn't sure whether they were looking at me or the god beside me.

Blake leaned over my shoulder, lightly touched my hip, and whispered into my ear, "Follow me. I have VIP seats." His breath licked at my earlobe and prickles swept across my chest. If he didn't stop with the sexy, I was going to lose it.

He walked around me and proceeded up the aisle, leaving me to admire his perfect male form. The way he held himself was so confident, powerful. You could see the muscles in his back gliding beneath his black T-shirt. Peeking out of the back pocket of his jeans was a folded notebook, which only drew more attention to the most perfectly round ass I'd ever seen. Maybe because I'd never looked before, but still, it was unnerving.

I tried to shake off what he'd somehow just done to me without even *doing* anything, and on wobbly legs, I did as he said and followed him. He stopped at the back corner of the room and slid into the last seat, furthest away from everyone else. Dropping a long fingered hand onto the desk beside him, he tapped, signaling that was where I should join him.

I obliged.

What am I doing? I should have run straight to the registrar's office and changed my class, not saddled up next to the only person in the world who seemed to have thrown all my guards down with one wink.

But something about him had me feeling protected and wanting to do whatever he said just to catch another glimpse of that smile.

A satisfied grin played on his lips. "Now that you can't run, we can get to know each other better."

Oh no you don't, dimples.

"Who said I was running?" I picked at the edge of my desk. "And shouldn't we be paying attention? I told you this is my favorite subject. It's the only class I don't mind being in."

He leaned over his arm so we were almost nose to nose. "Oh, you were running, sweetheart. You were about to leave me in a cloud of dust again." His deep laugh was like music as he tugged at a lock of my hair. "And don't you worry that pretty little head of yours. I'll be sure it's still the only class you can't wait to get to every day."

For the first time, he was serious, his eyes lit with sincerity, and it was even sexier than when he was smiling. The insinuation was obvious, and he meant for it to be. His gaze held me hostage, each twinkle in his eye pulling me further into his trance.

Needing to take back some form of control, I made a point of rolling my eyes, feigning indifference. I inched even closer until the space between us was barely visible, then I stood my ground and went toe-to-toe with him in this staring contest. "You seem so sure of yourself. Better be careful that head of yours doesn't explode."

You want to dance? I'll dance. I will not back away, I will not back away.

"I'm not trying to be conceited, Angel. I just have no intention of it being any other way." Blake had no smirk now. No smile. No hint of sarcasm or sense of banter on his gorgeous features. His gaze was so fierce, I felt myself falling into him. Those hypnotic eyes weren't sparkling now, they were glowing.

Breathe, you idiot!

He held my stare just a second longer. Then, taking note of my paralysis, he tossed the proverbial bone back again. "So what's your major?" He relaxed back in his chair, and the air between us snapped like a rubber band.

I sucked in a deep breath, making a desperate attempt to compose myself and use the organ between my ears as I stiffly sunk back in my own chair. "Psychology. Then I'll move on to med school to get my degree in psychiatry."

His eyebrows shot up. "Whoa, girl. You don't do things small, huh? No regular freshman with the undecided liberal arts major for you?" He chuckled.

I shrugged with a small smile. "I know. I set a hard line for myself, but I refuse to deviate from it." This fucked up brain of mine decided my career goal should be psychiatry of all things. I couldn't even help myself, yet I felt I should be helping other people? As if I were capable enough to do that. "It was on the short list of best careers for women, and I plan to be nothing less than the best. Always."

Rolling his bottom lip between his fingers, he studied me like I was a puzzle he was trying to decipher. I couldn't help but stare at that attention-seeking lip, and for a fleeting moment I wondered how it would taste.

What's this guy doing to me? Get off the topic of you, damn it!

I cleared my throat. "How about you? What do you want to be when you grow up?" I laughed at my funny.

Any amusement in his eyes faded, and was replaced by a forlorn expression.

My heart might have just broken a little, and I had to restrain myself from reaching out to touch his face and smooth away the lines. *Why do you care? You don't know this guy from Adam. You're letting him get too close!*

"Er, that's kinda complicated," he started. "I'm majoring in criminal justice so I can eventually go to law school just like dear ol' Dad wants me to, but it's the last thing I want." Blake gave a short shrug and looked out the window.

"So, tell him it's not what you want for yourself," I offered like it was the obvious solution. "Welcome to the modern day. Your parents no longer get to decide your future." Problem solved. I pulled my book from my bag and placed a pen on top of it.

He let out a sarcastic laugh. "Easier said than done. You've never met Judge Turner. Let's just say if I want to remain in his will and his good graces, I better get very familiar with our judicial system."

My mouth hung agape. "He would cut you off? For not wanting to be a lawyer?"

One simple nod told me all I needed to know.

I narrowed my eyes, frowning. "Who cares then? Screw his will. Why be miserable for the rest of your life?"

He noticed my mood change, and appreciation shone in his eyes. "This is all a story for a different day. I'd rather not waste any of my minutes with you talking about my dad and his overbearing tendencies." He raised his hand mid-sentence, never breaking eye contact with me as he called out to the front of the room, "Here." Then back to me, his voice discreet, "These are precious minutes." He licked his lips and his eyes gave a little twinkle.

Slick. Okay, he was better than I was at roll call. *Oh no. Roll call! I missed my name!*

His unrelenting stare went right through me. Unable to take it any longer, I cleared my throat and forced myself to look away. In a quiet voice, I muttered, "You know we really should be paying attention." And I was back to biting my fingers.

A second later, a packet of salt landed on my desk, and my head snapped up to see his mischievous grin. I couldn't stop the noise that escaped my nostrils and the back of my throat as I tried desperately to stifle the laugh behind my hand.

The professor shot a disapproving glare to the back of the room, and the entire class swiveled to see what all the fuss was about. I must have turned one hundred shades of purple as I slouched down in my seat.

"As I was saying . . ." the professor continued.

When the focus returned to where it belonged, I whispered out the side of my face, "You did not just throw a packet of salt at me." My eyes were wide with shock, my smile huge as short laughs snuck through my lips.

"Uh, yeah I did." He looked so proud. "I had a feeling you'd go back to chowing down on those fingers." Blake laughed openly at my still stunned expression.

"Oh, I gotta say, that was ten points right there. You win that round. Well played." I found myself relaxing and enjoying the moment.

"Thank you, thank you." He patted his own shoulder.

"Now hush before we get thrown out. I'm not off to a very good start here." I sent him one last little smirk and focused my attention on the front of the room.

"Fine, fine. Have it your way," he said, nudging his seat a couple of inches closer, as if that was his way of getting the last word.

For the most part, he was compliant for the remainder of the class. Every now and then I'd steal a glance his way and catch him staring. Each time he would play it off casually like he was only trying to copy my notes.

Knowing I'd have to make a quick getaway, I started packing up my books a couple of minutes early. My knee bounced up and down as I waited for the professor to announce the end of our session, and I jumped up before he could complete his sentence, slinging my bag over my shoulder. "Well, it was nice meeting you officially, Blake. I'm sure I'll see you around."

He got stuck in his haste, his large form struggling to get out of the seat so quickly, which gave me time to make it to the front of the aisle. When he was finally free and on his feet, he held out his hand as if to stop me and yelled, "Wait! I'll walk . . ."

Too late. I speed walked to the door, glancing back just in time to see the sullen look on his face as his hand slowly dropped down to his side. The only difference was this time I was the one causing that look.

That thought upset me.

Why? I was a pro at this. I'd seen that look cross many handsome faces before, but he was too beautiful to wear that expression. And I was just a fucked up bitch.

Just keep walking. What were you thinking anyway?

That I felt normal and happy . . .

Even if only for a little while.

Chapter 5

AFTER SCOURING THE CITY MONTHS ago, I'd finally found a place I could swing. Given my need for privacy and solitude, I'd been saving every penny since I was fifteen to make sure I could afford an apartment once I got to college. I'd be damned if I'd allow anyone to witness what went on with me when the lights went out. It was on the top floor, and it cost a pretty penny, but it was more than worth it to me. It had two things I considered priceless—my own private balcony and direct access to the roof. They were the perfect places I could go to forget about the world and throw myself deep into my two vices, writing poetry and singing. Music had always been a Band-Aid to my soul. The words resonated deep within me and resounded through my veins. Some nights, when the boogeyman came, it was my only means of escape. Go up there and sing out my sorrows while the world was asleep and oblivious to my heartache.

My parents only condition moving to the city was that I lived in a building with a doorman. There was no way I could afford that, so they paid the difference. Walking into the lobby, I waved to my white haired guardian without much enthusiasm as I headed for the elevator. The girls would be here soon, and I had to pull myself together and shake off the rattle Blake put in my insides.

I busied myself with endless cleaning, while belting the lyrics to my trusty Pat Benatar CD. I could always count on Pat to brighten my mood. I was hopping around the apartment, bopping and swaying and singing into spatulas, when the girls knocked on the door.

"Coming! Gimme a sec." I wiped the sweat from my brow, slapped my yellow gloves on the counter, and scurried over to the door to let in the giggling combo.

Jessie threw her arms around my neck like she hadn't seen me in years. "Eva, I missed you!"

"Jes, it's been six hours." I chuckled and rolled my eyes.

Sandra walked past me with an overflowing grocery bag and kissed my cheek. "I swear she would marry you if she could. She hasn't stopped talking about you."

"Aw, Jes, I'm flattered." I batted my eyelashes at her.

"Yeah, yeah. Shut up, both of you. Don't make fun, or I won't be your friend anymore." She stuck out her tongue.

Sandra was in awe, staring at the view out my kitchen window. "I really love your place, Eva. You scored with this one."

The city skyline was beautiful with all the lights and scattered buildings of varying sizes. The world was hustling about just feet below, but from up here it looked so calm. Once I saw it, it called to me. This is "the city that never sleeps". Well, neither did I. We were a perfect match.

Jessie hopped onto my couch, squatting back onto her heels. "I know, right? I'm so jealous. We're stuck in those tiny little dorms, and you're living like royalty over here."

I plopped beside Jessie and tucked one leg underneath me. "Hey, this tiny little *royalty* comes at a pretty ridiculous price." I lifted my eyebrow. "Which reminds me, it's time I find a job, or I'll be sleeping at the foot of your bed soon." I nudged her with my shoulder.

"What do you have in mind?" Sandra called out from the kitchen. She was bent over, watching for the flame to spring to life beneath a pot of water and my mouth watered thinking about the spaghetti dish she'd promised.

I shrugged. "I think I'll make the most money bartending. I can probably get away with only working three nights a week if I can snag a Friday or Saturday."

I could see the light bulb go off in Jessie's head. "My friend Rick owns The Backdoor. He'll hire you in a heartbeat. With your body and that face, you'll make a killing! I'll call him when I get back to my room later."

"You think?"

She nodded. "I *so* think."

"'Kay. Thanks, chick." I gave her a squeeze.

"No problem. Now let me at your notes."

I pulled out my book as divine scents wafted toward me from the kitchen. "San, you can come over any time. My kitchen's always open."

She tossed a spatula and caught it behind her back like Tom Cruise, then started a little jig. We all giggled in unison, and I sighed in contentment, somehow feeling more comfortable here in this chaotic city than I had in years back home.

An hour later, Jessie was all caught up, and I was wiping my plate clean with a piece of Italian bread. "My god, Sandra, that was amazing. If you're not supposed to be a chef, I don't know who is." A little burp escaped my lips. "Scuze me! See? Compliments to the chef." We all laughed again.

"Thanks." She beamed.

The girls helped me tidy up and then they were gone, leaving me alone . . . again.

I made a cup of hazelnut coffee in my nifty little Keurig, then grabbed a pen and my journal. I brushed my fingertips along the fraying edges of the tattered, leather bound book. Loose poems and scribblings from the last few years or so were clasped behind a heart-shaped snap closure. I headed out to the balcony, and my pen began to flow without thought as it had so many times before.

Icy blue waters wash across a blackened sky
A dark ceiling outlines creamy white sand
The shore is broad and powerful, casting off perfection
Twinkling white stars smiling down to where I stand

My pen stopped mid-stroke, and I realized the double entendre staring back at me. I'd just unknowingly described Blake. Great, he'd gotten to my subconscious now, too. I closed my book and ran a clammy hand over the top of my most prized possession, then dropped it on the coffee table with a loud thump. He should be the furthest thing from my mind.

Running a bubble bath, I relished in the sweet sounds of Sarah McLachlan pouring from my iPod. I tied my hair in a messy bun of curls, then stepped into the warm water. Laying back, I covered my eyes with a cool washcloth and buried the day.

"In the arms of the angel . . ."

Really, Sarah? It had to be that song?

"Ugh!" I threw the cloth off my eyes and rubbed my throbbing temples. Looked like this wouldn't be the relaxing time I'd envisioned after all.

Back in my room, I slipped into my favorite cotton shorts and a white tank, then slid under the covers and began to pray, as I did every night, for a peaceful night's rest.

After a few minutes, my eyes drifted shut.

I'm holding giant bags as I mindlessly glide through the halls of Columbia. My arms are tired, weak, and I'm straining under the weight. Looking into each passing classroom, I'm searching for something, but when I don't see it, I continue walking forward.

He steps out of a room two doors away, and my heart lurches in my chest. My eyes lose their emptiness, and a light shines in them as a smile creeps up my lips. Eager to reach him, I hurry my step, drop all of my baggage at his feet, and stare up into the blue depths of his eyes.

He kicks the bags aside as if they're nothing and picks me up so we're nose to nose. An overwhelming feeling of completeness washes over me, and I can tell by the gleam in his eye he feels it, too. Our eyes remain open as we begin to kiss through smiling lips. I'm lost in the feeling, savoring each flick of his tongue when brown starts to tinge the sapphire perfection.

I think I'm seeing things and blink my eyes, only to see even more brown when they reopen. I try to pull away, but the arms that were just lovingly holding me close now feel like a vise imprisoning me.

It's hard to breathe. My walls are constricting.

A dirt-colored hue has now completely covered the sapphire crystals, and when I pull back to break the kiss, I'm staring at someone completely different. Someone terrifying.

"Hey there, beautiful." He's smiling that hateful smile of his. *"I've missed you so fucking much."*

I shot up to a sitting position, shaking and sweating. My sheets were twisted around every part of my body, restraining me to the bed. Writhing frantically, I tried to free myself—ripping and clawing, legs and arms flailing. Once untangled, I drew my knees into my heaving chest and buried my head in them. Things could never be normal. *I* could never be normal. It was silly to entertain the thought.

I rocked until I was calmer. Next to the silhouette of my trusty stuffed lamb, the clock read a quarter after four. I was screwed. There was no getting back to sleep. I dragged myself to the kitchen and gulped down large amounts of water so quickly it took what was left of my breath away. Then I put a pair of gray, broken-in sweatpants and an old sweatshirt with the collar cut out over my pajamas. Climbing the rusted metal steps, I made my way to the place where I'd spent several late nights and early mornings trying to find my sanity—the roof.

A layer of sweat still clung to my skin, shooting a chill through my body, but I was numb to the vibrations. I lowered myself onto the lounge chair I'd placed up here and curled up into a protective ball. The sun wouldn't show her face for a while longer and, knowing no one could hear me, I began to pour out my soul aloud.

I don't know how long I sang or how many songs I'd gone through. I was belting lyrics now. Tears stained my cheeks, and I didn't stop until my throat was hoarse and the words were stuck deep inside it, scratching on its walls. When the sun peaked on the horizon, I knew it was time I went back in.

Time to start day three.

My outpouring of emotion was successful in washing away the internal scars of my night tremors, but not the physical ones. I showered and then layered on my under eye cover-up. I'd need plenty of reinforcements today. Carefully, I brushed my eyelashes and when I was confident my demons were well hidden, I made a to-go cup of coffee and went to knock on Jace's door.

"Morning sunshine." I smiled as Jace pulled back the door, grumbling.

He put a hand in my face. "Don't talk to me yet." He turned his hand, palm up. "Where's mine?"

I handed over his steaming French vanilla. He closed his eyes and took a sip, sloshing it around in his mouth like mouthwash and shut the door behind him.

Looking down at his feet, my eyebrows screwed together. "Um, Jace. I think you forgot something."

"I didn't forget, sugar. This was intentional." He dragged his slipper-clad tootsies down the hall.

I raised my eyebrows. "You're going to class in slippers?"

"Sure am. Let somebody say something to me." He put up a claw and hissed.

With a giggle, I hooked my arm through his. "You're too much, you know that?"

He kissed my cheek then looked at me from the corner of his smiling eye. "Good morning."

CINEMA 101. THANKFULLY, WE WERE all in this class together, so it should be an easy and pleasant one finally. There were so many people in this giant lecture hall that we were able to have our fun without drawing too much attention.

As the class wrapped up, Jessie nodded in the direction of the sleeping beauty. Sunglasses on and hands folded over his chest, Jace was laying back in his cushioned seat.

I nudged him awake. "You better start paying attention. If you get kicked out, I'll never forgive you."

He rubbed his eyes and gave a good stretch. "Oh please. You're taking my tests anyway. You won't let that happen. I'm stuck here and you know it. Although, I must say, the assortment of men is much greater here. I probably should be thanking you." He wiggled his eyebrows.

Cackling and planning out the rest of our day, we left the darkened lecture hall. The sun blared, taking me by surprise. I forgot how bright it was outside after spending so many hours in a room without windows.

I drew my elbow up, shielding my eyes to the blinding pain when—

"Hi, Angel."

That voice.

I whipped my head around, catching a blurred glimpse of Blake at the bottom of the steps, resting against the railing.

Stumbling, I fell down the short flight, grabbing unsuccessfully for the rail before landing in his arms. Holding me at an incline, his face was only an inch away from mine. The way the sunlight played on his features, was nothing short of hypnotizing. I was stuck in the tiny sparkles dancing around in his crystal blue eyes. Eyes that could suck you in and drown you in their depths. He smelled of soap, musky man, and what I imagined heaven must smell like. I instinctively inhaled, sending my senses into a frenzy.

He flexed a perfectly chiseled jaw. "I couldn't have planned that better if I'd tried." His lip twitched, and his arms tightened around me.

After what felt like an eternity, Jace cut in. "So, *Angel*, who's your friend?" Of course he said my new name in a sarcastic tone.

I scrambled out of his embrace and righted myself. "Um, Jace, this is Blake. Blake, Jace."

"So very nice to meet you, Blake." Jace licked his lips. "Any friend of *Angel's* is a friend of mine. Though she neglected to tell me she'd made a new friend. Why is that, Angel?" He cocked his head.

"Back off, Jace." I shot him a warning glare.

"Meow." Jace wrapped an arm around my waist and pulled me close. "Don't go there, honey." His tone dismissed my bitterness, and just like that, he was forgiven. I knew he was only trying to assess the situation. I could hear the wheels turning as he tried to figure out if he needed to save me or let me be, though an outsider would have never been able to tell.

Blake extended a hand. "It's nice to meet you, Jace. I'm suddenly very jealous of you."

"Join the club there, gorgeous." Jace shook Blake's hand, still keeping his protective hold on me with the other. He turned to me. "I have to get to this killer fucking calculus class, thanks to you showing off during my placement test. You good, sugar?"

"Yeah, I'm okay." *Am I okay?* "Go ahead. Come see me later."

He studied me one more second and, when my eyes didn't give anything away, he kissed my cheek. "Love."

"Love."

"Come on, bitches." Jace snapped his fingers, summoning the two open-mouthed, wordless zombies to follow him. They adhered to his command, but their jaws hung slack as they stumbled over each other, staring at Blake.

He didn't seem to notice. "Did I just witness telepathy?" Blake watched Jace walk away. The puzzled look on his face was adorable.

"At its finest. Don't sneak up on a girl like that. I could've broken my neck." I lightly shoved him.

"No, you couldn't have. I'd never let you fall." He was serious again, intently looking into my eyes to be sure I knew he meant it.

Oh, I'm falling all right.

He inched forward, and I backed away. "Where the hell did you come from anyway?" I looked around.

"Cinema." He shoved his hands deep into his restraints again.

"Liar, I was just in cinema."

"And so was I. I never lie." He cocked his eyebrow with a smirk.

"Oh yeah? Where? I didn't see you." *Don't throw your dimple at me, liar.*

"Ah, but I saw you. You're cute when you're not trying to hide yourself. I just sat back and enjoyed the show. And I don't mean *American History X*. I have VIP seats, remember?" He *was* there. *How'd I miss him?* Kind of hard to overlook a giant hot guy.

He was inching closer again. Quicker than I could react, his hand was out of his pocket and grabbing mine. "Come on. You're coming with me."

"Where?" He walked at such a brisk pace, my shorter legs were scrambling to keep up with his longer strides.

"You'll see." He wore such a boyish grin, I couldn't deny him.

After a few minutes, he relaxed and we began walking at a more leisurely pace. "So what was that little stunt you pulled yesterday after class? You're not going to make a habit of that are you because you're only allowed three bug-outs and that was number one." He smirked. "I'm purposely wearing my running shoes today, so I should warn you, you'll have a challenge on your hands. What do I have to do to get you to stay put, anyway?"

I ducked my head and tucked my hair behind my ear. "Sorry

about that. I don't do strangers well or, um, guys in general and you're just . . . Well, you're . . ."

"Magnificent? Charming? Exceptional?" There was that dimple again.

"Yeah, sure, all of those." I laughed.

He shrugged. "I don't know what the big deal is. We're already BFFs, so I'm not a stranger. And you're the most magnificent creature walking this earth, so I know my charms can't intimidate you."

Number one—*BFF?*

And number two—he just nonchalantly slipped in one of the nicest compliments anyone's ever given me and seemed to have genuinely meant it, not like he was just trying to get into my pants.

I smiled up at him and raised my eyebrows. "BFF?"

"That's what you focus on, silly girl?" He shook his head, laughing. "Yes, BFF."

"Tsk, Tsk. So sure of yourself."

"I'm not sure of anything when it comes to you, but I'll take what I can get at this point."

We were far from school grounds, and it hit me that I'd just allowed a complete stranger to pull me off to God knows where. Maybe I was a little nervous, but not for the reasons I thought I would be. Or thought I *should* be.

"So now that you've kidnapped me, where, might I ask, are we going?"

"If I tell ya, I'd have to kill ya," he said, straight-faced.

I stopped walking and pulled back on his hand.

Blake rolled his eyes. "Joke, Angel. Lighten up. The last thing I'd ever do is hurt you. Trust me." He tugged my arm, moving me forward once again.

I relaxed. I wasn't sure why I trusted him, but for some reason, I didn't question it. Didn't want to. Something about him made me feel safe.

Blake guided me down what seemed to be a never-ending stone staircase, leading to the giant, open green field of a breathtaking park. He wore a smile reserved for five-year-olds as he picked up his pace again and walked with determination, pulling me along the grass.

Squinting, I tried to take in the sites. It was enormous. Vibrant colored trees of red and orange hues lined trails that stretched for what seemed like miles. There were fields set up for different types of sports and activities, and set to the back was a duck pond filled with turtles and different wildlife. It would be easy to forget you were in the city once you entered this space.

Slowing his pace, he maneuvered me where he wanted me, then turned so we were face to face, hand in hand. "Just what I suspected." The corner of his mouth tipped up.

"Huh?" I was mesmerized by his blue diamonds glittering in the sun.

"You. The way the light looks behind that golden head of yours. Like a halo. You really *are* an angel, aren't you?"

I touched my hair, looking away. "I'm far from an angel."

He took my chin and brought my gaze back to meet his. "Bullshit. It's right there." He reached up and slowly caressed the top of my head where my imaginary halo rested. His hand lingered there before twirling a lock of my hair around his finger on its descent. He tucked his hands back into mine.

Snap. The fuck. Out of it. "Maybe you're delusional," I retorted.

He was unfazed. "Doubtful."

"Need your eyes checked?"

"Twenty-twenty."

Self preservation kicked in. "I have a boyfriend, you know."

He didn't even flinch.

Crap.

Instead, he leaned in, caressed my ear with his nose, and whispered, "Well, then you should probably warn him you have a new BFF." His breath danced on my earlobe before he moved to look me in the eye. "And this one's all male."

Oh shit.

His lips, only a breath away, had stolen every ounce of mine. It felt as though he was taking inventory of my skin, and pins and needles erupted everywhere. Just when I thought I couldn't take the closeness anymore, he winked and tugged me forward once again.

Catching my breath, I tried to figure out what just happened.

Is "my boyfriend" now a moot point? Do I push the issue?

Reaching his destination, he turned abruptly, and I walked straight into his hard chest. My heart banged against its shell, and my breath was coming out in hollow spurts. *I might die if this keeps up.*

He looked down at me, and his jaw flexed, momentarily giving away that whatever this was going on between us was painful for him as well. "I'm about to let you in on my best-kept secret," he said calmly, quickly composing himself. He walked two fingers up from my chin and placed his index finger to my lips as if to hush them. "But you have to promise," he brushed his finger gently over my mouth, "to never," *brush,* "ever," *brush,* "tell anyone."

Brush.

My eyes closed for a moment as that one touch sent signals to all my buzzing nerve endings. *Oh my god, what is this?*

When I opened my eyes, he was still staring down at me. Bent slightly, his face was so close, I could see every fleck swimming in his gorgeous blue pools. He smirked at my obvious discomfort and my eyes followed the curl of his lip.

"Hi, Angel."

I was so lightheaded, I felt like I was swimming on a cloud. "Hi, Blake."

"Wanna know my secret?"

"I don't know, do I?"

He opened his mouth, then shut it and was silent for a moment, trying to decide something. I could see an internal struggle ensuing and his jaw had developed a serious tic. He must have decided to go with the angel rather than the devil because he straightened his spine, turned, and sat, putting his back against an enormous weeping willow. He patted the space to his left and squinted up at me.

I slid down onto my backside, thankful for the reprieve because my legs were weak. For the first time, we weren't looking at each other. Rather, we were staring into the horizon, and it felt . . . comfortable.

"This is my favorite place in the world," he told me. "I feel like it belongs to me. I don't know how no one has found it yet."

We were hooded by the hair of the oversized tree, staring out across the pond. Shimmering twinkles danced across the water. Little by little, the pressure in my tightly wound up body subsided.

"It's so peaceful here. I may have to steal it from you."

"You don't have to steal. I share. This can be *our* place now. It's only fitting the most beautiful place be filled with the most beautiful creature." He made that word sound so endearing, I pushed back the chill that coated my spine. "When I first saw you, I knew I had to get you here."

Focusing on my hands, I started picking at the skin surrounding my nails. "You've got to stop saying those things to me. I don't know what to do with it." My brain was riddled with conflicting emotions.

He let out a frustrated sigh. "I'm sorry. I'm getting ahead of myself. I do just want to be your friend. I'll be good." He lifted my chin, and raised three fingers on the other hand. "Scout's honor. Just get that look off your face. I can't stand it." He smiled, willing me to do the same.

The corner of my lips turned up in a half smile, and he dropped my chin and relaxed against the massive trunk. "I come here at least once a week. Sometimes things with my dad are too much, and I can't think unless I come and sit with Bertha."

I bit down on a chuckle. "Bertha?"

"*Yes,*" he drew out the word, "Bertha." He patted the bark behind him as if I should have known.

"Oh." I stifled my chuckle, not wanting to insult him.

"Don't laugh. This is my other BFF, so I need you two to get along."

"I'm sorry." I cleared my throat. "Hi, Bertha. Nice to meet you." I looked up and waved, still choking through my giggles.

A subtle wind blew, and she swayed as though she was actually waving back.

My mouth dropped open, and Blake grinned. "She likes you." He turned toward me. "You have to come visit her now, or she'll get upset. They don't call them weeping willows for nothin'."

I nodded because somehow I thought he was right. "Understood."

Scrunching his eyebrows together, he tilted his head. "I just told you my best friend is a tree that I sit and talk to once a week, and you actually look like you understand."

"The girl just waved back at me." I squeaked. "How could I not?" We both laughed and leaned back together.

A slight breeze sent tendrils of my hair in Blake's direction. The way my golden strands looked laying across his tanned arm felt somewhat intimate. I wished I had nerve endings there so I could actually feel his smooth, taut skin. Heat rushed to my cheeks, and a drumming started in my girly nether region. *Shit*. I needed a distraction. Something else, anything else.

"So what's the deal with your dad anyway?" I knew I shouldn't pry because I didn't want him reciprocating with personal questions, but I couldn't stop myself. The look on his face when he talked about it made me want to help him in any way I could.

His shoulders slumped, and he started picking at the grass and flicking it toward his feet. "He's a judge on the Supreme court. I think I was born and bred for the sole purpose of following in his footsteps. When I was little, I was so proud of that. I couldn't wait to be big and be strong and powerful like him." He wore a reminiscent smile, seeming far away again. The corners of his mouth slowly dropped and he snorted. "People run around, hanging on his every word, and I was always one of them. But as I got older, I was interested in other things. Sports, writing, photography." He sent me a fleeting glance. "None of them were good enough." He fingered more blades of grass and tugged out his aggressions. "No matter what I wanted to do, he knocked it down. He'd tell me they were 'frivolous hobbies, not fitting for *his* son'." He straightened. "So I hid it. Trophies stayed in my closet. Pages and pictures were stuffed under my mattress and in my drawers. My whole existence was hidden from him." He glanced at me. "Still is."

He shrugged casually as if it was no big deal, but hurt radiated from his eyes. He looked like a wounded child, which is probably exactly how he felt, constantly vying for his father's approval. "It's cool, though. I'm not a kid anymore. I'm over it." He chucked the last blade he'd been toying with toward his feet.

An overwhelming urge to comfort him and take this from his shoulders washed over me. To let him know he *was* good enough. I instinctively reached over and touched his hand. "It's so far from cool, and you should *not* be over it."

One corner of his mouth quirked up. "Calm down, Angel. I'm a big boy. I'm past my daddy issues."

My face screwed inward and I made a sharp turn at my waist to face him. "Like hell you are. You sit by yourself once a week talking to a tree because she's all who'll listen. I haven't even taken one psych class yet, and I can assure you that's a problem." I slanted my head up briefly. "No offense, Bertha." I looked back to him. "We have to fix this."

"We, huh? I like the sound of that." He wiggled his eyebrows.

"Don't make a joke." I slapped his shoulder. "This is serious. It's your life. You're what, a junior?"

"Yeah, so?"

"So that means you've just started your third wasted year. Don't you see how ridiculous that is?"

Um, Eva, what happened to distancing yourself? And don't you have enough of your own problems?

Shut up, you.

He shrugged. "It's okay. I take extra English classes, and I'm never without my camera. I get my fix, and I'll have a good career when I'm done."

"And you'll be miserable every day of your life. How is that okay?" Even with my problems, I was trying my best to push past them and make myself happy somehow.

"Look at you all ferocious and shit. You're like a wild beast. I like it." He growled into my neck, sending goose bumps across my flesh.

I shied away from him. "Don't make jokes. And *I'm* the only one who gets to growl. Grrr." I poked him in the side.

He flinched and covered his ribs. "I'm not making jokes. I'm seriously scared you might bite me."

"I don't bite. Only on Tuesdays," I teased, finally making light of the situation.

"Damn it!" He threw his hands down. "I missed it by one day!"

I could tell he was trying to brush off the topic, and I didn't want to push him, so I dropped it . . . for now. "We're not done with this conversation. Not by a long shot. But this place is too relaxing to talk about something so frustrating."

"Good. Thank you." He took my hand and kissed my knuckles before lacing our fingers and placing them on his outstretched legs. My body unconsciously rested its head on his shoulder and leaned into him. I felt his head fall on top of my own and, like pieces of a puzzle, we sat in silence for a few minutes. The only movement was the tiny circles he was drawing on the back of my hand with his thumb.

What's happening? Look at yourself, lying under a tree with this guy cozying it up. Seriously?

What was I doing?

I pulled my hand away, scrambling to my feet, causing his body to fall into the spot I'd just vacated. He looked as if I'd just thrown a bucket of cold water over him.

"I should get back. Jace'll worry if he comes to my apartment and I'm not there."

"Wait." He was righting himself, but I had already turned and was rushing away. I heard him get to his feet and start after me. "Angel, please!"

I stopped in my tracks. My head dropped and my shoulders sagged forward. I turned to face him, but I didn't look him in the eye. I couldn't.

"Have dinner with me."

No, Eva. NO!

"I can't, I have plans." My feet worked on their own, backing up, making a futile attempt to escape.

Walk away from the model!

Shhhh.

I'm fucking answering myself now. Awesome.

"Lunch, then? Please?" He sounded desperate.

"I, um . . ."

He took advantage of my hesitation and closed the gap between us in one large step. Electricity bolted through me at his touch, forcing my eyes to meet his, instantly clouding me in the depths of his stare.

My legs stopped the pretense of trying to flee.

"Please." His eyes were imploring. It was as if he was staring straight into my soul, trying to will me to do what he wanted.

Well, hell.

"Okay," I murmured.

His mouth slowly turned into the biggest Cheshire cat grin I'd ever seen. "Come on." He held onto my hand like it was his lifeline and he was scared I would evaporate.

"How do you keep talking me into these things?" I asked, still stunned at the turn of events.

He shrugged. "Because, you love me. You just don't know it yet."
And there was that dimple again.

Fuck.

Chapter 6

BANG! BANG! BANG! BANG!

"It's me. Open the door."

At the sound of the familiar, albeit angry, voice, I pulled back the door. Jace stood in my entryway, foot tapping, arms crossed over his chest, and a scowl on his face.

"Come in before you scare the neighbors, psycho." I stepped aside as he stomped past, nose high in the air. He turned on his heel, and I had to stop short to avoid crashing into him.

"What's up your ass?" I crossed my arms over my chest.

"What the hell is going on, *Angel*?" He made the word sound filthy. "You want to explain to me what that episode was all about today? How do you expect me to protect you if you hide things from me? *And* while we're on the topic, *why* are you hiding things from me?"

This degree of mad had never been directed at *me* before. "Calm down. I wasn't hiding anything." *Not really.* "There was nothing to tell. He's the guy who helped me that day at the frat party, remember?" *The super hot, model sexy one.* "I saw him again yesterday in the cafeteria, and he's in my English class. That's it." *And suddenly we're BFFs, and my world has turned topsy turvy. No big.*

"That's it?" he asked suspiciously.

"That's it." I crossed my arms over my chest and nodded.

He narrowed his eyes at me. "You're fucking lying. It's all over your face. Did you forget who you're talking to? Hello, Mcfly." He knocked on my head. "You're talking to me." He pointed a finger at himself. "Jace. You might as well be trying to fool your own self. Not possible, sweetheart. Now spill it before I physically beat it out of you. I saw the way you looked at that boy."

I threw my hands down in frustration. "Okay, okay. Just chill out. Geez, you're like an animal right now. What's gotten into you?"

"Evangelina, so help me god . . ."

Oh man, I was in trouble. He never used my full name.

"All right!" I snapped. "Come sit down at least." I stomped to the couch and slammed myself down in a huff. But he was still looming over me, arms crossed, foot tapping, and his tongue shoved into his teeth.

"Well?" I raised my eyebrows at him.

"I'm not sitting. Speak."

"You're really going to stand over me like this is an interrogation?"

"E-vang-e-lina, Now!"

I let out an irritated sigh. "Ugh, you're such a bitch sometimes. Fine. That night at the frat party I had this weird attraction to him I didn't understand. I tried to brush it aside because it didn't make any sense. After, when I was lying on the ground, the minute he was near me I just felt . . . calm. I think *that* freaked me out even more. He was touching me and stuff and I didn't care. I almost wanted him to . . . I think." My eyebrows puckered as I contemplated that notion. "Then yesterday I was in the cafeteria, trying to get my head on straight, and all of a sudden he was just there. He was so close and something came over me. I've never felt like that before. I was all tingly and sweaty and couldn't breathe right. I was a fucking mess, but not a nervous mess or a scared mess. A hot, turned on mess. I mean did you look at the guy?"

He wasn't budging yet, so I gave him the rest. The part he was looking for.

"Anyway, I didn't know how to handle it, so I tried to get away from him. Turns out, since I have the luck of a degenerate gambler, he's in my class too. So I was stuck with that very hot, very sweet, fine piece of ass for the next two hours. Which, by the way, I spent panting and squirming in my seat every time he turned those unnaturally gorgeous fucking eyes in my direction. It's freaky. It's like there's an electric current running between us or something. I ran away from him as soon as the class was over, and left him with his mouth hanging open, but the damage was already done. Let's just say I had a very rough night."

Looking away, I hung my head in defeat and lowered my voice. "Happy now?"

Unfolding his arms, he relaxed his stance. Very gently, he lowered himself down next to me and pulled me into his chest. I wrapped my arms around his waist, putting my legs over his lap as he pet my hair.

"No, Eva. I'm not happy now. Why would that make me happy?"

"I don't know what to do, Jace." I sniffled. "I'm scared."

"Don't be scared, baby girl, and don't you cry either. There's been enough of that. What happened when I left you today?"

"We spent the afternoon lounging and talking at the park, and then we went to lunch. It felt so . . . *normal.*"

I unwrapped myself and concentrated on his face. "I'm in serious trouble. First of all, he likes me. I mean, abnormally likes me. And the guy's persistent. I told him I had a boyfriend, and he didn't even blink. I'd be able to handle it, except . . ." I threw my gaze away from him, unable to bear the scrutiny.

He took my chin between his fingers, bringing my focus back to him. "Except you feel the same way and don't want to push this one away."

"Jace, what am I gonna do?"

He took me by both shoulders, his eyes understanding and sympathetic. "Listen to me, sugar, it's okay. *This* is okay. It's normal. You're supposed to let yourself feel these things. You *deserve* to feel this. That wasn't why I was coming down on you. You don't know this guy. I didn't know how far it went or why you were keeping it from me. You can't hide things from me, Eva—ever. You understand that, right?"

I nodded.

"Promise. Out loud," he demanded.

"I promise," I said solemnly, hooking my little finger with his and sticking our thumbs in our mouths. It was the familiar pinky swear we'd been doing since we were five.

Jace finally relaxed. "I have to say, though, when you do something you sure do it right. That guy is sex on legs." He fanned himself.

I shot to my feet and began the endless pacing I did when I was nervous. "He's perfect! I've tried a million times over to find something, anything, wrong with him. All I find is another reason why he's so damn perfect. This is so bad. You know I can't pursue this. It's impossible. But I don't know how to get rid of him. Every time I try, he won't let me, and I don't have the strength to force him. He breaks everything down inside me. I'm like jelly the second he looks at me. It's complete insanity. And, if that wasn't bad enough, the guy is a total fucking chivalrous sweetheart."

I stopped pacing and turned abruptly as the answer to my prayers slapped me in the face. "You. You need to get rid of him for me. Yes, that's it!"

He sat back and casually crossed his legs, stretching his arms across the back of the couch. "I'm not so sure we should be getting rid of him, Eva. We have to talk about this."

"No! You have to, Jace. You have to! It won't work. He'll either find out, or think I need to be placed in a psych ward once he spends a little time with me."

I slammed down to my knees in front of him, propping my hands together in the begging position. "Please, Jace. Pretty please, with sugar on top." I batted my eyelashes, trying to persuade him.

He jumped off the couch. "Girl, get it together now. You're acting crazy. And get up off your knees. That look does nothing for me." He grabbed me by the shoulders and yanked me to my feet. "I can't believe how you're carrying on." He held me still so I'd have no choice but to focus on him. "Listen to me. This might just be a blessing in disguise. You need to start moving on, and I can't think of a better distraction."

"Are you insane?" My voice squeaked. "You've actually lost your mind. It's happened." I tried to pull away, but he held me tighter.

"I'm serious. I'm not doing this for you. Not yet, anyway. Let's see where this goes. Just trust me. Have I ever done anything to hurt you?"

My shoulders sagged in defeat. "No."

"Okay, well I'm not about to start now. Have a little faith, huh?"

"Ugh, whatever," I huffed and yanked myself away. "I hope you know what you're asking. You're throwing me into the lion's den here, and I'm the steak."

"Oh, please." He rolled his eyes. "I'm the dramatic one in this relationship, honey. Take it down a notch. You're gonna throw us off kilter. Now get your shit together. You're sleeping with me tonight, and you can tell me all about McDreamy. I need to keep my eyes on you."

"Yes, master." I reluctantly dragged myself down the hall to change into my pajamas.

Back at his apartment, Jace safely tucked me beneath the covers. I told him all about my time with Blake in explicit detail; he wouldn't have it any other way. Amid the oohs and aahs, he expressed over and over how hot Blake was. I had to be careful, or he might just go after him for himself. He'd been known to turn a few to the other team.

Yawning, he looked over and grew serious. "Just be careful, all right? I'm being hard on you because I want you to move on and try your hand at a regular life, but I know what this means for you and that you won't have an easy road ahead. Do *not* keep anything from me. You feel something, tell me. You're scared, tell me. He hurts you, you better fucking tell me."

"I will, if I even go through with this. For now, I'll just let him be my friend. He's not asking for more than that anyway."

"Okay, it's a start." He tucked me into his side. "Love you, mama."

"Love you too, crazy."

"Now, get some sleep. You look like shit."

JESSIE DROPPED HER LUNCH TRAY on the cafeteria table and sat across from me. "So, I talked to Rick. He says you can come tonight to meet him, and if it works out, you can stay and train." She was super excited. "Did I do good?"

I looked up from my cell phone. "Um, yeah!" I smiled. "Thank you. I'm slacking. I was supposed to be all over getting a job and studying, and I've done nothing. I needed a push in the right direction."

I was struggling so bad to keep my head on straight lately, I was starting to question whether coming here was even going to help. So far, I wasn't any different from before, except for the ease I felt knowing I was alone and safe.

"Well, here's your first nudge." She beamed with pride. "Glad I could be of assistance. Rick's a great guy and, shall we say, easy on the eyes." Her demeanor turned from bubbly to scandalous. "Speaking of incredibly good looking men, who was that smokin' piece of male specimen that swept you off your feet yesterday? I almost fainted. The way he was holding onto you and looking at you, I swear I thought my clothes were going to disintegrate off my body. I actually stopped breathing for a second. Not to mention the cold shower I had to take when I got home. I get the chills just thinking about it." She made a show of shivering and fanning herself.

"Oh, yeah. That's Blake. He's just a friend." I shrugged, trying to portray indifference.

She waved her fork around. "Friend, shmend. He likes you, Eva, and I've never seen anything so gorgeous in my life. He seems really sweet, too."

And oh how he is, damn him. "Yeah, well I'm taken, so he's out of luck."

Her mouth dropped open, displaying salad fragments and all. "You're serious?"

"As a heart attack. And close your mouth." I wrinkled my nose.

"Well, step aside then, sista. I wouldn't mind taking a ride on *that* express train." She wiggled her eyebrows, forking another bite.

I laughed, but something inside me unhinged, and I had to fight to keep my claws tucked away. *What the hell was that?* Composing myself, I plastered on my huge phony smile. "Go for it."

Jessie's face turned pale just as a deep voice rustled the hair beside my ear. "This seat taken?"

My belly fell out.

My body went rigid while my insides became languid, and the combination was so contradictory, it sent me into shock. The sound of the chair scraping beside me knocked me from my paralysis. I looked over to see a familiar dimple plunged deep into his smooth cheek.

He leaned in so close, I could smell the mint on his breath. "Hi, Angel."

I swallowed my tongue. "Hi, Blake."

If he's going to keep doing this to me, I'll probably go into cardiac arrest.

Jessie kicked me under the table, her eyes popped out so far I wouldn't have been surprised if they'd fallen out of her face. She was glancing back and forth wildly from me to him to drive home the point I hadn't introduced them yet.

I cleared my throat. "Um, Blake, this is my friend Jessie. Jessie, this is Blake."

She donned her signature smile and shot her hand across the table at him. "Nice to meet you, Blake."

"Likewise." He flashed those sexy-ass dimples politely back at her, and then turned a heated gaze back to me.

"So, are you following me again? Do I have to call campus security and tell them I have a stalker?" I chided playfully.

"You just might." Blake's smile turned mischievous. "Actually, you know I'm here at this time, so I'm thinking *you* might be the one following *me.*" He placed a hand on his chest, looking at me adoringly. "Don't break my heart and tell me I'm wrong, sweetheart."

"You're wrong," I stated matter-of-factly.

"Ow!" He clutched his chest and leaned back, making an overly dramatic show of faking a heart attack. "Someone call nine-one-one!"

I laughed, pushing his shoulder. "Stop it! You're making a scene."

He grabbed my hand and held it against his hard chest so I could feel his heart frantically flying beneath it. His voice lowered. "See, I told you. I'm not lying. It's short circuiting, and it's all your fault."

My lungs ceased.

Feeling his chiseled chest and the organ that drives this man beneath my palm was not something I was equipped to deal with. Tingles crept up the tips of my fingers with every erratic jump of his heart. I swallowed the cotton ball shoved inside my throat and nudged him, trying to play it off. "I can't take you."

His grip tightened and he tugged me toward him. "You can take me any time, anywhere you'd like." The double meaning behind his words didn't go unnoticed.

It felt like the intensity of his stare would burn a hole through my retinas. I had to look away, but I couldn't. I was mesmerized, and so help me god, if I went blind, then I went blind. At least I'd have that image engrained in my mind.

"Have dinner with me tonight," Blake said.

"Um, tonight? I, um . . ." *have lost the ability to control my tongue apparently.*

"She's training at The Backdoor tonight," Jessie's voice was so small I barely recognized it. Her eyes were timid and uncertain as to whether or not she should have spoken.

I blinked, forgetting she was still here, or that anyone else was even in the room for that matter. I nodded to reassure her.

Giving myself a little shake to rattle the spell off me, I redirected my attention back to Blake, more in control of my flesh and bones. "Right. Jessie has a friend at The Backdoor. He's been kind enough to offer me a job as long as it works out tonight." I smiled.

"Bartending, huh?" Blake grimaced, finally setting me free.

"Yes, bartending. What's that look?" The smile faded from my face and my eyebrows pulled together.

"I don't know. Are you sure that's a good idea?" His leg bobbed up and down as if the news of my new job made him nervous, but I didn't understand why.

I shrugged it off. "Why not? I'm fully capable, and I need the money."

"I didn't mean to imply you weren't capable. I'm sure you are. It's just, well . . . guys can get a little . . . pushy." Blake rubbed his forehead and looked like he was searching for words that would change my decision.

"Oh, you don't have to worry about that," Jessie reassured him. "Rick's very protective of his employees. He has a no tolerance policy for that sort of stuff."

Wait, she's reassuring him?

"Rick?" His brows drew together, a hard line breaking between them.

"The owner," she clarified. "He's my friend, the one giving her the shot. She'll be able to pay for her rent after one night of tips with those looks." Jessie smiled, pointing in my direction. She wasn't helping my case. Not that I should have a case.

"Oh." He looked disappointed. "Well, what time do you start? In case I get . . . thirsty."

I shrugged. "I don't know. I didn't even meet the guy yet. Who knows if he's even going to like me."

Blake's voice lowered as he scowled. "Oh, he's gonna like you all right."

"Boy-friend," I reminded him. "Why does no one remember this?" My patience was wearing thin.

Blake's eyes softened, turning my insides all gooey. "Just watch your back. I don't trust it."

"I always do." My voice was soft yet firm.

Jessie pushed away from the table. "I'm heading out to class. Call me later, Eva, and I'll give you the details."

"Will do. Bye, Mama. And thanks again." I waved.

Blake stood and extended his long fingers in my direction, offering me assistance. "I'm here to escort you to your next class, m'lady."

I smiled and took his hand. I'd let him have this. Besides, with him around, my shaky ass could probably use the help. "Why thank you, sir. You're so kind." I tried my best to cover up the chills coursing through me. I thought they were good chills; they felt different, like warm, fuzzy little effervescent bubblies.

He kept my hand in his as we began the short walk to our English class. I looked up at him and raised a questioning eyebrow.

"What? Best friends hold hands. Don't they?" He squeezed my fingers a little tighter and looked ahead.

"Yes, but . . ."

"But what?" he pressed. "Don't tell me we're not best friends anymore. I can only handle one heart attack a day."

I sighed, muttering under my breath, "What am I gonna do with you?"

"I can think of a few things." A smirk played on his lips.

"You're so bad." I nudged him with my free hand. "How am I supposed to be your friend when you're always saying things like that?"

"I'm just kidding, Angel. Lighten up." He began to swing our hands like we were regular old sweethearts. "So how 'bout that weather, huh?"

"Yeah, yeah." I laughed.

We arrived at class, and he escorted me to his VIP section, twirling me before lowering me into my seat.

"Such a gentleman." I looked up at the chivalrous man before me. Wanting to reach out and touch him, I knotted my fists together.

"Always."

He sat on top of my desk and peered down at me. Moving one finger across my forehead, he pushed aside stray hairs, then twirled the ends between his fingers. His sparkling eyes began to look heavy as his gaze slipped to my lips. "So how about Friday then?"

"Huh?" I muttered, staring at his plump bottom lip.

"Dinner."

"Oh." *Crap.* Lie! "Studying."

He eyed me warily, as if he could see through my ruse. Unaffected, his finger left my hair to trace my jawline. That one fingertip was like a lighted match to my skin. "Saturday then?"

Time for my go-to.

I sat up straight, bringing my game-face back, although I felt the disappointment simmering beneath the surface of my mirage. "Going to visit my boyfriend."

He didn't flinch—again. He just kept moving his thumb back and forth along my chin, driving me insane.

Damn him!

"Sunday then. And I won't take no for an answer. I need to feed you." His eyes stayed trained on my lips as his thumb stroked dangerously close to them.

I swallowed, ignoring that fact. "You *need* to feed me?"

"Yes. You're wilting away." He moved up to caress my cheekbones now. "What kind of best friend would I be if I didn't feed you?"

"I am not wilting away. I'm the same weight as always," I said defensively, even though my voice lacked authority.

He leaned in, placing his full palm to the side of my face to steady my gaze. His glinting eyes raked the length of my body before settling his determined stare on my green ones. "Sunday. You're all mine on Sunday."

The air lodged in my throat, fighting with my esophagus to be set free. It felt like my insides were replaced by a swarm of fluttering butterflies.

Is my heart quivering? Can the heart actually quiver? I can't breathe. Oh god, I can't breathe.

"Are you all right?" His eyes widened as he dropped his hands to cup my shoulders. "Breathe!"

Oh no. Oh no. Oh no.

Full. Blown. Panic attack.

Run! Don't let him see you!

"I can't do this." I sprung up on shaking legs, grabbing my bag as an afterthought, and darted past him, making a run for the door.

"Angel. Wait. I'm sorry!" he shouted, panic evident in his voice.

Not as sorry as I am.

My legs ran and ran. I didn't know where I was going, but I couldn't stop. If I stopped, I would feel this and I didn't want to feel it. I didn't want to feel anything anymore. I kept trying to shut off my nerve endings, but they wouldn't listen. They just hardened their resolve to continue the endless torture, making me victim to constant lashings day in and day out.

My subconscious drove me to the last place I had felt happy and safe—Bertha.

I threw myself at her feet, panting, and then it began. Uncontrollable tears and gut-wrenching sobs took over, and I curled up into a protective ball, shielding my face with my hair.

When I finally opened my eyes, I was garnished in leaves, and I couldn't help but wonder if Bertha was trying to conceal me from prying eyes while I broke down. The long hair atop her head seemed like it was hanging lower today and, when the wind blew, strands swept across my cheek, consoling me.

I was so physically and mentally drained that I didn't notice him approach. Startled, I couldn't hide the look of panic that stretched across my face. He rushed to reassure me, jutting out his hands in a stopping motion.

"Don't run. I won't come near you, I promise. Not until you say it's okay. Just stay. Please." He dipped his head in a non-threatening manner, searching me for reassurance. Lowering himself in front of me, a short distance away, he crisscrossed his legs. "I'm so sorry, Angel—"

"Please, don't. I'm embarrassed enough."

His eyes turned sharp, serious. "No! It's not your fault. You have nothing to be ashamed of, do you understand me? It's me." The harsh line of his shoulders curled in. "When I get around you, I just can't help myself. I know I said I just want to be your friend, and I do, I swear I do, but something comes over me." Pain showed through his eyes. "It's weird, ya know? I don't even think *I* understand it. We barely know each other. I know how crazy it seems, trust me, but all I can concentrate on is touching you in any way you'll let me."

His focal point settled on my mouth. "Like right now. The hair you haven't noticed is trapped in your chapstick. All I can think about is freeing it." He gripped the blades of grass beside his thighs like he needed his hands distracted.

I reached a finger to my lips, finding the object of his attention and plucking it loose. I hadn't even felt it.

Blake smiled shyly. "I thought it was okay and I pushed too far. I'm sorry." He sighed and raked a frustrated hand through his hair. "God, when am I going to stop fucking this up?"

His admission left me stunned, and I wasn't sure if I had the energy left I'd need to deal with it.

"Say you forgive me. God, I never want to fucking see you cry— ever. I only want to make you feel good things, never bad. Please, don't hate me."

The heartbreaking look he wore actually made *me* want to comfort *him*. My heart felt like it had just melted and was leaking through my nervous system. I needed to make it better as badly as he needed for it to be better.

Truth.

He needed the truth.

He'd done nothing wrong and he was here groveling as though he had. "It's not you. It's me. I'm fucked up." I closed my mouth quickly, unable to believe I'd said that out loud. "I overreacted. Let's just drop it, okay? We'll pretend it didn't happen."

Blake relaxed a little, and I was grateful he wasn't harping on what I'd just said.

I gave him a shy smile. "And I don't hate you. I couldn't if I wanted to. Trust me, I've tried." I rolled my eyes.

"Is it all right if I come closer now?" He looked like he couldn't stomach the distance anymore. It was cute. It relaxed my insides.

"Yeah, it's okay." I scooted over to give him room and patted the space beside me. "Bertha misses you."

Blake inched toward me on his butt like a worm, skeptical of every move he made in my direction. When he finally reached me, he was rigid by my side, leaving more distance than necessary. He sat on his hands as if he didn't trust he could keep them to himself.

"Relax, I'm fine. It was all too overwhelming. I'm sorry I reacted that way. I just don't trust myself when I'm with you. It makes me nervous. You must think I'm out of my mind, huh?"

"I'll never think anything bad of you, Angel. I don't want to tell you what I do think of you. You might run away again, and I forgot to wear my running shoes today, obviously."

I laughed, and the mood shifted between us like we'd been doing this for years.

Pulling his hands from their place underneath him, Blake turned toward me. He lifted his thumbs to the swollen, tender flesh beneath my lower lashes and smoothed away the loose tears and streaks of mascara, letting his hands cradle my face once he'd cleaned it all away. The act was so compassionate and gentle, I couldn't help but close my eyes and just feel. Feel him. Feel safe. Just . . . feel.

When I opened my eyes, he was staring at me as if there was so much he wanted to say. I had to put a stop to this. "Blake, I—"

"Come on." He smiled sweetly. "Let me take you for some ice cream."

"Ice cream?" I cocked my head to the side.

He winked and pulled me to my feet. "Sure. Ice cream makes everything better. And I already told you, I'll take whatever I can get."

Chapter 7

THE BAR WAS EMPTY WHEN I arrived, but I could already tell I liked it. It was small, clean, and surprisingly homey.

Immediately at ease, my gaze wandered, taking in my surroundings. A jukebox to my left flashed, alongside a computerized game. In front of me, an enormous bar sparkled. Behind it, a massive back, wearing a white button down shirt stood, counting the money in the register. He was bopping his head to the familiar nineties song playing over the sound system, his longish, ashy blond hair swept over his collar as he continued to rock-out.

When he finished counting, he used his hip to push in the drawer mid-lyric, then did a double take as he turned around to find me standing there.

I put my hand up and slowly waved, embarrassed for having found him that way.

Not the least bit ashamed, a big smile spread across his face. "And you must be Evangelina."

"The one and only." I flashed a toothy smile at him. I needed this to go right.

He walked over, extending his tanned hand. "I'm Rick. Nice to meet you." He was a bit older than me, possibly mid-twenties. His eyes were a light, cloudy, friendly blue, and his features were kind of . . . pretty.

"Eva. Please." I gripped his hand in a firm handshake. "It's nice to meet you, too. Thanks for doing this for me. I really appreciate it, especially on such short notice."

"No problem. Jessie's my girl. There's nothing I wouldn't do for her. Come, have a seat and we can get to know each other a little better."

"Lead the way."

We walked through a large opening, down a couple of steps to a dance floor where there were a few tables and chairs set. Pulling out the closest one, he gestured for me to sit before walking around to take the seat across from me.

"So, Eva, tell me a little about yourself."

"Well, I just moved here from Colt's Neck, where I spent my whole life. There isn't much to do in a small town so, of course, I grew up mixing drinks at house parties."

He nodded his head, giving me a friendly smile. "Didn't we all?"

My body relaxed even further, seeing how relatable he was. "I left because I wanted a fresh start and just enrolled in my freshman year of college. That's where I met Jessie. I know Jersey isn't a ways off for most people, but it's a ways off for me, so this is all pretty new."

The corners of his eyes crinkled, and he folded his hands on the table, allowing me to continue.

"Anyway, I have a very nice, very expensive apartment that needs to be paid for somehow. I figure this kind of job is probably the only one that can afford me to do that and," I shrugged, "I'm good at it. Plus, I'm sure it's good times. Am I right?"

He nodded and chuckled. "Indeed."

"So Jessie mentioned she had a friend and that she thought I'd do well here and . . . well, here I am."

"Fair enough. My turn." He leaned back in his chair, extended his legs, and crossed one over the other. Clasping his hands behind his head, he looked like he was sitting in his living room, talking about a baseball game rather than conducting a job interview. "This bar is my home. It's my life. My family. It's everything to me. If you want to come on board, you become my family and you treat it the same. Those are the rules."

I looked at him through a tilted view. "Are you saying I have the job?"

His lips spread into a bright smile. "Let's see how you do tonight. If all goes well and we mesh, then sure, you have the job." He sat up straight and leaned in, taking inventory of me from head to toe. "I think you'll fit in perfectly. Just remember how important this place is to me and always respect it. No drama. No jealous boyfriends. Just, as you say, good times. Deal?"

"Deal." I nodded, unable to contain my excitement. "Thank you so much! You won't regret it, I promise. Just tell me what you want me to do."

He laughed at my rambling. "You're starting to sound like Jessie now. Come on, let's show you the ropes." He stood up and made a sweeping motion. "This is where the bands and deejays set up. We have a dance floor and a few places to sit and hang out. Pretty standard stuff."

He walked toward the back corner to a long staircase that led to the lower level, which was set up like a cushy lounge. It was a different atmosphere from the bar area we'd just left. Deep plush couches and giant ottomans were scattered inside purple walls with bubbles crawling up them. There was another bar in the far left corner. It was just as big, and even shinier than the one upstairs.

"This is really nice. I'm thoroughly impressed," I said as I completed a full circle. He'd obviously spent a lot of time designing this space, and his love for it shined through.

He smiled. "I appreciate that. I try to cater to everyone. We're your neighborhood pub if that's what you're in the mood for, but a more modern, upscale lounge if that's what tickles your fancy. We support local bands and deejays, while still maintaining the old time feel of a jukebox. We have it all." He clapped his hands together proudly. "You'll be switching between here and upstairs, but I think you'll enjoy both. Dress code is whatever you like, just don't get too daring. I have a strict no touching policy, and you'll only make my job harder. But keep in mind you'll want the greatest amount of tips. Everyone should believe they *can* go home with you, even though no one actually will. Get my drift?" He raised his eyebrows, waiting for my reply.

"Got it." I nodded once. "I really can't thank you enough for this."

"Thank *you*." He started back toward the steps. "You'll be upstairs with me tonight. It's more beer and less extravagant drinks, so it'll break you in easy. Let's go up and I'll show you what goes on behind the scenes."

Around nine o'clock, patrons began to wander in. Working with Rick was smooth and comfortable; you'd never know we just met. I could tell he was a good guy, and I didn't feel on edge around him. After everything I'd been through, I'd become a good judge of character.

By eleven o'clock, the place was hopping. There was a deejay tonight with a large, very thirsty following. Rick and I had fallen into a rhythm, and I thought I was doing my job impressing him. We were entertaining the crowd, singing at each other into makeshift bottle microphones. He grabbed me by the hand, and twirled me into him before pushing on my hip, sending me spiraling outward. I swirled to the opposite end of the bar, laughing, spinning, and playing the role. Stopping myself abruptly on the edge, my head jerked forward, sending my hair cascading over my face. I flipped it up in an overly dramatic fashion to play with whoever was seated there when my eyes locked on blue diamonds.

His stare was fierce, primal and possessive. "Hi, Angel."

Chest heaving, I stared right back at him, because I hadn't figured out how not to yet. "Hi, Blake."

The background noise faded, and all that existed was me and him, locked in our own private universe.

"Eva . . . Eva." Noise funneled into my ears. I forced my gaze away. Rick stood at the other end of the bar with an unspoken question in his eyes.

I gave him a thumbs up and mouthed 'friend', then I turned back to the god perched on the stool before me.

Exhaling, I rubbed my palms over my thighs. "You got thirsty?"

Blake's eyes flitted over my shoulder in Rick's direction, assessing him before returning his attention to me. "Parched."

I leaned my hip on the bar. "What can I get you to quench your thirst?" It may have come across a bit provocative, but I didn't care. I was sick of being the only one left to squirm.

Take that, Dimples!

I watched his breath become strangled by his Adam's apple as it made a slow and deliberate travel, first up and then down the glorious length of his neck. Seeing it up close did things to me and I instinctively crossed my legs.

His hands gripped the edge of the bar, turning his knuckles white, and his eyes portrayed the struggle going on beneath them. He opened his mouth to say something, and I knew it was killing him not to bite at my outward insinuation. Then a devilish grin spread across his face.

Leaning as far forward as the barrier between us would allow, he stared at my lips and threw my sass back at me. "Sex On The Beach sounds perfect."

Flames sparked instantly in the sweet spot between my thighs. The heat that started there pricked down my legs and then slithered up every pore in my body before slamming into my cheeks.

Get a hold of yourself. You asked for that, idiot.

Playing his game, I peaked one wicked eyebrow. "Sex On The Beach it is." Giving a wink, I turned to work on his drink, feeling his eyes boring into me the whole time. I swore they could touch me. All over. Everywhere.

What's gotten into me? This has to be those few shots talking. I'm so going to regret this. I just know it.

When I returned with his liquid sex, a straw poked from the corner of his mouth, and he was working his jaw mercilessly. I instantly felt bad for leading him on. It was stupid of me. I didn't want to give him the wrong impression, so I played it off as best I could. "I have to work. It's my first night, so I can't really stay and chat."

"That's okay. I'll just be here, quenching my thirst." His eyes deliberately raked the length of me, pinning me in place. It sent a chill down my spine, and I almost believed *we* just had sex on the beach. He tipped his glass to me, showing off his dimple. "Cheers."

I tried to shake it off and appear unaffected, my body feeling as though it was vibrating back over to Rick.

Blake sat there the rest of the night, watching my display, an inscrutable look on his face. I made him a few more drinks, careful not to linger too long.

When my shift ended, my eyes immediately sought out Blake. He was gone. He'd left without saying goodbye. All that remained was the twenty dollar tip he'd left hanging over the edge of the bar with his empty glass on top of it. My heart sank to the pit of my stomach. I cleared away the glass and threw the twenty into the oversized fishbowl. Trying to cover up my disappointment, I cheerfully turned to Rick. "So, how'd

I do?"

He gleamed. "Phenomenal! Seriously, Eva. You were awesome. The job is yours. How'd you like it?"

"I loved it. I had such a good time, and we worked so well together, don't ya think?"

"I couldn't agree more. So what nights are you free?"

I beamed. "I'll make myself free. You just say the word and I'm here."

"Let's start with Monday, Wednesday and Friday for now. Deal?"

"Deal."

We shook on it and I was elated. I plucked my cell from my bag to text Jes as I walked out the door.

> Me: *I so owe you a months worth of pedicures. I got the job! Rick's great and I couldn't be happier. Thanks, girl!*

My fingers worked quick as I walked absentmindedly. Smiling, I slid my phone back into my bag. When I looked up, my steps halted. Blake's magnificent form was only a few feet away, illuminated under a street-light. He was standing how he normally did—leaning against the side of the building, one foot perched behind him, pieces of his silky hair falling into his eyes.

God, the man was gorgeous.

I approached him the way you would a butterfly you didn't want to fly away. "Hey, I thought you'd left without saying goodbye." I gave a flirty little pout.

Stupid shots!

One corner of his mouth tipped up. "Come on now. Would I do that?"

A smile crept up my lips. "No, I guess not."

"So, how'd it go?"

"So great! I got the job. I start tomorrow. I guess studying will have to wait again."

He gave a smile that didn't quite reach his eyes. The faintest look of something short of distress flickered there instead.

I didn't like that smile.

"I can always help you study, you know."

"Really? You would do that for me?"

Blake rolled his eyes. "Angel, I'm starting to think there isn't much I *wouldn't* do for you at this point."

I didn't know what to do with that. Blushing, I tucked my hair behind my ear and ducked my head. "Thanks. Well, I guess I'll see you around campus then?"

"Uh-uh. I'm walking you home. You didn't think I was letting you walk alone this time of night, did you? I didn't just stand here to hold this wall up." He pushed off the side of the building, landing nearly chest to chest with me.

I fought the urge to step forward, while at the same time fighting the urge to step back. *Friggin' head case.*

"Lead the way." He enveloped my hand, and we began to walk toward my apartment.

We had such a nice, easy stroll, you'd think it was the middle of the afternoon. I was so comfortable with him; it was like we'd known each other for years. We talked easily and somehow he managed to get me to open up. Every time I was with him, I felt like I could actually be myself. It'd been so many years since I'd done that, I thought I'd forgotten how.

Rounding the corner, my building came into view. I hadn't considered he would wind up knowing where I lived. Too late now.

We reached my front door, both dragging our feet, prolonging the inevitable.

I looked at my toes, my voice small as I said, "Hey, Blake?"

"Yeah, Angel."

I peeked up at him. "I'm glad you waited."

A slow smile swept across his lips. I wondered if he realized he was chewing away at my resolve. "Ditto. Actually, gimme your phone."

"For what?"

"Stop being so difficult all the time. Can you do that? I want to give you my number in case I'm ever not here on the nights you're working and you have a problem. That okay?" He reached out his hand, waiting.

I considered what he'd said a moment and the fact this would put us one step closer before fishing my phone from my bag and placing it in his waiting palm. His fingers made quick work of the buttons and with a smirk he passed it back to me. When our hands met, he wrapped his around mine and tugged me in.

He hesitated a moment, watching my eyes for trepidation with every descending inch.

Somehow, I had none. I was sure he was going to kiss me and I wasn't moving. I wanted this.

My breathing sped up, and I wondered if he could see my pulse knocking on the skin at my throat. The slow torture of him inching toward me, blue diamonds blazing, had my knees ready to buckle. I locked them to keep myself upright, the swift rise and fall of his chest a giveaway of his own weakness. When he was finally close enough that I could feel the tiny flicks of his ragged breath, he turned his head ever so slightly and brought his attention to the place where the corner of my mouth met my cheek and settled his lips there.

The second his mouth made contact with my skin, it was like I'd been branded. I was sure I would forever feel his lips seared in that very spot.

My chest heaved and my breaths sputtered through my lips. Pins and needles pricked every inch of my being and those butterflies were battering my insides again. I was worried I might pass out. I wanted to run away, yet I wanted to hold him to this very spot at the same time. I wanted to say no, and I wanted to say yes. I wanted to get mad, and I wanted to get happy.

Lunatic.

Slowly, he reached up with the hand that wasn't holding mine and laced it through the hair at the nape of my neck. He buried his nose in my throat and inhaled deeply, taking in my scent.

My eyes closed and my head dropped back. *God, this feels good.* I tried to memorize each sensation. It was my first experience with this and I never wanted to forget the details. The smell I'd come to know as Blake and the feel of his hand, secured at my nape. The way he explored me seeming to want to do the same. *This is what this should have been.*

His breath caressed the soft spot behind my ear sending a fresh wave of tremors through me. He took me in just a heartbeat longer, rubbing his nose up the length of my ear, then said in a breathy whisper, "Sweet dreams, Angel."

He released me and, just like that, he was gone. After a few unblinking seconds, I hugged my core, found my legs, and forced them to take me inside. I couldn't ignore the disappointment I felt, even though I knew I should be grateful he stopped.

What's wrong with you? This is what you wanted.

Right?

Chapter 8

U P ON THE ROOF, I popped in the ear buds to my iPod. Sarah McLachlan had always been my medicine, and I needed the good stuff right now. I listened to her songs on repeat sometimes, and they dissolved the salt in my wounds. Tonight, it was only fitting I play the first song that drew me to her, contemplating the first guy who drew me to him.

Possession.

I sang alongside her into the night, my voice heard by no one. The words resonated with me so deeply, I would have sworn this woman knew me.

I'd come to a realization tonight, after that almost kiss—I didn't want this sleepless solitude anymore. This was no life. Constant fear and worry. Constant feelings of filth and betrayal. I just wanted to forget. I wanted to feel good.

I wanted . . . Blake.

No, you don't.

Yes. I do.

I was talking to myself again. That was never a good thing.

But I couldn't do that to him. I was too screwed up to drag him into my mess. He wouldn't understand, and I wouldn't want him to. He was too good of a person. I didn't deserve him, and he didn't deserve me. He needed someone who could reciprocate everything he was looking to offer. It was time to push back a little. Make him forget about me.

I wrapped my arms around myself and hung my head, feeling uncomfortable at the prospect of not having him in my life. He made me feel good. Made me forget.

Why not me? Why do I never get to be happy?

I was constantly running. I came here to find a standstill, and I was *still* going round and round. The problem was, I couldn't escape myself; my demons were locked deep inside my soul. Persistent little fuckers. Would they ever go away? I could feel them in there. They were the ones whipping my nerve endings and causing the nausea. Keeping me barricaded from the rest of the world, sealed inside myself.

Fucking assholes.

"Leave me alone!" I screamed into the foggy night air. My words reverberated through the silence, becoming further and further away. My iPod chose that moment to begin *Blackbird* in Sarah McLachlan's soothing tones. Ugh, why was every song on this playlist so appropriate?

Fucking playlist.

I drew my knees into my chest and began to sing. In hysterics, my fingernails gouged holes in the flesh on my shins. The words barely made it past my lips as salty tears invaded my mouth. Right here, I wanted to forget the person who did this to me, who made me this way.

You were only waiting for this moment to be free.

God help me. I couldn't do this anymore. I just wanted to end it. That would be the only way to make it better. Free myself of the agony. Living this way just wasn't worth it anymore. I might as well finish myself off all at once instead of shutting down one cell at a time.

I ripped the portals of torment from my ears and threw them down in disgust. "Please, God. Give me a sign. Something. Anything. What am I supposed to do?" I shivered, a weeping lump of flesh.

The silence around me was deafening. The only sound was the sporadic hitch of air that came from your chest after a good bout of hysterics.

Breathe in. Breathe out. Hitch.

Breathe in. Breathe out. Hitch. Hitch.

Frantically wiping up and down my face, I dragged myself off the lounge chair. Going to the perimeter of the roof, I peered down, wondering what it would feel like to free fall to the bottom. Take hold of my fate and say fuck it. Break these chains and finally be free.

I pulled myself up and over the cold cement rail and settled my back against it. Holding on, I stared down at the tiny cars as I inched up on my tippy toes and leaned forward. *Maybe I could fly like a blackbird.* Dragging my bottom lip between my teeth, I creeped further, teetering on the edge. My stomach lurched, and I swallowed hard.

Pussy.

Another breath and I pushed back, unable to go through with it. That prick wasn't worth ending my life over. He'd already taken too much of me; I couldn't allow him that as well.

You were only waiting for this moment to be free.

I SPENT THE DAY GLIDING about the halls of the university. At least it was Friday, but making it through work tonight would be a challenge after the night I'd had.

Sandra let me copy a bunch of her notes, God bless her heart. She didn't say anything, just seemed to take notice of my zombie-like state. I wasn't doing a very good job of covering it up today. She merely gave me a half smile and pushed her notebook in my direction. Praise quiet, intuitive girls. I was doing a terrible job of concealing things here; worse than I'd done back home where I'd had constant reminders. *Go figure.*

Walking from my calculus class, my phone rang. I was so tired, I answered without looking at the caller I.D. "Hello."

"What the fuck, Evangelina!"

Shit! I stopped walking and tensed at the tone of the familiar voice on the other end.

"Did I not get the memo that we don't talk anymore?" She sounded irate.

"I'm sorry. You have no idea what I've been going through over here."

"You're right," she bit out. "I *don't* have any idea because *you* have apparently cut your only sister out of your life."

Oh no. I didn't want her to think that. This wasn't her fault. "That isn't true. Don't act that way. I'm really sorry."

"You know, I've been trying really hard for a long time now, but you just keep pushing me further and further away. Did I do something to you that I don't know about, because if I did, I'm sorry." Sadness laced through her angry tone.

"No, you didn't do anything. I love you. I'm the one who should be apologizing. Please don't feel that way. I'll make it up to you, I swear."

"Make it up to me, huh?" The skepticism in her tone told me she didn't believe me.

"Yes, I promise." I was desperate to take away the pain in her voice.

Stale air buzzed as she contemplated my words. Like always, she made it easy on me. "Don't worry about it," she replied, her voice soft now. "I'll see you soon enough. Just stop ignoring me."

I let my eyes close and sighed. "I didn't mean for it to seem like I was ignoring you. I'll be better, I promise."

"That's more like it." She let out a long sigh as well. "Now, tell me all about what's been going on with you. How's New York? How're your classes? Your apartment? Any hot guys?"

"Whoa, slow down." I giggled, loving her spunk.

"It's not my fault. I wouldn't have to cram them all in if I heard from you every now and then, little sissy." More guilt.

"My classes are okay. I'm still trying to figure it all out. I'm in love with my apartment. I just got a job last night, actually. Bartending so I can afford said apartment. You'll have to come for a drink one night. You'd love it."

"And? Hot guys? Hello, I need details. You skipped the best part." She jumped right back into our regular flow.

"I don't know. I haven't been paying much attention." I tried to steer clear of this topic.

"My ass! There is too someone. I can hear it in your voice. Don't lie to me, missy, or I'll call Jace next."

I rolled my eyes.

"Don't you roll your eyes at me."

I frowned. "Hey, how do you know I'm rolling my eyes?"

"I know everything."

Not everything.

"There might be one guy." I closed one eye and winced, preparing myself for the barrage of inquiries.

"I knew it! Spill!" I heard the foam seeping from her lips.

"Close your mouth." The smile could be heard in my voice.

We both laughed. God, I missed her.

"Eva?"

"Yeah?"

"I'm waiting." I could almost hear her tapping her foot on our mother's kitchen tile.

"Calm down, you piranha. There's nothing to know. Just some cute guy who keeps conveniently showing up wherever I am. He's really nice, but he's just a friend."

"Why?" She sounded aggravated. "Come on, Eva. You do this every time. Why can't you go out with him?" she whined.

"Not you, too. Just drop it for now, okay? I don't even know him."

"Bring him home winter break."

Um, no. "I'm not asking a stranger to come home with me for winter break. Be serious."

"Well, who knows? Maybe by then, he won't be a stranger." That time I did hear her eyebrows wiggle.

"You sound like the devil right now. You know that?"

"Mwahahahaha," she attempted an evil laugh, then added, "Or however the devil sounds."

I laughed, but the thought of going home made my armpits sweat. I hadn't contemplated the going back part when I left only a few short weeks ago.

"I'll follow up with this topic in a couple of weeks, and I expect a full report. You better tell me if anything happens in the meantime, or we won't be sisters anymore. I'll cut you off for good." She covered the receiver, and I heard her muffled voice say, "I'm coming. I'm just talking to Eva." Full volume resumed as she removed her hand from the mouthpiece and a low voice drawled, "Tell her I can't wait to see her."

"Damon says he—"

"I heard what he said," My knuckles turned white as I fisted the phone.

"Well, we're headed out to the mall. I love how he pampers me. Time to burn some of his plastic. Love you, sissy. Call me."

I muttered a weak, "Love you, too," but she didn't notice. What else was new?

Chapter 9

ARRIVED AT WORK HALF an hour before my shift, mind-fuckingly exhausted. This would be rough. Thank you, Blake. Like I didn't have enough of these nights to begin with. Fortunately for me, I was used to functioning on little-to-no sleep. The quadruple espresso from Starbucks had better kick in soon.

I cut up all the fruit and filled the ice in the beer buckets that lined the inside of the bar. Going around to the other side, I removed all the stools from the top of the bar and then wiped it down until it shined like the Emerald City. Pleased with myself, I turned and began to count the opening cash in the register.

"You're a pro," Rick's voice came from behind me.

"That's me." I smiled over my shoulder.

He sauntered behind the bar. "You should have a good night. Friday's our best crowd. Just holler if it gets to be too much, and I'll call in reinforcements. Jasmine is on with us. You'll like her."

"Don't worry. I'm good." I flashed him my award-winning smile, affirming that 'I got this'.

We fell into the same comfortable rhythm as the night before. He bobbed and I weaved. We sang and danced, tossing bottles back and forth. He wasn't kidding. The crowd was dense and rambunctious. It was nothing I couldn't handle, though. I liked crowds. I was used to crowds. Bad things didn't happen with a lot of people around. They happened when you were alone.

"Hey, sweetheart. I have a tip for you," came an intoxicated slur.

I looked from some drunk douchebag's glassy smirk to the dollar bill resting beneath his tapping fingers. *Gee, thanks.*

He started to slide it toward me, his drooling sneer making me nauseous. When I went to grab it, he *mistakenly* shoved it in my direction a little too rough. It flitted past me, cascading to the floor. Asshole just wanted to get me to bend over.

I dazzled him with a smile, not taking the bait, and said, "Thank you so much," and bent awkwardly, trying at all costs to avoid giving him a show.

Ugh, where did that friggin' thing go?

"Excuse me, miss. I'd like a drink please. I'm mighty thirsty again," a low, sexy baritone called out from above me.

I bolted upright, banging my head on the side rail. "Ow!" Wincing, I rubbed the top of my head.

"I'm sorry." Blake leaped forward, concern etched in his face. "Let me see." He took my head in his hands and moved it back and forth, the way you would examine a child's wounds, then he let out a relieved sigh. "I think you'll live." Still holding my face, he tipped my head forward and kissed the boo-boo on top. "There. All better."

Or worse. Now I'm on fire.

His hair was wet from a recent shower and falling free, framing his perfect features. His nose still had a shine at the tip, and he was wearing the fitted black T-shirt that did unruly things to my insides. The smell of his soap mixed with his cologne floated toward me and my eyes flitted closed for a fraction of a second, taking in the combination.

This should be fun.

"So, what can I get for you before you give me a concussion?" I asked, still rubbing the sore spot.

A coy grin spread across his face, and he drawled, "I'd love a slippery nipple, please."

"A s-slippery nipple?" *I stutter now?* I bit down on my bottom lip, hard.

His grin got even broader. "Yes, extra wet. I just love a wet, slippery nipple. My mouth waters just thinking about it." Blake let out a noticeable shiver. "Oh, and a cherry on top. Please." He licked his lips, and my eyes instinctively followed his tongue.

God help me.

I exhaled the breath caught in my throat. "One extra wet slippery nipple coming right up."

With shaky hands, I managed to keep the two different liquids separate in the shot glass. I deserved props. I topped it off with a cherry, knowing I'd probably regret it. I should have just said we didn't have any.

I placed the horny glass in front of him. Staring at me, he extended his index finger, and lightly traced circles around the rim. I swallowed deep, my eyes trained on that finger. And those hands. Even they were gorgeous. I had a thing for hands. Weird, yes, but a thing nevertheless. Blake's were strong, his nails well kept. Tight, tanned, skin-covered, thick veins.

Yum.

Now I was picturing what they would look like gliding over my ivory colored skin.

Awesome.

"Thank you," Blake said, his eyes sparkling with mischief.

"You're welcome. I hope I did it to your liking."

"Oh, you did it *just* right." He winked.

I knew I should get back to work, but apparently my feet were cemented to the floor.

Carefully, he picked up the cherry by the stem, twirled it around, and placed the tantalizing fruit between his teeth, eyes still glittering into mine. He did a short tug, freeing it into his mouth. I gasped. I wasn't sure which would taste better, but I'd bet the combination was mouthwatering.

Swirling the ball of fruit over his taste buds, he closed his eyes and groaned out a noise equivalent to an orgasm. Moisture pooled between my legs, and I found myself gripping the edge of the bar for support. That was the most erotic noise I'd ever heard, and I wondered what it would feel like to drown it out with my mouth.

When Blake opened his eyes, they were electric. His gaze flitted to the lip I had clasped between my teeth, and the corner of his mouth tilted up. In one drawn-out motion, he opened his mouth and slid out his tongue, still red with the juice of the cherry he'd just fucked, and placed the stem on its tip. He curled his tongue around it and pulled it inside.

I watched him assault that stem, doing god only knows what. Rolling, flicking, sucking. Each movement feeling like it was *me* gyrating around his tongue. I was one flick away from going into convulsions.

Moist lips parted as he pinched the end of the stem and revealed a perfectly tied knot. Twirling his victory between his fingers, those damn sexy fingers, he said, "You know what they say about a person who can tie a cherry stem in a knot in their mouth . . ."

Yeah, I knew what they said about that. I also knew I was turning into putty. My breathing was so erratic, I wondered if my brain was getting any oxygen at all.

He raised his glass to me and tipped his head back, gulping down the sweet liquid in one long swig. I watched his Adam's apple ride his throat, and I ached to follow it with my tongue.

Blake licked the full circle of his lips and breathed out, "Now, that was one hell of a slippery nipple."

And that's when I fell on the floor.

Literally.

I scrambled around, trying to find something, anything I could have been down here for.

The dollar! Yes!

Jumping to my feet, I waved the bill around like I'd found treasure. At least I was discreet about it.

My subconscious rolled her eyes at me. *I don't even know who you ARE anymore.*

Blake lifted his chin and settled back in his chair with an exaggerated casualness.

Smug bastard.

I wanted to slap him, or kiss him, or slap him.

Ugh!

"You okay, Angel?" he asked through an arrogant chuckle.

"Couldn't be better. Why?" *That's it, play it cool.*

"Because you just dive-bombed that rubber padding on the floor, you haven't blinked for about five minutes, and um . . ." He pointed to my head.

"What?" I spun around to look in the mirror behind the bottles, becoming instantly mortified. My hair was thrown upside down, coming over the top and then falling over the sides of my head, making me look more Afghan Hound and less beauty queen. I scrambled to put myself back together in every sense imaginable.

"A little help here, Eva." Rick's voice threw me back into reality. He didn't look happy.

"Coming! Sorry." I put the last strand in place and turned my attention back to Blake. Leaning over the bar, I hissed, "You're going to get me fired."

Unaffected, Blake leaned back in his chair and clasped his hands behind his head. His shirt rode up, revealing a sliver of bronze, toned skin with indents placed perfectly adjacent to his hipbones and, God forgive me, I loved that inch more than I should. I swallowed the puddle of saliva in my mouth with a long, hard gulp.

He shrugged, "Why? This is a bar and I'm a paying customer. All I did was order a drink."

I wanted to kick him off that stool. I narrowed my eyes at him. "You know *exactly* what you did with that porn show in your mouth."

Blake leaned forward, sending his hair to the edges of those gorgeous eyes. The tips of his fingers covered my own, electrocuting me. His voice was husky. "Did you enjoy what you saw?" Arching one perfect eyebrow, he continued, "There could easily be an instant replay." Reaching out, he traced my lips with his index finger, and it tasted like the wet nipple and the cherry and him and . . .

Oh god.

My mouth opened and closed like a fish, and I fought the urge to roll my eyes behind my head. Trying to regain some dignity, I straightened my back, clamped my fish-mouth shut and turned my attention to the parched, yelling crowd.

Blake's deep, hearty laugh bellowed from behind me.

I was glad he found it amusing.

For the next hour I found a way to block him out and took my game up a notch. I satisfied every customer, making them all feel loved, and redeemed myself with Rick. Jasmine was cool. She didn't talk much. Just did her thing and tended to the customers.

I turned as Jace, Jessie, and Sandra bounced through the door. Jace, ever the eccentric, was wearing blue sunglasses, his hair perfectly coiffed. *Thank you, sweet baby Jesus.* I was being rescued. Thankfully, we all had kickass fake IDs, and Rick was cool people, so we'd all be able to enjoy ourselves. He didn't care if I drank as long as I kept it clean, thinking it'd help business for me to accept shots and be social. I was happy to take the edge off.

"What up, girlie?" Jace hopped over to the bar and propped himself up, leaning all the way over to give me a kiss. "We came to see your new digs."

He pulled his glasses down his nose and looked around. "Not bad." His eyes caught hold of Rick. "Well hell-O there." He took a step in his direction.

"Jace," I warned. "Don't even think about it. That's my boss."

"Well, maybe I can put in a good word for you." He wiggled his eyebrows and tried to veer off in that direction again.

"Jace, I'm serious. No!"

"Oh, fine." He pouted perfectly plump lips. "You're such a grandma Mary. Why do you hate me?"

"You're so dramatic. Go find a different piece of meat. There's plenty to choose from." I waved him off, dismissing him into the crowd.

He stomped off in a huff, which only lasted a few feet before I heard, "Heyyy . . ." And he made a sharp left turn, honing in on a group of tasty men.

I shook my head, grabbing a bottle of Jameson.

Sandra looked over at me, eyes bright and hopeful. I knew how long it'd been since she'd been on a date. "I, uh, think I'll go stick by him."

"That's probably a good idea." I laughed.

"Hey, Ri—" The sight of a goo-goo eyed Jessie, kneeling on a stool, and talking to Rick, interrupted my thoughts. My mouth hung open as I watched him stare back at her with a similar expression.

Jasmine nudged me. "Grab the tequila for me, would ya?" When I didn't respond, she followed my line of sight. "Didn't know they were sweet on each other, huh? He'd never admit it, though."

I shook my head. "Guess not. But they're a good match."

"Probably not gonna happen. I've never seen Rick tied down." She reached over me and grabbed the liquor before walking off.

"Ahem," Blake cleared his throat. He was on his fifth nipple, but I hadn't stuck around to witness any more of them.

"Ready for another?" I glanced over.

His lip curled. "I don't want to spoil myself with too many nipples at once. I'll take a Blue Moon this time."

He *was* a blue moon.

"Sure thing."

As I set his glass down on the bar, a familiar voice overtook the speakers coming from the cover band. I turned so fast, the air whooshed around me.

No. He. Was. Not.

Jace was behind the mic as *Kryptonite* by Three Doors Down blared. Our eyes locked and with one finger, he summoned me over. This was our song.

Oh, he was *not* doing this to me right now!

Rick looked back and forth between Jace and me. Eyes twinkling with excitement, he shoved me out from behind the bar. I straightened my legs and pushed back, trying to gain traction, but it was no use. I stumbled next to Jace, who was proudly belting lyrics like a rock star, and he grabbed me by the waist, pulling me close so we could both sing into the microphone.

I started out weak at first, mortified, but then the familiar rush took over. We rocked out together, the way we always did. That song summed up our friendship, and we sang it proudly.

The crowd turned wild as we finished off the last note. Blake had vacated his post, and I spotted him leaning against the entryway, his expression a mixture of awe and turned on.

My body got knocked about as the screaming crowd bombarded us with hugs, but my eyes stayed locked on my sexy new admirer. At this point, I wasn't quite sure I *could* walk away from him unscathed.

In my preoccupied state, I'd almost missed Jace's announcement. "You guys didn't know your gorgeous new bartender could sing, did you? Would you like to hear her do another?"

The crowd roared to a deafening decibel, banging on any flat surface they could find while cat-calling and whistling through their fingers.

"Uh-uh." I waved my hands back and forth, shaking my head. "No way."

Jace grabbed me by the belt and tugged back forcefully as I tried to make my getaway. "Come on, guys, we aren't letting her get away that easy, are we?"

I thought they couldn't get any louder, but they did. Rick was laughing hysterically behind the bar, starting a hateful chant, "Eva, Eva, Eva." Within seconds, the entire place was shouting my name.

Note to self—make him pay for that.

I looked at Jace and mouthed, "I'm gonna kill you."

Jace smiled and kissed the air in my direction.

With only a few seconds to make a song choice, the perfect one popped into my head. Turning to the band to ask if they knew it, I was pleased when the beginning notes to Demi Lovato's *Heart Attack* sprung from the P.A.

Would Blake know I was singing it to him? Would he understand what was happening to me? That he wasn't just anybody?

Yes, he would.

As soon as the opening lyrics passed my lips, claiming my defenses were up and I didn't want to fall in love, Blake pushed off the wall and stood at attention. He'd gotten the message all right, loud and clear. I continued to sing, knowing full well he'd get the meaning and know he made me actually *want* to be with him, but that I was too nervous to go through with it. So many emotions changed those beautiful features as I witnessed his internal roller coaster.

Our gazes locked and, at the start of the first chorus, he prowled toward me like a hungry lion claiming his territory. His focus trained on me as he meandered through the crowd, authoritative and powerful, his eye on the prize.

I kept singing my heart out to him, arms banging on my chest and being thrown about. I hit the last high part, right before the ending chorus. By that point I was so lost in pouring out my soul, the crowded bar might as well have been empty.

By the last chorus, Blake was standing directly in front of me, fists clenched at his sides. His eyes were wild as he worked his jaw. The last note echoed off the walls, and I stared at him, my chest heaving with the exertion of that song.

His quizzical eyes desperately searched mine for an answer as I stepped around the mic stand. "Angel?"

"Yes?" My scratchy throat made my voice sound hoarse.

"Just so we're clear, you were singing that to me, right?" He was so close, but made sure not to touch me. He looked hopeful and scared at the same time.

My chest constricted. I murmured, "Yes." I couldn't look away. He needed to know.

Blake took a sharp intake of breath and straightened his body. Squaring his jaw, his eyes turned determined yet silently pleading. "Be with me." It wasn't a question.

I stood silent for a moment, trying to work through this internal tug-of-war. Not only was all of this happening so fast, and so foreign to me, but I couldn't let him get too close, no matter how badly I wanted to. "I can't."

"Why not? If you feel the same way, I need to know why not." His pointed glare commanded an explanation.

"I just can't, I—" I closed my eyes.

"Don't do this." I couldn't tell if it was a plea or a threat. *Or both.*

I didn't respond.

"Angel?"

Was I really going to do this to him? My first shot at something real?

Yes, I was.

Eyes still downcast, I delivered my famous line, "I have a boyfriend." Then I forced myself to look up. Though I'd recited it countless times, this was the first time I felt the lonely, empty desperateness it encompassed.

Blake flinched, disappointment flickering across his face before his jaw clamped shut. I watched a wall go up as his eyes iced over. He gave me a few more seconds to change my mind, staring at me mercilessly. When I didn't respond, he hardened his resolve further. "Fine. Have it your way then." He turned on his heel and walked out without even a backward glance.

A hairline fracture made its way down the center of my heart.

My soul ran after him, kicking and screaming, and then turned back to glower at me. I instantly turned arctic. I couldn't feel my limbs and nothing was responding. Though I could feel each knock of my pulse at each pressure point, I felt dead inside.

How did we get here? I wanted to run after him and stop him. Take it all back and tell him I was sorry . . .

But I couldn't.

Self-preservation prevailed and no matter how badly it stung, the possibility of anyone finding out was worse. I instantly regretted singing that song. For giving him hope I would act on my obvious feelings and then ripping the rug out from under him.

Jace rushed to my side with a huge smile on his face, talking through his teeth so no one would know what he was saying. "I don't know what the fuck that was all about, but not now, okay? Look at my face."

I looked up, being held together by old, brittle threads that were ready to snap at any moment. I felt myself crawling backward into my hidey hole and he knew it.

"Look in my eyes, Eva. My eyes."

I did as I was told, but my focus was still far away.

What have I done?

"Not now, baby girl. This is your first night, and you have a new boss to impress. Time and place, sugar. You'll be fine. We'll deal with this after hours. Okay, love?"

He was met by my blank expression.

"The words, Eva. Come on." Jace pinched my side hard, and it worked.

"Ouch!"

"There you are." He stepped behind me and pushed me toward the bar, while whispering in my ear, "Pull yourself together, you hear me? Excuse yourself to the bathroom, do a few shots or whatever you have to do, but do not let anyone see you like this."

His words finally sank in. What was I doing? I brushed him off and turned my neck side-to-side. Giving my hands a little shake, I took a deep breath and regained my composure. I could do this. I *would* do this.

My body did as it was told the rest of the night. My face smiled and flirted, and my limbs rushed around making countless drinks. Rick was none-the-wiser, and I ended the shift with a wad of cash and a pocket full of phone numbers from people claiming to be in love with me.

Jessie stayed to close up with Rick, and Sandra left with a new love interest. Jace, of course, waited to escort me home.

When I walked out the door, I instinctively looked around, hoping Blake would be waiting.

He wasn't.

My heart sank to my feet, and I trampled over it.

"Why are you doing this to yourself?" Jace's voice snapped me back to reality.

I looked at him through wet, blurred vision. "You know why."

"But you want this—bad. What're you doing? You obviously can't be his friend, so you either have to go through with it or walk away from him. He seems crazy about you. It's not right to lead him on."

I wiped the tears away with the back of my hand. "I'm not trying to lead him on," I said a little too forcefully. "I'm confused, all right? He rattles my brain, and it's not too stable to begin with."

"Look, I know this is hard on you. I told you it wasn't going to be easy. Maybe you should just go for it, love. Take the plunge."

"Come on, Jace. You know better than anyone that I can't." I sniffled, searching my bag unsuccessfully for a tissue.

"Just put the both of you out of your misery already. And me too while you're at it. It's fucking painful to watch. Can't you tell how much he likes you? He's the real deal, Eva. I know you can see it." He grabbed my face so I couldn't avoid his eyes. "Come on, mama. Let yourself have this. Free yourself. You deserve to be happy."

I shook my head free and gritted my teeth. "No. *He* deserves to be happy and I have *nothing* to give him, Jace."

He didn't fight me. "Go grab your things and meet me in my apartment."

"No, I just want to be alone."

Jace flinched as if I'd just slapped him. I'd never said that to him before. "So now you're going to push me away, too? What's happening to you, Eva?"

I seemed to be hurting everyone tonight. I placed my hand over his, trying to reassure him. "Please, Jace. Don't push. Just go and I'll talk to you tomorrow."

He hesitated a moment, evaluating me. "Fine. If you need me, you know where to find me. Love."

"Love." I turned and trudged into my chamber.

In my bathroom, I scrubbed my face vigorously as if the soap could wash away the emotion from it as well. Bracing myself on the edge of the sink, I looked into the mirror appraisingly. Freckles dusted a red, runny nose, and my eyes were leaky and bloodshot. My mouth was set in a scowl and I wondered if it would wind up there permanently. I looked broken down. Correction, I *was* broken down. This was the bare bones of me.

Reluctantly, I dragged myself into the living room and picked up my cell phone. I owed Blake an apology. My eyes glassed over when I scrolled, looking for his name and noticed how he'd programmed himself into the phone.

BFF.

I choked past a sob and sent the quick text.

Me: I'm sorry.

It was all I sent. I couldn't say any more. In a daze, I stared at my phone for an undeterminable amount of time, squeezing it as I waited for a response, but nothing came. With a thickness in my throat, I tossed it aside and stepped out to the balcony, clutching my journal to the stabbing ache in my chest.

This was a whole new kind of pain. It made my guts hurt. My soul ached. I'd survived a lot in my short life, but I wasn't sure I would make it through this one. This one really drove home all that I'd sacrificed and had to live without. All that was taken from me. What girl doesn't dream of a prince? Her knight in shining armor.

First love.

Real love.

I think he could have been a real love. Something in me was sure of it.

I peeled my journal from my dismembered rib cage and rested it on my lap, caressing the top of it before I creaked it open. This book was me. Bound up and battered, with its pieces falling apart and eaten away, holding all of my emotion and secrets in its heart.

I closed my eyes, took a deep breath and let the visions that scudded across the inside of my eyelids move my pen.

Nails on a chalkboard
Needles pricking flesh
My heart an open wound
The sores oozing and fresh

The pain is unbearable
But it is mine and I am its
I've been living this so long
I've been smashed and torn to bits

I'm dying a slow death
Body parts frayed and chewed away
Demons come and find me
And claim me as their prey

You're my hope when I have none
A gleam of light inside my grave
Oxygen when I feel I'm drowning
Rescuing me on a gentle wave

I want to curl up within your being
Breathe your air and feel you move
Be the liquid in your veins
So I could fit into your every groove

I'll keep this secret guarded
The pain's too bad, I will not share
You push and pull at my emotions
But your life I have to spare

So I'll sit inside my dungeon
My shell, my walking corpse
Locked away, a living nightmare
As it twists and turns and morphs

In time you'll understand
This is a horror made for one
I won't drag you into darkness
Your sun cannot out run

A teardrop hit the page, smudging my heartbreak, and I watched the words splay out in the tiny pool, the letters blending and smearing into one another. I allowed the tears to take over and mourned the death of what might have been. What would never be.

This was for the best.

He'd move on, find the right girl for him, and realize one day that I'd done him a favor. I'd eventually forget all about him, and my secrets would remain just that.

My. Secrets.

"Yes." I straightened in my chair, sniveling and wiping away the evidence with the back of my hand. "You did the right thing."

So why do I feel like I'm breaking?

Chapter 10

THE NIGHT WAS NOT KIND.

It seldom was, but this was one of the worst in a long time. Night terrors raked through me, claiming me as their bitch. My body wailed and trembled until I was able to pull myself out of it. Usually, my own screams were what woke me. A low cry at first, almost distant. Then it would get louder and louder, closer and closer, until the shrill pitch was so loud in my ears, it would rattle my brain.

My eyes burst open and my arms were wrapped around my core, my nails rooted deep in my flesh. Still partially lost in an abyss, I pounded my fists against my thighs in an effort to break the trance and fully wake myself up. A mixture of sweat and tears soaked me from head to toe. Pink droplets surrounded me on the sheets where blood from the wounds I'd inflicted seeped into the moisture.

When I'd straightened and realized it had happened again, I allowed the real sobbing to begin. The pitiful weeping as I'd rocked back and forth, holding onto my knees for support, becoming aware of just how fucked up I really was and realizing I'd never be normal again. I'd been stripped of that, too.

How could anyone ever love me? Get close to this?

They couldn't. I just had to accept the fact I'd spend the rest of my life screaming alone in a dark room. Logically, I knew I wasn't solely to blame, but the guilt of betraying one of the people I loved most in the world sat on my shoulders like a boulder.

My sights fell on the stuffed lamb that had been keeping vigil by my bedside since childhood. It didn't seem to be doing its job anymore and I wondered why I continued to keep it there.

"Eva, come out and dry off."

I squint through the bright sun and take in the warm lines around Nonna's eyes. My face splits in a huge grin. It was the week I always looked forward to in the summer when I got to stay with her. I'd swim all day and do crafts and watch old movies with her at night. She always let me stay up later than my mom, cuddling with me and eating sugary snacks.

I run toward the towel outstretched between her waiting arms. She wraps it around me, rubbing vigorously. "You'll be warm in a minute. I made you girls some lunch."

Abby looks up from her spot on the lounger. "Thanks, Nonna," we sing in tandem.

A few hours later, I lie beneath the covers, staring wide-eyed at the shadows on the wall. They always crept up them, different from the ones at home. Abby decided to come this year, so I thought that'd make it easier to sleep, but it didn't. I roll to the other side, trying to ignore the way the one that looks like a creepy clown is staring at me.

"Go to sleep," Abby's groggy voice mutters beneath the duvet.

"I can't. I'm spooked again and I miss Mommy."

She exhales and sits up. "Here." She pushes her favorite stuffed lamb into my arms.

My eyes glass over. "You're giving me Mary? But she's your best friend."

"I don't need her anymore." She shrugs. "She always helped me sleep and you can use her now. She keeps the bad dreams away." She smiles softly.

"Thanks, Abs." I squeeze Mary. "I'll keep her forever." I snuggle deep into the warmness and bury my face in Mary's soft tufts, humming the childhood rhyme until I was able to peacefully fall asleep.

Its fleece was white as snow . . .

I focused on Mary a while longer, waiting for the hiccupping and body jolts to subside. When the worst had passed, I clambered off the bed and dragged myself to the bathroom to assess the damage. Amongst the mangled golden knots, sweat pasted the baby hairs framing my face to my skin, and my eyes were practically swollen shut. Barefoot on the cold tiles, I trembled as a chill coursed over my dampened body. Craving

warmth, I turned on the shower as hot as it would go and stepped under the scorching stream. I bit my lip and cried out as the water scalded
me, blood invading my mouth from the newest wound I'd inflicted. But
I needed to cleanse my body of the filth crawling through my veins like
angry little centipedes.

It was as though his hands and tongue were still all over me. Wincing, I washed away the dried blood my nails had left behind until the water ran cold. No amount of makeup or cold compresses would conceal
the night I'd had. Thankfully, it was Saturday and everyone thought I'd
be away visiting my *boyfriend*.

I put on a pair of old sweats and a long sleeve shirt to hide as much
skin as possible—*just in case*. Popping a hazelnut coffee into the Keurig,
I closed my eyes and enjoyed the aroma. There was no way I could eat.
Night terrors always left me feeling nauseous. Caffeine, on the other
hand, was a necessity, and I'd need lots of it to keep away those haunting
visions.

I thumbed through my phone to see if Blake had replied to the text
I'd sent.

He hadn't.

Though it hurt and a wave of disappointment washed over me, it
was for the best. The quicker he forgot about me and got on with his life,
the quicker I could do the same.

I hope.

Truth was, I doubted I'd ever truly forget about him. In the short
time I'd known him, he had burrowed his way into my heart and shattered all my make-shift walls. I didn't know how he managed to do it. I'd
never allowed anyone into that place inside of me before. It was the only
thing I was able to control in my life. I didn't know the first thing to do to
expel him from there. All I knew was I had to. For his sake, I had to.

I shook my head clear and took a big gulp of my coffee. Today called
for a day of regrouping and studying. It'd been such a whirlwind since I
got to New York that I was beginning to lose sight of my goals. I had to
forget about Blake and bury my nose in my studies. Exams were coming
up this week, and I needed to focus on my life, my future, and my career.

For the next four hours, I sat in my living room, books sprawled everywhere as I tried to block everything out and retain as much information as possible. Every now and then, my body jolted in a half-spasm as my head fell forward and I started to doze off. Needing some air, I pulled my hair back into a ponytail and changed into a sports bra, T-shirt, and leggings, then covered up with a small hoodie. A good run should help even me out.

I stopped at the front doors and used the steps to stretch, then started a slow jog. I needed to get off the busy Manhattan streets and clear my head. Once I reached the park, I was able to pick up the pace a bit. It wasn't raining, but the sky was overcast, so the place was relatively empty. I ran the path more than ten times and made sure I waved at Bertha during my laps. I didn't want to upset her.

I'd lost count of how many times I'd gone around, but my legs were beginning to feel rubbery, and I had a sharp pang in my side that wouldn't let up. I stopped, grasping the pain and panting. I turned my nose up to the gray sky, closed my eyes, and wrapped my arms around myself, helping my heart rate descend.

Feeling better, I started the slow trudge back to my apartment, focusing on the music flowing into my ears. I smiled as *Eye of the Tiger* by Survivor began to play. The song did its job of perking me up. Feeling thoroughly exhausted but better, I picked a flower and tucked it behind my ear, then decided to grab Jace, order Chinese, and watch *True Blood* reruns. I could never resist an afternoon spent with some sexy vamps.

"Well, look who finally decided to show her face," Jace said, opening his door. "Hurry up and get in here before you embarrass yourself. You look like road kill, honey."

I snickered, tripping over my own feet as he yanked me inside by my arm. "Nice to see you, too. So glad I stopped by."

He turned and looked me up and down. "What the hell happened to you?"

"Can we not talk about it? I'm finally starting to feel a little better." I walked past him to his kitchen and peered into the refrigerator.

He gave me a doubtful glance. "If you say so, but I just need to let you know, I'm really worried about you, Eva. No joke. I don't know what to make of all this."

I screwed the cap off a bottle of water, and took a long gulp. "Thanks, but I'll be fine. Really. I've gotten over worse than a stupid crush."

"That's the thing, you *haven't* gotten over *any* of it." His eyes were lit with concern. "You're still having those god awful dreams. You finally have a chance at a real relationship, but you're pissing all over it. And what happens when you go back home, huh? Or are you planning to never see your family again? Have you thought any of this through? You really need to tell them, Eva."

I slammed the bottle down on the counter, tears budding in my eyes. "How many times do I have to tell you I can't? Stop asking and just be here for me, okay?"

His shoulders lost their sharp edges, and he huffed. "Fine. For now." He waved a warning finger at me. "But we're not done talking about it."

"We never are." I frowned, picking up the bottle for another sip.

"And, just to let you know, if you ever shut me out again the way you did last night, I'm ripping out your va-jay-jay hairs one by one."

"Pfft." I spit out a laugh full of water. The look on his face told me he was not happy I wasn't taking him seriously and I cleared my throat. "I'm sorry. I didn't mean to laugh, I just . . ." I stifled another bout of giggles and wiped the water dripping from my chin. "Go on." I sucked in my cheeks, trying not to laugh again.

"Uh huh," he huffed. "Laugh all you want. Just don't try me, missy. You won't be laughing when you feel the pussy burn."

At that, I laughed outright. When I'd finally got ahold of myself, I looked at my best friend adoringly. "I'm sorry I upset you last night. It's just sometimes I need to work through stuff on my own. Don't be mad."

"I'm not mad, Eva. I'm nervous. And I wouldn't care if you *were* actually working through stuff and not on some drawn out suicide mission. You're giving me early wrinkles for Christ's sake. Do you see these lines?" He pointed at his temples and the imaginary creases he believed were forming there. But we both knew his genes were way too good for that.

"Oh please, stop it. You're gorgeous and you know it. But point taken." I jabbed him in the ribs with the water bottle. "Now, come back to my place and you can braid my hair while we drool over Eric and Sookie. Well, Eric." I corrected with a smirk.

"Okay, but you're not off the hook just because you're distracting me with visions of a hot vampire Viking."

I sat on the floor between Jace's legs as he braided and unbraided my hair countless times. It was one of his favorite pasttimes. We'd gone through our ritual of what we would do if we ever got our hands on Eric, voiced our shared jealousy of Sookie, ate Chinese, and fallen asleep curled up together.

When I woke the next morning, Jace was already showered and bouncing around my apartment. I, on the other hand, felt like someone had taken a baseball bat to my entire body. Between the prior night of beating the shit out of myself, the first run I'd taken in longer than I cared to admit, and then a night spent face down on the carpet, I wasn't sure I'd be able to move from the spot on the floor I was stuck to like a chewed-up wad of gum.

"Oh boy, am I in trouble." I rolled myself onto my back and winced. "Why do you look so good already?" I scowled.

"Honey, I always look good. Trust." He reached his hand down and hoisted me to a standing position with one sharp tug. "Gimme a kiss. I'm going home."

I kissed him and rubbed the knot at the back of my neck. "See ya later." I started to walk him toward the door then stopped. "Hey, Jace?"

He turned, his hand on the doorknob. "Yeah?"

"Thanks." I gave him a half smile.

"You're welcome." He kissed the tip of my nose and stepped into the hall. "Now go do something with yourself. You look dreadful." He pulled the door closed in my face.

I shook my head. I should be used to that by now.

What *was* I going to do with myself today?

I stretched out my aching muscles and cleaned up my apartment before showering. My stomach grumbled, reminding me I hadn't eaten more than a little moo shu in the last two days. I opened the refrigerator, and scanned the shelves. Not even an egg.

Great.

I let out a huff, gathering my belongings to make a trip to the store when my cell phone pinged with a text.

Come open the door.

Chapter 11

STOPPED COLD IN MY tracks and felt all the blood drain from my face.

Blake.

He was here? Opening the door just a crack, I peered out with one keen eyeball. Nothing.

What the hell?

I peeled back the door and poked my head out, looking around the empty hallway. He must have sent the text to the wrong person. Feeling a sense of relief, I locked the door behind me, smiling at his choice of names for himself, but with an ache in my belly at how we'd left off.

"Hey, James." I waved.

"Hi there, Miss Eva." He returned my greeting with a warm smile.

I hurried out the front door and tried unsuccessfully to stop short before tripping over the broad shoulders seated on the top step.

Blake twisted, dropping the bags he had clutched in his hands, and caught me as I fell over his shoulder and onto his lap. "Whoa," he huffed out, just as surprised as I was. His eyes twinkled mere inches from mine. "I gotta say, I'm starting to like the way you come down a flight of stairs."

Am I dreaming? I squeezed my eyes tight and reopened them. Nope, still there, and the hardness forming beneath me told me this was definitely reality. Warmth swarmed my cheeks, and I squirmed in an effort to move away from it.

A low growl emanated from his chest. "I strongly advise against any movement like that unless you want a very public display of exactly what it is you do to me." He trailed his thumb along the piece of exposed flesh at my waistline, and my hips inadvertently twitched. Our faces were so close, he jutted his nose upward, tapping my own, and gave me a wink.

Sudden awareness of what was going on washed over me. I peeled my arms from around his neck and scrambled awkwardly off his lap, hopelessly trying to avoid his happy member. On hands and knees, I continued to clamber off the ground as he sat, calmly staring, dimples in full effect.

"You really *are* trying to kill me, I'm convinced," I said, brushing myself off.

He threw his head back and let out a hearty chuckle, "Au contraire. I'm trying to do exactly the opposite."

I planted my hands on my hips and narrowed my eyes at him. "What do you want?"

"Exactly what I said I wanted." He stared up at me like I should know what that meant.

I didn't.

He must have seen the question in my eyes because he stood up, grabbed the bags he'd tossed, and held them out to me. "I'm here to feed you."

My mouth dropped open. *Feed me?* I thought we had established that whatever this was, it was over. "I'm sorry, did I miss something? I thought we were fighting."

"We were." He shrugged. "I got over it. And I told you, as your BFF I'm deeply concerned for your well being." He placed a hand on his chest and forced the corners of his eyebrows together, making a show of looking overly troubled. "Now come on, chop-chop, bring me inside." He stared at me expectantly.

I balked. "Inside? Like, my apartment?"

"Yes, inside. Like your apartment," he repeated tiredly. "You're gonna have to get with the program, Angel. You're a little slow today."

Maybe I was, but I'd missed the part where I'd agreed to be alone with him behind closed doors. Nevertheless, I found myself wearing a dazed expression and doing exactly as he said, walking up the stairs in a clouded haze, and holding the door open for him as we made our way back into the lobby.

I unlocked my door and stepped inside, signaling with my hand for him to follow me. When he stepped over the threshold, I immediately felt like Alice crowded into a small room in Wonderland.

He looked massive standing there, barely inside my doorway. I opened my mouth to tell him he should leave, but he scooted past me and made his way over to the bar that separated my living room and kitchen, and placed the bags down.

Blake unloaded the contents with his back to me, and my traitorous eyes roamed over his masculine body, from his silken hair, past his broad shoulders, down his sculpted back, and landed on the tightest, roundest, most perfect ass I'd ever seen.

He turned, and I jutted my eyes upward, but a knowing smirk played across his lips.

Damn it! My cheeks flushed, and I fidgeted with my fingers.

"I got you a grilled chicken sandwich with fries, and a strawberry salad. If you're a good girl, I'll even let you have some of this *Crumbs* cupcake." He dipped his hand into the bag and raised it, exposing a mouthwatering hazelnut cupcake propped inside a clear shell. I licked my lips as he turned the tantalizing package. *Crumbs* was my weakness and hazelnut was my favorite flavor.

Eye on the prize, I determinedly stalked toward him, lifted the plastic heaven-containing package from his fingers, and placed it on the counter out of harm's way. That baby was all mine. I reached up to extract two glasses from the cabinet when a familiar warmth overtook my whole back side. I was beginning to recognize the feel of his gaze on me. Turning, I caught him while his line of vision was still glued to the lower half of my body.

Unlike me, he didn't try to make it seem as though he wasn't looking, but rather let his sights linger there just a little longer before he painfully, slowly sent them traveling up the length of me. He patted the stool next to him.

"Come, I'm starved."

I had the distinct feeling he wasn't talking about the chicken.

Or the salad . . .

Or the cupcake . . .

Everything smelled delicious and my stomach rumbled. My eyes went wide as I tore into the packages, shoveling French fries in my mouth while I unwrapped my sandwich and forked through my salad. "Thanks, I'm starving. I was on my way to get something when you sent me that text."

His eyes twinkled as he stared at me with a huge smile.

I stopped chewing, cheeks full, fingers dripping with grease. "What?"

He stared a moment longer. "You're cute when you're hungry. You're like a little lion. I like it."

Crinkling my nose, I growled at him and we both laughed. I wiped my hands and started eating my salad one calm mouthful at a time.

"So how'd it go with your boyfriend yesterday?" Blake asked pointedly. "Did you tell him you have a new BFF?"

I coughed, almost choking on my food, then cleared my throat. "No." I looked away.

"Tsk, tsk, Angel. I'm disappointed in you. Don't you know all relationships are built on honesty and trust?" He raised his eyebrows, accentuating his dissatisfaction.

The chicken felt like cement scraping down my throat. Suddenly, I wasn't so hungry. I did, however, have a good topic change. "Speaking of BFF . . . that was a nice little touch in my phone."

He beamed a satisfied smile that seemed to take up most of his face. "You like how I did that, right? Ten more points?"

"Twenty." I couldn't help but smile.

I stabbed a forkful of salad and chomped down, searching for my napkin before runaway dressing could slide off my chin, when I heard the distinct click of a picture being taken. My head snapped up as Blake was lowering a very fancy looking camera. Straight faced, he examined the image he'd just captured of me.

"You could warn a person before you do that." I glowered. "Do you regularly take pictures of people with lettuce hanging off their face?" I dropped my fork and wiped my lips.

Eyes still on the viewfinder, he murmured, "Don't worry. You look perfect." And then he ran his thumb over the screen and looked up at me with a half-smile. Our eyes lingered on each other a heartbeat longer than necessary. He raised his hands and, without looking at the screen or deviating from my stare, he clicked the camera in my direction once more.

I blinked rapidly, thrown out of my trance. "Stop it! What's wrong with you?"

Blake looked down and examined the image, a satisfied grin on his face. "Got it. I've been waiting to get that look since I met you."

"Look? What look?"

"This look." He turned the camera in my direction, and I saw a girl with her eyes locked adoringly, staring in awe, features soft, cheeks flushed, lips full and parted.

Oh. *That* look.

"Now I'll have it forever. Even if you run away from me." He slowly lowered the camera and placed it protectively in the crook of his arm, tapping it twice.

"So what're your plans for today?" I tried to lighten the mood.

"You're looking at it." He smiled, a toothy grin.

"Seriously? It doesn't take all day to feed me. I'm not *really* malnourished."

He cocked an eyebrow. "Oh, I don't know about that. I still have to show you the proper way to eat a cupcake. That could take some time." His eyes shimmered with mischief, and my belly did a flip flop. I could only imagine what he considered *proper*. In fact, I was certain it would be anything *but* proper.

Needing to divert his attention, I gestured toward his capturer of torment. "So what's with the camera?"

He raised the equipment, angling it toward me. "I told you, this is what I love. I'm always looking for beauty in unlikely places. Once in a lifetime seconds that would be lost forever." He shrugged and the corner of his mouth tipped up fondly. "You'd be amazed at all the things you walk past every day and take for granted. But there's beauty in everything. Even pain and sorrow, or a child's disappointed face. Everywhere. Like right there." He brought the camera up swiftly and snapped another shot. Smiling, he turned the viewfinder in my direction to show me.

My face looked strained, my lip strangled by my teeth. The light from the window created blurred streaks across my face and through my hair. It actually *was* beautiful somehow. He was right.

I grabbed the camera from his hands, disgusted that my face was so telling. "Give me that thing. It's my turn." I fumbled with the heavy apparatus. There were a bunch of dials and buttons and moving parts. I had a better shot of assembling a Rubik's Cube than knowing what to do with it.

"Would you like a lesson? First one's free." Blake's voice in my ear startled me, and I jumped, almost dropping his most prized possession. I glanced over my shoulder, nearly brushing his lips with my own. Swallowing, I brought my gaze back to the contraption in my hands. "Yeah, sure."

The hairs lining my body stood at attention, the awareness of his body moving closer to mine undeniable. Prickles raced up my back as the space between us disappeared and he settled himself in the seat behind me. His fingers lightly grazed my throat and then slid across my neck to sweep my hair over my shoulder, exposing my vulnerable flesh and causing a deep shudder to erupt. I sucked in a sharp breath as he placed his chin on the spot where my neck met my shoulder. Bringing his arms around either side of me, he grasped the shaky camera firmly between his hands, trapping mine beneath his. They felt so strong but soft at the same time. I imagined they would glide over my skin like silk, while being powerful enough to protect me from anything that might harm me.

"This is a heavy duty piece of equipment," his voice rasped in my ear. "You have to stroke it *just* right, and it'll do exactly what you want. It can bring you lots of pleasure and happiness when the moment's right." His breathing was calm as every syllable excited each nerve ending that lined my oversensitive skin, causing my own breath to be jagged and erratic.

I hated him for that.

His thumbs never stopped caressing the tops of my hands as he raised the camera at the flower I had picked during my run through the park.

"Let's keep it simple for now and leave this baby on automatic. I wouldn't want to scare you away during your first lesson." Blake took my index finger and placed it over the button on top of the camera, keeping his own above it. Twisting and turning the lens with one hand, he thoughtlessly traced circles over my finger with the other. I could feel each swirl between my legs and squeezed my thighs shut, trying to alleviate the ache building there. It was as if he was actually stroking my most delicate parts. I thought I'd be frightened, but I wasn't.

I wanted more.

Hard biceps curled around me, leaving little room to move as his front pressed against my back, essentially trapping me in. But I didn't feel threatened.

I felt protected.

He pushed his nose into my hair as though he was learning my body. No longer paying attention to anything he was doing or saying about the camera, my face instinctively turned toward his and I licked my lips, breathing in his manly scent. *God, I want this man.*

"You paying attention?" His words hurled me back to reality.

I hadn't noticed he'd finished adjusting the lens. I quickly straightened my head. "Uh-huh." I cleared my throat and made my best attempt to look like I was concentrating.

His chin dipped deeper into my shoulder, and I knew he was grinning at my expense. "Okay, now that we're zoomed in exactly where we want it, all you have to do is push down lightly on the shutter release button. Don't click all the way. It'll start to focus itself."

His finger gave a slight nudge, and the screen blurred in and out as it adjusted.

"Just make sure once you have it where you want it, you don't let it go. You wouldn't want to lose your shot." His words seemed to take on a double meaning. "There you go. Perfect. Now . . . push." He added more pressure to my finger and the photo snapped.

So did my insides.

Squeezing my legs together, a gasp escaped my lips. My body ached with a need I'd never experienced before. His one swirling, pushing finger felt like it was probing the most sensitive parts of my anatomy.

"Let's look at your handiwork." He clicked a button, and the image appeared on the screen. "See how nice?"

It *was* nice. What I thought was just a plain, ordinary flower was now sitting there, shining beautifully among streaks of sunlight. It seemed to be angling toward it, drinking it in. Loving it. Needing it. Much like I must have looked gravitating toward Blake.

My head inclined toward him, drinking in his energy. I was beginning to need this man. Desperately. My head screamed at me to run away and never look back, but every fiber of my being wanted to melt into every fiber of his.

It was too much to handle and I couldn't think straight with him so close. I needed space before I did something irrational. "It's pretty," I murmured. Then I slid off the stool and put some much needed distance between us.

Taking a moment to study me from across the room, Blake plucked the bud from its vase and rolled it between his long fingers. He smelled the petals. "To some people flowers symbolize death. But to me, they symbolize life."

I stared at him. Where was he going with this?

"There are certain flowers you can plant and, even when the cold comes and they die, they aren't gone. When the pain of winter is gone and the ground thaws the next spring, they come back." He looked at me with a serious expression. "They get a new chance at life. No matter *what* happened to them in the past. They regrow and are even more beautiful than before. To me they're a sign of hope. Hope for tomorrow. Hope for the future. Hope of new life and possibilities. Different circumstances. Second chances. Hope." He stood and began to make his way toward me.

My feet were rooted to the ground.

He tucked a loose tendril behind my ear and placed a finger beneath my chin, slanting it back so I could look into his fiery sapphire eyes. "Love." He swept one finger across my forehead, smoothing wayward hairs. "Living." His thumb traced my lower lip, and my eyes closed at the warmth flooding my belly. He put his palm to the side of my face and searched my eyes for an answer and I instinctively leaned into his touch. Cradling my cheeks between his hands, he lowered his face so slowly, so gently, toward mine.

As if trying to commit every contour to memory, he used his nose to caress each of my features. It was the most sensual and erotic thing I'd ever felt. Traveling up past my cheekbone, he circled my temple and continued across my forehead. After circling the opposite temple, he came across the right cheekbone and up to each of my eyes. He placed a soft kiss to both and then moved down my nose, toward my jawline.

My lips parted in invitation, my body relaxing forward as I willingly released myself to him. My breathing labored when his lips grazed mine, but he didn't linger there, barely even touching them. I wondered if I'd even felt them at all or if it was just my imagination running wild with desire. My body caved into his, the need for him growing fierce within me.

He skimmed his nose from the spot below my ear, along the length of my jaw, past my chin, to the other ear, and caught the lobe between his teeth, igniting prickles throughout my body. I hissed a guttural sigh, my body noticeably trembling. His touch evoked something animalistic inside of me, and it was banging on the walls of its cage, begging to be set free.

He sensually stroked his forehead along the area he'd just traced moments before, gently rolling his head back and forth, like he was trying to seep me into his brain and melt me into his being.

My chest rose and fell rapidly. I needed his lips on mine. I'd never wanted anything so badly in my life. I felt like he was making himself part of me, molding himself into a piece of my anatomy. When he made his way back toward the center of my face, I couldn't take much more.

I tilted my head up toward him in a silent plea. He peered down at me through long lashes, his eyes hooded. Then his mouth descended toward mine, excruciatingly slow.

I closed my eyes in anticipation as I felt his being come within centimeters of my own. The seconds he lingered in that small space were pure agony and I wanted to grab the back of his head and crash my mouth to his.

He kissed the tip of my nose, and my eyes fluttered open. My heart sank to the pit of my stomach as I blew out the air trapped in my throat in wispy gasps. He rested his chin on the top of my head and wrapped me in an embrace. I knew he was thinking, trying to figure out where to go from here and what to do with me. If I were anyone else, I was sure he would have kissed me. He let out a deep exhale, rustling my hair and kissed the top of my head. Then he backed away.

With weak limbs, I stumbled back and grasped the counter to steady myself. I should have known he'd be too much of a gentleman to do anything without my explicit consent, but I couldn't give it to him.

"I want you so bad, Angel. I'm not gonna lie. All you have to do is say the words, and I'll do the rest. Just tell me you want me, too." He searched my eyes for a response, his expression desperate, hopeful, and pleading all at once.

I remained close-mouthed, unable to form a thought. I wished it were that simple. I wished I could just tell him I wanted him too and let him take away my misery. But I knew it wasn't possible. There was no future for us. I didn't have a heart to share with anyone. It'd been destroyed years ago.

A brief look of disappointment flashed across his face as he realized I wasn't going to cooperate. He gave me a weak, halfhearted smile, and took my hand. "Come. I have another surprise for you."

Steering me toward the living room, he stopped momentarily to retrieve something from one of the bags, hiding it behind his back. He propped me on the couch and ordered me to stay, then walked over to my DVD player. Making quick work of the buttons, he came and sat close enough beside me that I could feel the heat from his leg radiating into my skin through my jeans. I still hadn't recovered from our previous encounter, and I wasn't sure if I could handle him in this close proximity yet. I rubbed the tops of my thighs to alleviate the scolding burn. He appeared unaffected and didn't seem to notice my discomfort.

How did he recuperate so quickly?

Maybe you've misread him all along, and he doesn't feel as strongly about you as you thought. I told you this was a bad idea.

Shut. Up.

"Oh wait, I almost forgot." Blake jumped up from his spot, and I was thankful to feel my temperature begin to decline.

I heard pots and pans clanging and, a few moments later, kernels were popping. I strained my neck to see what was going on in my kitchen. A moment later, he reappeared holding a giant bowl of fluffy popcorn.

"Did you just make that fresh?"

"Yep. It's the only way I'll eat it. It's so much better than that microwave crap. You ever have it this way?"

"Sure. My mom used to make it all the time when I was little." That one sentence built a lump in my throat. It was hard to think about how things used to be, how innocent *I* used to be. Softly, I added, "I haven't had it in forever, though."

He held the warm bowl out to me. I popped a few pieces into my mouth and closed my eyes, savoring the flavor.

He grabbed the remote, pressed play, and snuggled into my side, dipping his hand into the bowl.

I stiffened at the initial contact.

He didn't look at me, just muttered through his mouthful, "Lighten up. I don't bite. Only on Tuesdays." Then he smiled that lopsided grin and settled even deeper into my side.

Ah, what the hell. If you can't beat 'em, join 'em.

I rested my head on his shoulder as the beginning of *The Notebook* emerged on my television. "Seriously?"

"What? Can't a guy enjoy a good romance?"

"Actually . . . no." I laughed.

Blake tipped his nose in the air. "Well, you don't know me very well then. I happen to appreciate a good heart-throbbing tearjerker."

"If you say so," I teased playfully. Whether he was telling the truth or not, *The Notebook* was one of my favorite movies, and this was just what I needed. Or so I thought.

We weren't very far in when I noticed the similarities between Blake and Noah. The way Noah tried to get Allie to go out with him with all of his cute, quirky ways. Never giving up and following her around, asking her to do things she wouldn't ordinarily do. The realization made me squirm.

"Don't you even think about it," he grumbled. "The qualifications for watching a movie are . . . we snuggle. So saddle up, sweetheart." There was no question in his demanding tone. Though I hesitated, something about the playful way he'd said it made me do exactly as he'd requested.

I melted further into him, and he let out a contented sigh, then wiggled a little closer into my side. He took my hand in his, brushing his thumb along every surface of it absentmindedly. His easygoing, sweet and thoughtful personality made it easy to feel comfortable with him. He was passionate about the things he cared about and was a genuinely good person. I mean, what guy *wanted* to watch sappy love stories? I'll give you one hint—none.

Toward the end, I tried so hard to hold back the waterworks that my throat burned with unshed tears. Eventually, I succumbed and let them out. When the movie ended, I was embarrassed I'd let Blake see me bawling like a baby.

He passed me a tissue. Was there anything he hadn't thought of?

Looking at me through glistening eyes, he wiped away the tears pooling under my lower lashes. That simple, compassionate act made my heart open up a little bit more to him. My heart felt heavy, swollen with emotions I didn't want to feel flying through it.

Needing to freshen up, I began to move away from him, but he gripped my arm and pulled me back. My heart flew into my throat, panicked. Numbness shot out to each of my limbs, tingling my brain.

Oh please, God, no.

Very calmly, as though he didn't notice the alarm raking through me, he drawled, "These movies are like sex. You can't just jump up and leave me after. We have to spoon a little. I need a few minutes to come down from it." Then he nudged his head into my shoulder while wrapping his arms around my waist. There was nothing malicious or insincere in his eyes. He was telling the truth. He wasn't going to hurt me.

The tension in my body dissipated and the ringing in my ears was reduced to a low hum as I relaxed. "I was only going to clean myself up, you know. I'm a mess."

"You're perfect."

"Yeah, okay. My makeup is everywhere, I probably have snot running down my face, and my hair—"

He put one finger against my lips to quiet my ramblings, articulating each syllable, "Per-fect." His eyes bore into mine.

Gulp.

His finger felt like a weight against my lips, and I resisted the urge to slip my tongue from my mouth and take a taste.

Before I lost my cool again, I looked sternly into his eyes. "I'm getting up now."

He nodded and inched toward the other side of the couch, looking as though he needed to get away from me too. Making sure I didn't miss my opportunity to escape, I jumped up and made a beeline for the bathroom.

I splashed water on my face and wiped away the runaway mascara. Applying a cool compress to the back of my neck, I leaned across the porcelain and looked at myself in the mirror.

Pull it together. You wanted this, you got it. Now figure out what you're going to do with it.

I inhaled and exhaled ten deep breaths, smoothed my clothing, then made my way back to my guest.

Blake was still in the spot where I'd left him—leaning back with his arms draped over the back of the couch, exposing a slice of his belly and his very happy trail. My fingers twitched, wanting to trace that blissful path.

As if he could sense my thoughts, he yawned and stretched his arms up high above his head, widening my view of his perfectly sculpted abs and revealing those hip bone divots that drove me wild. I gasped and he smiled his adorable lopsided grin. Being this good looking was just sinful.

"Come. Sit." He patted the vacant area next to him.

I sat and turned to face him, noticing the mischievous glint in his eyes. "What?"

He reached behind him and pulled out the clear shell that housed the most delicious cupcake in the world, and twisted it in front of me.

"Hand it over." I stuck out my hand.

"Uh, uh, uh . . . not so fast." He backed away from me. "I told you there's only one way to eat these puppies. I'll break you in slowly, but next time you're getting the full effect." With hungry eyes, he popped the lid and the sweet smell immediately flooded my nostrils. I closed my eyes, my mouth instantly watering. I had an insatiable sweet tooth, and I couldn't wait any longer.

"Gimme a bite," I said in a breathy whisper.

Still smirking, he raised his eyebrows. "How bad do you want it?"

Oh, he was going to play games with me? Well, I wasn't giving in. *Screw the cupcake.* I clamped my lips shut and frowned, crossing my arms over my chest.

He raised his eyebrows, completing his cocky grin. "Tell me, Angel, or you're not getting any. I have no problem eating it all by myself." He swiped his finger through the icing and held it out to me. My lips parted and I inched toward him, waiting to taste the sweet goodness, but then he yanked his finger away and submerged it into his mouth.

"Hey!"

"Come on. Say it." He licked his lips, closing his eyes, and savoring the taste. "How bad do you want it?"

I slumped my shoulders in defeat. "Bad."

"Doesn't sound like it to me." He licked a piece of icing slowly, curling his tongue around the smooth topping and letting it linger there.

My mouth itched to suck it off his tongue. I licked my lips and bit down, inching closer to him, my heart racing from a damn dessert. "Come on, gimme a bite. Pleeeease." I dragged out the word, doing my best puppy dog impression.

He shook his head, being just as obstinate as me. *Damn him.* "Not until I hear you say how bad you want me . . . I mean it." The glint in his eyes told me he'd meant for that slip up.

Playing his game, I pushed my face as close to his as I could without physically touching him and steadied my gaze. Something flickered behind his eyes, and he took a sharp intake of breath. "I want it."

The corner of his mouth quirked, delighted I was complying. "How bad?"

"Bad." I settled myself closer, fingering his arm. "More than anything I've ever wanted. My mouth waters for it. My body aches for it. If I don't get it soon, I think I'll die." I let my eyes settle on his mouth and then trapped my lip between my teeth. I could play the double meaning game too.

He began to peel the paper down each side, taking his time. "That bad, huh? Sounds pretty serious. It must mean more to you than you let on." He looked up at me through his long lashes.

"It does. It means . . . *everything* to me." Though I wasn't sure how or why, I genuinely meant those words and I needed to get my point across.

He dragged his finger through the icing once more and brought his finger to my lips, tracing the salivating circle. My tongue slithered to one corner and followed the same path he'd just taken. His eyes widened, not expecting my boldness. Hell, I wasn't expecting my boldness but it felt good and I wanted to test the *normal* waters for a change.

"Sure you can handle this?" I said through shortened breath.

Mouth tipped in a cocky grin, he grabbed my finger, dipped it into the icing and brought it to his parted lips. His eyes seared into mine as he flicked his tongue over the tip, and I gasped. Slowly, he licked the inside of my finger clean. I squirmed, feeling each swipe between my legs. He made a circle around the top before pushing it inside his mouth.

I almost fell off the couch.

Oh. My. God.

His tongue was warm and soft, curling around me. Lost in his ministrations, I wanted to feel it everywhere. A tremor followed my exhale.

His voice was husky. "You taste delicious. I'll bet every inch of you tastes just as sweet." And then he nipped the tip of my finger with his teeth.

I swallowed the moisture pooling in my mouth. How I wished he would find out whether or not that was true.

He broke off a piece of the cake at the bottom, containing the rich frosting in the middle and held it close to my lips. "Take a lick." Though it held no threat, his tone left no room for disobedience.

Letting myself enjoy this, I dragged my tongue up the center of the cupcake, and his eyes blazed with desire, his pupils dilating. He put the cake to my lips, and I took it inside my mouth.

Following its path, he slid his thumb inside my mouth as he breathed in ecstasy, "Beautiful."

Immediately, my walls slammed down, reinforcing my icy fortress. My eyes widened in horror, and I snapped my head back as I was propelled into a different time and place. Remembering the fear, the panic, the disgust.

I scrambled to the opposite end of the couch and blanketed myself with my arms. "Get out."

"What?" His breathing was still labored while shock engulfed his features.

"You heard me. Get. Out. Get out now!" I was in full panic mode.

He reached for me. "What did I do?"

I recoiled from him. "Don't touch me. Don't you dare put your hands on me. You're just like him."

"Just like who? Tell me what I did!" He looked desperate. He didn't understand. Logically, I knew he couldn't possibly, but there was no reasoning with my emotions right now.

"Just. Leave. Me. Alone—Go!"

He set what was left of the cupcake on the coffee table. With a frustrated but calm voice, he leveled his eyes on me. "This is number two, Angel. Your second bug out. I'll go because I can tell that's what you need right now. But when you calm down and come to your senses, you're going to have to explain to me what it is exactly that I did so it doesn't happen again. And, by the way, I don't know who the *him* is you're referring to, but *I* would never hurt you. Remember that." Without another word, he stood and walked out, slamming the door behind him.

I flinched at the abruptness. The half-eaten cupcake lying in front of me only fueled my anger. Tonight had gone from great to disastrous and it was all my fucking fault. I screamed, tears flooding my eyes as I hurled the damn cupcake as hard as I could at the door Blake had just retreated from. Pieces of cake exploded, crumbling into scattered pieces, much like my insides.

"You fucking psychopath. What is wrong with you!" I screamed out loud, watching the icing drip down the door.

You did it again.

I pummeled my legs with my fists before throwing myself into the cushions and crying myself into oblivion.

Chapter 12

AWOKE THE NEXT MORNING in a blanket of anger and dread. How had I let myself react that way? And worse, I'd accused him of being just like *him*. Flipping out and making him leave was bad enough, but now he'd surely know I was hiding something.

Groaning, I rolled myself off the couch and into the shower. I closed my eyes as I rested my forehead against the tiles, letting the water cascade over my slumped form. Memories from yesterday invaded my thoughts, and I tried my best to push them away. My body seemed to be getting lighter as I allowed the water to cleanse not only my physical being, but my soul as well.

This too shall pass . . . right?

Shirt over head, mascara to lashes, blush to cheeks. I went through the motions of getting ready in a zombie-like state.

You need to end this. You're making mistakes.

I didn't bother to answer myself this time. I didn't have the strength. Not trusting myself, I checked my belongings three times to make sure I didn't forget something in my current condition. Then I unlocked my door and froze.

At my feet lay a stunning arrangement of dainty, sky blue flowers. At the heart of them, a silver star-shape rested behind a sunny yellow center. I slowly dropped to my knees and caressed the smooth petals, my brows worrying a line between my eyes. As my fingers glided over the tops of the sprouting buds, I spotted the scroll at the bottom of the box.

"To plant a garden is to believe in tomorrow." ~ Audrey Hepburn

My hand came up to cover my mouth. He was forgiving me . . . again.

Tucked behind the scroll was a card that read, *"Open Me"*.
With shaky hands, I withdrew the hard paper.

Angel,

These are forget-me-nots. I chose them hoping you'd do just that. They're the annual flowers I was telling you about that are forever getting a second chance at life. Each leaf symbolizes something I want you to remember.

Forget Not in life there are do overs

Forget Not you're cared for

Forget Not you're a strong and incredible person

Forget Not . . . Me

Forget Not you only get one more bug out, so choose it wisely ☺

I giggled at that last line through teary eyes and rubbed my thumb across the winking smiley face he'd placed beside it.

I'm not giving up on you, and I'm not letting go of life's second chances and what I know we could have. I know it's sudden and maybe it's crazy. I don't fully understand it myself, but I've never felt this way about anyone before and certainly not in this short amount of time. There's something about you that draws me to you, makes me want to protect you. Consider being mine and you'll always be cared for. It might not be easy and I may have to put you over my knee every now and then ;) But I'll suffer the consequences of that for you.

Plant your feet with mine and stop running from me and from yourself. I promise I won't hurt you, but don't take my word for it. Just try with me. That's all I ask. I'll be there when you're scared, and remind you of your feelings when you want to run. I'll be your friend, your companion. Remember to always re-member. Remember to forget-me-not.

Your BFF, Blake

I looked down at the glistening flowers as another drop rolled from my chin, landing on them. I wiped my face with the back of my hand and replaced the card in the envelope. I was openly sobbing in my hall-way, but I didn't care anymore. Why did he have to make it so hard to say no? Why did he have to be so persistent and so sweet? He said the perfect things and gave me hope. I'd given up on hope so long ago, but he always managed to ignite a spark, my glimmer of light in a dark tunnel.

I had to make him stop. There'd be no second chances for me. I didn't deserve them. He had to understand why this could never happen.

I tucked my head between my knees and curled into a ball.

Two strong arms lifted me up and cradled me against a familiar chest. "Come on, love. Let's get you inside."

He lowered me to the couch, the pressure of his hand smoothing down my hair. Through my sobs, I heard the rustling of paper being extracted from an envelope. When I opened my eyes, Jace was staring at me through a tear-stained face. "Eva . . ."

"Don't. Don't, Jace, please." I hopped to my feet and retreated to the bathroom to fix myself. I felt his presence in my doorway, his stare burn-ing a hole into the side of my head as I focused on the mirror. "I know what you're going to say, and I don't wanna hear it. I have to get to class. And, by the way, so do you."

The sympathy in his voice vanished and was replaced with convic-tion. "I'm giving you until the end of the week to make a decision. I'm not standing by and watching this anymore. You're either going to be with him or you're going to cut him off. Or I'm leaving, Evangelina, be-cause I can't stand it anymore."

I scowled at him, even though I knew he was right. I knew what I had to do, and I would. Just not yet.

I wasn't ready to let go of him yet.

OBLIVIOUS TO THE HUSTLE AND bustle of the cafeteria, I sat, staring off into space, picking at the plastic lid on my coffee cup.

"You okay, hon?"

My finger halted, and my eyes flickered toward Sandra's concerned voice. She and Jessie sat across from me, pity etched on their faces as though they could see all my broken pieces.

I squirmed in my seat, feeling exposed and vulnerable, and put on the best phony smile I could muster. "Fine, why?"

Her gaze descended to the contorted cup being strangled in my grasp. I would really have to pay better attention to my tell signs. Clearing my throat, I pushed it aside.

"Where've you been? We haven't heard from you since the bar on Friday," Jessie asked.

"I laid low this weekend," I told her, carefully putting the lie together in my head. "Went to visit my boyfriend on Saturday, and the rest of the time I pretty much spent at home."

"Boyfriend, huh?" Jessie raised her eyebrows, her mood shifting as she curled her torso over the table. "I was sure you were going to end things to be with the panty-dropping Blake."

"Now why would you think that?" I asked, trying to bide time while I found all of my pieces and stuck them back together.

"Oh, I don't know. Maybe because the two of you are so madly in love, you practically make babies just by looking at each other."

"We are *not* in love. We hardly even know each other." I shoved her arm and averted her attention away from me. "What about you? You and Rick looked awfully fond of each other. I saw you making goo-goo eyes at him."

Jessie's body deflated as she sank back into her chair. "I like him. *A lot.* But he always keeps me at arm's length. Every time I think he feels the same way and he's going to make a move, he pushes back and we have to start from square one. It's so frustrating." She grimaced. "He's around so many hot girls. Maybe I'm just not pretty enough." Lines formed across her forehead.

"Stop it. You're gorgeous and you don't even know it, which makes you even prettier. Besides, he likes you. I can tell. Maybe he's just not ready for a relationship," I tried to reassure her.

Jessie blinked. "I didn't say I wanted to marry him. But the guy's gotta date, right?"

I shrugged. "I don't know him well enough yet. I'll try to feel him out if I can, though. Promise."

"Thanks. You're the best." Her smile returned, and I was thankful. I liked this Jessie better. The girl was too sweet to be upset.

Sandra cut in, "So where'd you learn how to sing like that?"

My spine stiffened as the attention shifted back in my direction. "My whole family is musical. I guess you could say it's hereditary. I never really thought about it." Growing up with a dad who played in a band, music was always just around. It was a staple in our household.

"You were seriously amazing," Sandra praised. "I've never heard anyone sing like that. The way you belted those notes. You need to be famous."

I laughed. "I wouldn't go that far. I'm all right."

"You're a lot better than all right," Sandra argued, dipping a fry in ketchup and stuffing it into her mouth. "You're amazeballs. Blake seemed to think so, too," she trilled in her sing-song voice.

At the sound of his name, my belly did a summersault. I swallowed past the lump in my throat. "Thanks."

Must. Change. Topic.

"So, Sandra, who's the guy you met? You were gone before I got a chance to meet him." I pulled my coffee in for another sip.

She instantly sprung to life, her whole demeanor changing as she gushed. "His name is Jeremy, and I think I'm in love. He's a grad student, studying graphic design. You have to see his drawings. They're incredible. And he's so nice and sweet and hot!"

"Whoa, slow down." I put my palms up, smiling. "You think you like him a little?"

Her face softened. "I do. I really do. He gives me the tingly wigglies." She shivered.

We all laughed. "Sounds serious."

"It is," she sighed. "At least I hope it is. We're meeting at the bar again tonight, so we'll see." Sandra checked her watch. "Crap, it's late. We gotta go."

We all jumped up, blowing kisses goodbye and running in different directions.

THE SOUND OF CHAIRS SCRAPING the wood floor as they were brought down from their resting place greeted me when I walked into work. As much as I needed the money, I was hoping for an easy night. I hadn't been able to pull myself out of this funk all day.

Rick looked up, and a friendly smile spread across his face. "Well, hello there. I got a head start prepping stuff for you."

"Great. Thanks." I smiled back.

"Not a problem. So how'd you like your first real day? The chatter hasn't stopped about the gorgeous new bartender."

"Oh boy." I rolled my eyes. "Well, it'll keep the tips flowing nicely," I joked.

"You're right about that, darlin'. They all fell in love with you. And that voice . . . whew, girl. You've got some set of lungs on you." His eyebrows lifted in appreciation. "I think I'm gonna have to make that a new requirement when you're working. You had the place jacked up. We made a killing." The excitement in his voice was palpable.

I twirled a long lock of hair between my fingers. "I don't normally sing. That was my friends doing. He's a pain in the ass, but I can't say no to him. Usually I get all shaky and sweaty and dry mouthed."

"Hog wash. You're singing."

"Hog wash?" I laughed.

"Yes, hog wash," he repeated with a good natured grin. "I don't wanna hear it. A person can't have a gift like that and keep it to themselves."

"But—"

"Singing," he demanded.

"We'll see." A nervous laugh escaped my lips. I tried to think of a way to ease into my next topic and get away from this me-singing business. "So Jessie might stop in again later."

"Really? That's cool. I guess I'll be seeing a lot more of her now that you're here," he said nonchalantly as he counted the opening register.

"Yeah, probably." I grabbed the cutting board and dug into some lemons. Forging on, I asked, "That's a good thing, right? You guys seemed pretty, um . . . friendly the other night."

He looked at me briefly, and I thought I saw adoration flash across his eyes, but he quickly replaced it with something noncommittal. "Yeah, they don't come any sweeter than Jessie girl. That girl can have whatever she wants from me."

"Were you guys ever an item?"

"Nah, we're just friends." He acted like none of it mattered to him, but I could tell by the nervous tic in his neck I had touched a nerve.

I glanced at him out of the corner of my eye. "That's a shame. I'm pretty sure she likes you, and you guys would probably be good together."

"Oh, yeah, well, I uh . . . *like* her, too. But I don't date my friends." He pushed the drawer in and walked away, dismissing the conversation.

A short while later, random bar-goers were scattered on stools, playing pool and throwing darts. I dragged a damp rag along the bar and glanced over at the door, wondering if Blake would show again. I shouldn't care . . .

But I did.

Shortly after, Jessie and Sandra, toting a guy who must have been Jeremy, strutted in. "Hey, chickadee." Sandra beamed, gesturing toward her new man. "This is Jeremy. Jeremy, this is Eva."

"Nice to meet you, Jeremy," I yelled over the music, extending my hand over the bar.

"Likewise." He smiled a friendly smile that made his eyes shine. He was on the shorter side, five-nine possibly, with choppy, sandy brown hair, and hazel eyes.

"You've got a gem on your hands. Take care of her so I don't have to hunt your ass down," I warned playfully.

"Duly noted. No worries. Your girl is safe with me." He wrapped his arm around her waist and pulled her close to his side while she stared at him in awe.

"So, where's Rick?" Jessie cut in, her eyes searching the area.

"He stepped away for a sec. He'll be right back." I eyed her warily, unsure whether or not I should broach the conversation we needed to have. "Hey, Jes?"

"Yeah," she said, still not focusing her eyes on me. The girl had it bad.

"Does he know how you feel? I mean, have you ever told him?"

Jessie looked at me. "No, not directly, but the signs are all there. I know he knows."

"Okay, because I kind of asked about you guys in passing, and he says he would do anything for you, but that he doesn't date his friends. He seemed pretty adamant about it, Jes." I reached out a sympathetic hand and covered hers. "I know you two would probably make a cute couple, but maybe it's not in the cards. I mean, Rick's an awesome guy, don't get me wrong, but I can tell you really like him and I just don't want to see you get hurt."

"I know. I get that." Her lips dipped in a frown and she looked away. "I just can't get him out of my head and he always acts like he feels the same way. Just when I think I can move past it, I see him again and it starts all over. I just don't see what the big deal is." Her gaze scudded to the right as Rick resumed his place behind the bar. Conversation over.

"Hey, Princess," he called over to Jessie, a huge smile on his face.

"Hi," she answered, giving him a shy smile.

Princess? Really? I wondered if he had lovie names for all of his so-called *friends.* No wonder she thought she had a chance. He stretched across the bar and placed his lips flush against her cheek, making her blush.

Friend my ass.

He wanted her as bad as she wanted him, and he was messing with her head, acting like he didn't. I tapped my fingers on the bar and made a mental note to get to the bottom of that.

After a couple hours spent laughing and playing pool, Sandra and Jeremy remained lip-locked in a corner. He caressed her face and played with her hair. She had such a big heart and a lot of love to share. I was glad she had found someone, but I couldn't help the pang of jealousy.

My eyes sought out the door for the umpteenth time at the very moment a familiar silhouette filled its frame. A slow smile spread across my lips as I let out a huge breath of air. My body relaxed and a sense of comfort encased me like a warm blanket. It was as though I'd been walking around without a limb all night. I sprung to life in that instant, feeling my missing piece return.

Blake's eyes locked on mine and we stilled at the sight of one another. We drifted toward each other like magnets drawn to an opposite pole. He sauntered over to the end of the bar and took his standard post, where I knew he'd be keeping his eye on me for the remainder of the night. I wasn't going to admit to anyone how much I liked that—feeling his eyes on me, his sights seeming as though they were lying on my skin, touching me. Feeling protected—safe.

Clad in faded denim jeans and a baby blue button down that accentuated his eyes, the top two buttons were left open, exposing a slice of his perfectly smooth, tanned chest and the v-shape it created right below his neck. I wanted to explore that whole valley with my tongue. Dip in and out of it and swipe across the broad spectrum, nibbling the bones that housed it. On its own accord, my tongue flicked out to wet my lips.

He seemed to be evaluating me and my response as he took the seat I now thought of as his.

"Hey," I breathed, my cheeks warm from my inappropriate thoughts. We didn't leave on the best of terms to say the least, so I knew this would be a bit awkward.

"Hi," he responded. Curt, and unsure of me, but still polite.

"Thank you for the flowers. They're lovely." I scratched my nail along the smooth surface of the bar.

"Glad you liked them." His smile didn't quite touch his eyes, but I could tell he was beginning to soften.

I rubbed my palms up and down my thighs to rid them of the sweat lining them, and bit my lower lip. I needed this off my chest. "Blake, listen, I'm sorry about the way I reacted last night. You didn't do anything wrong—"

He put a hand up, halting me. "Not the time. You can tell me all about it later." Good to see we were still tossing that bone back and forth.

"Fair enough. So, what can I get you?" I reached between the bottles and grabbed the Stoli Razz and Seven I'd hidden there earlier. I took a sip, trying to quench the dry mouth my nerves had created.

The corner of Blake's mouth twitched as he tried to keep his expression serious. "A blow job please."

A gush of liquid flew out of my mouth, my hand rushing up to try to catch it. The stream narrowly escaped hitting a patron in the face, who looked at me in horror and decided to vacate his seat.

Son of a bitch. I forgot how loaded of a question that was for his smart mouth.

"Excuse me?" I croaked, the vodka burning the inside of my nose and the back of my throat, causing my eyes to glaze over.

"A blow job. Shot glass . . . Baileys . . . amaretto . . ." he dragged out as if he was stating the obvious.

"Oh," I coughed out.

"Call your friends over. I'll buy a round. It's time I get to know them a little better."

"Hey, Jes," I choke-shouted. "Grab Sandra and lover boy and come on over with Rick. Blake here wants to buy you guys a shot."

Still leaning all the way over the bar, she tore her gaze away from Rick, but left her hands clasped in his. "'Kay."

"What's up, bro?" Eric slipped into the seat beside Blake, slapping him on the back. I hadn't seen him come in.

"Just in time." Blake beamed. "You in the mood for a blow job?"

"Music to my ears. It's been a while since I had a good blow job, and if it's coming from this fine lady," he gestured to me with a smirk, "I'm sure it's going to be good enough to make my knees weak." Eric winked.

I looked at him with disgust. "Don't get cute."

"Too late, sweetheart. I'm as cute as a button, wouldn't you agree?" His eyes twinkled with amusement. I needed to learn how to put up with him if I was planning on keeping Blake around. *Awesome.*

Squinting my eyes, I pointed my finger at him, opening my mouth to spit out a witty comeback when Blake sent his palm into Eric's chest. "Back off this one." He wasn't kidding and his face held no room for mis-interpretation.

"Take it down a notch, bro," Eric defended himself. "I was only jok-ing. I know this one's yours. She's just so easy to mess with." He turned his mint green eyes back on me. "You forgive me, don't you, sweetheart?" He smiled his flashy smile.

"Only if you stop calling me sweetheart." I flashed a set of sarcastic pearly whites.

"Sure thing, *Angel*." His eyes glowed with excitement at his goading.

"Don't push me, dude." Blake's face turned red, the veins in his neck visible.

He raised his palms. "Okay, okay. I'm sorry. Eva. That good?"

"There you go." I patted Eric's forearm, condescending, and got back to business. By the time I returned, all was well, and Blake and Eric were laughing like nothing had ever transpired between them.

I poured the liquid that made up the dirty shot, topped it off with some whipped cream, and lined them across the bar. Jessie came bouncing over with Sandra and Jeremy, and Rick stood next to me behind the bar.

"Ah, ah, ah. Don't forget yours now." Blake winked a beautifully mischievous eye.

I rolled my eyes and turned to grab the bottles again but was handed a shot overflowing with whipped cream. Rick was far ahead of me.

"Thanks," I said unenthusiastically, turning back around. "Okay, guys. Who'd like a blow job?" I teased.

"A what?" Jessie cried. Her hand came up to cover her chest, shocked at my audacity. "Eva!"

"What?" I laughed. "Blake here wants a blow job and thinks you would all like one too, so drink up." I raised the glass to my lips when Blake's hand shot out to cover the glass before I could guzzle it.

"Oh, no you don't, babe. Not so fast." The corner of his mouth tilted up. "I told you, there's certain ways you have to go about *consuming* things."

My cheeks caught fire as I remembered the last thing he showed me how to consume. I didn't want to do it again in front of an audience. He applied pressure to my hand, forcing the glass back down.

"Everybody ready?" Blake looked around.

Seeming to know more than the rest of us, Rick's face split into an enormous grin.

I hated them both.

"Everyone put your hands behind your back." He moved his arms behind himself and looked around, waiting for everyone to follow. Rick and Eric, enjoying every second of Blake's show, were next to join in.

Jessie, then Jeremy, then finally Sandra, followed suit. I looked around at them in amazement as they all stared at me, waiting for me to comply.

"Oh, hell," I threw my arms behind my back and stuck my tongue in my teeth, giving Blake a look that said *you happy now.*

His smile told me he was delighted. "Now, lean forward and put your mouth around the glass. Pick it up, drop your head back, and swallow. On the count of three. One . . ." His eyes locked with mine. "Two . . ." I looked around at everyone gearing up to dip their heads. *Were we really doing this?* "Three!"

Everyone's heads leaned forward, and their mouths circled around their glasses.

We were really doing this.

Blake lifted his eyes to me, keeping his head low.

"We're waiting."

With a scowl, I lowered my head to the fluffy-filled glass and encased it with my mouth. One by one, each of us shot up, drinking down our share. White froth lined all of our mouths. I rushed to wipe mine away with the back of my hand, feeling dirty, and like everyone was seeing something private, even though in reality it *was* just whipped cream.

Washing his away, Blake licked the full circle of his lips, his tongue leaving a glistening trail in its wake. Reaching across the bar, he wiped a stray piece of cream from the corner of my lips, and then stuck his finger in his mouth, licking it off. He closed his eyes as my taste invaded his senses. My belly clenched at the intimateness of the gesture.

"Oh my god, that was so good." Jessie fanned herself. "I think I'm turned on."

"Jessie!" Sandra nudged her.

"Now there'll be none of that talk." The humor was gone in Rick's voice as he leveled his gaze at her.

"Why?" Her eyes challenged him. "It's not like you're interested anyway. I'm not dead. I can get turned on, and I can find a guy to take care of it for me if I want to." Jessie puffed out her chest. "As a matter of fact," she slipped her arm around Eric's middle, "there seems to be quite the delicious selection tonight. What do you say, cute stuff? Wanna show me a good time?"

"Jessie," Rick warned, narrowing his eyes.

"Rick," she shot back in the same warning tone.

Oh boy. She wasn't playing. And she wasn't backing down, either. Good for her. Maybe this needed to come to a head.

Eric put his hands up. "You're cute, sweetie, but something tells me I should stay out of this one." Slipping out from under Jessie's arm, he said, "Oh, would you look at that, I think I see an old girlfriend of mine. Catch you guys later."

Still noticeably livid, Rick glowered at Jessie. "We'll talk about this later."

"Maybe we will, maybe we won't." She glanced in my direction, hands crossed over her chest. "Eva, I'd like another one of those please."

I looked over at Rick for a cue. It was his bar, after all, and he was my boss.

With his disapproving glare pinned on her, his voice could cut ice. "Go ahead. Give it to her. Let her have her fun."

"Thank you." She stuck out her chin like a rebellious child.

He looked like he wanted to say something, but then a look of disappointment washed over him, and he turned and walked away.

She kept her tough stance, not budging as I made her drink, but her eyes betrayed her. I knew that took more out of her than she let on.

I slid the glass to her and leaned forward, talking as low as the atmosphere would allow to retain some form of privacy. "You okay, sweets?"

"Yeah, I'm fine." Jessie took a steadying breath, waved her hand in a dismissive fashion, then spit out, "Fuck 'em. I'm gonna have a good time. It's his loss." She tossed her head back, downing the shot. Then she looked to the end of the bar and made eye contact with Rick as her tongue darted out to lick the cream from her lips.

Well, this was a whole different kind of Jessie.

"Come on, Eva," she said, still looking at him. "Give us all one more round—on me."

Rick shook his head and turned his back to pay attention to the other customers.

Before I knew it, the place was clearing out and it was time to wind down. Jessie left without saying goodbye to Rick, and Sandra and Jeremy followed behind her to make sure she got home safely. I hadn't kept tabs on Eric, but my guess was he hadn't left empty-handed.

Blake tossed a twenty dollar bill on the bar. "I'll wait for you outside."

I nodded and made quick work of cleaning up and counting the drawer.

I eyed Rick. "I don't know what that was all about, but she really likes you, ya know? It would be a shame to let a good thing slip away. I can tell you're a decent guy, and I'm sure you could do far worse."

Rick looked over at me as if I'd broken him out of a trance. I put up my hands. "Just an observation." With that, I slung my bag over my shoulder. "Night, Rick."

"Night, Eva. Get home safe," he replied catatonically. "Oh, and Eva . . ."

I twirled around. "Yeah?"

"I could say the same to you." He cocked an eyebrow at me.

I paused, briefly taken aback. Not knowing how to answer, I simply nodded, ducked my head, and walked out of the bar. Shaking that off, I smiled up at Blake and slipped my hand into his. "Come on, Romeo. Walk me home."

"If you insist." His dimple smiled down at me, and I wondered for the hundredth time what that divot would feel like beneath my fingertips.

I looked down at my feet, biting my lip and trying to figure out how to start the conversation, planning out the words in my head before I lost the nerve. "About last night . . . It wasn't your fault. You couldn't have known what you did. I thought about what you said and it made sense. If we're going to be spending time together—and based on the fact you just won't go away, I suspect we will—then you're going to have to be aware of some of my," I gulped, "triggers."

There. That's a good word.

"I'm all ears." Blake kept his focus straight ahead, knowing this wouldn't be easy for me.

I couldn't believe I was about to admit this to him and give him a glimpse inside my world. "The word beautiful." I shivered involuntarily just saying it now. "Though I appreciate the sentiment, and I've tried to push past it—trigger." I was keeping things honest, yet simple.

He glanced down briefly at me and I continued. "Putting your thumb in my mouth—yes, sexy as all hell, and yes, you taste delicious, but—trigger."

He still looked concerned, but the corner of his mouth twitched.

"Both of them together, well, you witnessed that one firsthand." I peered up at him and braced myself for the look one gives when they're in the presence of a crazy person. I mean, who goes berserk when a guy calls them beautiful? This psycho, that's who.

Instead, a broad smile stretched the spectrum of his perfect features, and his dimple winked at me. "You think I taste delicious, huh?"

"What? I . . . um . . ." *Oh my god, I did say that, didn't I?*

"It's okay, I think you're pretty scrumptious yourself." He chuckled. "Don't be embarrassed. I'm flattered. And glad you finally admitted you feel something too for a change. I was beginning to get a complex."

I blinked at him. That hadn't gone at all like I pictured. "Yeah, so um, anyway, now you know. Steer clear of those things, and we should be okay."

"Noted. Thanks for the heads up. And you're forgiven." He squeezed my hand. "But now you owe me a cupcake. Those bad boys are *not* meant to be wasted. Your punishment for the way you reacted will commence upon the next lesson on how to eat them." His eyes blazed, dripping with humor and promise. And again he'd managed to evoke the little sexy-place tingle that let me know I was alive, sending a buzzing thrum that started in my most intimate parts and traveled throughout my entire body.

I forced myself to respond without giving away my disability. "Deal." Then I smiled at how easy that was. Every time I turned around, there was another reason why Blake was so amazing. Instead of making me feel self-conscious or ashamed, he'd just made a joke and accepted my apology, making me feel comfortable during an awkward situation. The guy just kept proving himself over and over, and I wondered for the millionth time why I was fighting this so hard.

Tonight was chillier than it had been, and by the time we reached my steps, I realized I wasn't dressed appropriately in my jean skirt and halter top. A cool breeze sent a chill snaking over my skin, and I shivered.

Noticing how cold I was, Blake turned toward me and wrapped me in his arms. "Thanks for sharing that with me. I know it probably wasn't easy for you."

"Thank you for understanding after what I did." My head instinctively burrowed into his chest, and his scent invaded my nostrils, weakening my resolve further.

He slid his finger under my chin and tilted it up so I couldn't avoid the seriousness in his eyes. "I'll always understand. I want you to open up to me. There's nothing you can't tell me, remember that. I've meant everything I've said since the day I met you. Let me in. I won't judge you. I want to help."

There was no helping me. I couldn't *be* helped. Taking a small step backward, I dropped my arms, but he caught them in his hands, keeping us close. "Well, thanks for walking me home. I guess I'll see you in class tomorrow?"

His mouth pressed into a hard line at my curtness. As understanding as he always was, he recuperated quickly and lowered his lips to place a soft kiss to the top of my head. I wondered how long it would take before he gave up on me. I dreaded that day.

"Goodnight, Angel." He stood back and stuck his hands in his pockets, his jaw tense as he rocked back on his heels.

Reluctantly, I walked away, feeling him staring, waiting for me to make it safely inside. But when my foot hit the step, I halted as a wave of emotions rolled through me. I needed him to know his efforts weren't in vain. That I was grateful to him—for him.

I turned and rushed back to him before I lost my nerve. His hands dropped from his pockets, and his eyebrows knitted together, uncertain of me and my rapidly changing mood swings. I placed my hands on his shoulders and pushed up on my tippy toes, placing a soft kiss on his cheek and letting my lips linger there for a moment longer than necessary. When I pulled back, his eyes were wide and he was trying to tame his breath.

"Goodnight, Blake." Then I turned and sprinted into my apartment without looking back.

Chapter 13

TAPPED MY PEN AT a feverish pace as Professor Sorrenson handed our graded exams back. This was the first grade of my college academic career, and I was anxious to see how I did. Lord knew I studied enough. It was hard to believe a month had passed since I arrived here, alone and scared. So much had happened in that short period of time that it felt like a lifetime ago.

I'd already forged irreplaceable bonds with new friends—which, besides Jace, was something I hadn't done in a very long time. I also saw Blake on an almost daily basis. True to his word, he was slowly becoming my new BFF. The flirting never ceased, but I knew it went further than that and he truly did care about me.

I'd grown a habit of messing with him, trying to hook him up with random females, but he always managed to come up with a new excuse as to why they weren't his type. "Her hair is too short," or "Her eyes are too close together," or my personal favorite, "She smells like a wet Band-Aid". The longer it went on, the more outlandish his reasoning became. It was a fun game we'd adopted, where I pretended not to care, but to tell you the truth, I didn't think I could handle it if he ever took me up on one of my offers.

"Nervous, babe?"

"Huh? Oh . . . yeah." I blinked out of my haze, glancing over at Blake and his concerned face.

"Don't worry, I'm sure you did fine. This is your favorite subject, remember?" He reached over and brushed his thumb over the top of my hand. He was always doing this, touching me in little ways to soothe my nerves or comfort me.

"Thanks. I just have so much riding on all this, and I've been such an unfocused mess since I got here."

"Evangelina Ricci." The sound of my name had nervous-queasies spiraling through my belly.

Here goes nothing.

I sent Blake an anxious smile. He patted my hand before pulling his away and folding them on top of his desk.

With trepidation, I made my way to the front of the class from all the way back in the V.I.P section. I hoped I wouldn't be doing the walk of shame on my retreat.

I could tell as I approached the professor's desk the news wouldn't be good.

"Evangelina, I think you need to apply yourself a little more. I can tell you have great potential but your work is lacking." With a disappointed look on his face, Professor Sorrenson reluctantly handed over the same little blue booklet I'd held in my hand the week prior.

I glanced down at the red, bold-faced seventy-three staring back at me. "Sorry, sir. I'll try harder next time." I trudged on back to my seat and slid into my desk, shoulders hunched, clutching the mocking pieces of paper.

But I studied! How had I let this happen? I'd have to kick my own ass to get my GPA where I needed it to be now.

Fanfuckingtastic.

Blake slid back into his seat. His lips were dipped low in the corners, and he wouldn't look me in the eyes. By the look on his face, I didn't have to ask how he'd done. Better than me. Peering at my paper, he offered me a sympathetic smile. "It's not so bad."

"Shut up. It's bad and you know it," I bit back.

"Well, it's not great, but it could be worse."

"I'll never be able to salvage this." I threw the booklet down in frustration.

"Sure you will, if you let me help you." He looked at me hopeful.

I dreaded having to agree to this since the first time he offered. I didn't like asking people for help. I buried my face in the crook of my arm and swayed my head back and forth.

No. No. No.

"Come on. I'll make it fun. I promise." He rubbed soothing circles on my back.

I talked into my arm. "Fine." I could feel satisfaction oozing from his pores and was already second guessing my decision. "Don't make me regret this."

"*Me?*" He acted shocked and hurt at my insinuation.

I snapped my head in his direction. "Yes, you. And quit acting all innocent. I know you better than that, Mr. Turner."

Blake turned his attention back to the front of the room, but he couldn't help the huge grin slithering across his face. "I don't have a clue what you're talking about."

MY FOOTSTEPS ECHOED ON THE wood floor as I searched for an unoccupied table. I couldn't believe I'd agreed to this. I claimed a vacant seat, and thumbed through my nasty little blue book while I waited, unable to figure out where I'd gone wrong.

"May I?" Blake whispered loudly in my ear, gesturing to the empty seat beside me. His warm breath prickled my skin.

"Stop doing that to me," I chastised in a harsh whisper, grabbing my chest.

"Doing what? It's a library. We need to whisper."

"Just behave. No funny business or I'm leaving."

He held up his hands and leaned back, adding space. "I didn't know we needed to be so formal. Is this an acceptable distance, Miss Ricci?"

"Yes, thank you." Truth was, I couldn't concentrate with his heat so close. His aura wrapped around my brain like a snake, smothering it until I couldn't think straight. Which is probably why I had failed in the first place. Who could concentrate with a sex-exuding god sitting mere inches from you?

"Hand over your booklet. Let's start with that."

Reluctantly, I slid the horrid little book across the table.

His beautiful fingers glided back and forth over his squared off chin while he read through my pages. That one action only amplified my awareness of him.

"Hmph."

"What?" I stretched my neck over his shoulder, wondering what he saw.

"Your use of superlatives is excessive, don't you think?"

I frowned. "Super-la-*what*?"

"Superlatives. Best. Most. Widest. Longest. I know you're trying to make a point, but *everything* can't be superior. Calm down with that."

"Okay," I drew out. Now he'd piqued my interest. Originally, I wasn't sure what I would take away from this little study session besides some wet panties, but maybe he knew more about all this than I thought. I couldn't help but stare as he drummed his fingers against his lips. Giving the bottom lip a little tug, oblivious to my growing discomfort, he continued, "And you're misusing your vocabulary."

"What do you mean?" Professor Sorrenson had given us a bunch of words to use in our essays, and I meticulously memorized every single one of them. I was sure of it.

"The words. You're mixing them all up."

"That can't be. I studied them so much, they're imprinted in my brain for life." I squeaked in a harsh whisper.

"I'm telling you, Angel." He read from my booklet, "The digital *nascent* in which we live is making human interaction non-existent? When technology was *milieu,* one could never have predicted the solitude it would bring forth?" He raised his brows, waiting for the light bulb to go off.

I snatched the paper from his grasp, scanning it in disbelief. "Oh my god, I did! What's wrong with me?" The professor must think I didn't even bother to learn them. I banged my head on the desk.

"It's okay. I'll teach you my little trick." He folded a page vertically and began to write words down the left margin. Then he opened it and inside the hidden piece, he wrote the definitions. "When you're not with me, this is how you're going to test yourself. Keep the answers hidden and don't stop until you get them all right. Also, we're going to make sentences for each of them you couldn't possibly forget. Trust me." There was that evil glint again.

"You really know your stuff, huh?" I rested my chin in my palm and looked at him, even more impressed than before.

"It's a gift, what can I say." He rubbed his chin, deep in thought. "So, nascent—to begin to exist. There is a nascent ache burning in my chest for you. Say that sentence three times." His lip twitched, trying to contain his amusement.

"Wise-ass."

"I'm serious."

"Come on," I whined.

He tapped his pen on the paper impatiently. "I'm waiting. I don't have all day."

I let out a puff of air. "There is a nascent ache burning in my chest for you."

"Again."

I rolled my eyes. "There is a nascent ache burning in my chest for you."

He smirked. "One more time." He inclined his ear in my direction and tapped on the lobe.

I rushed through. "There is a nascent ache burning in my chest for you."

His hand covered his chest as he batted his eyelashes. "Why, Evangelina, I'm flattered."

"Very funny," I said sarcastically. But he was right—I would never forget that word again.

The next twenty minutes consisted of every word on that list being used in more *unforgettable* sentences. I never realized the word quell could be dirty, or any of the words for that matter. The guy had a talent.

Staring at my booklet, I was oblivious to the fact he'd inched closer to me during our testing session.

His warm breath at the soft spot below my ear made my belly clench. He pressed his chest against my side and pointed to the page in front of me. "Also, see right here where you keep using the same words over and over? That's called an echo. You need to find other words and substitute them. It'll flow better and be easier to read," he whispered, burrowing his nose into my hair.

My head tilted into him, his pull on me as magnetic as ever. I swallowed long and hard, willing my lungs to cease their need for oxygen so I didn't have to breathe in his intoxicating scent. "You're in my personal space." Damn my voice for sounding so shaky.

He brushed his nose down the side of my neck. "I just wanted to be sure not to disturb anyone else. We *are* in a library, after all."

"I can assure you, you don't have to be that close in order for them not to hear you."

He chuckled, the sound deep and sensual. "True, but it was a good excuse to get close to you for as long as I could get away with it." He dragged his lips up the length of my neck and nipped my earlobe.

I gasped. "What're you doing?"

"It's Tuesday." He smiled and chomped down on his jaw, reminding me of when we'd first met and that he too bites on Tuesdays.

Although my body was reeling, I covered it up with a burst of laughter, then quickly stifled it under my palm. "Remind me to steer clear of you on Tuesdays then. Sheesh. I didn't know I needed to take you seriously if I didn't want to become your next meal."

He leaned dangerously close, forcing me to bend back so far in my chair the top of it bit into my shoulder blades. "Angel, I would make you the appetizer, main course *and* dessert if you'd let me. You have no idea what my mouth is capable of. I would devour you inch by delicious fucking inch, and lick my fingers clean afterwards."

I was wordless, unable to form a coherent thought. Even here, in a library, he had my heart pounding and my hormones raging. I itched to plunge my fingers into his hair and pull his mouth to mine. This attraction was all-consuming and it was becoming harder and harder to say no.

"You just let me know when you're ready." His eyes flicked to my lips, and my cheeks turned to flames.

"Why do you do this to me?" My voice gave away my weakness.

His serious gaze never faltered. He almost looked pained and the sincerity in his words shocked me. "I need you to know how I feel, Angel. I'll try every chance I get to convince you you're made for me. No regrets. I've never felt this way about anyone before, and I can't just ignore it. Whether you admit it or not, I can tell you're drawn to me, too. You just keep fighting it." He moved closer still, pinning me to the pressed wood at my back. "Give into it, to this." He brushed his fingertips along my jaw and my eyes fluttered closed.

I took a fortifying inhale but didn't move from his touch. "Why don't you stop? You're relentless."

"I can't, I told you. As long as you'll have me around, I'll never stop. Not until you're mine. You should just accept that you want me already so we can move on from here." With a confident smirk, he ghosted his fingers down my arm and squeezed my hip.

How did he always get the upper hand? I swallowed hard and my voice came out in a barely audible whisper, "You forget I have a—"

"Boyfriend?" He scoffed. "Yeah, I've heard. *You* forget, I don't really care. Let me ask you this, where is he, Evangelina? Not a very worthy adversary if you ask me. How can he go weeks on end without seeing you? Hell, I can barely stay away from you now. I'd rather not hear about your poor excuse for a man anymore. You need a real man." He snaked his hand through the hair at the nape of my neck and inched me close. "One who's right here. Flesh and blood. Who can take care of you." He dragged his knuckles along my cheek and scraped his thumb across my bottom lip.

Lost in the weight of his eyes, and the possessiveness of his touch, I fought to tear my gaze from his. Looking down in my lap, I toyed with a thread hanging from my shirt. "I told you . . . He's away."

His focus darted from my pouted lip up to my eyes as he analyzed me. A disbelieving *humph* escaped his lips. Then he backed away, taking his heat with him, and didn't say anything more.

My façade crumbled into dust around me. He was turning me to putty and somehow could see right through my shields, my lies. Like an intimate little chisel, he was breaking me down piece by piece. I was beginning to worry all that would be left was bare bones. "You promised you'd be good," I whispered.

His eyes glowed with promise. "Oh, I *am* good. Make no mistake about that. I'll be the best you'll ever have. Rock your world and make you beg for more. And *that's* a promise."

"Stop." My voice was so small, so meek I could barely hear it in my own ears. If I wanted to be convincing, I was doing a poor job.

He leaned in again. "Make me."

"Excuse me?"

"You heard me, Angel. Make me stop." His lips were so close to mine, a mere hiccup would push them together. The air around us was as thick as a swollen cloud about to combust.

He was right—everything he said. And as much as I should tell him to go to hell and get as far away from him as I could, I couldn't bear the thought of not being near him. I liked the way he made me feel. For the first time, I felt alive.

I had to get out of here or I would do as he asked because, damn it all to hell, I couldn't take it anymore.

"Want to watch a movie?" I suddenly blurted.

His head tilted to the side and his brow furrowed, the brisk change in topic catching him off guard. "A movie?"

"Yes, a movie." I took the brief opportunity to regulate myself.

He contemplated my request for a quiet moment. "Sure, let's go." He grinned. "I told you, I'll take what I can get."

BY THE TIME WE REACHED the hallway in my building, all awkwardness was gone and we were laughing and joking.

"Thanks for the help. If I fail another test, I'm gonna kill myself."

He rolled his eyes. "Oh please, you're such a drama queen."

"Am not!" I swatted at him playfully, but he skillfully dodged me.

Out of the corner of my eye, I glimpsed a ginormous, skeevy monster dash out from under a door. With its beady eyes and giant wings, it was raging at me, fists flying.

"Ah! Oh my God!" I yelped. Before I could think better of it, I jumped up and wrapped my legs around Blake's waist, nearly strangling him with my arms. "Kill it, kill it, kill it!"

He secured me by my waist and spun around. In every attempt to keep my eyes on the ferocious beast, my head flew to the right and left as he swirled and whirled, trying to see past me to the ground.

"Calm down, it's only a water bug, sissy girl," he said through his laughs.

I didn't care. "Come on! Get it!" I screamed.

He twisted, maneuvering me on his hips, stomping his foot, trying to extinguish the hideous demon. I shrieked into his chest. My body was jolted and shaken, flying from side to side as Blake danced a jig, thrashing madly.

As the pounding died down, awareness prickled up my body. I suddenly realized the severity of what I'd done. My face was buried in the soft hardness of his chest, feeling his heart beat against my cheek with each rise and fall. My nose taking in the scent that was just . . . Blake. My hands were buried in the hair at the back of his head, and my legs securely wrapped around his . . .

Oh my God!

I could feel his *appreciation* of me spearing me in my girl parts. The skirt I'd decided to wear did nothing to create a shield against his prodding tip. It tantalized me, teasing me, begging to be set free and touch me without any barriers. Of its own free will, my body opened up to him, welcoming him. Telling him to come inside and take a seat, stay for a cup of tea. The feeling was so strong, I was nervous I'd leave evidence of my own appreciation on his clothes through my thin undergarments.

Feeling him nuzzle his nose on the top of my head, all movement ceased, other than his chest still heaving from exertion. At least, I thought it was still exertion.

My voice was muffled in the peaks of his chest. "Is it dead?"

"Yes, you're safe." He smoothed his hand down the length of my hair, keeping me tightly clasped with the other.

I lifted my head, then immediately regretted it. Our faces were so close, I could see flecks of white mingled into his blue eyes. They flicked to my lips and he took a deep, long swallow, then his gaze moved back to my eyes, seeking approval. The tension in the air was massive, the pull to each other fierce. It would be so easy to give in to what we both knew we wanted, what we craved. My stubbornness was the only obstacle.

Abruptly, I wiggled and unhinged my legs, signaling he should set me free, but his grip tightened, preventing me from hopping off. The corner of his mouth raised and he slid me down excruciatingly slow, my body pinned to the front of his, dragging down his length, feeling every—*every*—bit of his . . . length.

Fuck.

As I traveled down, his hands traveled up, feeling each curve of my body, and coming to rest on my shoulders. I swallowed hard and realized my hands were still rooted deep into his hair. That as much as I was trying to tell my body to relinquish him, it was grasping at straws, defying me.

I uncurled my fingers, one at a time and dropped my hands to my sides, willing him to do the same. Realizing this would not be the time, a look of disappointment came over him. He dropped his arms but didn't back away.

"See. Drama queen." His voice was gentle now.

I smiled weakly. "Shut up."

"Shut me up." Typically his eyes were wicked when he said things like that, but right now they were devoid of any humor. Longing and desire replaced his usual snarky confidence.

Seeing another notch in my already strained resolve break away, he moved closer, closing the small gap that remained between us. "Shut me up, Angel." He brushed the pad of his thumb over my lower lip. "I dare you."

My body was in flames. It took everything I had not to jump back into his arms and burrow into his pores. But I couldn't do that to him; he was too important. I looked at him, trying to think of a witty response, but came up empty.

In truth, that was all I really wanted to do anyway. Catch his bottom lip between my teeth and slide my tongue over his. Learn the curves of his mouth from the inside out.

"It's impossible to shut you up. I learned that already." It was a struggle to get the words out when I could smell the mint on his breath. His proximity made the hairs on my entire body stand at attention, and they all seemed to be bending toward his electric current.

"Try me." He hooked his hands underneath my arms and slowly lifted me back up effortlessly so we were eye level again. "Wrap your legs around me."

I did as he said.

My body was aching to please him. To feel him. To surround him and be consumed by him.

He kept one arm securely fastened around my waist and buried the other in my hair before bringing his nose to the sensitive flesh beneath my ear. "God, you feel so good wrapped around me. You were meant to be where you are right now. Do you feel that?" He pressed his chest tightly against mine, and our hearts beat against each others in rhythmic thumps. Aching to get to one another and finally mesh into their other half.

I licked my lips and nodded. I couldn't deny it.

His gorgeous blues followed the trail of my tongue. "You kill me when you do that." He brought the pad of his thumb to the glistening trail, yearning in his eyes.

"Sorry."

"Don't ever be sorry to me. You have nothing to be sorry for. But I do suggest you refrain from any gestures involving this mouth." He tugged at my bottom lip while staring at me with a fierce, carnal longing to claim me once and for all.

He saw the desperate look in my eyes, the shattering of my resolve. The aching desire and need coiling and twisting like a wicked little tornado. "Tell me it's okay, Angel. Tell me what you want me to do. That you want this as badly as I do."

"I can't," I panted out my words in forced gasps, my eyes watering under the pressure of trying to keep it contained.

"Why not? Tell me why not. What're you doing to us?"

I cupped the side of his face. "You're a beautiful soul, Blake. I don't want to ruin that. I wouldn't be able to live with myself. You're too good for me. I don't want you to feel the anguish I go through every day. It isn't right to drag you into that." I blinked as the tears swelled over my bottom lids and trailed down my cheeks.

"It's too late. I'm already there, baby. Can't you see that? I'm not scared, and I'm not running. I'm right there along with you, whether you want me to be or not. When you hurt, I hurt. You reside right here." He took the hand still blanketing his cheek and placed it to the center of his chest, each pulse reaching out to touch me.

"You've taken up permanent residency. Give it to me. Let me take it away from you. Protect you. Be with me and I swear, you won't hurt anymore."

His words wrapped around my heart and clenched. Helping it beat in its weakened state. I wanted so badly to believe I could do this. To believe it would be okay. That I wouldn't destroy him.

"Just be sure when this happens, you're ready because you'll be mine from that moment forward. I don't intend on letting you go—ever." He slid one finger under my chin and lifted my tear-stained gaze to his. "Be with me, Angel. Be mine. Be my forever."

My insides shook violently. My whole body went numb, both un-feeling and feeling everything at the same time. All I had to do was say yes.

Three little letters.

One word.

Yes.

I felt weak, my head all fuzzy and uncertain. "I can't be what you want."

"Wrong. You're already all I could ever want. There is nothing else for you to be. You just . . . are."

His admission left me speechless. This man was bearing his soul. Leaving it all out there for me to either take hold of or crush in my grasp. "It isn't right. You deserve so much more. You're perfect. You're everything. You deserve someone just as perfect."

"That's you, you silly girl." He smudged away the tears now pour-ing from my eyes. "You can't see it yet, but let me show you. Please just let me in. Don't push me away. I can't handle it."

My bottom lip trembled as my body wracked with uncontrollable sobs. Still snaked around his body, I buried my head in the crook of his neck and wept.

"Shh. It's okay. Everything's going to be all right. I promise." He comforted me, petting my hair. "Where are your keys?"

Without moving my head, I pointed toward my bag that I'd tossed on the floor in my haste earlier. Buried in the soft contours of his neck, his smell enticed my senses. My body clinging to him for support, he lowered himself and fished my keys from my bag before collecting it from the floor and making his way to my apartment at the end of the hall.

He shifted me on his hip, but still kept a secure hold while he un-locked my door. Setting my bag down on the coffee table, he walked around it and sat down on my couch.

My face still buried, body still encircling his in a cocoon, he ran soothing circles over my back. "Look at me."

Dread loomed over me at the thought that I was letting him see me like this. So vulnerable. So insecure. A broken mess.

"Look at me, Angel." He tilted my head back. "I don't want you to ever cry because of me. I'll never hurt you. I want to make you feel good things. Cry happy tears. And you will. When you're ready. Do you understand?"

I nodded my head.

"I won't pressure you. When you're ready, I'll be here waiting. It might be the death of me, but I'll be here waiting. Got me?" He smoothed his thumbs over my cheeks.

I nodded my head once again, feeling like even more of a burden to him. "Blake, I'm so sorry I can't give you what you need. I want to. Really, I do."

"Shh. You will, baby. I know you will. It'll be okay." He kissed the tip of my nose, and I leaned in to hug him, content to stay like that forever. His hand smoothed the length of my hair as he buried his nose, collecting my scent. "Your shampoo drives me wild. Peach. I bet you taste like a peach. My little peach." He curled the long strands of my hair around his finger.

And here, right here, in the midst of everything, I let it happen. I don't know how I let it happen, but I did. With him petting my hair and rubbing my back, with the enormity of both our admissions, with the low, soft beating of his heart in my ear, his steady slow breathing . . .

Right here, in his arms, I was lulled to sleep.

Chapter 14

'M WALKING INTO WALLS, SPITTING back my reflection at every turn. *I need to find a way out of this maze. Wiping away the sweat on my brow, I watch as one hundred different arms repeat the same motion. Every corridor looks the same. There are no deciphering marks to help me find my way to freedom. All I see are a million visions of myself.*

My. Pathetic. Self.

I run and run, needing to get away from them, but they're always there, staring back at me. A fleeting glimpse of a male figure pierces my periphery. More sweat beads as horror invades my senses. I'll be trapped in this never-ending dungeon with him, unable to escape.

Run!

It can't be. I try to convince myself it was all my imagination. I'm seeing things.

Run! Run!

There he is again. I scamper around a corner, clutching the mirror lining the wall for support when he slams into my chest.

No!

This can't be happening. I try to free myself but his hold, it's too tight. Unbudging. Frightened and shaking, I look up into the eyes of my captor. But instead of the sickening brown eyes I always see, I'm met with angelic blues, and a warm rush washes over my sweat-soaked body.

Blake.

The glistening sheen coating his skin tells me he's been running just as desperately as I have. Trying to find me, no doubt, as changing imposters flitted past him. Pinning me, he holds on tight. To me. The real, flesh-and-blood me. Not a reflection.

Me.

His eyes, wrought with awareness and purpose, see me. Inside my mirage, my walls, my fortress—me.

How did he get in here?

He holds on and won't let go and I'm trapped. Trapped, and I've never wanted anything so badly. Even so, instinct tells me to push away. To continue my flight. To run.

Desperation in his eyes, he holds on for dear life, knowing if he releases me, he may never get a hold again. His fingers bite into my upper arms.

I make an attempt to escape, but he pins me into a corner with my hands clasped above my head, sending hundreds of dancing images of us slamming into their surrounding walls. He holds me steady with his hips as moisture seeps from my eyes, the raw passion he exudes rolling off him in waves.

He releases my arms and cradles my face. No longer able to handle the pressure, my body collapses forward, and he dips and picks me up effortlessly. Cradling my limp body to his chest like a child, he walks the easiest route out of the maze. I don't know how I didn't see it before. It's such a clear path.

My maze. My façade. My fortress.

Light hits us as a loud, continuous beeping blasts, and I hear what sounds like a building cracking at the seams. Peeking out from his shoulder, I watch the walls crumble and dissolve. They ripple to the ground in a cloud of dust as if they never existed. Blake walks forward, determined, staring straight ahead, undeterred, and I feel a sense of release. Nothing remains behind me but the beeping.

Beep. Beep. Beep.

Beep. Beep. Beep.

The alarm blared.

My arm snaked out from the covers, slamming down on the pesky device. With a groan, I rolled onto my back and draped my arm over my eyes, visions of my dream floating through my head. I wondered how much of that dream was reality. How much of me Blake could actually see.

Blake . . .

I rubbed my eyes and threw back the covers to find myself in only a T-shirt and underwear. I sat up, dangling my legs from the bed and noticed the skirt and shirt I'd worn yesterday neatly folded on my night-stand. Recounting the previous night, my last memory was coming into my apartment with Blake and being cradled in his lap. Him trying to soothe me . . .

Reaching for the clothes, a piece of paper fluttered to the floor. I scrambled off the bed to retrieve it.

You fell asleep. You looked so peaceful, I didn't want to disturb you.

Sweet dreams, my angel. Talk to you tomorrow. —B

Blake put me to bed? And undressed me? And tucked me in? Then I real-ized how nicely I'd slept and the enormity of the dream I'd had. Though it felt nightmarish at first, I couldn't get the visions of him cradling me and freeing me from my tortured dungeon, out of my head—the walls cascading to their ashy deaths behind me.

Oh my God, did he see me naked? I yanked the collar of my shirt and peered inside to make sure I was still wearing a bra. *Phew.* My shoulders relaxed forward. Worst case scenario, he saw a little of Victoria's Secret.

I padded my bare feet to the kitchen and guzzled down some or-ange juice. Leaning against the refrigerator door, I tipped my head back. I couldn't remember the last time I'd felt so refreshed. I might just have Blake sleep over every night.

I punched the security code into my cell phone, and sent Blake a quick text.

Me: Did you enjoy your free feel?

I filled a cup of water and went out to the terrace to water Blake's flowers when my phone pinged right back. I rushed back to the kitchen, eager to see his response.

B: Every handful. Pink lace is so your color. ;)

My face turned every shade of crimson.

Me: You pervert!

B: Relax, LOL. I only saw the back. But I had visions of the front all night long. ;) ;)

Ugh, this boy.

Me: You better not be lying!

B: I told you, I never lie, sweets.

Me: Well, thank you. I don't remember the last time I was tucked in and wrapped all snuggly in a blanket. I slept nice.

B: You're welcome. I only wish I could've stayed to unwrap you from said blanket.

Me: Maybe one day you will.

My thumb hovered over the send button while I chewed my lip, debating whether or not to go through with it. *Eh, fuck it.*

Send.

I closed my eyes and waited, my lungs devoid of air, to hear the next ping.

Ping.

Expelling the air, I looked down through one winking eye.

B: In my mind, I already have. Every day. For the last month.

Heat.

Ping.

B: However, maybe tomorrow morning I'll take you up on your offer. Show you what you've been missing.

Me: A little presumptuous, aren't we?

B: Determined. You must admit my perseverance is unsurpassed. I'll wear you down eventually. And then I'll wear you out ;)~

Me: Is that a threat, Mr. Turner?

B: That's a promise, Miss. Ricci. A very delicious promise.

Me: I look forward to it.

B: Coming around I see. I knew you were a smart girl.

Me: The smartest ;)

B: Study session at my house tomorrow 4:00. Be there or be square. You can show me how smart you really are.

Me: I'll be there. See ya later, Romeo.

I SAT IN THE CAFETERIA, intently focused on pieces of folded paper that were strewn about. Blake made them for me yesterday, but for some reason the information didn't quite sink in the same when he wasn't with me. I smiled softly, reminiscing on our afternoon.

Ringing my nervous fingers together, I crossed the threshold into Blake's apartment. Without a glance at them, he took my hands in his and slid a hazelnut coffee between them. My body instantly lost its stiffness and a smile skimmed across my face at how easily he always relaxed me.

Guiding me to the dining table, where he already had books and notes sprawled out, I noticed his apartment was surprisingly tidy for a bachelor pad and secretly wondered if he was a neat freak or if it was for my benefit.

A slice of yellow tape caught my eye and I paused, looking down the hall. What I assumed was Blake's bedroom door was cautioned "off limits". I raised a questioning brow at him.

"Just taking the necessary precautions." A smirk donned his gorgeous lips as he led me to my seat.

I laughed around my cup, loving his cute quirkiness and his ways of slipping himself under my skin every chance he got.

"Don't be boring."

Jace's voice pulled me from my daydream as he plucked my study sheets from my fingers and threw them down.

"Hey, I need those." I swiped my hands across the table, trying to put them back in order.

"You can have them back later, fuddy duddy." Jace grabbed my notes once more and shoved them into his bag.

"You're such a bad influence." I stuck my bottom lip out in a pout.

"Hey, I gotta live up to my name. How can I be called the corrupter if I don't cause any corruption? Where's the fun in that?" He winked.

"Yeah, yeah," I muttered. "So what're you up to besides ruining my academic career?"

"Although that sounds like loads of fun," he rolled his eyes, "I actually missed your ass, though I'm starting to regret it already."

"Oh stop. I missed you, too. I've just been busy."

"Think fast," was all I heard before an apple flew at me. I instinctively reached out and snatched it with one hand before it could bounce off my forehead.

Blake's eyes were animated as he turned the chair next to me around and straddled it, crossing his arms over the back. "Nice catch. You play softball or something? Not many girls can catch one-handed."

I dropped the apple to the table and scraped my palms on my thighs to try to rid them of the offending fruit. "That wasn't at all sexist," I said sarcastically. "No, I don't play softball. I'm just talented. And why, might I ask, are you throwing food at my head?"

He grinned back. "I told you it's my duty to feed you. You were looking a little frail sitting there, and I figured you could use a pick me up. You know what they say, an apple a day . . ."

Jace snorted out a laugh somewhere in the back of his throat. When I snapped my head in his direction and shot him a warning glare, he looked away, whistling. I glanced back at Blake. "For your information, I'm perfectly healthy. And I'd prefer to remain concussion free. Not exactly the softest object to throw, wouldn't ya say, killer?"

"Sor-ry." Blake put up his hands as if I'd offended him.

Jace and Blake fell into back and forth banter about something, but I couldn't concentrate. The apple sat on the table, staring at me. I tried with all my might to hold a conversation and ignore it, but my eyes repeatedly wandered back to where it rested, taunting me with its shiny glare. The harder I tried to ignore it, the more I could feel my eyes itching to glance at it again.

My focus was now locked and I was trapped far away.

I'm sixteen and it's Halloween. Quarters shoved into apples peek out of a basin of water that's stained with murky costume makeup. I stare at the red, blue, and brown swirls, dreading my turn. That thing has to be unsanitary.

I wrap my hair into a knot and try to be conscious of the constraints of my Dorothy outfit. I hadn't wanted to stand out, showing up to my first high school house party as a nun, and this was the least revealing of the assortment at the costume store. It seems they make everything slutty these days.

Kneeling, I tuck the skirt into my heels, bend forward, and dunk my face, fishing around for a few desperate attempts. The water tastes like a combination of sweet, metallic, and gross old makeup. Traces of hairspray swipe along my taste buds as well.

Through the water, I hear a muffled, familiar laugh, and I stiffen. Two fingers drag along the length of my spine and then yank my skirt from where it's securely fastened behind my heels. Bolting up, I cough, choking on the water. His fingers find the spot between my legs and slide from the very top of my center, all the way up my slit, and then push inside me swiftly. Trying to push myself up to escape, his other hand wraps firmly around my waist, securing me to him. Still coughing, I frantically wipe away the water coming out of my nose and burning my eyes, and I try to clear away the little hairs plastered to my forehead.

My eyes dart around the empty room. Where did everyone go?

I try to calm my ragged breathing, water stinging my eyes and makeup running down my face. His mouth is on my ear, his hand caressing the soft flesh between my legs as if we're sharing an intimate moment.

When his weight leaves my back, I glance behind me.

"Hey there, beautiful. I want you so fucking bad right now. You look tastier than any of these apples bent there on your knees. I just couldn't help but sample the forbidden fruit." He removes his fingers, slides them into his mouth, and then slowly drags them out, keeping his eyes on mine. Bile rises in my throat as he hovers over me and brings his hand back to cup my sex once again.

Paralyzed, I fight the urge to heave into the colorful basin. "Please, someone's going to see us. What're you doing?" I can't hide the panic in my voice.

His eyes glaze over as he rubs my ass, staring at it. "Calm down, beautiful.

They were all finished and tired of waiting for you. I sent them to do shots downstairs."

I'm panting, wondering how far this will go. My chin trembles as traces of salt seeps through the seam of my lips.

Still anchored by his other arm, his hand leaves my delicate area, sliding up my ribcage, and around to the front where he grabs a handful of my breast. The crease of his smirk presses against my wet cheek and I squeeze my eyes shut, willing this not to happen.

A sharp pinch stabs my nipple as he tweaks it, the burn of it blistering out from the center sending a small cry tumbling from my throat.

Slowly he releases me and my body slumps forward in defeat. He hooks an arm around my waist, lifting me upright. "Come on, I can't wait another second to feel you where I need you."

"Angel, did you hear me?"

Blinking rapidly, my head snapped in Blake's direction. Short of breath, I could feel the wildness behind my eyes. I glanced down at my white knuckles balled up in my lap and winced at the pain my fingernails had created against my palms.

Breathe, Goddammit!

Jace looked from me to the apple as realization finally hit him. Snatching it, he flipped it up in the air, caught it and took a big, overdramatic bite. He chewed for a few beats and then spit it out into the trashcan beside him with an exaggerated, *"Pew.* I hate apples." Then he tossed what remained into the pail. "All gone." He brushed off his hands and looked me dead in the eyes, willing me to come back to him.

I took a hard gulp, attempting to steady my breath and compose myself quickly. Our eyes were still focused on one another as I nodded my head and turned my attention back to Blake, who appeared dumbfounded.

"Did I just miss something?" he asked, glancing back and forth between me and Jace, trying to crack the secret best friend code.

"Not at all." I exhaled. "I just hate apples. You can keep those to yourself from now on and catalog them next to the name 'beautiful'." My eyes trailed back to the garbage can, wondering if there'd ever be a time I could see one of those things and not get dragged back into my past.

Jace planted two fingers on my cheek and forced my focus back in Blake's direction. "So you're coming, right?" He directed the question at Blake, making a swift change of topic.

Blake blinked at him, and then shook his head. "Where are we going again?"

Jace rolled his eyes. "X.L. and I have it on strict authority Evangelina will be there too."

"Where will I be?" I looked to Jace. Clearly, I'd zoned out for that part of the conversation.

"X.L.," Jace annunciated. "God, doesn't anyone listen to me?"

I relaxed back in my seat and folded my arms across my chest. "And when exactly did I agree to be there?"

"When you said you loved me and couldn't live without me and wanted me to stay in this dreadful place." Jace's mouth split into a devious smile.

I raised an eyebrow. "Ah, blackmail at its finest. Well played, love."

Jace lounged back in his chair and brushed his knuckles along his chest. "Hold the applause, please."

Jace looked to Blake. "Well, lover boy. You in or what?"

"Um, yeah sure. I guess."

"In for what?" Eric chimed in, dropping himself in the empty chair next to Blake.

Blake looked to his left. "Some place called X.L. Wanna come?"

Eric's eyebrows drew in. "Never heard of it. Is it new? I thought I knew all the hot spots around here."

Blake shrugged. "No clue."

The glint in Jace's eye was unmistakable to me, but went unnoticed by the two unsuspecting bystanders.

"Well, either way, I can't make it. I got a hot date tonight." Eric slapped Blake's back.

Blake rolled his eyes. "When do you not?"

"Don't blame me. I gotta keep the ladies satisfied. They depend on me." Eric smiled his wicked smile and then leaned all the way back in his chair, tipping it to the point that I didn't know how he was keeping it balanced. "Speaking of which . . ." He trailed off, bringing the chair back to an upright position and hopping off. "Gotta go. Lunch just arrived." He darted over to the leggy blonde standing in the center of the cafeteria, searching for a place to sit, and snaked his arm around her waist.

I looked at Blake. "He's such a dick. How do you put up with him?"

Blake lifted his lips in a dismissive gesture. "He's not so bad. He's got his issues, but I've known him my whole life. He's like a brother. Once you get to know him, you'll understand him a bit more. He's harmless really, and he'd give you the shirt off his back. He's just got . . . female issues, I guess you could say."

I shook my head. "If you say so, but he still gets under my skin."

"He just likes to push your buttons. Give him a chance." He dipped his head low and gave me a small smile. "For me?"

"I'm sure I could think of a few ways to rectify his female issues." Jace's eyes were glued to Eric's lower half.

"Behave, you," I told Jace before turning my attention back to Blake. "So you're definitely coming tonight then?"

His eyes became warm. "If you're there, I'm there. Where should I meet you guys?"

Jace made a show of quivering as he pulled his line of sight from Eric. "Eva's apartment at ten." Jace gripped my arm and pulled me to my feet, then blew Blake a kiss. "Don't be jealous. I'd still do you, too. See ya later, hot stuff."

Blake reached out and snatched the invisible kiss from the air and planted it on his cheek, playing into Jace's charade. "Bye, honey," he said in the sweetest voice possible and flitted his fingers in a wave.

"Oh God." I laughed at them both, wondering when they'd gotten so close. It felt good to know Blake was comfortable with Jace and not freaked out by his eccentricities, but the two of them scared me. I could barely handle them separately. Together, those two could totally railroad me if they wanted to.

Note to self: Pay better attention to what the fuck is going on.

Chapter 15

HOW DID I ALWAYS GET suckered into these things?

Pulling the skin taut at the corner of my eye, I skillfully applied a thick black line across the edge of my lashes. Then I twisted the cap back on the eyeliner and dropped it into the bag on the sink. Standing back, I combed my fingers through my mane, fluffing it out as I examined my handiwork. With a pout to my lips, I glazed on some shimmer. Done.

Wearing only a black lace bra and matching thong, I exited the bathroom as Jace walked in my apartment.

"Hey, bitch."

"Hey," I called over my shoulder as I padded down the hall toward my bedroom.

I heard him skip up behind me. "Meow." The swat on my ass echoed through the apartment.

"Ouch, dick!" I rubbed the sore spot with a scowl on my face.

"Oh, hush it. You know you loved it. Now, gimme a kiss and tell me how pretty I am."

I kissed his cheek. "You look fabulous. Love the mohawk." I patted the top of his head.

He jerked his head away from my hand like I was holding a lit torch. "Careful! Don't mess with the masterpiece."

"Sor-ry. What was I thinking?" I held up my hands.

"Get it together, girl. You know better than that." He rolled his eyes at me, turned, and peered into the full length mirror, fingering his hair and making sure every strand was just as he'd left it.

Stepping into my black booty shorts reserved only for these occasions, I looked at Jace's reflection. "Poor guy has no clue what he's in for. You didn't tell him, did you?"

"Hell's no. I get few pleasures in life. Why would I give up the opportunity to see the look on his face when he figures it out?"

With a huge smile, I shimmied into a spaghetti strapped, ice-blue silk shirt. "You're evil. Pure. Evil."

"This'll be a test of his worthiness. If he loves you, he has to love me. And if he doesn't love me . . . well, then he can go fuck himself." Jace fingered the corner of his mouth and puckered his lips at his reflection, then turned to the side, inspecting his ass.

A knock at the door caught my attention. I swatted him on the shoulder and shooed him out of my way. "Go answer that. I'll be right out."

Jace fawned over himself one last time, did a spin like Michael Jackson, and planted a kiss on my cheek.

I bent down to retrieve a pair of knee high, black leather boots, as Jace trilled, "Coming, loverboy."

Their voices were muffled as I put the finishing touches on my ensemble. I glanced in the mirror, satisfied. "Good enough."

My heels clacked on the hardwood floor as I made my way to the kitchen, the good time they were having becoming more audible with every step. Glasses clinked and, as I rounded the corner, the boys brought shots of my reserves to their lips.

Blake's eyes locked on mine as the liquid fire went down his throat, and he choked. His hand flew up to cover his mouth as he bent forward, coughing uncontrollably.

"You okay?" Jace pounded him on the back.

Using the counter for support, he let out a few more of those nasty little chokes that linger as his glassed over eyes found mine again. "Yeah, I'm okay." He scanned the length of me, from the tips of my toes all the way to the top of my head as he regulated his breathing. "Damn, Angel. You look . . . breathtaking . . . apparently." Another stray cough passed his bewitching lips.

I fidgeted, swaying back and forth and picking at my nails. "Thanks. You clean up pretty nice yourself." And man, did he ever. I tried my best to play it cool, but the boy had to have been carved from the gods themselves.

I took in the faded jeans that hung low on his squared off hips—the hips with the perfectly placed indents at each corner. A tremor passed through me as my eyes roamed over the muscles that bulged from beneath a fitted white V-neck. He tried to cover them with a blazer, but I knew they were there, pressing up against the thin cotton.

The smooth skin below his collarbone taunted me, begging to be nibbled. Between the round peaks of his chest lay a shiny silver cross. My fingers twitched, wanting to grab it, pull him to me and hold him there. I dug my fingernails into my palms to stop from doing just that and shifted from one foot to the other. Crossing my legs, I stood there, nervous the sensations traveling through the lower half of my body would be visible. Heated vibrations pulsed through my core making it difficult to stand, let alone hold a conversation.

I licked my dry lips, wondering what the smooth curves of his neck tasted like, and then my eyes roamed past the juiciest lips I'd ever seen. Rosy and plump and glistening with the moisture the last swipe of his tongue had left. The rum he'd just downed probably lingered at the corners and would make them taste even sweeter. Visions of plunging my fingers into his perfectly mussed hair and anchoring him to me danced before me. It was shiny and darker than usual and styled to look as though he'd just been fucked. My sights landed on his glittery, gorgeous eyes. The shimmer of water that remained from his bout of choking was enough to make his blue diamonds dance.

I bundled my hands into balls at my sides as my body warred with my mind. All I wanted to do was grab him, drag him to my bedroom, and put a stop to the endless torture. Tell him I surrendered and was his to do with what he wished. The pull on my soul was intense. It felt like he was reaching out for me, begging mine to meet it halfway. I don't know what stopped me from caving right then and there, and I didn't understand where these foreign feelings were coming from.

"Care to join us for our pre-gaming extravaganza?" Blake raised a glass and tipped his head toward it, breaking me out of my reverie.

"Sure. I could use a stiff one." My eyes were lit with humor as I made my way over to them, making sure to sway my hips just right.

Violent coughing raked through him once again. When he was able to catch his breath, he looked at me out of the corner of his eye as I rounded the edge of the kitchen bar. "You're killin' me. You know that, woman?"

The edge of my mouth quirked up in a sly grin. I reached up on my tippy toes, making sure to elongate my body as I grabbed another shot glass down from the cabinet. When I turned around, Blake's eyes were glued to my legs, or ass, or both. His mouth hung agape.

"Fill 'er up." I placed the glass in front of him. Since he was always messing with me, I thought I'd have a little fun with Blake tonight, but now that I was so close, it was hard to play this game. The smell of his cologne curled its way up my nostrils and into my brain, causing my eyes to close for the briefest of seconds while I took it in. The scent of him freshly showered had me picturing him standing under the hot stream. His head tipped back, dragging his fingers through his hair, water beading up on his tanned skin.

Oh, dear God.

I panted under the weight that was placed on my chest. Standing this close to him was out of the question, so I rounded the bar to distance myself. He slid the now full glass in my direction and, when I went to pick it up, my fingers brushed his, sending an electric shock up my arm.

My hand recoiled from the buzz, and I spilled a little of my drink on the counter.

"Damn."

"It's okay. No worries." Blake topped off my glass, then filled the other two for him and Jace.

Jace looked back and forth between Blake and me. "Seriously, you could cut the sexual tension in here with a knife. Just go at it already. My dick's getting hard just looking at you guys. Go ahead," he brushed both hands toward us, "unleash your sexy beasts."

"Jace! Seriously? Shut up, wise ass."

"I'm not being a wise ass. I'm *seriously* tenting over here." He gestured to the bulge in his jeans where the material actually did look a little strained.

"Wow. Now *that's* an accomplishment. I must be better than I thought. It's usually *you* turning people to the opposite team." I raised my eyebrows, amused.

He rolled his eyes up to the ceiling. "Yeah, well, I'm not proud of it. And if you tell anyone I'll kill you, but what the fuck, guys? This is like watching porn that never goes anywhere. It's torturous! Are you two for real? Do you not see what's going on?"

Blake replied to Jace, but kept his eyes on me as he spoke, "I told Angel all she has to do is say the words and I'll handle the rest. But she just . . . won't . . . say it." He shrugged.

"Well, what the hell are you waiting for, *Angel*?" Jace asked, impatient.

"Shut up, Jace. And enough with this conversation. Come on, let's go." I lifted my glass, raised one arched eyebrow and glared at them with a look that said 'you better shut the fuck up and join me'.

"Brute. You don't scare me, ya know." Jace raised his glass.

"Oh no? Then why are you doing what I said?"

He jutted his chin out in a sulk. "I'm just being polite. I don't want to embarrass you in front of Blake. And besides, I never turn down alcohol."

"Yeah, okay." I giggled, holding the glass in the air. "To fresh starts."

In unison, Blake and Jace repeated, "To fresh starts." We all kicked our heads back and swallowed the sweet liquid.

Our glasses came slamming down, and my eyes sought out Blake's once again. It was like they didn't know how to look anywhere else when he was around. He was magnetic. He had a way of looking right through me, like he was actually looking into my soul. His eyes stayed trained and focused on mine, barely pausing to blink. It was unsettling and yet I couldn't help but do it back.

"You ready to get this party started?" Jace's voice broke through my thoughts.

"Sure." I tucked a piece of hair behind my ear and gave Blake a half smile.

BLAKE STOOD PROTECTIVELY IN FRONT of me as our bodies were jostled about on the number one train heading down to Forty Second Street. I was pressed against the metal doors, and to my left, a man lay spread out across four seats, the stench deep within the threads of his worn and tattered clothes.

Jace, feeling good I could imagine, was skipping through the car, wrapping his arm around the poles and twirling around them. "Wanna see something?" he asked before spinning around with his arms extended like a ring leader at the circus. "Ladies and gentlemen, can I have your attention, please. What you are about to witness will leave you breathless. It will blow your mind."

Only a handful of people glanced warily to observe Jace's spectacle. This was New York, after all. Weirdos came a dime a dozen, and most people just went about their business uncaring.

"Please, stand back," he called out again, and a few more heads rose.

I bit my lip and shook my head, knowing what he was about to do. Blake stayed close, but turned, curious.

Jace raised his arms above his head, sought out my eyes to give me a wink, and then took off down the subway car in a round off followed by three back handsprings, missing the poles by mere centimeters. He landed with a bounce to his step and a huge smile on his face as the car erupted in gasps, applause, and whistles.

I had to admit, he was good. It took a lot to get the attention of people in Manhattan.

He circled his arm in front of him himself as he bowed three times. "Thank you very much. Don't forget to tip your waitress," he joked.

People stuck out their hands, waving dollar bills at him.

"Why, thank you," he clutched his chest, blushing. He came back to us with a fistful of money. "Drinks are on me, guys."

"That was awesome, bro. I didn't know you could do that." Blake was genuinely shocked.

Jace rubbed his knuckles over his chest. "I know. I'm just a bundle of talent bursting at the seams." We all laughed and Jace leaned forward looking through the Plexiglass window. "This is us, guys."

The subway car came to a stop, letting out a puff of air, and the doors glided open. Blake placed his hand on the small of my back and guided me off the train onto the hot, smelly platform. He took my hand and I let him. I liked when he did that.

Jace looked around and found his bearings. "Follow me."

We emerged from below the belly of Manhattan into the cool night air and began the short walk to the club. Underdressed, I shivered and curled inward to block the wind. I probably should have worn a jacket, but I hated bringing them inside.

Blake noticed and wrapped his arm around my middle, bringing me closer to his insane body heat. I welcomed the warmth and nestled myself further. He looked down at me with a little smile playing on his lips, and I thought how nice it was that he was always so attentive and how comfortable it felt to be wrapped up in his arms.

"Thanks," I said through lowered lashes.

"My pleasure." He squeezed my hip.

As we neared the club, I noticed the familiar rainbow flag proudly hanging from the side of the building, and I was at ease. Jace knew these were the only clubs I was comfortable in that didn't have a bar separating me from the patrons. No threats I couldn't handle. No one was interested in me.

Blake seemed to be in his own world and hadn't noticed yet. We walked up to the velvet ropes, and Jace happily hopped us right to the front of the line where a very large, bald man stood, wearing a black T-shirt that looked like it was about to burst at the seams under the pressure of the muscles bulging beneath it.

"Man, that's a big dude." Blake eyed the bouncer as though he'd just shrunk to my size.

"Hey . . ." Jace called out, smiling and waving.

"Hey, boy. Get your ass over here," the bouncer called back, gleaming.

Jace peaked up on his tippy toes to plant a kiss on the man's cheek. "Henry, you remember Eva." He gestured to me.

"Hi, Eva. Looking stunning as usual." Henry smiled warmly at me.

"Why, thank you, Henry." I smiled back.

Jace motioned to Blake. "And this fine fellow is her new boy-toy, Blake."

"Yum." Henry eyed Blake like dinner.

"Down, Henry. This one's off limits," Jace chided.

Henry stuck out his hand. "Nice to meet you, Blake."

Blake returned the gesture. "Um, nice to meet you, too." The curious expression on his face was adorable.

Henry unclipped the velvet rope and held it to the side. "Go on in, guys. Enjoy yourselves."

"Thanks, Henry," I called back over my shoulder as we scooted inside the darkened club.

The vibrations emanating from every wall beat deep into my chest. No matter how many times I felt it, I couldn't help the thrill that washed over me every time I took the first few steps into a club. It was invigorating. I loved to dance, and a gay club was the only place I could really let loose and enjoy myself.

We paid at the ticket counter and stepped inside. Fluorescent lights swirled around the dance floor in countless shapes and sizes. It smelled of sweat and musk and raw skin and sex. Gyrating bodies and people singing loudly consumed every inch. Usually, I'd panic and feel claustrophobic, but not here. Here I was safe.

Blake looked around, taking in his surroundings. The shocked expression on his face was priceless. Big men, small men, fit men, out of shape men, all groping at each other and all having the time of their lives.

"A gay club? You guys took me to a gay club?" He looked back and forth to me and Jace, who was grinning wider than I'd ever seen. "I'm gonna get eaten alive in here."

"Calm down, handsome." Jace petted Blake's chest. "No one's gonna bother you. We stick to our own kind." Although he was smiling, I could tell he was gauging Blake's reaction and was ready to pounce if it was the wrong one.

Blake raised his eyebrows. "Whatever, but I'm telling you right now, the only hands that touch my ass better be attached to this gorgeous little blonde girl, or I'm outta here." We all laughed, and Jace relaxed.

"Come on, Romeo. I'll buy you a drink for being such a good sport." I tugged at Blake's arm.

"Way to totally emasculate me. Thank you, but I don't think so. Come on, I got you. Besides, I probably have a better shot of getting us drinks quicker than you do in here, anyway." He moved behind me and placed his hands on my hips, ushering me through the crowd.

We walked to the glowing bar and waited among the sea of men. Blake leaned into my ear. "I'm so gonna get you for this. You better not leave my side. You're not even allowed to go to the bathroom tonight."

I turned, putting my back to the bar, and wrapped my arms around his neck. I gave him a peck on the cheek, giggling, "Just relax, you're fine. Try and have a good time." After a couple of rounds and a few shots, I collected my Ketel One and Seven with a lime, and Blake scooped up his Corona. "Come on, dance with me. It'll loosen you up."

We squeezed our way onto the crowded dance floor, and I twirled around to face Blake. Raising my glass, I grabbed his free hand, swirling my hips in smooth, languid movements, inviting him to join me. Distracted, his eyes darted around as his feet shuffled to an awkward rhythm. Wanting him to relax, I secured his chin between my thumb and index finger and brought his sights back to mine. Tension left his body as I took my two fingers and pointed them toward his eyes and then back to my own, telling him to stay focused on me.

A freeing feeling came over me and I stepped closer, leaving only a couple of inches between us, and began to move. Taking my invitation, he grabbed my hip and mirrored my motions. I slid my hand up the front of his firm chest, enjoying the way it twitched under my fingers. Cupping the back of his neck, I rested my forehead against him, closing my eyes as our bodies swayed. This was the first time I'd allowed myself to touch anyone in this capacity; felt a man's body against my own and liked it. Actually, I thought, I loved it. I'd spent weeks pushing Blake away, scared of this very moment even though I was constantly dreaming of it. And now that it was here, I wanted more.

Blake's hungry hands grabbed my drink and set his and mine on a stage behind us. He leaned forward, curving his body into me. It fit like a piece to a puzzle. His leg moved between mine, and our bodies, closer than ever, rocked in perfect sync. He slid his hands to the base of my spine, just bordering my ass and locked his arm there, pressing me to him. In that moment, I wanted him to want me. To want *only* me. I laced my fingers through his hair and pushed my pelvis forward.

Blake growled in my ear. "I'm seriously going to bite you." He flicked his tongue on my lobe, and I nearly lost it. I pressed my forehead against his and held him firmly to myself, making sure every piece of me was touching every piece of him.

Our hearts were banging against each others, amplified by the pounding of the bass pressing in on us. I curled my leg around his hip, and he snaked his hand around my thigh, pulling me deeper into him and tipping me back. I gasped as the hard fabric of his jeans bit into the thin material covering my most delicate area. My head dropped back, unable to withstand the pressure building inside any more. *My God, this feels amazing.*

Blake leaned into me, raining kisses down the length of my neck, nipping and sucking at my collarbone. My grip tightened in his hair, and I pushed my hips further into his as I slowly lifted my head and sought out his eyes. His pupils were dilated, his blue irises noticeably darker even beneath the bright fluorescent lighting. Our breathing was labored as we stayed motionless in that position, staring at one another. After a moment, Blake released my leg and ghosted his fingers up my back before burying them deep into my hair. Dragging his teeth up my jawline, he sucked my lobe into his mouth. My knees buckled and I fell into him, using his body as support.

He breathed into my ear, "Let's get out of here. What I want to do to you can't be done in the middle of a dance floor."

Those words should have scared the shit out of me, but I wanted this. I was tired of being *that* girl. This all felt so good. I wanted to finally see where it would take me.

I nodded my head.

Wasting no time, Blake took my hand and headed for the front door.

"Wait." I stopped him and his head fell forward as he took a deep breath. His eyes started to fill with disappointment, thinking I'd changed my mind again.

I squeezed his hand, reassuring him. "I have to find Jace and tell him we're leaving."

A relieved smile spread across his lips. He guided me back, scanning the crowd. I was too short to see over everyone, so it was up to Blake to find him. Then it hit me. I knew exactly where he was. "Follow me."

We weaved through the masses until Jace came into view, twirling around a pole and dancing for some lucky stranger. The guy was staring at him in awe. Blake hoisted me up, and I climbed on top of the box with Jace.

Excitement filled Jace's eyes as he pulled me into him. He grabbed onto the pole and thrust his hips at me in an attempt to put on our usual show for the crowd. But I just couldn't play tonight. I was too worked up, and my mind was too preoccupied to focus on anything but Blake and getting the hell out of here.

Not giving myself the opportunity to change my mind, I leaned into his ear and told him we were leaving, then I gave him a kiss. "Get home safe. Text me when you get there and don't bring home any strangers." I swatted his behind playfully.

"Okay, but I make no promises to your last request." He wiggled sweaty eyebrows.

I waved Blake closer, and braced myself on his shoulders. The corner of his mouth hitched up, and he placed his palms on my bare thighs. He rounded the backs of my legs and slid them up, scooping me under the ass and pulling me down to him. Flying forward, I let out a yelp as we collided, and then he braced me against him.

I landed with my belly lined up with his face, and he placed a kiss in the center before dragging our bodies along one another. Lowering me, his face came closer, and when our lips were finally adjacent, we lingered there, less than a breath away. I ached to rid ourselves of our clothes and feel his skin against mine. Keeping me pressed to him, he lowered me until my toes hit the floor.

With his fierce eyes locked on me, he extended his fist up toward Jace. "Later, my man."

"Later." Jace pounded Blake's fist. "Oh, Eva, darling?"

I tore my eyes from Blake, the delicate area between my thighs throbbing. "Yeah?"

"Come here, would you?" Jace lowered himself onto his belly and hung forward on the box.

I walked up to him, and he grabbed me by the back of the head and searched my eyes before leaning into my ear. "You okay with this? You *want* to leave with him?"

I didn't know if it was the alcohol or if I'd finally had enough, but I wanted nothing more than to get the hell out of here as fast possible. I nodded, knowing he could see the fight in my eyes, but also what I was ready to be rid of—the past. Then I saw the blessing there as he released me. "Then go, but call me if you need anything or if you change your mind."

"I will. Love."

"Love." Jace stood back up and Blake grabbed my hand, turning to leave.

"Oh, and Blake?"

Blake stopped and turned back him. "Yeah?"

"Take care of my girl."

Blake's smile stretched across his face. "Oh, I intend to. Don't you worry about that." He ran his thumb over my palm and a quake rocketed down my spine.

Tugging him beside me, I waved to Jace with my free hand, and we made our way to the exit.

Cool air coated my overheated body. Although it sent a shiver coursing through me, I welcomed the temperature change. I felt like I was on fire. Groaning, I threw my head back. "I'm so not in the mood to walk."

"Well, why didn't you say so?"

"I did say so."

Blake chuckled and stepped in front of me, causing me to stop short. He squatted a bit and looked back over his shoulder. "Hop on."

"What?" I looked at him confused.

"Hop on. I'll carry your lazy ass."

"Don't be ridiculous." I veered to the side to walk around him, but he side-stepped in front of me once again, and I walked straight into his back.

"What're you doing?" I put my hands on my hips and waited impatiently for him to move.

He didn't blink. "I don't think I stuttered."

"I'm not getting on your back like a five-year-old."

"Oh, I think you are," he replied. *Cocky son-of-a-bitch.*

I tried to move to the side, but again and again he blocked my path. "I can do this all night, Angel."

I sighed as he bent down to my height and reached his hands over his shoulders. "Gimme your hands."

I blew out a breath of defeat and slid my hands over his. He tugged them around his neck and straightened, draping me down his back as he began to walk us to the subway. Giving up completely—and already getting used to the warmth of his back against me—I wrapped my legs around him. He scooped his hands under my thighs and we walked to the train, piggyback style. I let my chin rest on his shoulder and tried to evaluate what was happening now that I was in the fresh air and able to clear my head a little.

What was I going to do once we got to my apartment? Could I go through with this? Was I going to back out again like a scared little girl? I wanted him so bad. And I wanted to be a woman in control of my own body. I just hoped the damage that was done to me wasn't irreversible.

Eventually, I decided I wasn't going to think about it. I was going to let whatever happened happen. Regardless of the outcome, I was grateful for Blake. For his relentlessness and for him caring enough to finally bring me out of my shell. Tightening my grip around his shoulders, I kissed the back of his neck and lay my head there.

He let out a gasp and his body trembled before hitching me up higher. Together, we clung to each other, showing just how scared each of us was of losing the other.

Chapter 16

"WHAT TIME IS IT?" I kept my legs wrapped tightly around Blake's waist as he lifted his arm to check his watch.

"Twelve-thirty. We didn't last very long, did we?"

"No, but that's okay. I like this better." I placed my chin on Blake's shoulder and rested the side of my head against his, content. "You did good." A big smile spread across my face as I recalled the look on Blake's face when he realized where we'd taken him.

"I still can't believe you guys did that to me." Blake peeked over his shoulder. He raised his eyebrows, and I bit back a smile. "It wasn't so bad, though. They were all kind of cool."

"Yeah, they're good people. Jace'll be happy. You passed his little test."

"Did I now?" He looked forward and smirked, all happy with himself.

"Yes, you did. With flying colors, my friend."

He shook his head. "I knew the little fucker had something up his sleeve."

"He always does." I laughed.

When we reached the subway entrance, I hopped down, a bit reluctantly. I'd enjoyed that more than I'd thought I would. "Thanks for the lift."

"Anytime." He winked.

Blake laced his fingers with mine and together we entered the subway, coming one step closer to being behind closed doors. As the blinding white lights approached, my heart rate kicked into high gear. We entered the car and sat down beside one another in silence, listening to the sound of the jangling car. My head rested on his shoulder as he traced circular patterns on top of my thigh.

At the sound of our stop, Blake stood and guided me from the train. We walked a few feet and through the turnstiles when he stopped out of nowhere, his sweaty palm tightening around mine.

Rubbing his free hand over the side of his face, he forced out, "Listen, Angel, I don't want you to do anything you're not comfortable with. I know things got heavy back there, but if you're not ready . . . my feelings for you won't change. Got me?"

"I know. I wouldn't." I fidgeted from foot to foot, still unsure of how this would unfold.

"Good." He lightly brushed his thumb over the top of my hand in a soothing manner.

Seeming content with my answer, he relaxed and tugged me alongside him once again. We ascended the stairs, and the cool October breeze hit us. Blake shrugged out of his blazer and slipped my arms into it before he tucked me into his side, sheltering my partially unclothed form from the bite in the air.

I wrapped my arms around him, grateful for his warmth. I could feel the hard muscles of his abdomen through his thin shirt. It was a mystery to me how someone could be so hard and so soft at the same time.

As much as I was attracted to him, the cool air and dissipation of alcohol from my system had me second guessing my earlier reasoning for leaving with him. I didn't think I was ready for this.

When we reached my door, I fumbled with my keys, my hands trembling. Blake watched my failed attempts to get the key in the lock and delicately lifted them from me. "Here, let me."

I didn't say anything. I just looked at him, the uncertainty of what I was about to do swimming through my mind.

The door popped open, and Blake stretched out his hand. "After you."

With trepidation, I stepped over the threshold, rubbing my shaky, sweaty palms over my hips. I walked to the middle of the room and stood there in his blazer; the sleeves hung below my hands, the bottom hem falling below my shorts. I should probably have taken it off, but I didn't want to. I was enjoying the way his scent was wearing off onto my skin, imbedding itself in my hair.

Blake stepped forward, his eyes soft and reassuring. "It's just me, Angel. Relax."

"I know," I whispered, fiddling with the oversized sleeves.

We stood about five feet apart. A long awkward silence passed, neither of us brave enough to break the barrier. Something I needed to confess was knocking around in my head, fighting to make its way out. Finally, I figured it was better out in the open and decided now was as good a time as any.

I gulped and cleared my throat. "I have to tell you something. Something no one knows besides Jace. Not even the girls." My voice was shaky as I continued to mangle the sleeves.

Blake's stance sharpened. I'd never opened up to him before and I could see the eagerness in his eyes to know what I was about to share. "Okay. I told you, you can tell me anything."

I inhaled a deep breath and dropped my hands that now tingled from loss of circulation. "I . . . I don't have a boyfriend. I never did."

I chanced a look up at him, expecting to see shock, but instead, he looked embarrassed as he averted his gaze from mine and shuffled his feet back and forth. "Yeah, I um . . . kinda knew that."

I stared at him openmouthed. "Wait. You knew? But how? H-How'd you know?"

He puffed out his cheeks and expelled a big breath of air. Shoving his hands in his pockets, he rocked back on his heels. "Promise not to get mad?"

I wasn't about to agree to that. I cocked an eyebrow and placed my hands on my hips, waiting for him to proceed.

"Remember that weekend after we first met when I wanted to hang out with you, but you told me you were going to see your boyfriend on Saturday? It was right after the night in the bar when you sang that song, and we got into the fight—"

"Yeah, I remember. What about it?"

"Well, I came here that Saturday." When I didn't react, he continued.

"After you sang that song, I knew you wanted me too, and I needed to talk to you about it. I got here as you were coming back from a jog, so I figured you were just getting cleaned up and ready to leave, but you never came back out." He paused for a moment, taking in the realization sweeping over my face. A small blush crept over his cheeks. "The next day when I showed up here, I asked how it went as a test. I wanted to see if you'd tell me the truth, but you lied and said you'd gone. At that point, I pretty much knew there was no boyfriend. I just didn't know why you were lying."

"You were spying on me?" I clutched the jacket, bringing it tighter around myself as a shield.

"I swear it was innocent and I wasn't spying. I was just desperate to show you he wasn't worthy and convince you you'd be better off with me. I didn't expect it wasn't true, and I never planned to hide it from you. Please, don't be mad." He was cringing, waiting for my outburst.

"Blake, it's been over a month!" I shouted, mortified he'd made a fool out of me. "Why didn't you tell me when you came here the next day? And why did you keep acting like you didn't know?" My voice was escalating and my scalp felt prickly and hot. Trust was a huge issue after everything I'd been through. I never thought he would mislead me in any way and it was like he just slipped a big, ugly feeling under my skin.

He raked a hand through his hair and began to pace. "I wanted to tell you, but I never found the right time. I didn't want you to get mad or weirded out and stop talking to me. I have a hard enough time with you as it is. So I figured I'd wait until you opened up and told *me*. You obviously weren't ready for me to know, and I didn't want to push you. I don't want you to feel pressured, and there must've been a reason you went to such lengths to keep it from me." He stopped pacing and placed his arm against the large picture window.

I looked away and contemplated his words. What he said made sense and *I* had been the dishonest one here. I understood why he did it, and I shouldn't hold it against him. If this was going to work, there'd have to be a give and take. I took a deep breath and continued through my admission, "I've never been on a real date, either."

I looked back to Blake and this time got the reaction I was expecting. He dropped his arm and turned to face me, his eyebrows pulled together in the center, and he scrubbed the side of his jaw. "I'm sorry, did you just say you've never been on a date?"

"Yes."

He blinked in shock. "You, Evangelina, the most gorgeous girl I've ever laid eyes on, have never been on a date?"

I straightened my spine. "Yes."

"You're gonna have to help me out with this one because I'm not following."

I swallowed down the pain, the irregularity of my past, and the fact it always came back to haunt me. "Let's just say, there's a lot about me you don't know. Stuff I'm not sure I'm ready to talk about yet. I want to give you the chance to know me a little better. I promise, I do. Just . . . one step at a time."

"I know. I believe you." He took a tentative step toward me. That one truth told him more than the few vague words I actually spoke, and I could tell it struck a nerve.

I went back to strangling the sleeve of his jacket as I watched his advance. My body quaked from the inside, nervousness and want warring within me. I felt light on my feet as he stood before me, looking down, flexing his jaw repeatedly. His hands were balled into tight fists at his sides but his eyes were different this time.

Knowing.

Understanding.

A flitter of nerves passed through my stomach, wondering if he was going to press the issue, looking for answers. He seemed to gauge the panic in my eyes, and his tension eased a bit. "So do I get to take you on your first date?" His mouth pulled at the corner.

I relaxed a little. "Maybe. If you're a good boy."

"Tsk, tsk. Come now. I'm always a good boy."

"That's true." I slanted my head and pretended to study him. "But I just don't know if you're my type."

His mouth dropped, and he stared at me wide-eyed.

"I'm kidding, don't go getting all skittish on me." I laughed, nudging his shoulder.

As he swayed back, he grabbed my wrist, staring into my eyes with warmth and want. "Do you have any idea how sexy you look right now in my jacket?"

"Sexy? I look homeless." I laughed.

"Oh man, you have no clue." He took one more step and closed the small gap that remained between us. And as much as I was scared, I was also calm. This was unknown territory, but I was in it with Blake. Nervous and scared but not for negative reasons. For typical, never-done-this-before reasons. The butterflies fluttered and I clenched my belly, willing them away.

Blake inched forward with caution. "I'm going to try something, okay? Just don't move."

I swallowed past the lump in my throat. My tongue flicked out to wet my lips, and he let out a soft groan. It was his undoing.

His hands traveled up the lapel of the blazer, and he curled his fingers around it at my collarbone. Giving a slight tug, he pulled me to him so our bodies were flush against one another.

My breathing caught in my throat, and I could feel his heart hammering against his chest. I wondered if he could hear mine, the thrumming was so loud in my ears. His breathing was labored, but his eyes were determined as he very slowly lowered his face to mine. He stopped when our noses touched, and stared into my eyes. I knew he was giving me one last chance to back out, but I couldn't. Though my heart was flying, a sense of tranquility and security washed over me. I wanted this.

No—I *needed* this.

His hands trembled in the fabric of the jacket, and I knew it was taking everything in him to restrain himself. Unable to withstand the pressure anymore, I pushed up on my tippy toes, quickly breaking the tension surrounding us, and locked my lips with his.

We stared at each other, taking in the fact this was really happening, and then our bodies instinctively took over. He closed his eyes and drew my bottom lip into his mouth as I clasped his upper lip between my own, my tongue gliding across it. I let out a soft groan as his taste flooded my senses. He paused briefly, never breaking contact, and I felt his smile widen beneath my lips.

This. Was. Happening.

His kiss was slow and cautious at first. He kept me firmly pinned to him by his jacket as he tilted his head and parted my lips. Allowing him in, our tongues danced in my mouth, circling and sliding as we tasted one another for the first time.

We explored each other gently, our tongues flicking and caressing. He dipped in and out of my mouth, following each with a kiss. It was so soft and sensual I found myself building, needing more. Desire coiled, bubbling up inside me, consuming me until I felt like I couldn't take it anymore.

A rush swept through me and I plunged my fingers deep into his hair, deepening the kiss. I wanted to pull him inside, make him a real piece of me. This first was stolen from me, but here and now, this was my true first kiss. That thought gripped my insides and spiraled in my belly.

My back bowed as I kissed him with a fervor I didn't know I possessed. He growled into my mouth, released the lapels, and wrapped his arms around my back, pulling me tighter to him as he fisted the jacket behind me. We clung to each other like a lifeline, neither one of us willing to let go.

Sliding his hands up my back, he buried his fingers in my hair and broke the kiss as he pressed his forehead against mine. Our chests heaved as he stared at me once again and placed a small peck to my swollen mouth.

"Wow."

"Yeah," I breathed.

"You have no idea how much of a struggle it's been for me to not do that all this time." He rolled his forehead over my own. "I could die now and I'd die a happy man."

A little laugh escaped my lips. I never imagined it could be like this. That feelings could run so deep, like your survival was dependent on that other piece of your soul. The piece you were born without and could only hope to find so you could finally feel whole.

He kissed me again, soft, light pecks as he tilted his head back and forth, getting me from every angle. "Incredible." He sighed and released my hair. "You really *do* taste like a peach."

He took my hand in his and walked me over to the couch, pulling me on top of him.

I placed my hands on his chest and noticed they were trembling.

Embarrassed, I withdrew and clasped them in my lap.

Blake eyed them, his mouth draped at the corners. "You okay? That was okay, right? You're not uncomfortable are you?"

"No, I'm perfect. *That* was perfect. Really. These are good shakes," I promised. "At least I think they are." I knotted my fingers tighter, forcing them deeper into my lap. "I think my hands are just shaking because they want to touch you."

His body relaxed, and he grabbed my hands and placed them back on his chest. "Well then, by all means, touch away."

His eyes darkened as he massaged his fingers into my hair and brought my lips down to his once again. His tongue swept through my mouth, learning every curve and then dragged along the roof on its retreat before placing a gentle kiss to my lips. "I could kiss these lips forever." He placed his hands on the sides of my face, and clamped my lower lip between his teeth, giving a small tug that shot straight down between my legs.

My head was spinning. I didn't know how far this was going to go or how much I should tell him. I knew he deserved the truth. He should know what he was getting himself into. Who he was falling for. It was only right.

But if I told him, I'd be taking a chance he'd run away from me. My stomach knotted as I pictured my life without him. I didn't know if I was capable of going back to that anymore. That thought made me realize just how far this had come. How close we'd become. My heart began to race and I felt sweat bead on the surface of my skin.

"I just need a second."

He dropped his hands and nodded. I unwrapped my legs from his lap and shut myself in the bathroom, slamming my back against the door. "You can do this," I whispered to myself, closing my eyes. I repeated those words over and over again like a mantra, banging my head against the door, trying to convince myself. Moving to the sink, I ground my palms to the porcelain and leaned forward, looking myself square in the eyes.

"Come on, Eva. Pull it together. You owe him this much. Fuck, you owe him everything." I spoke to my reflection, thanking my lucky stars for a chance at normal. A chance I'd never have had without him.

He deserves the truth.

And there she was—the voice of reason.

I rolled my eyes at the face looking back at me, dampened a washcloth with cool water, and held it to the back of my neck to calm my nerves. I took ten deep breaths, feeling better by the seventh but finishing the cycle to bide my time. Deciding I couldn't put it off any longer, I put one foot in front of the other and stepped determinedly back into the living room, removing Blake's jacket and draping it over my forearm.

Blake was staring down at his lap. He looked engrossed in something. His leg bobbed up and down at a frenzied pace and his eyebrows pinched together, forming a hard line between them.

Then my eyes drifted to the leather bound book between his fingers as the sound of a page turning splintered my heart in two, sending it on a wild frenzy.

My journal.

Chapter 17

TIME STOPPED AS I INCHED forward. Mortified, I wanted to crawl into a dark hole and bury myself. No one has ever read my journal. Not even Jace. Blake was so immersed, he didn't even hear my approach.

"What do you think you're doing?"

He jumped as my voice cracked the silence. I threw his jacket down and snatched my most prized possession from his grasp.

Blake blinked as if seeing me for the very first time. "Is that really how you see yourself?" His eyes searched my face like he was trying to find the answer buried inside somewhere. Head tilted to the side, his features were pinched, tortured.

I tucked my hair behind my ear and dropped my gaze.

He moved to his feet and let out a shaky breath. "What happened to you?" He reached for me, and I backed away, clutching my journal to my chest.

"You had no right. What's in there is private." My voice cracked, escalating with each word. Tears stung the corners of my eyes.

He took another step forward, and I backed away again, but he grabbed my wrist, halting my retreat.

"Let go of me!" I shrieked, trying to yank away from him. My legs were itching to run. To protect myself.

"No!" The force in his voice shook me, stopping me dead in my tracks. His grip lightened a fraction as he caught himself and softened his tone. "No, Eva. Not anymore." Sorrowful eyes stared back at me as he released me. "I shouldn't have looked, okay? I know that and I'm sorry, but I did and now I can't let it go. Talk to me, Angel." His nickname for me was strangled as if my pain had become his pain.

That did me in.

I dropped the book and covered my eyes with my hands as the tears spilled over. My shoulders shook with force and I hunched forward, feeling as though I might heave. He was never supposed to see that. *No one* was ever supposed to see that.

His body wrapped around mine, his hands creating soothing circles over my back, sending me into deeper hysterics. The scars inside were so deep and one by one, they were ripping open, producing fresh wounds.

Bolting upright, I grabbed fistfuls of his shirt and held myself to him for support, my tears soaking a wet patch in the center of the fabric. I wasn't sure how long we stayed that way, but he never wavered. Never pushed me. In that moment, I think he knew I needed his stability more than anything. And he gave it to me, without question, without fail.

Eventually, he pulled back. Sliding his finger under my chin, he turned it up to him. "Talk to me. Tell me what happened to you. Someone hurt you, didn't they?" His jaw tensed and his hands bit into my upper arms.

"You weren't meant to see that. Just leave it alone. For me—please." My lip trembled.

"No, Angel." His voice was determined yet gentle. "*For you*, I won't. You're going to trust me and tell me what happened."

I'd planned to do just that, but now, seeing him in front of me, so close to knowing the truth, the words wouldn't come out. "I can't! Don't you see that I can't?" My fists pounded on his chest in quick succession as he stood there, absorbing every strike like it was simply the flit of a butterfly wing. Finally realizing what I was doing, I withdrew, covering my mouth, fresh tears glassing over my eyes.

Without a word, he studied me and I saw it, clear on his face. He was seeing *me*. And he wasn't backing away.

Oh God, this can't be happening.

But it was and it couldn't be undone. Part of me was relieved to finally give up the charade, and part of me was scared out of my mind, scrambling around inside to cover up like I was standing here naked, bared to his scrutiny.

For so many years, I was constantly on my toes, always with my guard up. Making sure to keep my lies in tact and stay buried within my skin so no one would know what was really going on. And then, like what happens when your body crashes after a serious high, mine went limp, almost catatonic. My shoulders bowed forward and I felt the life seep right out of me, seeming to melt down from my head and drain out of my fingertips as they hung toward the floor.

"Don't look at me like that." I fidgeted with the hem of my shirt, unable to meet Blake's eyes.

"Tell me what happened to you." He placed his hands on the sides of my face and erased my tears with the pads of his thumbs, lifting my gaze to his. His voice was so soft, so compassionate.

My lower lip trembled. "Do I have to say it? I think you know what happened without hearing the words."

The muscles in his neck worked to push down his swallow, and his eyes gave away his fear of what I'd just said. "Yes, you do. I need to know, and you need to get it out finally. Something tells me you've been holding it in since it happened. That shit'll kill you inside. The longer it festers, the worse it'll be. Give it to me. I told you, I can handle it."

I let out a jagged breath. *Was I really going to do this?*

If I wanted this thing between us to go anywhere, I knew I needed to.

Taking a little too long to compose myself, Blake cleared his throat, cutting into my thoughts. "When did it happen?"

I focused my eyes away from his, drifting off into that far away place as a lone tear slipped down my cheek. "I was fourteen when it started."

He sucked in a sharp breath. "When it . . . started?"

"Yes," I replied in a hushed whisper. It was the first time I'd admitted that to anyone other than Jace, and I felt dirty, ashamed. A pang of nervousness shot through my belly when I wondered if he would be thinking the same thing. I quickly prepared myself for the worst.

I watched the blood drain from his face as the depth of my words sunk in. He began to work his jaw again, and his eyes grew more intense. "Why haven't you told anybody?"

I squared my shoulders, knowing I hadn't told him the worst part yet. That, I wasn't ready to share. "No one can know."

His eyes tightened their focus on me as his eyebrows drew in sharply. "What do you mean no one can know? How can anything be done about it if no one knows? You have to tell someone."

"No! And please don't push. It took a lot for me to tell you that much." My breaths came in quick gasps as I stood my ground.

Sliding his arms around my waist, he buried his face in my hair. "My God, Angel, I'm so sorry. I didn't want it to be true."

"Don't be. It's not for you to be sorry about. You didn't do anything and I'm fine . . . really." I pushed away from him, needing distance. This was all too much for me, and the need to run was still festering beneath the surface.

Blake's eyes widened as he took in my guarded demeanor. He could tell he was losing me again. "Can I be honest with you?"

He snagged my pinky with his pointer. I looked down at our interlocked fingers in awe of how powerful that one connection felt. The smallest way two people could attach themselves to each other, but it felt like we were connected by steel.

"Sure . . ."

He took a moment to gather his thoughts. When his eyes met mine again, there was nervousness behind them, but it was hiding behind something more powerful. He blew out a slow breath, wiping his other palm on his thigh.

"I've been trying to hold back my feelings for so long because I didn't want to scare you away, but I just can't anymore. I'm falling for you, Angel. Hard." He took a long swallow. "I felt it the second I saw you tied to that guy in the park. Something draws me to you. You're my drug of choice and I'm a hopeless junkie. It's impossible for me to stay away. I have this sick need to be near you." He closed the already small distance between us. "To touch you." He brushed the back of his hand over my cheek.

Silent tears rolled from my eyes at his confession. My hands trembled, and I toyed with a strand of my hair to try to cover it up as I looked away.

Tell him to go.

I attempted to get my tongue to say the words, but it remained glued to the roof of my mouth as I stood popping my knees back and forth in a nervous rhythm. I couldn't do it.

The corner of Blake's mouth pulled in. "I knew there was something different about you, and I could always tell something was a bit . . . off. I just didn't want to press the issue. But I suspected it was something like this for a long time now." He hung his head. "I hoped I was wrong. Prayed for it actually. But . . ."

He swallowed hard, concentrating on my eyes again. "I want you to open up to me. I need to know the rest. Let me help you," he pleaded. "I know you think you're broken, but let me help fix you. I can handle what you can't. We can do this together." He sounded so certain.

I shook my head. "You don't understand. And you can't. There's a lot that you don't know, Blake. I'm no good. The sooner you figure that out, the better off you'll be." Tears rolled free as I built up the courage to do what I was about to do.

I plucked my pinky from his grasp, and looked him dead in the eye, reinforcing my barriers. "You should go." My voice didn't even sound like my own. It sounded automated, forced.

He flinched and hurt veiled his beautiful eyes. I looked away. I couldn't stand to see the pain behind those eyes. Pain that I had put there. This man was putting his heart out there for me, pumping and bleeding in front of me, and I was trampling all over it.

He caught himself and strengthened his resolve. "Don't do that. Not anymore. I'm in this with you and I'm not changing my mind. I want it all. The good, the bad and the ugly."

I bit down on my lip to stop it from trembling. "There is no good. Only ugly. Please, do yourself a favor and just move on. Find someone else. Someone who has a heart to give back to you. I don't have one anymore. I haven't had one for a long time. You can't change that."

He clenched his teeth. "That's not true and you know it. I can see you have feelings for me. You're just fighting it. You're stronger than you give yourself credit for." He took a step toward me and held out his hand.

"Be with me."

I couldn't look at his pleading eyes any longer. Neglecting his hand, I turned my back on him. My heart was breaking, screaming in my chest to go to him, but I was glued to the floor, picking at my nails all the while feeling his pull behind me.

Determined, he rounded me and snatched my nervous hand in his. "Angel, I know more than you think. Your eyes give it all away. I know you feel alone and I know you have no clue what you're worth. You can't blame yourself for what happened to you. It's not your fault, baby."

"You don't know!" I shook my head violently, feeling lost and hollow.

"I don't need to know!" Finally letting his frustrations spill over, his fingertips gripped my upper arms.

I flinched at his abruptness.

He bent down to my height and in a softer voice, pleaded, "Listen to me." His eyes were too intense. I tried to look away, but he grabbed my chin between his fingers and forced my gaze back to his. "I'm in this with you. I'm not going anywhere. What do I have to do to convince you of that?"

My mouth opened, but I was unable to push out any words.

Blake continued, "You're a good person. You care about other people and their feelings. Hell, you cared about my feelings and the shit that goes on with my dad after five minutes of knowing me. You can't see what I see, I get it. Just say yes. Let me show you you're worth it."

His words slapped me in the face, bringing me back to reality. My voice sounded hard, cold. "I'm not as good as you'd like to believe I am."

"Look, nobody's perfect, but you deserve to be happy and I can make you happy. I've seen it in the moments when you forget to leave that stupid fucking guard up. The smiles you forget to hide and that cute little blush that creeps across your cheeks when I get a little too close." He swept the back of his fingers across my cheekbone. "You need to stop being so hard on yourself."

His gaze intensified. "Be. With. Me."

I inched forward, wanting more than anything to take him up on his offer but I thought better of it. "Look, Blake. I admit I do have some serious feelings for you, but I'm just not ready. I'm trying, I promise. I just need time to think, okay? I need to figure out what to do with all this."

His body deflated. "Whatever you need." He placed a kiss to the tip of my nose and pulled my hair behind my shoulders, clasping it between his hands as he rested his forearms there. "I told you I'd be here and I meant it. Just try—for me. Think about it and I mean *really* think about it."

"I will." And I would.

He held me until the turbulence settled, brushing his fingers through my hair and smoothing his hands down my back until my breathing was even and I'd forgotten how intense of a moment we'd just shared. He always seemed to know how far to push me and when I couldn't handle any more.

He pulled his head back, a mischievous sparkle gleaming in his eyes, and just like that, in true Blake fashion, the shift in the air became more lighthearted. "Now, where were we?" He tapped the edge of his chin with his index finger.

I cocked my head to the side, wondering where he was going with that.

The corner of his mouth twisted into a grin, and he nudged my journal with his toe. "So . . . am I in there?"

"None of your business." I bent to retrieve the book I'd dropped in my haste and held it firmly to my chest.

"Come on, Angel. Am I in there?" Blake's smile was animated as he inched toward me.

Backing up, I said, "Maybe." I couldn't help but grin at his teasing manner. When my calves met cushion, I tossed the book down and sat on top of it, bringing my knees to my chest.

He prowled toward me with slow, fluid steps. "Let me see."

"What're you crazy? No way." I gripped the edges of the book tight, anchoring myself to it.

"Angel . . ." He dragged out my name, holding out his hand.

"Blake . . ." My voice mirrored his, and I cocked a brow, silently telling him not to mess with me.

"Come on. Show me. Don't make me tickle it out of you." He flitted all of the fingers on both of his clawed hands in a threatening gesture.

I narrowed my eyes. "You wouldn't."

"Oh, I would. And I should warn you, I've been the king of tickle wars since junior high. I still have the crown to prove it." He jabbed a finger to the side of my rib before I could see it coming.

I flinched to the left. "Don't!" I squealed.

"Show me the goods, or I unleash the fury." He wiggled two fingers into the opposite rib, and my body jolted to the side accordingly.

"Stop! I'm not in the mood. Don't make me kick your ass!"

Straddling me, he pinched my side while leaning in to nudge his nose into the soft skin of my neck. Bumps raised along my flesh as he dragged his bottom lip up to the base of my ear. When his tongue sucked the lobe, I swallowed my breath.

"That was the wrong thing to say. Now I want to do it just to see that," he whispered before pressing a kiss to my cheek. "But another time. I think you've shared enough for one night."

I silently thanked him with my smile for knowing so well what I needed. It was sweet of him to try and distract me, but it was kind of hard to laugh when your insides were spilling out. He brushed my nose with his own as his hands snaked around my back, holding me tight to him.

Enraptured by the feel of him, I gave up the fight of trying to ignore what his body did to me in this close proximity, my mind returned to what had brought us here in the first place.

"Kiss me."

The words escaped my mouth before I had a chance to swallow them down.

A smile dusted his face as he closed the small space between us and parted my lips with his tongue, sweeping in and out of my mouth slowly and delicately. But, like moths to a flame, one touch sparked a fire. Moaning with pleasure, he delved deeper, increasing his need with each stroke.

I breathed my air into him, loving how he received each pant, pushing some of his own back into my mouth. Unclasping our lips, I knotted my fingers in the hair at the base of his scalp, slanted his neck, and dipped my head to suck on the collarbone that had been teasing me all night. Sweet and salty and twisted with a hint of Blake, it tasted as delicious as I thought it would as I ran my tongue over it and gave it a little nip.

A quake ran through Blake's body as he expelled the air from his lungs. "Fuck, Angel." He dropped his forehead to mine, and I raked my fingernails from his scalp, down the hard contours of his back, exploring the muscles lining his spine. With trembling fingers, I attempted to do away with the thin piece of cotton standing between me and what I wanted.

His chest heaved, and his body retracted from mine a fraction. "We have to stop. This isn't happening like this. Not until you're sure."

I moaned in protest, wanting to tell him to shut up and keep going, but I knew he was right. I dropped my hands down to my sides and blew out the rest of the air in my lungs, a slow blush creeping across my cheeks.

He took a deep breath and must have noticed my embarrassment. "I want you, too. Fuck, I want you so bad I can barely think straight. But we can't. Not like this." He brought my hands around from his back and kissed my palm before settling them between us. Then he dipped his head once again to place a soft peck on my lips. "Come on." Securing my hands, he rocked back, pulling me up with him.

"What're we doing?" I asked as I was led to the back of my apartment.

He tugged me along. "Stopping myself just now was probably the hardest thing I've ever had to do in my fucking life, and I don't know if I'll be able to do it again." He shivered noticeably. "I'm putting you to bed since you said you slept so well last time."

I raised my eyebrows, looking up at him.

"Sleep, Angel. Just sleep. I still won't get to see the front of that pink lace, don't you worry." He smirked down at me.

Another warm blush met my cheekbones.

Like a gentleman, Blake looked away while I changed into my pajamas, then helped me under the covers. He kissed me, placing an arm on either side of my body, and pushed up to propel over me and onto the other side of the bed. Shucking off his shoes and socks, he turned to face me.

"What are *you* doing?"

"Staying with you. It's Thursday. I won't bite." He winked and slid his hands under the side of his face.

Knowing I didn't want him to go anywhere, I didn't protest.

I mirrored him, staring in awe at his beauty. Twinkling sky blue eyes looked back at me, and my subconscious gave me a pound for agreeing to have him in my bed. In the quiet of the moment, I reveled in that fact, taking note of my slow breathing and tame heartbeat. I was so comfortable around this guy. So secure.

No words were spoken as we took each other in, relaxing in the comfort of one another.

As the time passed, Blake's eyes grew heavy. Fighting against his lids, they'd flutter open each time they slid closed. I smiled at the cuteness of it. On one of the descents, I couldn't help myself and reached out to stroke one with the tip of my finger. Blake's mouth shifted to a smile.

"Thank you." The words tumbled from my mouth.

With his eyes still closed, he answered, "For what?"

Still caressing his lids, I answered, "For you. For this."

I leaned over and kissed him softly, making sure to breathe him in as I did. I wanted to remember this for the rest of my life. Every detail—the smell of his skin, the feel of his breath, of his lips, the divot in the center of his collarbone, and the swell of his biceps tucked under his perfectly relaxed face. All of it.

A lump rose in my throat at the beauty of this moment. At the sincerity and realness Blake was showing me. And at the lack of any lust or want swimming between us.

Just comfortableness.

Security.

I kissed Blake on the tip of his nose and rose from the bed, needing to get down all my feelings before I lost the words. "Sleep. I'll be right back."

My journal was still in the same spot I'd left it on the couch. Opening it, I went to the first clean page and let my hand take over. I'd crossed out and rewritten words like *love* and *meant to be*, not believing this could be real. The enormity of what I felt for this man petrified me.

Flipping back through the last few weeks of entries, my eyebrows knitted together as I realized that almost every single one was about Blake. From the second I'd met him, he'd dominated my thoughts. Invaded my psyche. Lived under my skin.

I held the book open to something I'd written when Blake had showed up at my apartment with lunch all those days ago. Making the decision, a smile slid across my face, and I determinedly walked back to my bedroom. Though he hadn't moved, Blake's face wasn't relaxed in peaceful slumber, and I could tell he was still awake.

The bed dipped with my weight, and I tucked one leg beneath me, watching as his eyes dragged open, then fell to the book resting on my thighs.

"I want to share a piece of me with you." I absentmindedly picked at the edges of the worn pages.

"I was only kidding. I know that book is special to you. I don't expect you to let me read it."

"*You're* special to me." I lowered my eyes. "And I want you to know. To let you in." My gaze met his. "To give you a piece."

Wordless, Blake sat up. Reaching out, he cupped my behind, and dragged me toward him to sit between his legs. He overlapped my legs with his and rested his hands on my thighs. "I'm all yours."

I smirked at the sentiment, and it relaxed me enough to open up the rest of the way and begin.

Flash.
He points the camera at me, and I swear he sees my soul.
Flash. Flash.
I wasn't ready for that one, and I scramble to cover up.
Flash. Flash. Flash.
Pieces of me, captured for him Images that he can hold
Try as I might to deflect, he pushes further
I'm anxious to hide, trying to find cover,
But he peels my layers back one by one.
I keep thinking it won't feel good
That I'll feel exposed and naked
Bared to him
But the more he reveals, the deeper he goes.

The further he pushes, the more he sees me,
The more comforted I become.
Flash. Flash.
With every bright light, he comes more into focus.
Each click stabs at my heart, trying to break through.
Each click reveals another piece of my soul.
Another inch of me.
For him
Flash.

Staring down at the page my cheeks warmed as the bared feeling of letting someone see a little bit of my insides swirled through me. *Had I done the right thing?*

Blake took my face between his hands, the emotion behind his stare quelling any insecurity I'd had a moment ago. "Your mind fascinates me." He searched my eyes as if he was trying to see past them, into the very place that intrigued him. "That was deep. And eloquent. And beautiful." He brushed his nose against mine and pressed a kiss to my lips. "Thank you for sharing it with me." His eyes shimmered. He looked like he wished he could reach out and erase my pain, change my past. And for a second, I wished he could.

But that was a silly notion.

Pasts are engrained in you forever. Deep little cuts on your soul.

"Thank you," I murmured in a voice that struggled to exist.

He kissed my nose and wrapped his arms around me, scooping me to his chest before laying us down. "Sleep, my angel." He burrowed his nose into the top of my head as his body relaxed into mine. "Sweet dreams."

"Sweet dreams." My body sank into his, molding to the curves like it was made to be its match.

Breaths slowed, muscles relaxed, consciousness ebbed away. I drifted off wrapped in a cocoon of Blake. Warm, soft, safe . . .

Chapter 18

I T WAS AS THOUGH MY being could sense his absence. Waking from a state of euphoric bliss, I was met by an empty space. A hole sank into my heart as my fingers sought out the vacant spot beside me, the warmth of his body still lingering on the rustled comforter. I leaned over, inhaling the faint trace of his cologne.

Rain pelted against my window, capturing my attention and I rolled over with a groan. I hated the rain. Like severely hated any form of precipitation. Snow could be pretty—once or twice a year—but that pretty white fluff always turned into nasty black mush, sloshing underfoot, and leaving dirty little marks along the bottom of your pants from what your feet kicked up. Rain, however, was my most hated. My mom used to keep me home from school when the weather was bad, and I never quite got used to it after that. I guess she spoiled me.

My phone buzzed on my nightstand. Resting beside it was a torn piece of paper that caught my attention. I lifted it and fell onto my back, staring at Blake's neat penmanship.

I wish I could've stayed to wake up with you, but I needed to wash off the club and get to class. I'll think of you, though. Thanks for last night.

♡ B

Smiling, I reached to the side, and fished for the phone that wouldn't stop its incessant ringing. Sandra's name flashed across the screen. "Hel-lo," my voice croaked. I cleared my throat and tried again. "Hello."

"Hey, soul sista." she trilled, sounding too cheery for such a crappy day.

"Why do you sound so uppity?" I draped an arm across my eyes.

"Oh my God, I had the most ah-ma-zing night ever! I need to tell someone. By the way, are you going to class? You have a thing with rain, right?"

"Jury's still out. Go ahead, spill it."

"Okay, so Jeremy—you remember Jeremy, right? So, he shows up at my door last night, telling me he loves me and that he's never felt this way before and that he wants to take it to the next level!"

I pulled the phone away, wincing as she squealed in delight. When I thought it was safe, I put it back to my tender ear. "That's awesome, San. What'd you say?"

"Duh, what do you think I said? I've been lusting over the guy for weeks. I contemplated playing hard to get for all of five seconds before I grabbed him by the collar and had my way with him—twice." She sang the happiest little giggle I'd ever heard.

"Aw, Sandra. I'm so happy for you." I rolled onto my side, brushing my palm over the spot in the bed where Blake had slept, recalling a memory of my own.

"I know, right? Come on, don't be a pooper. Meet me on the cor-ner. Don't make me sit in this boring-ass class alone, holding all this in. Please, come with me. *Pleeeeeease.*"

I hesitated for a second, picturing her disappointed pout. "Fine, give me a few."

I scooped up the pillow Blake had slept on in a bear's embrace, then I rolled onto my back, drawing in his scent once more so it would last me the day. Something felt odd and off, but I attributed it to the weather and the way my body repelled it. Shaking it off, I tossed his note in my bed-side drawer and dragged myself out from under the covers.

BY THE TIME I WAS leaving, the rain had stopped, leaving a film of nas-tiness in its wake. Thick, muggy air slapped me in the face, coating my skin in a sticky sheath the second I opened the door. It was so disgusting, even my eyelashes were having a bad hair day.

I stood in the doorway, contemplating running back inside and nose-diving under the covers; I could stay there until the sun decided to come back. Pulling the hood over my head, I hitched my bag further up on my shoulder, shoved my hands in my pockets, and began the trudge toward campus.

I couldn't shake a sense of foreboding that clung to the air, pecking at the back of my brain. I pushed it aside and pulled my hood further up. It was starting to rain again—the annoying, barely there rain that just spit at you enough to annoy the shit out of you.

I turned the corner and spotted Sandra hovering under a subway entrance. "You do love me!" She gave me a peck on the cheek and hooked her arm with mine.

"Yes, I do. I'm not a total bitch." I squeezed her arm. "Shall we?"

Huddling into each other, we maneuvered the slick New York City streets in a swift walk toward campus. Sandra chattered the whole way while I tried my darndest to dodge raindrops—hopping over puddles and tossing her long curls over my head to shield myself. We probably should have been more cautious, but feeling lighthearted with her, I was reveling in the fact that I was enjoying the rain for the first time and wasn't paying much attention to anything else. *Stupid.*

The campus was in sight. Just a few more feet. "Come on! I'll race ya." I dropped Sandra's arm and took off in a sprint. Hopping onto the curb, I completed a spin when headlights caught my attention. Fast moving headlights. Barreling straight for her.

Sandra.

Time stood still. Everything slowed while the pounding of blood in my ears intensified so it was all I heard banging on top of white-noise humming in the background. The air in my lungs pushed up and trapped in my throat. Tingles started at my spine and prickled down my legs making it an effort to put one in front of the other and force them to work right and ultimately, they failed.

I watched it happen.

Paralyzed and unable to do anything to stop it. Sandra's face contorted, registering the panic in mine. Her mouth dipped at the corners as her head slowly turned to focus on my line of vision.

It was too late.

Ginger curls.

All I saw were ginger-colored curls flying in the air before landing in a motionless heap on the sidewalk a few feet away.

"Sandra!" My voice shrilled in my ears, my feet finally remembering how to work. "No!" I scrambled to her side, scooping the top half of her limp body into my arms. I tried to assess her in any way I could. Smoothing her hair from her bloodied forehead, I prayed for any sign of life.

Her eyes were partially open—slits of emerald blankly looking back at me through streaks of crimson. "Sandra? I'm here with you, sweetie. Can you hear me? Please wake up." I cried, begging her. "Help! Somebody do something!" A frenzied panic whipped around in my chest.

A crowd began to gather, voices asking questions, but I barely noticed through the fuzz in my head. All I could do was rock. Back and forth. Rocking her in my arms

It felt like an eternity before I heard the sirens. Flashing, swirling lights approached and then the doors flew open. Instantly they were on us. Hands everywhere. All over me. Removing me. Dragging me away and laying her flat on the ground. I pulled my knees to my chest, tears mixed with the rain streaking down my face, and I watched and prayed. Why couldn't I have yelled to her to get out of the way? *This is all my fault.*

"No!" I screeched, my own voice piercing my eardrums. Crawling, I tried to get to where they were frantically pumping on her chest, feeling the bile rise and pool at the back of my throat. Each compression felt as though it was stabbing me in the heart. "Please, Sandra, please!" I hoped she could hear me.

This can't be happening.

With a gurgling sputter, the best sound I'd ever heard escaped her lips, and her chest heaved, choking. My body fell forward, doubling over onto my knees. *Oh, thank God.*

The paramedics worked desperately to stabilize her—strapping her to a board and immobilizing her neck before covering her face with an oxygen mask and hauling her into the ambulance.

It was then the police officer noticed me. "Miss, are you okay? Were you hurt? Paramedic! I need another paramedic!" he shouted over his shoulder, bending to appraise me.

I shook my head and whispered, "I'm fine. Just take care of her."

And then I shut down.

"Thank you, officer. I've got her." Blake was out of breath, his voice laced with worry as he squatted to my eye level. "You okay, Angel? Anything hurt?" He grabbed at my hands, my arms, my face, looking for signs of injury.

I looked up through soaked, swollen eyes and shook my head, unable to speak.

The police officer interrupted Blake's assessment. "We're going to need your statement, miss."

Blake laced his fingers with mine, showing me his support. I nodded. "Anything that'll help."

A few minutes later, I finished telling them what I could remember and the police officer thanked me, but it still didn't feel like enough. I sank into myself once again, falling into the black pit that surrounded me.

"Hold on to me, baby." Blake reached beneath my knees and behind my back, scooping me up effortlessly. I clutched fistfuls of his jacket and buried my face in his chest, sobs wracking through me. "You're safe. I've got you now." Blake soothed me before turning his attention to the police officers. "Thank you, gentlemen. Are they taking her to St. Luke's?"

"Yes."

"I'm taking her to the hospital to be with her friend. You can contact me if you hear anything from her." He gave the officer his number before solidifying his hold on me and walking away.

BLAKE CARRIED ME THE COUPLE blocks to the hospital. I was grateful for his strength since I didn't trust my legs to support me. He set me down in the front vestibule. "You gonna be okay?"

"I couldn't stop it. Why didn't I stop it?" I covered my face with my hands and began to sob again.

"Hey, don't do that to yourself." Blake lifted my chin with his finger. "There was no way you could've stopped it. You can't control things like that. You just have to be strong for her now. Can you do that?"

I took in a deep, trembling breath and sniffled. "Yes."

"That's my girl. Wait here." I watched Blake's broad back head to the service desk. He spoke to a gray-haired woman. As she searched her computer, he rested his forearm on the counter, his body twisted to watch me.

Blake nodded as she gave him the information we needed, and then he came over to take my hand. He guided me to the elevator, and my stomach sank with dread at what I would find once we got to her floor. Blake curled his arm around my middle, pulled me close, and pressed a kiss to my hair.

I spent the ride twisting my fingers until they lost circulation. When the doors glided open, I stood immobilized, my legs feeling as though they were replaced with concrete stumps.

Blake put his free arm out to hold the doors. "You can do this."

"I'm so scared. What if she didn't . . . What if she's . . ." *Dead.* I couldn't force myself to say it aloud.

Blake simply applied pressure to my back and guided me onto the floor. We walked over to a reception desk, and he gave another gray-haired woman Sandra's name.

"They have her in surgery already. You can sit in the waiting area and a doctor will come and see you as soon as they're finished," she said matter-of-factly.

Sitting. Standing. Pacing. Crying.

Mad. Sad. Scared. Restless. Numb.

I was numb.

By the time the young-looking doctor walked through the door, removing his mask, I'd become desensitized. My limbs prickled back to life with each step he took; my breathing hanging low in my chest.

Sandra's parents had arrived shortly after us. They leaped to their feet and scurried to meet the doctor halfway. Her mom's red-rimmed eyes were too much to bear. There was no consoling her, and I was in no shape to try. What a way to meet for the first time.

The doctor removed his surgical cap and addressed her parents. I stood behind them, hanging on his every word. "Your daughter's a fighter. She's banged up pretty bad, but I think she'll be okay."

"Oh, thank God." Sandra's mother sank into her husband's arms and wept.

"There's some internal bleeding, which we have under control, but we'll have to keep a close eye on it. She's got a few broken ribs, a broken leg, and a fracture in her skull. Right now it looks as though she only has a concussion, but we need to keep her under observation and continue to watch for any swelling in her brain. She's not out of the woods just yet, but I'm confident she'll be okay. You can see her as soon as she's awake."

"Thank you, doctor." Sandra's dad shook the doctor's hand, still cradling his wife. He looked like he'd aged a lifetime in these last few hours.

When she woke, I wasn't sure I was ready to see her. I sat with bated breath as Sandra's parents took the time they needed with her. Part of me was afraid she'd still look the same as when I'd left her—broken and bloodied, blank and lifeless emerald eyes staring at me.

Suddenly, I realized I'd never let Jessie and Jace know what was going on. I sent a quick text to each, letting them know what happened and that she was going to be all right.

"Eva, sweetie. She's asking for you." Sandra's mother's voice broke me from my thoughts. At my hesitation, she placed her hand on my shoulder. "I was nervous too, but she's okay. Do you want me to go with you?"

"I'll take her, Mrs. Neis." Blake placed his hand on my knee and smiled up at her.

She smiled weakly. "Go ahead. She'll be happy to see you both. Oh, and Eva . . ."

"Yes, Mrs. Neis?"

Her eyes glistened with new tears. "Thank you for taking care of my baby."

"I didn't do anything." I looked down at my lap, fighting the urge to bawl.

"You did more than you know, honey. Don't be so hard on yourself." She patted my hand. "Now, go see your friend."

Number 216.

I stood at her door, staring down at my toes flush against the seam of the threshold, my hands knotted around the door frame. Blake plucked my fingers free and laced them with his. "Go on in, baby. She's waiting for you."

One step in front of the other. That's what I focused on. Not the drab white walls, the green curtains or the beeping.

And there she was. A mess of a person, taped up with bandages and casts, laced with wires, and surrounded by machines, and somehow smiling.

"Eva," she rasped, reaching a weak arm out to me.

"Oh, Sandra." I ran to her side and scooped her hand in my own. "Are you okay?" Such a stupid question. Of course she wasn't.

"I'm okay." She gave my hand a small squeeze and looked up at Blake. "Hi, Blake." She smiled, bashful.

"Hey, sweetie. You gave us quite a scare there. How you holding up?" He patted the hand I held.

Her eyes rolled a bit as she tried to focus on him. "Like stir-fried shit, but it could've been worse. I could be feeling nothing right now." We all fell silent, unsure of how to respond to that. "Besides, things were getting boring. Figured I'd liven them up a bit." She offered a slight smile and we chuckled at the unexpectedness of her statement. Sandra winced, drawing her arms inward to cover her broken ribs. "Remind me not to do that again for a *long* time."

"Is there anything you need?" Blake offered.

Her head feebly rolled back and forth. "No, thank you."

I turned to Blake. "Mind if I have some alone time with her?"

"You sure you'll be okay now?"

"Yeah." I gave him a small, appreciative smile. "Thanks so much for everything. You always seem to be rescuing me."

"I'm just glad you're both all right." He glanced down at Sandra, who was starting to drift off. "Call me if you need anything. Anything at all. Doesn't matter what time it is. And try to get some rest, young lady. Don't overdo it."

She smiled weakly. "Thanks, Blake."

He patted her leg and placed a kiss on top of my head before walking out of the room.

I turned my attention back to Sandra. "You sure you're okay? You look like you hurt all over." My eyes searched her body, taking count of all her injuries, and I couldn't help my frown.

"I'll be fine." She looked as though she was fighting fading off.

"I'm so sorry, San. So sorry. I don't know what happened. I froze. I should've stopped it and I didn't."

She blinked, her eyelids heavy. "Stop that . . . couldn't do anything . . . I was there . . . not your fault."

"I know that, but—"

"But nothing. You did everything you could. I might be dead if it weren't for you."

"But look at you . . ."

That must have struck a nerve because her eyes popped open and she replied with more force than I thought she was capable of. "Yes, look at me. I'm alive and I'll heal." She winced at her effort.

"But you could've been . . . you could've—"

"Died?" She relaxed again, covering her throat. "Can I have those ice chips?"

I grabbed the pink container and slipped a couple pieces onto her tongue.

She rolled them around, and swallowed the water. "I know how close I came. But now we get to live, right? Every day like it's our last."

I closed my mouth, unsure of how to respond, but she continued, "Eva, you let your life slip by every day and I can't stand it. I'm actually grateful for what happened today because it opened my eyes." She covered my hand with her own. "Just find what makes you happy. Don't wait till it's too late." She smiled weakly and I looked away, ashamed.

Had I been that obvious? Clearing my throat, I looked back at her. "You should get some rest." I kissed her on top of her head and she cringed again. "Sorry."

"It's all good . . . just glad you're here with me." She sank deeper into the pillows.

"I'll be right here." I covered her hand with my own.

Her eyes got heavy and her head lagged to the side. "Think about what I said." As Sandra drifted off, she said one more thing, her whisper barely audible, "You gotta live, Eva. You haven't been."

I leaned back in my chair and stared at her. I'd almost lost her. Hell, I'd almost lost me! It could have easily been me standing in the path of that car. I mashed my forehead into the off-white waffle blanket that covered Sandra's body and listened to the monotonous beeping that filled the room.

Flashing back to this morning, our conversation played in my mind on an endless loop. Everything she intended to do with her life. All of her ambitions. Her dreams. Nearly shattered in a split second of time. Just like that, it all could have been over.

I groaned into the blanket when I pictured myself lying there. Cold on the concrete. Unmoving. "I don't want to die." The words stumbled out of my mouth as quickly as I'd thought them, but there was no one to hear them but me, as usual. *Always alone.*

The enormity of what could have happened came crashing down around me like a ton of bricks, rocking my world on its axis. Everything I thought I had figured out no longer made any sense. In that one moment, I knew everything could be ripped from you in the blink of an eye. Your life—over.

Life.

I needed mine back. Needed what was taken from me all those years ago when I was still just a kid.

And I needed *him*—Blake.

I'd fought it tooth and nail. Fought it with everything I had. But he was it. I needed to live before my time on this earth was ripped out from under *me* as well. Enjoy what was important and pay attention to the fact I was still alive.

It was time to take Blake's advice. No regrets. I wanted to love the things I loved again. I wanted to be happy. I wanted to do this life and not look back and I didn't want to die without ever really living.

Through my veil of tears, I watched the cloudiness that hazed my mind flake away into particles in the air. What stood behind it was the most adoring and understanding face I'd ever seen staring at me.

Waiting.

Always waiting.

A smile spread across my face while water still streamed from my eyes.

Live. I'm going to live.

Chapter 19

T HE AIR WAS SO FOGGY, I thought I must have been walking through a cloud, but I couldn't walk quickly enough. My brain was whirling so swiftly, my feet scrambled to keep up. Night came fast and my body was physically and emotionally drained, but something stronger drove me, propelling me forward. I seemed to be functioning on overdrive.

Just a little further.

With a frantic smile, I waved to the doorman as I ran past. I jammed my finger on the elevator button five times as if that would make it come quicker. My legs were restless while I stared at those metal slats, waiting for them to part—up to the illuminated numbers—back to the slats.

Fuck this.

Unable to stand the jitters any longer, I veered to the left and slammed the door open, taking the steps two at a time. Short of breath, I reached my destination, and pounded my fist against the door in a frantic rhythm.

Be home. Be home. Be home.

A minute later, the last barrier swung open, and there he stood in all his gloriousness. His eyebrows pulled together as he looked me over, propping the door open with his leg. "Angel? Everything okay?"

I couldn't speak. I remained in Blake's entryway, chest heaving, trying to calm my heart as my eyes raked his entire body. His muscles bulged from beneath my favorite black V-neck and he was wearing faded jeans, tattered in all the right places. I bit my lip as my gaze fell to his bare, sexy-as-hell feet, and I was done for.

My eyes darted back up to meet his, and I placed my hand to the center of his chest, moving him inside his cushy apartment.

Backing up slowly, the confusion on his face was adorable. "What's going on?"

I pushed him down on the brown leather couch and sat on his lap.

His frown deepened. "Angel? You're freaking me out. Say something, please?"

"Today was crazy, right?" I huffed out.

"Yes . . ." he drew out the word as if he was waiting for the other shoe to drop. I hated that I always had him so on edge.

"It just got me thinking, ya know? How quickly it can all be over." I looked up into his gorgeous blue irises and felt myself sink into them, getting lost. I continued before I lost the nerve. "I don't want to die."

"Hey, what's that talk?" He sat up straighter, his eyebrows pulling in.

"It could've just as easily been me, Blake. And I don't want to die." Panic rose in my voice with every octave.

His expression softened, and he smoothed a tuft of hair behind my ear. "Stop that. You can't think like this. What happened to Sandra was a freak accident. There's no controlling things like that, sweetheart. But you're not going anywhere, any time soon."

My eyes welled up as I took a deep breath. "Okay," I stated simply.

"Huh? What's okay? What'd I miss?" His eyebrows knitted together.

I reached one finger up to the space in between them to smooth away the creases. Shifting, I sat up a little straighter and looked at him with determination. "Okay, okay."

All the confusion slowly faded from his features, the taut, drawn-in lines relaxing as his eyes searched mine. He looked scared to death. Scared to let himself believe I was actually saying the words. Scared of the let down if I wasn't. He took my face between his hands. "Are you saying what I think you're saying?"

"Yes." I nodded. "I don't want to fight it anymore. I don't have the strength to deny it—to deny us anymore." I lowered my voice and looked down in my lap, fidgeting with my fingers. "Just . . . be careful with me. Please. All I've ever known of this is pain." I gulped before I added, "Make me forget."

He swiped the pad of his thumb under my eye, brushing away an errant tear. "I'll never hurt you, Angel. You're safe with me. I promise."

I scrambled into his arms, hooking my leg over the other side of him to straddle his lap. "You're too good to be true. It scares the shit out of me." I nuzzled into his neck.

"I'm not as good as you'd like to believe I am," he repeated what I'd said to him, a smirk in his voice.

"Oh, bullshit." I swatted his shoulder playfully, looking at him through glassy eyes. "So are we really doing this?"

"I'm all in if you are. I've been waiting to hear those words since the day I met you. I just want you to be sure. I don't think I could take it if you woke up in a day or two and changed your mind."

"No, I want this. I've never been more sure of anything in my life. It's you I'm worried about. Running away once you realize what you're dealing with." My posture slackened and the corner of my mouth pulled in. I felt so vulnerable voicing my insecurities.

"I'm well aware of what I'm dealing with. I told you that. And I don't scare easy. Bring it."

A light giggle escaped me. "You're gonna get sick of me sometime."

He laughed into my hair. "Well, it's not today. Tomorrow's not lookin' so good either."

I threw my head back, keeping my hands on his shoulders, and let out a full belly laugh. He laughed along with me and curled forward, nuzzling his face in my neck. Little by little our laughs dissipated and, when I sat upright, I noticed the shade of his eyes was slightly darker.

I dragged my bottom lip between my teeth and bit down, cocking my head to the side. "You really are kind of beautiful." There really was no other word.

"Beautiful, huh?" His eyes twinkled as the corner of his mouth pulled up.

"Mm-hmm." I bashfully traced a circular pattern over his chest with my finger.

"I'd say the same thing to you, but I don't wanna chance you bolting." He reached up and tugged a tendril of my hair.

I laughed and slapped his upper arm. "Ha-ha, wise guy."

He flinched. "I'm serious. I always feel like you're gonna disappear. You're like a unicorn."

I cocked my head to the side, scrunching my face. "A unicorn? I'm a horse with a horn?"

He let out a slight laugh and curled his arms around my waist. "Not a horse with a horn. A unicorn is a fabled creature, a myth. They're impossible to catch. Didn't you ever see *Gone in Sixty Seconds*, woman?" He looked at me in bewilderment, and I laughed.

"They've always kind of fascinated me. When I was younger, I thought if I looked hard enough that one day I'd find one. I guess I was right." He winked at me and my heart fluttered. "I finally found my unicorn. That's probably why I feel like I always need to keep my hands on you. I feel like one day I'll turn around and you'll be gone." His eyes showed true signs of worry, like it was something that had kept him up at night.

I laced my fingers behind his neck and leaned my forehead against his. "Well, I'm not going anywhere. I don't think I ever was. You can relax now."

Without warning, he pulled back, his expression serious. "Say it, Angel."

"Say what?"

"That you're mine. I need to hear the words." He cupped my face in his hands.

I took a deep breath and stared him right in the eyes so he knew how serious I really was. "I'm yours."

His eyes flared to life. "Again."

I licked my lips and brought my face a few inches closer to his. "I'm yours."

His fingertips bit into my thighs as he rooted me deeper into his lap. The corner of his mouth tilted up and those gorgeous baby blues sparkled. The dimple I loved so much poked into the smooth skin at the side of his mouth. "One more time . . . so you never forget."

Very cute. His study tactic. I leaned in and did what I'd wanted to do since I first saw it and dipped my fingertip into that adorable little divot. Feathering my lips across his, I breathed against his mouth. "I'm. Yours."

A growl rumbled low in his chest before reverberating into mine, and he sunk his fingers into my hair as his lips came crashing down. I dug my nails into the muscular flesh of his shoulders and scooted deeper into his lap, needing to be closer.

His tongue probed my mouth, and I parted my lips, inviting him in. I gulped down every last drop of his breath, panting and clawing at his back. This was nothing like the sweet, timid kisses we'd shared before. This was fervent, carnal. Months of pent up emotion and longing bled from each stroke of our hungry tongues. My senses were overloaded, every one of them blanketed in Blake. His taste, his smell, his touch, the look in his eyes, the sound of his moans, and the feeling of them hitting the back of my throat. My heart exploded, opening up to scoop him inside.

His hands left my hair and dropped to my hips. He slid them over the mound of my ass, then yanked the hem of my shirt into his fists. I raised my arms and he broke the kiss just long enough to pull my shirt off the rest of the way, sending my curls cascading in waves over my breasts.

His eyes widened as he took me in. The erratic pulse in his neck was visible, and his chest looked like his lungs were struggling for oxygen. "So fucking perfect." He stared at me with a deep longing. His thumbs traced the round peaks beneath the thin silk of my bra, spreading warmth throughout my body. This was the first time I'd felt desire and need when being touched like this, rather than disgust and filth.

I wanted his hands on me. Around me. In me. The feelings were foreign, but I invited them in, welcoming them. I closed my eyes and allowed the sensations to take over, feeling every stroke lick through my body. It felt so fucking good, and I longed to feel good for a change.

My eyes dropped to the moisture glistening on his lips. I reached out with three fingers and pressed them there, knowing it was my saliva covering his mouth. I wished it could stay there forever, my mark on him. Show the world he was taken.

Suddenly, a fresh wave of panic coursed through me, starting in my chest, quickening my pulse and spreading through my limbs like wildfire. I never wanted to be without him again. What if he couldn't handle who I was? What I was? What if he got sick of all my baggage?

As if he could read my mind, he cradled my head in his hands, and his expression softened. "You're stuck with me, ya know. I'm not going anywhere. You'll have to beat me off with a stick."

I huffed out a short, nervous chuckle. "Am I that easy to read?" I wanted to believe him, and I prayed that was the truth. I didn't think my heart could handle any other outcome.

"C'mere." He clasped my chin between two fingers and brought my mouth to his. He teased my bottom lip before pulling back to look in my eyes, his dimple peeking out slightly as a sexy, soft smile played on his lips. His hands came around to the back of my neck as he leaned into me, parting my lips with his tongue for another mind-numbing kiss. "Angel?" he breathed into my mouth.

"Yeah?" I answered, rubbing my lips back and forth along his.

"Wrap your legs around me."

Without hesitation, I unfolded my legs from where they straddled his thighs and hooked them around his waist. His hands instinctively dropped lower to cradle my ass.

"Hold on," he said through a devilishly sexy grin.

I wrapped my arms around his neck and let out a yelp as he stood and walked us toward the back of his apartment. I felt drunk on him, my body buzzing on a high.

The sound of his footsteps hushed as he crossed the threshold to his bedroom. He lowered me to the bed—my legs still hugged firm around his waist—and broke the kiss to look at me. His fingers toyed with the strap of my bra. "You okay with this?"

"More than okay." I looked directly in his eyes.

"You're sure?" He slipped his finger between my bra strap and my skin, and slid it slowly up and down, leaving trails of fire in its wake.

I took his face between both hands. "Blake, if you don't touch me right now, I think I'm going to spontaneously combust."

He laughed at my candidness and then looked down at me with dark, hooded eyes. "Then your wish is my command, sweetheart."

He licked his lips and brought them toward me, but instead of my mouth, he dropped a kiss right below my ear. His warm breath on the sensitive area raised bumps along my flesh. I sucked in a sharp intake of air as his mouth trailed kisses down the curve of my neck and then along my collarbone.

He slid his hand up my ribcage and closed it around my breast as his mouth made its descent lower still. When he reached the edge of my bra, he ran his tongue along the strip of skin bordering the fabric. Closing his teeth around the silk, he tugged and slipped the strap off my shoulder. My breast now fully exposed to him, he circled my nipple with his tongue, still teasing the other one through my bra. With shallow breaths, I watched him lavish my body and yearned for him even more. Leaving a glistening trail, he dipped his head to the side and nipped a love bite into the hardened mound. My eyes closed as I let every sensation surround me. Blake reached under my back and unclasped my bra, freeing me completely. He tossed it to the floor and sucked the other waiting nipple into his mouth.

With a moan, I arched my back, pushing my breast further into his mouth. "I need to feel your skin on mine."

My fingers fumbled with the hem of his shirt. Raising off me, he crossed his arms at the bottom of the cotton and pulled his shirt up over his abs, pecks and finally, his head.

Holy fuck!

Smooth skin rippled in waves over rock-hard abs, trailing to a deep V that plunged mercilessly into the low rise of his faded jeans. At the sight of my wide eyes, his dimple returned. "Like what you see, baby?"

I bit my lip and nodded, my fingers reaching out to trace the cut line beside his hip.

Blake smoothed his index finger over my bottom lip and then tugged at the corner, freeing it from my teeth. Then he placed a kiss full on my lips, nipped it himself, and licked the tender flesh. He let out a shiver. "I've been dying to do that."

My mind toyed with the fact I didn't feel nervous. Not one jitter, not one bead of sweat. I was willing to trust him so completely, opening a door inside myself that had been locked for so many years. So many *lonely* years.

Trying not to ruin the moment, I pushed all my thoughts aside and just enjoyed the feel of him. I skimmed my hands up the hard, smooth contours of his back and, when I reached his shoulder blades, I eased him toward me. His skin coated mine, his heat bleeding into me, causing a trembled wave to pass through me. The feel of my breasts pressed against his bare chest was euphoric. Our torsos one as his arms enveloped me, bringing us as close as we could get.

God, he felt so good. So right.

"I want to kiss you," Blake breathed into my ear.

I cocked my head to the side. "Um, I think we've covered that, don't you?"

Blake's grin spread, and his eyes glowed a dark sapphire. He dragged his finger along my mouth. "I'm not talking about *these* lips." He skimmed his finger along the side of my body, igniting sparks along every inch and nestled it between my legs. "I want to kiss *these* lips."

Mother hell. Heat swelled through every cell, coiling in my belly and mingling with the swarming butterflies.

He twirled the string of my sweat pants around his finger and fisted the fabric. "Would that be okay?" He kissed my jaw and looked back at me for confirmation. The fact he was asking made my heart open up to him even more.

"Yes," I breathed. "I'd love that."

"You'd love what?" He smirked before running his nose along the outside of my ear.

"For you to kiss me."

"Kiss you? Like this?" He pushed his tongue inside my mouth and kissed me soft and slow, his thumb rubbing circles into the throbbing flesh between my legs.

My body was going haywire. "Yes. No. You know what I mean."

"Say it. Tell me what you want me to do to you." He applied more pressure and slid his tongue into my mouth again.

Moaning, I broke free of the kiss and dug my nails into the roundness of his shoulders. "Kiss me. Down there."

"Down where?" he asked innocently. "Here?" He removed his thumb from my sex, leaving my body reeling, and skimmed it along the inside of my thigh.

"Higher," I panted, my chest heaving with built-up tension.

"Here?" He circled my belly button with his index finger and licked my earlobe.

Fuck! "My pussy! Kiss my fucking pussy!"

His eyes widened in excitement, but there was a seriousness mingled with it. "That's my girl. Don't hold back with me, Angel. Say what you feel and let yourself go. When I say I want you to be with me, I mean I want *all* of you to be with me. Tell me what you want and I'll be there for you every time. But I can't know unless you tell me."

"Okay, Blake, just please . . . touch me. I can't take it anymore," I whisper-panted.

He put the full weight of his body over mine and licked his words into my ear, "You drive me in-fucking-sane, you know that? I wanna taste all of you. Know you're mine as I push my tongue deep inside you and watch the look of pleasure on your face knowing I put it there." He pulled his head back and focused on my eyes. "And I'm not gonna stop until your legs are numb and shaking around my head."

Fuck. I was already shaking. My body couldn't withstand the pressure anymore. I pushed my pelvis against him, anxious for relief. Raising my head off the pillow, I licked up the smooth expanse of his neck then sucked his earlobe into my mouth. "Now. Please."

Blake's body shuddered before he lowered himself to suck one rosy nipple, rolling the other between his fingers. He gave it a tug as he pinched the one in his mouth between his teeth then licked the soreness away. Nipping and sucking, he made his way over each of my ribs, and continued down to my belly button. His tongue circled around it and then dipped inside. My fingers knotted in the sheets beside my thighs, trying to contain the random convulsions.

I glanced down just as his blue diamonds found my gaze. His face split into a broad smile as he took the string of my sweatpants into his mouth and tugged them untied with his teeth. Watching him, I couldn't help but picture what he'd done to that cherry. Something told me I was about to find out, and I squirmed in anticipation.

He hooked his fingers into the waistband and slid my pants down, tossing them to the floor behind him. Stopping for a moment, he stared up the landscape of my body, exposed and open for him. "My God you're so fucking beautiful. I'm sorry, but you are." His eyes were unapologetic, yet soft.

My chest constricted as that small and simple word left his mouth, but I knew he genuinely meant it, and I appreciated the sentiment. I didn't flinch. I thought I would, but I didn't. Instead, I reached down between my legs and caressed the side of his face, not wanting to ruin the moment. I wasn't sure if he was testing me, but I wanted him to know I meant what I said and was undeniably his. "It's okay. Thank you."

He smiled, dragging a finger up the center of my folds. "Jesus, you're so wet. I'm going to enjoy every . . . last . . . drop of you."

He removed his finger and put it in his mouth, closing his eyes as though he was savoring the taste, and then placed it to my clit, rubbing slow, tantalizing circles. My head dipped back into the pillow, and my back arched as he pushed two fingers inside me, keeping his thumb pressed to the tight bud the whole time. His fingers moved in and out of me, swirling deep, and driving me insane.

"Blake, your mouth, please. Kiss me." The words came out in a breathy whisper.

He removed his fingers and I gasped, feeling empty.

"Look at me," he commanded. "I want you to watch me. See what I do to you."

When I looked down, Blake's eyes held a sense of possessiveness I'd never seen before. He turned his head to the side and kissed the inside of one of my thighs before biting the meaty flesh and then licking it. He repeated the same thing to the other leg, sending quivers prickling up my spine. It felt like he was marking his territory. His gaze locked on me as his tongue snaked out from between his lips, and he very slowly dragged it from my opening, up the length of my lips, and over my clit. Then he closed his mouth around my throbbing heat and sucked it into his mouth. I let out a whimper, twisting the sheets even further.

Releasing his suction, he licked one more time and then took two of his fingers and spread me open, kissing me the same way he would my mouth. Slow. Delicate. Mind numbing sensations rippled through me. He kissed and licked and circled my sex, making love to me with his mouth, and I nearly came right then.

"Blake. Faster. Please," I panted.

He put his lips to me with a, "Mmmm," sending vibrations into my sex. "I want you to come slow." He licked again. "Keep your eyes on my mouth, Angel." He kept his tongue visible and circled it around my clit and then sucked the swollen flesh into his mouth. His strokes were still slow, but he applied a bit more pressure and I found myself shaking, teetering on the brink.

I dove my fingers into his hair and pulled his mouth to me, feeling myself fall to the other side, whimpering in ecstasy. My body sunk, lax into the mattress, but the licking never ceased.

Blake began soft, lapping kisses once again, and my belly tightened in response. My breathing strained as I looked down at him. He showed no signs of stopping. Instead, from between my legs, he raised one eyebrow at me and stiffened his tongue as he pushed it inside of me.

Fisting his hair, my head fell back as he fucked me with his tongue. He slid both hands up my ribcage to find my breasts, rolling my nipples around in his fingers. My back bowed as I felt another orgasm taking shape in my core. He tugged both of my nipples, pushed into me once last time, and the sensations rippled outward, sending me spiraling into bliss.

Suddenly, all tension left my body. I felt weightless and spent, and my face twisted in ecstasy as I looked down at him, still perched between my legs, looking as eager as ever.

"My God," I gasped for air. "You're fucking incredible."

"Hold on, Angel. You have one more for me."

"What? I don't think I can." I couldn't hide the panic in my voice. I felt drained, numb.

"You can, baby. Come for me one more time." Without warning, he slipped two fingers inside me and began sucking on my sensitive flesh once again. The need returned immediately. He sent his fingers deeper inside with each thrust and, when he hooked them just right, the buildup was too much to hold on to anymore.

My body rose up from the bed as I cried out, "Blake!" and then collapsed back against the mattress. Small jolts wracked my body, and my legs fell limp. Blake brought me down slowly, lapping up every drop of my release before placing a kiss to my most delicate area, his arms still hooked around my quivering thighs.

Releasing them, he crawled up the length of my body, feathering kisses along every inch. His last kiss was to my lips before nestling his nose into the curve of my neck, curling up next to me, and dragging me into the cocoon of his body.

"I don't think I can move," I said with closed eyes.

"Ah, my plan to incapacitate you worked then? I knew I'd find a way to make sure you couldn't run away from me again." He kept tickling my neck with his nose. My whole body was super sensitive, and even that small gesture raised bumps along my skin.

"Mmm, I guess so. Very sneaky, Mr. Turner."

"If you remember I was very upfront about it actually." He drew light circles around my belly button. "I believe my words were, I'd wear you down, then I'd wear you out. I'm just making good on my promise." He sucked one sensitive nipple into his mouth and released it with an audible pop.

I laughed and swung my body onto my side, sheltering my delicate parts. Hooking my leg over his waist, I stared into his beautiful eyes, loving the intimate playfulness I saw there. I secretly kicked myself for holding out for so long and missing out on all this, but I knew I wouldn't have been ready. I was a different girl a couple of months ago.

I traced the outline of his brow with my index finger, then his cheekbone, and finally his lips, watching the path of my finger the whole time.

His features became serious, and I wondered what he was thinking. He closed his eyes, inhaling a deep breath.

"I'm glad you were so persistent, Blake." I leaned in and placed a kiss on his lips.

"So am I, Angel. So am I."

I burrowed myself as close to him as I could. I couldn't believe I was really here, wrapped up in his arms, and how good it felt. It felt like . . . home. Real home. What home's supposed to be.

"So how about you?" I asked with a smirk.

He scooted his head back on the pillow, a question playing on his face. "What about me?"

"Well, I know *I* feel relieved, but you've got to be pretty, um . . ." I reached between us and cupped his bulge in my hand. "Frustrated."

He laughed and pulled my hand away, tucking it into his chest. "Uh-uh. Professor Pleasure will have to be a good boy for tonight. Not till you've had your first real date." He placed a kiss to the tip of my nose.

I pushed up on my elbow. "You're serious?"

"Yes. I'm a gentleman. And maybe slightly old-fashioned," he said with a wink.

"Wait a second, did you just call your . . . *member*, Professor Pleasure?" I scrunched up my face.

"Sure did. He's an expert in his field." The serious look on his face caused me to fall onto my side, laughing.

Wiping tears from my eyes, I propped myself up on my arm once the hysterics ceased. "You don't see the irony in that? Professor Pleasure? PP? You named your pee-pee, PP!"

He gave a cool shrug, even though he tried to act offended I'd made fun of his happy member. Then a wicked smile hit his lips. "Hey, I could've called him King Cobra, but try to get a girl to *come* near that— pun intended. You wouldn't put your mouth on a king cobra, would you? But who wouldn't suck the fuck out of Professor Pleasure?" He wiggled his eyebrows at me, his dimple plunged deep into his cheek.

"This is true." I laughed whole-heartedly. "Is there anything about you that isn't perfect?"

He made a display of looking nervous while he looked left and right, and then pulled me closer to whisper in my ear. "Yes, I didn't want you to find out, but I'm secretly a serial killer who stalks beautiful women and makes them swoon, only to have them disappear once they're finally mine."

I slapped him playfully. "Idiot."

Blake rocked into my side. "So, what do you say?" He raised his eyebrows, cocking his head to the side like a nervous little boy. "Will you go on a date with me?"

"You're asking? I thought I was yours now." Resting my chin on his chest, I peered up at him.

A huge smile split his face. "Good answer. So Saturday then?"

"No good. I see my boyfriend on Saturdays." I smirked.

"Well then, that works out perfectly, doesn't it?" he said without a pause, enveloping me in a protective hold.

"Yes. Yes, it does." I breathed him in and felt myself drifting off into a blissful rest.

Chapter 20

"STAY JUST LIKE THAT." BLAKE leaped from the bed, and I heard his hurried steps scamper down the hall.

"I'm still naked. Where the hell do you think I'm going? And what's the big idea? I was comfortable." I pulled the cotton sheet up to my neck and burrowed deeper into the softness.

"Two seconds. Just don't move!" he yelled, sounding as though he was frantically rummaging through things.

I heard his footfalls getting closer, and then he whisked through the doorway, muttering to himself, "Of all the times . . ." Camera propped in his hands, he knelt beside the bed and brought it to his eye, only to lower it slowly. "You moved," he said through bowed lips.

"I was cold." I tucked the sheet further under my chin and put my hands out to him in a grabby motion, trying to get him to bring back his warmth.

Blake let out a dramatic huff and lifted himself from the floor. He rested his hands on the bed and peered down at me, his arms flexed so the muscles were protruding. I swallowed hard, paralyzed.

His eyes bore into mine. "When I say don't move, I mean," he leaned forward, sending me deeper into the pillow, "Don't. Move."

"Sorry," I whispered, looking up at him. I was lying on my side, one leg hooked over the sheet bunched between my thighs.

"Just be still." He took the sheet from beneath my neck and draped it so it rested just below my nipples. Tilting his head, Blake analyzed me intently. He twirled one long curl and laid it over the crest of my breast. My breathing became labored as I watched him place me back to the image in his mind. "There. Now. Hold still."

The bed dipped with the weight of his knee as he balanced himself above me, squinting into the lens. His body was taut, his muscles drawn in as he tried to remain as steady as possible.

Flash.

Blake took a few shots from above me and then lowered delicately so not to disturb my position. He walked to the end of the bed and captured a few more.

My eyes followed him the whole time as he rounded the corner, back to my side, and bent on one knee so we were eye level. He was making love to me for the second time. First with his mouth and now with his mind. The guy was intense.

Bent at the waist, he stretched across the bed to get closer to my face.

Flash.

Finally, he lowered the camera. "Perfect." With hungry eyes never straying from mine, Blake placed the camera on the nightstand and crawled the rest of the way toward me, leaving his legs hanging off the sides. "You're like a work of art." He plucked a curl that lay over my shoulder and lightly brushed it aside. His thumb grazed my bare flesh, sending goose bumps rippling down.

I couldn't speak. The words were trapped in my throat and my body felt pinned to the very spot he'd displayed me in minutes earlier.

Blake put his hand to my cheek, brushing it with his thumb, and then trailed one finger down my neck. He swiped his finger back and forth along my collarbone, searing my skin and bringing desire back to life in my core. "Do you have any idea what you do to me?"

Swallowing hard, I shook my head no, my lips slightly parted to ease the difficulty I was having breathing.

With the back of his hand, he continued down over the side of my breast, along my ribs, and then over the arch of my hip, coming to rest on my thigh. "You make me want to battle the world just to keep you safe. You do things to me I can't even understand myself half the time. You're everything to me, Evangelina. Every-fucking-thing. I never want to spend another minute away from you."

He walked two fingers up the side of my body like he'd found a treasure and was savoring it. My chest rose and fell in deep, drawn out successions.

His eyes moved to the spot in the center of my chest where my heart lay, battering my insides beneath it. He covered my heart with his hand, like he could see it racing and was trying to slow it down for me, but the feel of him pressed there only sped it up further. "I love that this body is all mine now, and I can't wait to make love to it, but *this* is the piece I want." He held his hand steady over my galloping heart.

"It's yours," I breathed in what little voice I could muster.

"No, it's not." He smiled softly. "Not yet. One day soon, I hope. You'll open up to me. Trust me fully. I want this piece of you whole-heartedly. I'm not going to settle for less."

"Blake, I—"

"Shhh . . ." He put three fingers to my lips, silencing them. "No words. They don't mean as much." Inching forward, he removed his fingers and replaced them with his lips, gently guiding my mouth to follow its lascivious rhythm.

I mewed softly and he drowned it out, deepening the kiss. A hint of myself still lingered on his lips, and I was reminded of how he'd ravished me earlier. The familiar heat of a blush creeped across my cheeks and spread over my chest. He was so selfless, even with this.

Reaching over, I grabbed under his arms and pulled, trying to get him to join me on the bed fully. Without breaking the kiss, he leaned up on his knees and crawled the rest of the way toward my body. Not wanting any barriers between us, I tossed the sheet aside, leaving myself bared to him once again.

That got his attention. Blake parted our lips and let his eyes roam my body, his index finger following his gaze, exploring. "I've dreamed about this very moment. So many times, I feel like I've actually lived it, but at the same time, I can't believe it's really happening."

The wetness pooling between my legs made it abundantly clear this *was* really happening. I'd dreamed about it too, but this was no fantasy.

His chest was still bare, allowing me the proper view to admire it. He was chiseled, flawless. His skin was smooth like velvet, showcasing rippling muscles. He still wore those sexy fucking jeans, the edges worn, exposing white threads. Sitting back on his heels, his bare feet turned me on more than anything. They looked strong and powerful. I'd never seen sexy feet before. Never imagined they could be.

As I drank in the sight of him, hovering above me, tracing every curve of my body, something pulled at me. The need to please him consumed me. To give him something I was still virgin to. Something that could be his and only his—something I'd never done before. My fingers itched to touch him. To claim him.

I scrambled to my knees, causing him to straighten. Taking his face between my hands, I guided his mouth to mine. Our bellies were flush together and he trailed his fingertips along my spine, sending a fresh wave of heat coursing through my veins. He cupped my ass and pulled me to him, pushing his hardness into my sex.

I couldn't take it any longer.

Dropping my hands, I placed my palms flat on his chest and ventured down until I hit the waistband of his jeans. I hooked my index fingers inside and slid them back and forth. His body bucked when I hit a sensitive spot. I smiled into his lips and kept moving toward the center until I reached the button.

Effortlessly, I popped it open and lowered his zipper. I tucked my fingers beneath the waist of his boxers and delved my hand inside the fabric, feeling his silken sheath throbbing and anxious. Curling my hand around it, I circled my thumb around the head, feeling the wetness of his arousal already atop it. I sucked his tongue into my mouth, while I spread his juices over him and he moaned, his eyebrows pinched together in ecstasy. Loving the effect I had on him, I let him go, and he gasped as my hands came around to his hips to slide his jeans off the rest of the way.

He looked as though he was straining for a breath as I slowly, deliberately lowered his pants inch by excruciating inch. My eyes widened when his erection sprang free. I pushed him and he bounced back on the bed. He helped me remove his clothes the rest of the way, kicking them off when they got to his feet before pulling me down on top of him.

I'd been dying to get close to him with nothing between us for what felt like an eternity. And now, as his warm, soft skin coated mine and our bodies molded into one another, from our mouths to the tips of my toes, we felt like one being. It was an intense connection, as if we were one living organism.

Evidence of his arousal sat between my thighs, reminding me of what had provoked this.

I wanted him.

I parted our lips, gave a small peck to his panting mouth, and began trailing kisses down his neck and along his collarbone before placing a love bite to the muscled peak next to his shoulder. Blake gasped as I took his erection in my hand and licked a path down his torso.

"Baby, what're you doing?" he asked, breathless.

"I want you, Blake. I can't wait any more." I placed a kiss right next to his belly button.

"But we're," his swallow was tight in his throat, "going to wait." The poor guy was having a hard time putting sentences together.

The lust-filled look on his face washed away any trepidation I had as I lowered my head, and breathed my words onto his swollen head. "I know. No sex. Just this. Let me do this for you." My tongue flicked out to wet the tip before I slowly dragged it from the base all the way to the tip.

Blake's body quaked, and he dove his fingers into my hair. "Jesus." His head dropped back, and his eyes pinched shut.

Desire to have this man overpowered me. I toyed with his slit, sliding my tongue around the base of the bulged tip, and he moaned. He was so swollen it looked painful. All I wanted to do was alleviate his ache. Sucking the head into my mouth, I toyed with him a little before gliding him down my throat. I was tentative at first, learning him and testing myself. Each time I reached the tip, I'd stop to suck on it before venturing down once again.

The muscles in his stomach pulled tight, his body partially raised as his grip on my hair tightened and I knew I was doing something right. "Holy fuck, Angel. You feel so good. I need to come."

Knowing I was giving him pleasure sparked something animalistic in me. His words shot straight down between my legs, and I tightened my thighs together, my own desire building. He used his hands to guide my head how he liked it, and I relaxed my throat, taking him as deep as I could. All I wanted was for him to feel a fraction of what he made me feel.

"Fuck!" he groaned, his eyes bursting open to watch me taking all of him.

I surprised myself when I began to move quicker, deeper, my own need fueling me, then he cried out my name, shaking and convulsing, and I felt his desire seep into my mouth.

Blake's body sunk into the mattress, and his cock gave one final twitch as I slowly dragged my mouth to the top and placed a kiss to the tip. "All mine." I licked my lips and laid my head on his belly.

"I sure as hell am," he sighed. He peeked down at me. "Get up here."

I crawled up his body and lay in the crook of his arm, resting my head on his chest. The steady rhythm of his heart was still beating in double time as he kissed my scalp. "You're amazing."

"Only for you," I replied, placing a kiss to his pec. "And I mean . . . only for you. That was a first for me. I wanted to give you a piece of me that could just be yours."

Blake's relaxed voice touched my ear. "Thank you, but you didn't have to. Just having you near me is enough." He released a contented sigh. "You feel like heaven. My own little heaven with my own personal angel." I felt him smile against the lobe.

Our legs tangled together and we both scooted a little tighter, as though we were trying to melt into one another. When the enormity of how that felt was too much to bear, I lifted on my forearm and kissed him until I wasn't sure which air was mine and which was his.

Blake feathered his fingers along my skin, touching everywhere he could reach. Laying my forehead against his, I wanted so badly to say the words hanging on the tip of my tongue. It amazed me how much I'd changed since meeting him, but I wasn't ready to admit it out loud. My heart tucked him into its pocket, content to hold him there and carry him around with me.

I laid my head back on his chest, listening to the steady rhythm of his heart, wondering if his had pockets, too. "This feels so right, no?"

"You're asking me? I've been trying to tell you that for months now. Maybe from now on you'll stop being so hard-headed and listen to me for a change. Blake knows best. Repeat that three times." I felt his smirk on the top of my head.

"Idiot." I smacked him on the stomach, and he flinched, expelling an 'oof'.

I settled back into him. "It's just been such a crazy day, I can't seem to shake it. It's one of the worst and best days of my life at the same time. Every feeling will stay with me forever."

"And with me." He smiled.

Thinking of Sandra, I reluctantly sat up. "I should probably call Jessie and check in. I'm sure she's at the hospital by now."

Blake unwrapped his arm and gave me a gentle pat. "Go ahead." When I glanced self-consciously at my naked form, he pointed to his dresser. "T-shirts are in the second drawer. Throw one on."

"Thanks." I retrieved my crumpled panties from the floor and pulled them on before choosing one of Blake's oversized white V-necks.

He propped his head in his hands and drank me in as I slipped it over my head. "So sexy."

I shook my head and gave him a shy smile.

My bare feet padded to the living room as I rubbed the back of my neck, the weight of the day bearing down on me. I grabbed my phone and settled on Blake's couch, tucking my knees to my chest. *Shit.* I had ten missed calls from Jessie, ranging from the time I first texted her until about a half hour ago. With everything going on, I hadn't even thought to look at my phone. I hoped she wasn't too upset.

Her frantic voice answered on the first ring. "Jesus, Eva. Are you okay? Where are you?"

I cringed. "I'm at Blake's. I'm sorry I didn't answer. I'll explain later. Are you at the hospital?"

"Yes. I can't believe this. Thank God you were there." She sighed. "This is so scary. How the hell did it happen?"

Fresh tears welled in my eyes as the picture played before me again. "I saw the whole thing, Jes. It was horrible. I was so scared she was dead."

Jessie expelled a trembling breath on the other end of the line. "I can't even imagine."

"How is she?"

"She's okay. Groggy and out of it, and she doesn't want anyone fussing over her. She's trying to make jokes but I can tell she's in pain. She nods off every now and then."

"Tell her I'm sorry I ran out, but there was something I had to do. She'll understand."

"Okay, babe." She sounded calmer now.

"I love you, girl," I told her, feeling emotional again. I guess this was the day for it. "I need for you to know that. You guys are my sisters from other misters."

She chuckled. "I love you, too. Soul sisters for life." Her voice went soft as she added, "I'm just grateful we're all still here."

I gulped. "Me too. Tell San I love her, okay? And tell her I'll be back tomorrow."

"I will."

I kissed into the phone and hung up, then made one more call to Jace and, without thinking, my fingers dialed the next number.

"Hello."

"Hi, Mom." I'd only made the necessary weekly phone calls home in an effort to distance myself. I saw now how foolish that was.

"Eva? Is that you? Are you crying, honey?" My mom's concerned voice made me feel so small. I missed her comfort.

"Yeah." I sniffled.

"What happened, sweetheart? Are you okay?"

"I'm all right. Just a little upset." I went into the story then, tearfully filling her in on all the details—how scared I was for Sandra and the what-ifs about my own mortality. Of course, I left out Blake. That was a story for another day.

"Oh honey, I'm so sorry." She sounded beside herself with worry. "Thank God you're all right. Where are you now? Maybe you should come home. I don't like the way you sound."

My spine straightened at the mention of home. If my poor mom only knew there was no comfort in home anymore. Although, if I was being honest, all I really wanted to do was crawl into her lap the way I used to and have her tell me everything would be okay.

Taking a breath, I composed myself. The purpose of this phone call wasn't to make my mother nervous. "No, I have to stay here. I'm at a friend's right now. I'll be fine."

"You sure? I'm sure it's okay for you to miss a few days."

"No, I want to be close to her. She's not in good shape." I inhaled a steadying breath. "I'll be all right. I just needed to tell you I love you."

"I love you too, baby. Always."

"Tell Dad I love him too, okay?"

"I will. Call me tomorrow so I don't worry about you, please."

"Okay. Thanks, Mom."

"Bye, sweetie."

"Bye."

I lowered the phone between my crisscrossed legs and stared at the grains in the wood coffee table. I missed my mom. Missed my family. I'd give anything to go back to the way it was—when I was innocent and whole and there were no secrets between us.

Movement out of the corner of my eye broke the deep trance I was in. Blake sauntered down the hall in only his boxers, his hair all mussed, his face drawn in with concern. The cushion dipped as he sat beside me. Bending forward, he rested his elbows on his knees. "I want you to stay here tonight. I don't want you to be alone."

I hadn't thought about where I would sleep, but a sense of relief washed over me. For the first time in longer than I could remember I didn't want to be alone either. "Okay."

His shoulders relaxed, and a relieved smile emerged. "Good, then it's settled." He inched closer and slid his arm around me, pulling me into his chest.

I closed my eyes, savoring the protectiveness I hadn't realized I'd been craving. "Thank you, Blake. Just . . . thank you."

He kissed the top of my head and then stood up abruptly, dragging me with him. "Come."

Pulling me by the hand down the short hall, he took me into his bathroom, picked me up, and placed me on the counter. He rested his hands on my thighs. "Lavender or jasmine?"

"Excuse me?"

He stepped over to the tub and turned on the faucet, testing the temperature. "Lavender or jasmine? Which would you prefer in your bath?"

"Lavender, I guess? Wait. You have bubble bath?" I gaped at him in awe.

"Yeah, my sister's a bath nut. When she stays over, she makes sure

I have her favorites. But I'm not gonna lie and say I don't enjoy a good bubble bath myself from time to time." He winked.

I shook my head. "You just get better and better, Mr. Turner."

He poured the soapy liquid under the stream of water, screwed the cap back on and placed the container on the ledge of the tub. Biting my lip, I watched him walk toward me like a predator stalking its prey. Settling between my thighs, he commanded, "Arms up."

I raised my arms above my head, never taking my eyes off his. He placed his hands on my hips and pulled at his oversized T-shirt, tugging it from under my butt, and then dragged his hands up my sides, his thumbs grazing my nipples on their ascent. He removed the shirt the rest of the way and then folded it neatly, placing it on the counter.

"You'll put that back on later. I like you in my clothes." He hooked his fingers into my panties and I lifted off the counter, helping him pull them off. "So perfect." He removed his boxers and kissed my neck. "Wrap your legs around me."

Hooking my legs around his waist, he hoisted me up. I couldn't ignore the feel of his hard flesh pressing against my bare opening. I blushed, wondering what it would feel like to lower myself onto it. Blake gave me a lopsided grin, seeming to read my mind once again, and I looked away.

What was happening to me? Was I turning into some sex-crazed psychopath?

Eyes on mine and with his hands cradling my ass, he lowered us into the warm, sudsy water. He dropped a kiss below my ear and then spun me around so my back was pressed up against his chest. I relaxed, enjoying how comfortable I was. Blake twirled my long hair in his hand and twisted it up, knotting it effortlessly.

Reaching over, he took the shower gel, squirted some into his palm, and began massaging my shoulders. I hadn't realized how tense I was, but as his fingers circled and pressed into the tightly wound flesh, I felt each muscle unknot and ease into his touch.

I leaned my head back against his shoulder and closed my eyes as he brought his hands to my neck, spreading suds. Sliding over my breasts, he came up around the sides, circling, kneading, and pressing his palms against the taut peaks before twisting my nipples between his skilled fingers. They hardened in response and I whimpered, dropping my head to the side as he began the process all over again. My core tightened in anticipation of him trailing his hands lower. I reached around Blake's thighs and held him to me, pushing my bottom against his swollen manhood. He was nestled perfectly between the crevice, the head of his erection resting on my lower back.

His teeth scraped along the curve of my neck and then finally bit into my shoulder and I moaned in pleasure. Trailing soap along my belly, his hands finally came to rest on my sex.

"Blake, I need . . ."

"Shhh." He took my chin, turning my head toward him, and covered my mouth with his.

Grabbing the insides of my thighs, he secured me against him while spreading me open. The need to have him fill me was overwhelming and I whimpered into his mouth, pleading. He circled and tugged on my clit, toying with it, before sliding his fingers inside. At the delicious intrusion, I sucked his tongue, his cock hardening against my back when I did. He worked himself in and out of me, massaging with his palm as he deepened the kiss, mirroring what he was doing to me. His other hand lay across my belly, holding me tight to him.

The pressure built until I couldn't hold it in any longer. My teeth sank into his bottom lip and I cried out, digging my nails into his thighs and then went limp in his arms, resting in a euphoric bliss. "What are you doing to me? I feel like I'm losing myself in you."

"That's exactly what I want you to do. Give yourself over." I sighed as he kissed the top of my head and wrapped his arms around me. "Come on. It's time for me to feed you." He squeezed me and then his hold loosened as he readied himself to stand.

I wanted to reciprocate. No matter how scared I was of what was going on, I needed to make him feel as good as he made me feel. I whirled around onto my knees, shoving him down by his shoulders. "Not so fast, loverboy." A devious smiled played on my lips.

"Baby, I'm not sure how much longer I can last with you in this tub. I *am* still a man, ya know."

"Yes, I know. I can see how much of a man you are." I smiled and gripped his throbbing flesh in my hand.

Blake closed his eyes and laid his head back against the wall.

"Angel . . ."

I poured shower gel into my palm and stroked his length. My first kiss was to his Adam's apple. His features settled and I knew he wasn't going to fight me. I traveled to the hard peaks of his chest, licking. My hand never let up, gliding and pulling. I pushed my tongue into Blake's mouth; loving the feel of his gasp on my lips. I felt his core tighten, his lips becoming taut while he kissed me feverishly.

His body trembled, giving away how close he was. I reached down and cupped him with my other hand, gently massaging and Blake lost it. He sucked my tongue into his mouth and moaned as his body quivered with his release. Panting, he rested his forehead against mine. "You're so fucking hot. I hope you're ready for when I can finally have my way with you. You might not survive it."

I laughed and kissed him on the side of his neck. "I look forward to it."

After rinsing off, Blake helped me from the tub and then proceeded to take his time toweling me off. He seemed to be enjoying it. I marveled at him, bent on his knees, drying between each of my toes. "Better and better."

Grabbing my hips, he kissed my belly button and then stood, dropping his shirt over my head. "You ain't seen nothin yet. Stick around." He winked. "Come on, you must be starving."

Escorting me down the hall, he passed the kitchen, heading for the living room. I tugged back on his hand. "Where are you going?"

"To put a movie on for you. I want you to relax. I got dinner."

"Oh no. I don't think so. You're letting me help or I'm going home." I crossed my arms over my chest.

"You're so stubborn. We're going to have to talk about that hard head of yours." He tapped the edge of my nose.

"Yeah, good luck with that," I chided before smacking him loudly on his ass, sending him scooting through the doorway of the kitchen.

"And now you're assaulting me. What's happening?" Blake rubbed his backside, walking over to the refrigerator. He opened the door and bent to peer inside at the contents. The roundness of his ass was so delicious in those boxers. I admired the muscles gliding along his back as he pushed items around on the shelves. Turning at the waist, he peered at me, breaking me from my thoughts. He pointed to a lower cabinet. "Grab a frying pan."

Blake moved about the kitchen effortlessly. I was right on his heels, helping where he needed without him saying anything, like we'd done this for years.

A lemon flew at me and I reached out quickly, snatching it in one hand. I cocked an eyebrow. "Still throwing fruit at my head?"

"I can't help it. It always amazes me you can catch it that way." He shook his head and turned the flame on beneath the pan. He deftly sliced the chicken, his fingers moving with skill as I made the first cut into a lemon.

Eyes on what he was cooking, Blake stated matter-of-factly, "You'll have to meet my family now, you know."

Slicing down with the knife, I responded sarcastically, "Yes, and I can't wait."

He looked up at me from the corner of his eye. "And I'll have to meet yours."

I gulped hard, momentarily taken aback as my brain scrambled to come up with a plausible answer as to why that shouldn't happen yet. "Blake, I left home for a reason. I don't plan on going back there any time soon."

He turned his focus back on his knife, disappointment clouding his eyes.

"Can we talk about this another time? Let's not ruin today, okay? Let's just focus on you wowing me with your culinary skills for now. Deal?"

Ever so slowly, the dimple appeared on the side of his cheek, the glimmer in his eyes telling me I was getting a pass. He placed the cutlets in the pan, washed his hands and turned to lean on the counter. "I thought I wowed you enough today with my . . . other skills. How much wowing do you need, woman?"

I ducked my body down and squeezed between his arms, wedging myself between him and the island. "I know. I'm very needy aren't I?" I walked my hands up his chest, circling his tanned nipples, and then dragged my nails around the hard curve of his shoulders.

With a grunt, Blake took a handful of sliced lemons and reached back, tossing them haphazardly into the pan. Pushing aside whatever was behind me, he hooked his hands under my arms and lifted me onto the counter, pressing himself against my parted legs. "Be careful what you wish for. I was letting you remain mobile today, but I can easily take you out." His eyes glowed into mine.

My belly clenched, the muscles drawing inward, loving the dominant tone he used. It should have scared the shit out of me, but something in me knew he would never hurt me. That anything he did to me would be for my pleasure. Leaning back on my forearms, my body inclined, I pushed my chest upward. "Show me."

His eyes opened a little wider, showcasing his dilated pupils. "Don't push me, Angel. You're getting your date."

"I know." I hooked my legs around his ass and pulled him as far into me as the counter would allow, pushing up even higher with my chest. "But can't we play just a little more?"

I knew Blake couldn't say no to me. I was his weakness. A rumble rolled in his chest as he reached one finger into the V of my T-shirt and pulled down, exposing one of my breasts. He laved his tongue around the taut peak and then used the pad of his thumb to spread the moisture over it while taking my other nipple between his teeth through the thin material.

My body bucked into his as I dipped my head back, feeling the pull in so many different points. Toying with the exposed nipple, he sucked and pulled on the other through the shirt and then released it, dragging his tongue from the center of my heaving chest, up along the curve of my neck. He smacked his hands to my ass with a squeeze. My eyes flew open as he looked right in them and said, "Saturday." Then he smirked and turned to tend to dinner.

My mouth fell open and my body was reeling. "You're kidding?"

"Not kidding." He pointed to a head of lettuce. "Chop that up. There's a bowl in that cabinet." He pointed above his head to the right, flipping the cutlets with the other hand.

With a scowl, I jumped down from the counter and hissed in his ear. "Payback's a bitch. Just remember that you asked for it when it comes— or when it *doesn't* come." With that I reached up onto my tippy toes, elongating my body, to grab the bowl that was the furthest back in the cabinet I could find.

Blake looked out of the corner of his eyes and licked his lips before focusing his attention back to the pan. "I won't crack, woman."

I huffed, walking around to sit at the kitchen bar, and began chopping the lettuce. "Your loss. So tell me about your family. This way I know what to expect when I meet them."

"There's not much to know. You know all about my dad. Mom's different. She loves me to death and tries to sympathize with me but always winds up defending him. I know she means well, but it gets old. And Victoria—she's a spit-fire that one. I think you'll like her."

"Can't wait. It should be interesting to meet the people responsible for Blake Turner." I drizzled balsamic vinegar and olive oil into the salad and began to toss.

He set the plates in front of me, and sat down beside me. "Trust me, no one is responsible for Blake Turner but Blake Turner."

"Well, either way, I'm grateful they brought me you. No matter how you feel about them."

Blake opened his mouth as if he wanted to say something and then closed it just as quickly. I felt bad he was still so in the dark about me, but for now, it had to stay that way. I leaned forward and breathed in the most divine scent. "This smells amazing." My stomach flared to life. I didn't realize how famished I was.

"Dig in. It's my specialty."

"Is there anything you can't do?"

Blake popped a forkful of food in his mouth and tapped his chin. "I can't sing worth a shit. But I make for a damn good show trying."

"Really? I'll have to see that one day." I laughed.

"Let's wait till you're really head over heels before you do. I wouldn't want that to be what sends you running."

My taste buds soared as the most delicious bite I'd ever taken flooded my mouth. "Wow."

"Good huh?" He wiggled his eyebrows.

"Of course. Why wouldn't it be?" My tone was sarcastic. "You know, if you weren't so cute, you would never get away with being so cocky."

"Confident you mean?" Blake tipped his head at me winking.

"Whatever."

"You know you love me."

He rocked his shoulder into mine and I smiled thinking maybe he just might be right.

Chapter 21

WE PAUSED BEFORE ENTERING SANDRA'S hospital room.
"You ready for this?" Blake whispered.

My smile answered for me. We were going to tell them about us, and I was more than ready.

Jessie and Jace were already there when Blake and I walked in hand-in-hand. We didn't earn any head tosses since they were growing accustomed to his constant hold on me. But when I clamped his face between my hands and pushed a big sloppy kiss to his lips, Sandra nearly rolled off the bed, and Jace leaped into Jessie's arms, howling, "Yazzzz!" His fabulous version of "yes", of course.

I giggled and rested my head on Blake's chest, hugging him tight. "You can all give a round of applause to Ms. Sandra here for opening my eyes."

Jace made the sign of the cross. "Praise baby Jesus! I said a million novenas for this."

"Stop being so dramatic," I chastised.

"Who's being dramatic? I was about to jump that boy's bones myself. For Blake's sake, of course." He winked, and we all laughed.

"So, I have *you* to thank for this then?" Blake asked Sandra, smacking my ass. I yelped and hopped away from him, but he caught me by the arm and yanked me back into his chest. "Uh-uh. I don't think so. Not anymore, sweetheart. You're all mine now."

A round of cat-calling and atta-boys erupted around the room as I rubbed my sore bottom. "Take it easy there, killer, or I'll cut you off before you can seal the deal."

"You wouldn't." He folded his arms around me and kissed the top of my head.

I leaned my head against his chest as a wave of butterflies took flight inside me. My hand slid against his thumping heart, and a warm smile spread, knowing he was feeling the same. "You're right. I wouldn't."

Blake's mouth descended toward mine, and I licked my lips in anticipation.

"Oh boy. I can tell how things are gonna go now that you guys can finally have at each other." Jessie fanned herself, folding her leg beneath her to sit on the bed beside Sandra.

I cleared my throat. Showing enormous restraint and willpower, we both took a second to compose ourselves and loosened our hold ever so slightly.

"Well, I'm glad there was some good in all of this." Sandra waved a hand over her battered form. "And I'm glad you paid attention to what I said. I love you, chick. I just want you to be happy."

"I love you more." I put a knee to the edge of Sandra's bed and brushed my thumb along the top of her hand. "How do you feel today? Any better?"

"Better than death? Yeah. I have a crazy headache twenty four-seven, but I know what it could've been, so I'm just grateful to still be here. Anything else is cake."

"That's my girl." I lightly patted her bruised arm, happy to see she was more herself today.

Jace took Sandra's hair in his hands, delicately fingering strands into a braid, careful not to disturb her bandages. "That hurt, love?"

"No, you're good. I must look like a train wreck." Sandra held the side of her head, self-conscious.

Jace waved her off. "You're gorg. Now shutty." He finished off his handiwork and twirled the edge of the braid between his fingers just as a knock sounded on the door.

We all swiveled to see Jeremy standing in the doorway, holding a bouquet of flowers in one hand, and a teddy bear and a balloon in the other. "Did I come at a bad time?"

A blush crept over Sandra's cheeks, and she strained to scoot up higher in the bed. "No, no, perfect timing. Come in."

I cleared my throat and nodded my head to the others. "We were just leaving."

Sandra sent a look of thanks my way as Jace hopped off the bed, looking Jeremy up and down. "Rawrrr," he purred, accentuating with a clawing, catlike motion. I loved how Jace needed to test the newbies.

Jeremy, bless his heart, didn't flinch.

He's a keeper.

"Don't worry about it, dude. He'll ease up." Blake winked at Jeremy who stood motionless, not three feet from the door. Lacing his fingers with mine, Blake bent to give Sandra a quick peck, and we all followed suit.

"When I come back, I'm signing that cast." I smiled over my shoulder as Jeremy moved to hover by the foot of Sandra's bed, looking lost for words. I'm sure, just like the rest of us, he was struck with the severity of what she'd gone through.

THE NEXT FEW DAYS LEADING up to my date were excruciating. They were divided between classes, work, visiting Sandra, and squeezing my legs shut so tight in Blake's presence, I was sure they'd lose circulation.

Jessie seemed to have the same life-changing moment as me and forgave Rick, thank God. I couldn't take the two of them being on the outs anymore with her quieter than I ever imagined was within her capabilities, and him a pain in the ass to work with. Jace popped in to see Sandra now and again, but was MIA for the most part, which could only mean one thing—man candy.

I sat, gnawing at the inside of my cheek, feeling Blake's eyes peering into the side of my skull.

"Something wrong, Angel?"

"Huh? Oh. No, I'm fine." I tried to focus on the white board at the front of the classroom.

"You sure?" He brushed his knuckle along my cheek. "You look nervous, and I'm afraid the inside of your mouth could use a stitch or two."

I released my clenched teeth and exhaled. "I'm fine. Really." *You're not fine.*

Blake paused, his head tilted as he studied me. "Does this have anything to do with our date tomorrow night? Because we can wait. There's no rush, babe."

"What? No." *Yes.* "Shut up!"

"What?" Blake's face screwed in confusion.

Fuck, I'd said that out loud. "Nothing. Just drop it." I leaned over and kissed him on the cheek.

Blake's features didn't budge—he knew me too well. But he acquiesced and leaned back in his chair. For the remainder of class, I felt his eyes on me periodically, but I pretended not to notice as I scribbled down an exorbitant amount of notes. Knowing we'd go our separate ways from here, I stilled my heart and forced myself to push all the racing thoughts from my mind until I could be alone. I didn't want him to know what a mess I was inside.

At the dismissal of class, I gave him a chaste kiss on the lips and tried to disregard the look of concern in his eyes.

"See ya tonight?" he asked, hopeful.

"Huh? Oh. I, um . . . I have plans with Jace, and then I have to work. I'm sorry. I forgot to tell you."

"Oh." Disappointment marred his beautiful features. "It's okay, I can give Eric a call. I haven't seen him much. He's been acting weird lately. We're still on for tomorrow though, right?"

"Of course." I flashed an unconvincing smile.

Blake hooked his finger with mine. "You sure you're okay?"

"Uh huh. I gotta go, or I'll be late for my next class." I lifted on my tippy toes to give him a swift kiss, but he caught me in a bear hug, tipping me back and pressing his lips firmly to mine.

Instantly, all thoughts flitted from my mind, and I became light on my feet. My legs turned to squishy fuzzballs while he held me there, long enough for all doubt to wash away. When he finally broke the kiss, his eyes were half lidded, his breathing slow as a soft smile spread across his lips. "See you tomorrow night, Angel."

Nervous queezies overlapped the underlying jelly still in my belly from that kiss, but I shoved them down and smiled. "See you tomorrow night."

Tomorrow night.

When I was sure Blake was out of sight, I turned and headed for my apartment. There was no way I could sit through class. My nerves were jumping out of my skin.

Slouching down on my couch, I dragged my knees into my chest and rested my chin atop of them. What if I disappointed him? Or worse, what if I couldn't go through with it? How much could one guy excuse?

I rubbed my temples and rocked back and forth. Sure, I was fine with the intimacy we'd already shared, but sex? I'd thought I was ready the other day, but what if I freaked out? There's a big difference between that and what we'd done. What if it was too much?

"Fuck!"

I shot to my feet and yanked the elastic band from my hair, releasing my curls. Twirling clumps around my fingers, I paced around like a caged lioness. I wasn't denying the fact I wanted him more than I'd ever wanted anything, but sometimes I wasn't in control of my stupid body. Things had a way of creeping in and taking over. Experience had taught me that, and I didn't want it to happen in front of him. I never wanted him to think he was the cause of something bad. Or worse, to figure everything out.

I threw open the drawer in my end table with so much force I thought it'd unhinge, and pulled my journal out from under a magazine. Opening the door to my balcony, I shivered as cold air rushed in, and closed it just as quickly. The balcony was not an option. Returning to the couch, my pen scrawled.

Torture
Pain
Worry
Refrain

Hurt
Mad
Alone

Sad

Dream
Free
Soar
Be

Caged
Wild
Extreme
Mild

Scrambled
Confused
Conflicted
Bemused

Locked
Strapped
Prisoner
Trapped

Lost
Found
Confined
Bound

Dead
Alive
Phony
Hide

Asleep
Awake
Live
Blake

My fingers danced across my phone in a familiar motion I could do with my eyes closed, and a second later Jace's groggy voice answered. "Well, I guess I'm not going to *that* class." He yawned.

"I need you."

"What's wrong?"

"Just come here, okay?"

"I need coffee," he groaned.

"Already done. Door's open."

Five minutes later, Jace stumbled through my door, wiping crust out of the corners of his eyes, his hair all mussed. "This better be good. Kostas Martakis was having his way with me when you called."

I pushed the steaming mug into his hand, and he dropped onto my couch, tucking his feet under himself.

"I can't do this, Jace. I need to call it off."

"What? Have you completely lost your mind?"

"Yes. No. Maybe. I don't fucking know!" I plopped down on the coffee table in front of him, fiercely fingering my hair. "How can I do this? What if he finds out everything? And how can I have sex with him?"

"I'll show you how." The corner of his mouth tilted with his eyebrow, and he raised the mug to his lips.

"Jace, I'm being serious."

"Chill, boo. I'm not awake enough for this shit. Let me rev up some brain cells first." Jace took a giant swig of his coffee, all relaxed as if I hadn't been in the middle of a panic attack. I wanted to knock him off the couch.

I crossed my arms over my chest. "Can we figure out my life now, or should I get you an I.V.?"

"Listen, bitch, you're giving me whiplash. I've had it with you already. That boy's going to run away from you if you don't stop it, and then what? Is that what you want?"

I stared at him, unable to form words.

Jace's lips pinched. "I didn't think so. And stop ripping at your hair. The bald look ain't for you." Jace grabbed my hands and pulled me forward so our noses were almost touching. "Look, Eva. I've supported you living in your shell long enough. You have a chance to have something really special here, and I'm not about to let you fuck it up."

I groaned, rolling my head to the side. "Jace, I don't know what I'm doing. All my instincts are telling me to protect myself, but then I get within five feet of his electric fucking eyes, and I'm lost in him."

"As you should be." He relaxed back on the couch, and I wanted to punch him in the face.

"I really hate you sometimes. Can't you just pretend to understand? What the hell did I even call you over here for?" I started to get up when he shot forward, pressing down on my shoulders and lowering me back down.

His eyes were stern, making me feel like a five-year-old being scolded. "You know exactly what you called me over here for. To talk you out of making the biggest mistake of your life. At least *part* of you is smart enough to know you're doing the right thing. Somewhere in there is a rational girl who called me here to talk you down from a ledge. Where's that girl? I want to speak to her. I don't like this one." He looked around as if he was searching the room for something.

Sarcastic mother . . .

I raised my chin in defiance. "That's not true."

"Oh, it's not?" He raised an eyebrow.

I huffed out a huge breath and looked away.

He let out a tired sigh. "You're broken, yes. But I haven't seen you this happy in years, Eva. You may not see it, but you've already begun to fix yourself. It's working, baby girl. Just don't give up on it yet." He paused. "Not when I'm so close to getting my friend back. I miss her." He maneuvered my chin to face him. It was one of the rare times he'd ever been serious, and I knew what he was saying meant a lot to him.

"I'm sorry I'm a mess and that you're always having to deal with me. You know I love you. But, Jace . . . tomorrow—God, I'm so fucking scared. What if I can't do it?"

"Then you don't do it," he said, simple and to the point. "Call me crazy, but I'm pretty sure if you're not ready, that boy's still gonna be there waiting till you are."

He was right. Of course he was. "I know," I whispered.

"So then what're we talking about? Hush it. Relax and let's pick us a sexy little number for you to wear." He slapped my thigh. "Come on, let's raid your closet."

"There's one more thing. I told Blake I was hanging with you until I had work later. He also doesn't know I skipped class. I may have had a *slight* freak out earlier." I pinched two fingers shut for emphasis.

"You're hopeless." He shook his head, exasperated. "So let me get this straight, you've already succeeded in insulting the guy and pushing him away. Am I reading through the lines correctly?"

"Maybe." I winced.

"Well then, I guess we'll just have to turn the sexy up another notch." I nearly tripped as he grabbed my hand, forcing me down the hall.

"Um, I don't think so." I snorted out a giggle.

"I'll call him and let him know you're a jerk and that he should come to the bar tonight. I swear I'm gonna put a dog collar on you and zap your ass every time you're out of line. I'll teach you."

Walking hand-in-hand, we both laughed as we retreated to the bedroom.

HOURS LATER, MY MIND WAS reeling, torn between wanting to find Blake and jump on him, and wanting to run away and live under an assumed name. I was staring off into space while my finger absentmindedly wiped sweaty beads of water dripping down my half-filled glass.

Rick's hand blurred my vision. "Earth to Eva. Thirsty people here."

I startled and my cheeks grew warm. "Sorry. I'm somewhere else right now. It's been a crazy week."

He placed a friendly hand on my shoulder. "It's okay. Wanna take off? I can call someone in."

"Nah. Jasmine will be here soon anyway and I could use the distraction. Thanks, though." I was lucky to have found such a considerate boss.

Time passed as though I was in a vacuum. Any attempt to turn off my brain was futile. Blake still hadn't shown up, and it was beginning to weigh on me. He *always* showed up.

Happy by Pharrell Williams, blared through the speakers from the cover band. It was an upbeat tune that I usually loved, but I just couldn't force myself to get into it.

Rick approached me, clapping his hands *along* and bopping his head. "You know what time it is, don't you?"

Head tilted, I frowned at him, too distracted to catch on.

"Time for you to get your butt up there and belt out some tunes." He grabbed my hands, forcing me to *clap along* also, while he jiggled his hips.

I pulled my hands free and dragged them along my thighs. "Oh, I don't think so, Rick. Not tonight. I'm just not feeling it."

"You have no choice. It's your gig now. People come here waiting to hear your pipes. You can't disappoint them."

"He's right," Jasmine chimed in. "At least five people asked me when you're singing already."

"Do I have to?" I whined.

"Yep." Rick spun me around and ushered me out from behind the bar.

Jace smirked. *One day I really* am *going to haul off and slap him.* He got too much enjoyment out of my misery lately.

The lead singer leaned into my ear. "What song do you want?"

I thought for a moment as a vision of Blake's eyes flashed before me, and I decided to get out my feelings through song tonight. "Demi Lovato. *Lightweight.*"

He smiled and turned to the guys, instructing them of my selection. "The lady wants Demi's *Lightweight.*" They nodded, coordinating as

I inhaled a deep breath. I swallowed hard, curling my fingers around the barrel of the mic, and getting into the moment.

The quiet beginning notes started, and I sang in a soft, breathy voice. My eyes were closed as I imagined all of Blake's sincere words and felt every bit as lightheaded as the song implied. I crossed my arms over my chest, rubbing the tops of them as my feelings bled out of the lyrics.

And then I sensed him. Legs like jelly, my eyes opened after the first chorus to find Blake's gaze fixed on me. My heart lurched at the sight of him, a full breath of relief filling my lungs. *He came.*

A sense of completeness and comfort washed over me and realization hit me—hard. I wasn't whole when he wasn't around. Like I was half a person in those times. He kept me glued together. Kept me from coming apart at the seams.

Locked into him, I started the next verse, asking him to promise he'd always be in reach. I wanted him to feel it, too. Feel the weight of the words bearing down heavy on my chest as they passed my lips. They meant so much to me. I needed him to know how scared I was, but that I trusted he'd provide a safe place for me to fall.

I kept on, letting him know how delicate I was and how hard I was falling for him. He progressed toward me, and my heart stuttered. Each time I saw him, I swore he took a beat away. Standing before me, his demeanor was intense. He wasn't smiling. Devotion and what looked like love showed in his eyes, coupled with something else that almost resembled pain. He didn't have to say the words. I was saying enough for both of us.

The ending lyrics—telling him he kept me from falling apart—echoed through the speakers as Blake leaned down and scooped me up, whisking me off my feet.

Arms tightly circled around my waist, he whispered in my ear, "Always, my angel. Fall into *me*. I got you."

I pushed my nose into his neck and inhaled a deep breath of him. "I already am."

Tingles whisked through my body. I was content to stay here, just like this—suspended in his arms. This man had me. I couldn't run from him. I'd be running from myself.

"Blake, I—"

"I know."

Moving so our mouths were a breath apart, his eyes flicked to my lips, and my insides squirmed, wanting to feel what I'd nearly denied myself of.

He brushed his nose along mine, and I watched the slow dip of his dimple as he lowered his head the rest of the way and covered my lips with his. I hugged his neck tighter, missing the feel and taste of him. Blake groaned into my mouth and then pulled back, clasping my bottom lip between his teeth. He carried me back to the bar, my legs draping down the front of him, and set me down behind it.

"That was beautiful, Eva. I'll never get used to hearing your voice. You really should do something with that," Rick called, tossing a rag to me so I could wipe up a spill at the end of the bar.

"I do. I'm a Backdoor exclusive." I winked.

With Blake here, my mood shifted exponentially, and I became more lighthearted and playful. Even while I was busy, I felt him staring, his aura surrounding me in a protective bubble, and my mind, body, and soul were at ease.

Jace twirled Jessie and then dipped her backward over the top of the bar so her head rested on it. She looked at me upside down, giggling and out of breath.

"Come dance! Your favorite song's about to start. I requested it," Jace yelled over the music.

"Can't. I'm working." I pinched the straw poking out of my glass between my fingers and placed it in the corner of my mouth. "Besides, who would Jessie dance with then?"

"Me," Rick cut in, his body rigid as he stared down at her tight curls lying across the bar. She scrambled out of Jace's hold and stood to face him.

Unspoken words traveled between them before she stretched out her hand to him. "Well, come on then. Song's about to start."

From the corner of my eye, I saw Jasmine smirk as she focused on the liquor she was pouring.

I smiled. "Hold on, we're missing one." I turned, motioning to Blake to meet me half-way. "This better be good," I said to Jace as I grabbed Blake's hand.

"Bitch, please. Never doubt me." Jace stuck his nose in the air.

"This next song is by special request, dedicated to our very own Eva!" The powerful guitar strums at the beginning of *My Own Worst Enemy* by Lit, erupted from the speakers.

"Yazzzz!" I squealed, hauling myself at Jace. "I love this song!"

We all sang-yelled the lyrics in a tight clump, bopping and jumping, heads wagging. Jace and I screamed into each other's faces while we held hands. More dancing and hopping ensued, and I was pretty sure bodies were tossed in the air. The place exploded with whistles and claps as the last note sprang from the speakers.

"One more! One more!" I called to the lead singer. "Play *Livin on a Prayer* for me!" I smiled, exposing all my teeth and grabbed Blake's hand, having more fun than I ever remembered having in my life.

"You heard the lady. One . . . Two . . . A one, two, three, four . . ."

We all yelled the familiar opening lyrics in chorus. The whole place was shouting, jumping up and down in unison. Blake whirled me around and dipped me. We rocked our bodies side to side and I felt so free. So alive. My blood pumped fiercely, and my heart was full.

With a tight grip on my back, Blake sang close to my face, telling me we had each other, followed by something so simple and unexpected heat spread to my girl parts instantaneously. He scrunched his nose in the sexiest way, sending my hyper-aware body into overdrive and with a wicked grin, he sang the rest of the words, exclaiming that we'd give this a shot.

I laughed as he propelled me out, then pulled me in and swung me onto his back, just in time for the ending few verses.

As the song ended, excitement buzzed through me. Panting, my face ached from laughing so hard. Blake maneuvered me around to his front and looked into my eyes as if he were meeting *me* for the first time. A different, fun-loving, *real* me. Not the broken, fragile girl he was used to seeing.

His lips crushed mine with a ferocity I'd never experienced before. My hands immediately knotted in his hair as his tongue swept through my mouth. My stomach fluttered wildly. His chest heaved as he released my lips and rested his forehead against mine.

His eyes told me he wanted to say something but was holding back.

I thought mine must have mirrored his because I had to bite down on my lip to stop the words *I love you* from flying out of them. I never thought it'd be possible to fall for someone so fast, but I couldn't help it, I was.

My toes touched the floor as he lowered me down and then bent to press his temple to mine, his breath caressing my ear. "Tomorrow, Angel."

Tomorrow.

Chapter 22

TOMORROW.

Today.

It was today. Saturday. My first date. With Blake.

My sweaty palms rubbed over my star-and-moon pajamas so abrasively I thought they'd start a fire. I stopped, wringing my fingers together, trying to ease the burn. I could do this.

Could I do this?

Yes. I could.

I stood and walked over to the large picture window. I tipped my head to the glass.

Nine hours.

I had nine hours to regulate myself. What was with me? I'd had a great time last night. I'd thought I was past this. I knew this was what I wanted, but something in my body was constantly fighting it, always determined to keep me miserable. And, unfortunately, in a fight of wills, that girl always won.

Bitch.

A knock at the door stole me from my reverie. I lifted my head, wondering who it could be. Pulling back on the handle, a delicious scent floated in.

"Morning, ma'am." A short man holding a brown paper bag smiled at me, the corners of his eyes crinkling.

"Good morning." I poked my head out and looked around. "I'm

sorry, but I think you have the wrong apartment. I didn't order any food."

A knowing grin adorned his face. "Señor Turner order for you. I just need you to sign here." He held a piece of paper and pen in front of my astonished eyes.

"Mr. Turner?" My head cocked to the side.

"Sí. Sign please."

I scrawled my signature across the bottom of the slip and handed it back to him. Only, he wouldn't take it. That knowing smile was back, and he nodded toward the half-crumpled paper. Blue hand-written ink caught my eye, and I flipped it around.

Good morning, Angel. You're going to need all your energy, so eat your breakfast and get yourself together. We're going to have a bit of fun today. I've laid a path for you. Follow the clues and they'll lead you to the treasure (That's me) ;)

Pulling his arm from behind his back, the delivery man handed me a single red rose. A card dangled below the petals. "For you." He grinned.

I took it delicately between shaky fingers and spread the flaps, revealing its note.

Muscle tension melts away,

For a once in a lifetime, special day,

They'll cater to your every wish,

By eleven, make your way over to Bliss.

XO

B

My mouth hit the floor. "Thank you," I stammered at the grinning delivery man. He just stood, smiling at me with a wide mouth of teeth while I fumbled with the door. "I'm sorry, let me get you—"

"No, no. Señor Turner took care of everything. Enjoy your day, señorita. He a good man."

"Thanks." Dumbfounded, I scooped the bag from his arms and shoved the door closed with my heel. I set it on the counter and sent a text to Blake.

Me: Suave.

Blake: Thought you'd like that. Eat up. There's plenty of protein in that bag. And try to relax today. I want you . . . pliable. ;)

Me: You're crazy.

Blake: Crazy like a fox. See you tonight, Angel. XX

My stomach growled. Since my nerves had been jumping out of my skin, I hadn't eaten much in the last couple of days. Peeling the bag open, the smell consumed me. Eggs, turkey bacon, home fries, whole wheat toast, and a container of mixed fruit. And, of course, a steaming cup of coffee.

This man had catapulted himself straight into the center of my heart.

I HOPED I HAD CHOSEN correctly when I crossed over the threshold of Bliss 57. A lady with a blonde French twist greeted me with a warm smile. "Can I help you?"

"Yes, I believe I have an appointment. Eva?" I fidgeted, unsure.

"Ah, yes. We've been expecting you. Your boyfriend was very explicit that he wanted you totally relaxed. He booked the works. If you don't mind me saying, he's a real looker, that one. You're a lucky girl."

I blushed. Hearing him referred to as my boyfriend for the first time just turned the *real* up a notch. I tucked a strand of hair behind my ear. "Thank you."

"Ready to get started?"

"Sure." I couldn't stop the grin from splitting my face.

HOLY HELL, THIS WAS AMAZING.

Delicately, she worked her fingers into every tension point my coiled body harbored, until I felt like a numb ball of jelly. It was like lying on a cloud, all pressure and tightness melting through the table beneath me and seeping out through the floor. She massaged my scalp, my nape, and every bone in my body, from my fingers down to my toes. When she finished, I needed to physically recall how to work my limbs, and it took me a while to get to my feet.

"Take your time, dear. No rush."

"That was fantastic. Thank you." I rolled my neck around on my shoulders, amazed at how loose it felt.

"You're very welcome." She turned away momentarily as I sat up, holding the sheet to my chest.

"I believe this is for you." She held a long stemmed rose in her hand, the same familiar card dangling below its petals.

My heart fluttered as I took the flower from her. "Thank you," I said shyly. I let the card slide between my fingers for a moment before I flipped it open, and she quietly backed out of the room.

From the moment I tapped on those pretty, manicured fingers,

I wondered what they'd look like on my skin.

What I've imagined them doing is something close to a sin.

When I picture even that small piece of you, my heart swells.

Hurry, or you'll be late for your appointment at Spa Belles.

Spa Belles. With the corner of my mouth tipped up in a smile, I hopped down from the table, anxious to get to my next destination.

My body was so loose and relaxed, I felt like I didn't have a care in the world. My brain felt empty and free of negativity for the first time in what felt like forever. That was priceless to me.

The door chimed, and an Asian woman looked up from the counter. The hesitant look on my face must have given away my identity. Each person I encountered seemed like they couldn't wait to meet the girl behind the rose.

"Eva?" she asked.

"Yes."

She smiled broadly. "Nice to see you. Come with me. Pedicure or manicure first?"

"Manicure, please."

Propping me in a chair, she offered me a cup of coffee, which I declined. I was above the clouds, soaring on Blake. I didn't need a synthetic high.

I imagined he was sitting back, picturing me following his notes, all proud of himself, his dimpled smile highlighting his sparkling eyes. The muscles in my belly drew inward at the thought. Who did this on a first date? Or any date for that matter. The man was gold.

Between the massage at the spa and the hand and leg massage during my manicure and pedicure, I'd been thoroughly rubbed and scrubbed.

The pedicurist helped me down, and led me to the drying area. I fidgeted in my seat, always restless to just sit idle and dry. When she returned, she slid a clear container in front of me and placed a long-stemmed rose diagonally across the top. A proud smile donned her lips, and then she left me to read my note in private.

Make sure that you have lunch,
So your fingers you don't munch.
Though by now you're probably wishing I'd sent you a butler,
Finish your meal and head over to Cutler.

I looked down at the grilled chicken sandwich and French fries inside the plastic. A salt packet was taped to the lid, and I smiled inwardly, knowing it was definitely placed there on purpose.

It was coming up on three o'clock, and I was getting nervous about the time, but I trusted Blake knew what he was doing and wouldn't leave me scrambling to get ready later. I was pretty sure Cutler was a hair salon and that made me a little nervous. Maybe I hadn't mentioned to him how highly I coveted my hair. I didn't trust it in the hands of just anyone.

A cheerful, elegant looking man greeted me. "Hello, young lady. What can I do for you?"

"Hi. My, um, boyfriend—booked me an appointment, I believe." Those words felt foreign on my tongue and made me slightly uncomfortable.

"Ah, Eva. I've been waiting patiently to meet you. You're as beautiful as he said you are."

My hand swept up to the messy bun pulled on top of my head, and I blushed. "You're being kind. I'm a mess right now."

"Sweetheart, with that palette, we're going to create a masterpiece. Natural beauty can never be misconstrued, even in its messiest of states." He rounded the counter and approached me, gesturing toward my lump of hair that I now wished I'd done a better job styling before I ran out that morning. "May I?"

With precision, he had my hair down and loose around my shoulders. He fingered it. "Gorgeous. You have the most beautiful, natural highlights I've ever seen. I don't think we're going to touch this. Unless, of course, you want to brighten up the front, but I don't think you need to. A wash and fresh cut, and we'll have you looking like the princess you are in no time. Rochelle is a master at what she does. You'll love it."

I beamed, excitement replacing my nerves as I headed back to wash the massage oils out of my hair.

An hour later, I stared in awe at my reflection. The stylist spun the chair and handed me the mirror to investigate her handiwork. My head was covered in curls that were looser at the top and then tighter as they swirled in waves down my back. It looked flawless. Tossing my head side to side, I smoothed my hand over a few strands, careful not to disturb it.

"I love it!"

"In a little while it's going to loosen up and fall at the bottom. Then you're really going to love it." She smiled, turning me around before pulling off my cape.

I stared at myself in the full mirror once again; long blonde waves framed my face, cascading over my shoulders. "It's perfect, thank you. I couldn't be happier."

Then a small pang of panic struck me. What I'd planned to wear was nowhere near as elegant as this hairstyle was. Now I'd need more time to choose a new wardrobe for tonight. I pushed out of the chair in a rush.

"Don't forget this." The hairstylist twirled a red rose between her fingers. "You bagged a real winner, my friend. You're a lucky girl."

"Don't I know it." I smiled, lifting the bud from her and opening the card.

I hope you enjoyed your day, but I hope you enjoy your night even more,

You'll need to be relaxed and ready for what I have in store,

Hurry up and get back to your apartment so that you're not late,

I'm getting antsy thinking about what

I'm going to do to you, so don't make me wait,

♡ B

Love. I loved him. I wouldn't say it out loud, and I'd never been *in love* before, but that had to be what this was. My chest was tight and heavy, and my heart was fluttering anxiously. I couldn't relax the smile glued to my face. My feet were restless, wanting to take me to him.

I flitted out of the salon and had to stop myself from sprinting home, wanting to turn the clock ahead so I could be with him already.

Chapter 23

BURST THROUGH MY DOOR and headed straight for the bedroom.
What the hell am I going to wear?

"Ouch!"

In my clumsy stupor, I had smacked my toe on the edge of the wall.
I brought my foot up and took my throbbing, but thankfully unchipped,
toe in my hand, hopping haphazardly the rest of the way.

"Damn, that hurt . . ." I dropped my foot, no longer conscious of
the pain as I stood motionless in the doorway.

What the . . .

I approached the bed as if it were covered in a flock of baby doves
perched to take flight. A red satin dress lay atop it, a single red rose
sprawled across the midsection. At the foot of the bed stood a pair of
silver strappy heeled sandals.

My eyes searched the room wildly, feeling nervous and violated,
wondering how he'd gotten in. When I didn't see anything else out of
place, I snatched the rose by the card and yanked it open.

I would've loved to be there to see the look on your face,

For this wonderful surprise you can thank your friend Jace,

You'll be an angel in a devil's dress,

A beauty, a vision—sure to impress

Now put this on so I can have fun taking it off later ☺

Warmth swarmed my cheeks as my hand smoothed over the silky material. I picked it up and held it to my chest, smiling. This must have cost him a fortune. And Jace, that snake, slipping in here without telling me. I was going to have a talk with him.

I wasted no time slipping into the beautiful ensemble Blake had chosen for me. Admiring myself in the mirror, I was in awe of his choice. A deep V plunged into the channel between my breasts, but not enough to be considered distasteful. The edges came up in a halter-type fashion to wrap around the back of my neck, showcasing my delicate shoulders. A tight bodice led to a fitted skirt, which flared slightly right above my knee. It was sexy and sophisticated and . . . perfect. I couldn't have picked a better dress myself.

I dabbed a Q-tip to my eye, putting the finishing touches on my makeup just as a knock sounded on the door. My breath caught in my throat.

This is it.

I knotted my trembling hands together in an effort to still them. Taking one more deep breath, I puffed it out and then peeled back the door, revealing Blake. One look at him, and my heart stopped beating.

He was stunning.

He had one hand in the pants pocket of a black suit, the other behind his back. Underneath was a black collared shirt, opened at the top. His hair was styled perfectly messy, his skin sporting a clean shine. Electric blue eyes widened as they took me in, giving his sculpted cheeks a rosy hue. They traveled from the top of my head, along every curve, finally stopping at my French manicured toes.

"You're exquisite."

Taking my hand, he kissed my knuckles and then pressed a rose into my palm. The best rose yet. I smiled.

"Thank you. You look . . . incredible." I sucked my bottom lip between my teeth and eyed him.

"Incredible, huh?" His clean shave showcased his dimple as he inched forward, causing me to stumble back into the apartment. "I knew that dress would look amazing on you. Turn around. Let me see."

Smiling, I held my hands out to the sides and completed a slow spin, letting him appreciate his handiwork.

"Perfect." His eyes drank me in as he took both my hands in his and placed a kiss to my cheek.

A familiar warmth spread there. "Thank you for today."

"My pleasure. I wanted you to relax and enjoy yourself. I hope I succeeded."

"More than you know." I elongated my body and kissed him on the nose, then wiped away the glisten of lip gloss I left there. "So where are we off to?"

He gave me a mischievous look. "Now what fun would telling you be? Let's go, we don't want to be late." He reached out for me, but I declined his hand.

"One sec." I scooted to the kitchen bar and added the most recent rose to the vase, making a half dozen. Smiling, I walked back and scooped up his hand.

"Now we can go."

"RESERVATION FOR TURNER," BLAKE SAID to the hostess.

The young girl blanched, clearly taken back by Blake's striking features. "Ah, yes, Mr. Turner. We've been waiting for you. Everything's ready."

"Thank you." Blake pressed his hand to the small of my back and led me through the dimly lit restaurant, his excitement barely contained. He looked like a five-year-old on his way to meet Santa Claus.

The hostess stepped aside, extending her hand. "Enjoy your dinner. Someone will be with you shortly."

Blake looked into the room, and his smile spread further. Gripping my hand, he guided me inside and I froze, just barely inside the door. "It's a wine cellar."

"Yes, it is."

"We're eating in here?"

"Yep." His proud smile showcased the twinkle in his eye.

"This is unbelievable," I breathed, looking around astounded.

Set inside a circular room was a small round table with two chairs on either side. A candle flickered in the center, accentuating the bottles lining every inch of the walls from floor to ceiling. My eyes landed on a rose which lay across one of the settings and I smiled. He had booked a private room—in a wine cellar.

In-Fucking-Credible.

I looked back to him and shook my head. "Better and better."

The corner of his mouth tilted up, and he helped me into my chair before pushing it in and rounding the table to join me, still looking like a kid in a candy store.

"So is this how you woo all your women?" I asked.

"Are you wooed?" He folded his hands and leaned forward, his eyes illuminated with each flicker of the candle.

"Oh, I'm wooed all right," I confirmed, curling my body over the table to close more of the distance between us, not liking even that small barrier. Blake balled his hand, pulling his elbow back while crinkling his nose as if he'd scored a winning goal, and it brought something to mind.

"I have a request."

"Anything."

"The other night when we were dancing, you did this nose-scrunch thingy when you were singing and you just kind of did it again."

"Nose-scrunch thingy?" He cocked his head to the side, laughter in his eyes.

"Yes," I wet my bottom lip. "I'm going to need you to do that more often. It's sexy as hell."

Blake let out a hearty laugh, leaning back in his chair. "Nose-scrunch. Got it." Then he scrunched his nose one more time and winked. "Like that?"

"Yes. Just like that." I shivered noticeably, and he smiled his famous dimpled smile.

Reaching across the table, he took both my hands in his. "Are you happy?"

I considered his question before nodding. "I am."

And I was.

He studied me. "Good." All the words that hadn't been spoken yet shone through his eyes.

A waiter cleared his throat beside us, breaking the moment of connection we were sharing. We both deflated back into our chairs, turning our attention to him. He offered us tastings of a few wines, and I thoroughly enjoyed watching Blake swirl the different colored liquids and swish them around in his mouth like a true connoisseur before making his selection. We chose our meals and then were alone once again.

Knowing how important honesty was to Blake, I needed to clear the air about a few things and make my feelings known. Smoothing my hands over the table, I began, "I have a confession to make."

"What is it?" Blake's lips twisted and deep creases appeared in his forehead. It was the furthest expression I wanted him to wear tonight.

I winced. "I may or may not have been *very* close to my last bug out yesterday. I kind of freaked out over tonight and almost called the whole thing off. You put a great amount of effort into today, and I just wanted to say I'm sorry."

Blake visibly relaxed. "You're here, so there's nothing to be sorry for. And for the record, I think I'm going to ban the use of that word from now on. I don't like that you use it so often." He scratched his chin. "Yes, that's it. I'm administering a 'sorry' ban."

I frowned. "Well, I *am* sorry. Look at all the trouble you went to, and I almost messed the whole thing up."

"Almost doesn't count. I know you need baby steps, Eva. It's all good." He put his hand over mine. "Now, this is your first date. No negative talk. How do you like the wine?"

"Please, I'm not finished. Let me get this out." I fidgeted, pulling my hand from under his.

Blake's gaze shifted to where his hand lay empty on the table. He leaned back in his seat. "Go on."

"I'm going to mess up. Most likely a lot. Just don't give up on me, okay? Even if I'm a bitch sometimes or a head case. What I'm feeling for you is serious, and it's scaring the crap out of me. I'm nervous you're going to wake up one day and wonder why you wasted your time with the crazy girl. It'll break my heart, even if it would be the best decision you could make." I lowered my head, twisting the napkin spread across my thighs.

Blake stood, walked around the table, and knelt at my side, scooping my restless hands into his sturdy ones. "Look at me, Angel."

I glanced in his direction briefly, giving him a half-hearted smile, and then looked back at my lap.

Blake cupped my chin, forcing my gaze to meet his. "My eyes. Look at my eyes. I want you to know how serious I am."

I slowly raised my line of sight until it locked with his penetrating stare. I'd never get used to those eyes and the way they pulled me into him.

"I need you to listen to everything I'm about to say and take me very seriously, okay?"

I nodded.

"A world without you could *never* be a decision in my best interest, so get that out of your head. It'd be the end of me. Your heart is safe with me. I'll build a metal fucking cage around it if I have to." He bore his stare deeper into mine. "*You* are safe with me. I told you I'll never do anything to hurt you." Blake swallowed hard and inhaled a deep fortifying breath. "I love you, Angel. I do. I didn't want to tell you yet because I was scared you'd run, but I think you need to hear it."

Tears filled my worried eyes, burning the back of my throat.

He loves me.

"But you can't . . . you can't . . ."

Blake hushed my lips with his finger. "But I do. Love isn't about sex. It's about a connection." He swiped the tear that spilled over onto my cheek. "A commitment. A bond." He straightened his spine and cupped my cheeks in his hands. "I'm bound to you, Evangelina Ricci. Fuck, if I could tie you to me and wear you as a fucking hat I would."

I laughed, closing my eyes, and covered his hand with my own, rubbing my cheek into his palm.

"I mean it. Please don't doubt what I feel for you. I'd do anything for you. Anything but walk away. I'm not strong enough for that. Now just relax. Enjoy this for once. Just . . . be with me." He shrugged, quirking a smile.

I threw my arms around his neck and held him to me. "God, am I ever. I don't think I could be anywhere else anymore."

I wanted to say it so bad, but I didn't know if I could. I thought I was incapable, but in my heart I felt it. I felt everything. Him, his words, his . . . everything. *He* was everything. My savior, my light, my hope. All I'd ever wanted.

But I still felt guilty doing this to him. It was the worst decision he could make for himself and by reciprocating his love, I felt like I was enabling him. Creating the illusion all would be okay when I still wasn't convinced it ever could be. But I'd selfishly agreed to this, and I'd selfishly go as far as I could with it, just to be as close to him as possible for as long as he'd have me.

I looked up as my voice trailed off, unsure if I could say the words. "Blake, I—"

"Don't. I don't want you to say it until you're ready and I can see that you aren't. Don't think I'm insulted because I'm not. I can tell it's not your feelings for me you doubt. Your doubt is in yourself." He smiled and cupped my face. "We'll have to work on that."

I sighed and dropped my forehead to his, closing my eyes. Somehow he always pinned down exactly what was inside me. "Thank you. For everything." I opened my eyes and kissed his nose.

A slow smile stretched across his face, and he slowly and deliberately scrunched up that nose and sent my panties into a frenzy. I leaned forward and bit him on the tip of that adorably edible nose, taking him by surprise.

Blake smirked. "It's not Tuesday."

"I know, but I'm starving."

He laughed. "Well, we can't have that now, can we?"

As if on cue, the waiter appeared with our food, and Blake reclaimed his seat opposite me. Conversation flowed easily as we learned even more about each other. I told him a little about my family and how much I adored them. He seemed surprised since I avoided talking about them and assumed I had a bad home life when it was quite the opposite.

He mentioned spending the upcoming holidays together and I agreed to consider it. Although it would be hard to have him there, I didn't really want to go back home alone, and Jace needed to be with his family. Of course, he always showed up for a portion of each holiday to polish off the vodka before his mother demanded he come home.

Blake and I enjoyed our evening, barely noting the staff's presence. It was just me and him. And I didn't just mean in that room. I meant in this life. I could feel it. The shift in the atmosphere as I opened up to him even more. It felt so natural. So good.

For the first time in years, I felt secure. And I hoped it would stay that way. It all felt too good to be true.

Dabbing my napkin to the side of my mouth, I placed it beside my plate. "I'm stuffed. That was delicious."

"I'm glad you enjoyed it." Blake checked his watch. "We'll have dessert at our next destination. Do you mind?"

"Not at all. I can't take another bite of anything else right now anyway."

"Even if I did this?" Blake scrunched his nose again, and I almost lost it.

I licked my lips. "Use that sparingly in public if you don't want me to be a walking pheromone."

"Maybe I do." He winked, and my belly fluttered.

After he paid, he lifted the rose from the center of the table and handed it to me. "For you."

I accepted it and slipped my palm into his. This was already the best first date imaginable, but he'd made reference to dessert, so I knew he wasn't done. "So, what's next?"

"Patience, my dear." He guided me through the front door and onto the sidewalk.

"Come on. Tell me," I pouted.

"Pa-tience." He dragged out the word, drifting his eyes to the curb and nodding his head.

I looked up, expecting to see a livery cab. What I saw instead halted my steps. A pristine white horse flanked with a carriage proudly stood before me. The driver hopped down. "Mr. Turner." He shook Blake's hand and moved his eyes to me. "And this must be your angel."

"Could she be anything else?" Blake regarded me with pride, brushing the pad of his thumb along my jaw. "After you."

A horse and buggy? Is he fucking kidding me?

Blake gripped my hips, hoisting me inside, and my eyes fell to the rose lying across the seat. I scooped it up with a grin, joining it with the other one I was holding. The driver placed a warm blanket over us, and proceeded to pour us each a glass of wine. Blake wrapped his arm around me, and I snuggled into his warmth.

The wine coupled with the blanket and Blake's insane body heat kept the bite out of the November night air. The horse clip-clopped through the streets of the upper west side, and I turned to Blake. "You're incredible."

"I could say the same to you."

"No, you can't." I laughed. "And don't downplay your fabulousness." I wagged a finger at him. "I don't deserve you."

"You deserve more than I could ever give you." He paused, studying me, his eyes holding a deep sincerity. "I'm glad you're enjoying yourself. Cheers, Angel." We clinked glasses, and then he looped his arm through mine, urging me to take a sip through interlocked elbows.

I was in awe of the beauty of the city this time of night. All of the twinkling lights when they weren't lost in the hustle and bustle of it all.

Eventually, the buggy came to a stop in front of one of the most expensive hotels in Manhattan, and my gaze traveled from the golden doors to the roof. I sat up straight. "We're going in there?"

"We are." Blake slipped a bill into the driver's hand and jumped down, reaching up to me. I supported my weight on his shoulders, and he dragged his hands along the full expanse of my sides taking his time, eyes locked heavily onto mine. His muscles expanded as he kept control of how slowly he slid me down against the hard front of him.

"I'm going to feast on you tonight, Evangelina. I'm a starved man," Blake rasped in my ear.

Warmth flooded my entire body and, when he set me on my feet, I wasn't sure I could walk unassisted. Sensing my vulnerability, Blake gave me a minute to steady myself.

"Is that what you meant by dessert?" I asked.

He licked his lips. "You have no idea what's in store for you. Let's just say, I intend to obliterate any doubts you might still have." His eyes penetrated mine.

I simply gulped, heated vibrations engulfing me at the prospect.

Blake didn't let me ponder his words for too long. He wrapped his arms around me and led me toward the door. "Come on, you're freezing." He must have mistaken the goose bumps lining my skin as a reaction to the cold when, in fact, my body was on fire. It was like a five alarm with a side of dizzy little chills.

Bypassing the front desk, Blake walked us straight to the elevator, not giving me enough time to appreciate the expensive looking lobby donned with golds and zebra prints and a floor that looked so nice I almost thought I should take my shoes off.

He pushed the button that would take us to the highest point where my eyes had drifted to minutes before when we pulled up. Resting against the back of the elevator, he pulled me to his front, wrapping his arms around my waist, and placed a kiss to the side of my neck while we took the long ride up to the roof.

I melted into his touch, closing my eyes and reveling in his closeness. I unconsciously pressed my backside into his length, purring like a kitten at the feel of it growing against me. Blake growled into my ear and caught the lobe between his teeth. "Patience, Angel. Or we aren't setting foot outside this elevator."

"I'm fine with that," I breathed, suddenly needing more and not caring what his plans had been. I turned abruptly and caged him with my arms, flicking my tongue out to brush his lips. "I don't think I can wait, Blake. I want you. Bad."

I didn't know what happened between yesterday and today and frankly, I didn't care.

At my sudden assertiveness, Blake's pupils expanded to take me in. With a grunt, he wrapped an arm around my waist and hoisted my leg up to hug his hip with the other, then he ground himself into me.

"You feel that?"

"Yes." I panted, throwing my head back at the feel of him. How could I ever have denied myself this? What the hell had I been so scared of?

"See what you do to me?" He skimmed his hand under my skirt and cupped my bare ass, making me whimper as he pulled me deeper into his steely erection. "You drive me in-fucking-sane." He dragged one long finger along the slim line of my sex. "And in a little while, I'm going to bury myself so deep inside you, you're going to think you grew a new body part. But right now—you're getting the rest of your date." His hand left me then as he forcefully grabbed my thigh.

My breathing was coming out in ragged spurts as I dug my

fingernails into his upper arms and ground my forehead into his shoulder. "Why are you torturing me?"

"Torture?" He chuckled. "What I'm going to do to you can hardly be classified as torture. Anticipation heightens everything. I can smell your arousal seeping out through your legs and my dick is aching to find it and claim it. It'll make it that much better when I finally do. And I'm going to. Repeatedly." He smirked knowingly.

"But just to ease your grief . . ." He slammed his hand against the controls, bringing the car to an abrupt standstill. Mischief, playfulness and need seeped out of his electric blue irises as he threw my back against the wall and slowly, deliberately lowered himself to kneel before me. He took my ankle in his hand and draped it over his shoulder. "Hold on. This is going to be quick."

Bracing myself on the metal rail, I did just that. Blake hooked his thumb inside the thin strip of my thong and pulled it aside, caressing my clit in slow, soothing circles as he did. "A fucking peach." His tongue started at my opening and slipped up to the bundle of nerves perched at the top. Then he closed his mouth around it, his eyes shutting as he sucked greedily.

The muscles in my belly drew in and my legs gave way. I held on tightly while Blake dug his fingers into my thighs, supporting me. "Come for me, baby. Show me what I do to you. That I'm yours." He slipped a finger into my tight channel and sent me over the edge. I clawed his head and ground my pelvis against his face, screaming out his name as my body bucked and pulsed with my release.

Blake moaned between my legs, careful not to miss a drop of my need as I folded myself around him, unable to remain upright. Then he brought my leg down slowly and scooped me into his arms. "All mine."

I nuzzled my face into his chest, panting and in a state of euphoric shock. "You spoil me."

"No, I treasure you. I just know how to properly express it." He reached around me and pressed the button that would allow us to ascend the rest of the way. When the doors parted, Blake swiped his thumb along his mouth, which still glistened with my juices, erasing the evidence of my lust that still clung to his lips. With a wicked grin, he stepped out onto the rooftop, taking me with him.

With legs like jelly, I followed. "Wow."

He smiled down at me. "See why we couldn't skip this?"

I gazed in wonder, trying to catalog every detail of this night into memory. It felt like we were on top of the world, walking across the pinnacle of the city through the clouds. Set up like a lounge, tables and cushy white couches lined it. The city glowed beneath us and I was secretly jealous this wasn't my rooftop. It was still fairly early so there weren't many people around and that was fine by me.

We ordered drinks at the bar and chose an out of the way table overlooking the bright lights of the skyline, the smooth voice of Frank Sinatra playing in the background.

"This is amazing. You're amazing. Where've you been all my life?" I admired Blake.

"Life?" he scoffed playfully. "What life?" Then his eyes were serious. "I don't think I lived until you. I thought I did, but now I know I was only just existing. Gliding along, waiting for you." He brushed at my lips, seeming to study me. "You're my life now. My feelings for you are deeper than you could ever imagine."

What do you say to that? I stared at him, my mouth close to touching the table.

He let out a soft chuckle at my loss for words. "I'll be right back." He pushed up, closing my mouth for me, and I leaned back in my chair, embarrassed.

I watched the tight muscles of his backside walk away, loving the smooth strides he took. The man was perfection and it blew my mind that he was mine. I intended on showing him how grateful I was of that fact later. This felt like a dream I would wake up from to find it was all something I'd conjured up in my mind. Things like this didn't happen to me. I reached down, pinching myself on the hand, expecting to wake up a sweaty, shaky mess, but it never came.

Blake returned moments later. "Penny for your thoughts?"

I felt a glisten in my eye as I struggled to keep my emotions at bay. "I love you." I threw my hand over my mouth. I hadn't meant to blurt it out, but as I watched the knowing smile spread across his face, that dimple I loved so fucking much showing itself, I lowered my hand and looked at him with determination. "I love you, Blake."

Blake scooped up that hand and kissed my knuckles before turning it around and pushing his lips into my palm. "Dance with me."

I looked around, self conscious even though there wasn't more than a stray couple here or there. But, if I was being honest, I was a little disappointed that was his only response to the most raw and honest thing I'd ever stated in my life. Didn't he know what a big step that was for me?

At my hesitation, Blake stepped behind me, sliding back my chair. "Please."

I could never deny him of anything and after the day he'd given me, it wouldn't be right to let my insecurities ruin the moment. I slipped my hand back into his and allowed him to lead me onto the dance floor.

The deejay nodded in acknowledgment, and Blake answered with a wink. God, I loved when he did that.

The familiar tune of a piano began, and Blake smiled a sexy, knowing smile. He dragged his hands along my hips, spinning me to rest in front of him, and then settled his hands on the soft curve of my lower back, holding me tight to him. He curved his body, coating mine, brushing his nose along my jaw before nestling his face in my neck. I melted into him as John Legend's, *All of Me* filled the expanse of the rooftop.

"Listen to the words, Angel. I can't sing, but it's everything I'm feeling right now."

I didn't have to listen. I knew every word by heart.

Blake hummed into my ear, every now and then singing the words that were most important to him. He told me how confused I made him as he tried to figure out my mysterious mind. Asking for the one thing I never thought I could give—all of me. This explained the extent of his love for me, and it took away all of my insecurities. That was why he ignored my admission. He was answering in his own Blake way. Telling me he even loved the rough edges, the bad parts.

I buried my fingers in the hair at the nape of his neck and covered his mouth with mine, emotion seeping from every pore.

Blake pulled back and brushed away a stray hair the wind had blown across my forehead, placing it behind my shoulder as he sang, "You're my end and my beginning . . ."

And then the part came that hit home.

He cupped my face, acknowledging what had happened in my life, assuring me he'd be there for every mood, and my heart burst at the seams, no longer in denial of what this was. All I'd ever yearned for was to be understood and not have to hide anymore. But I didn't think it'd ever be possible. And yet here I was, dancing with the man who had stolen my heart somehow and begged me to let him love me.

There was no question. No pretense of anything but what I felt in this moment. "You've had me for a while, longer than I even knew, but now I'm telling you . . . I'm yours, Blake. All of me. Even here." I lifted his hand to my chest, knowing that was the piece of me he'd been waiting for.

A huge smile split his face as he tightened his arms around my waistline, and spun so my legs swung out to circle us. "I love you so much, baby."

"I love you, too. All of you." It felt so good to finally say it.

Blake stopped turning then. Sentiment washed over his features as his mouth lowered to claim mine. Licking along my lips, he spoke into my mouth, "Come on, let's get out of here."

"I've been waiting for you to say that," I replied, breathless.

He laughed at my impatience and set me on my feet, giving a swift wave to the deejay before leading me back to the elevator. I blushed, remembering our first escapade in here, but then a familiar warmth spread throughout my limbs knowing that was just the beginning. Blake rubbed circles over my palm with his thumb the whole way down. His face gave away nothing as to what else awaited me, but anticipation hung heavy in the air and in my belly. I was wound so tight, I didn't think I could wait the next few feet to be near him.

Guiding me from the elevator, he slipped a key card into our room and stood back, extending his hand. "Ladies first."

When the door split at its seam, soft music seeped through and streaks of candlelight danced across the walls as I entered the corridor lined in different colored rose petals. A king-sized bed sat proudly in the center of the room, and hundreds more petals were scattered across it. My heart swelled in adoration as I stood there, taking in all of Blake's efforts.

I felt his presence come within inches of me, and then his hands were on my shoulders and he was kissing the top of my head. "This makes seventy-seven. One for every day I've adored you. They all have different meanings. The yellow is for the friendship we share, the pink my gratitude and admiration of you. Orange is my desire . . . there may be a few extra of those."

He winked at me, picking up a light purple petal and placing it in my palm, and a tear rolled from my chin, coating it. "Those symbolize love at first sight and the white, that's a symbol of truth and loyalty. It means I am worthy of you and that's probably most important of all. But the red," he picked up the one single rose that lay across the top, "that's for my enduring passion. True love is stronger than thorns. I won't let anything come between us. Ever." He feathered the soft bud down my arm. "You like?"

"I . . . love." I brushed a tear from my cheek.

Blake reached around to my chin and angled it toward him, taking my mouth in his as he wrapped his arms around my middle. I reached back, weaving my fingers into his hair.

He placed his forehead to my temple. "None of my plans could ever surpass the gift you've given me tonight."

"Blake, I'm going to remember today for the rest of my life. There's nothing more you could've done to make it any more special."

His dimple lightly skimmed his cheek. "Well, I wouldn't be too sure about that. The night's not over. I'm not done with you just yet."

My heart skipped a beat at the insinuation in his words. "Well then, by all means, show me."

I turned, placing my hands over the hard curves of his chest, and licked a line up his neck before nipping at his strong jaw. I gave him a nod so he knew he didn't have to be careful with me like he always was. Tonight I wanted it all. I was here. Mind, body, and spirit, and I didn't want to be treated like a fragile piece of glass.

Blake cupped my face in his hands and gently massaged my mouth with his. Feathering around to my back, he slowly lowered my zipper until it rested right above my backside. Slipping between the silky fabric and my skin, he rubbed his thumb over the dip of my spine, the tips of his fingers brushing the top of my ass and sending a chill rocketing through me. I molded into his touch, pushing my breasts against him, anxious to feel his skin on mine.

"I so enjoyed you in this dress, but I think it's time we lost it."

"Yes," I breathed.

Blake slipped the straps off my shoulders, ghosting his hands down my arms until the material pooled at my feet. I kicked my shoes off at the same time and was left standing there in only a black lace bra and matching thong.

"Nice choice." Blake mingled his fingers with the hair at my nape, dipping my head back. With his other hand, he dragged his pointer finger along my chin, down my neck, along my collarbone, barely touching me as he traced one long line down to the edge of my panties, eliciting a soft moan from me. He made his way back up, between my breasts, to circle my heart. "Mine."

"Yours," I acknowledged.

Lowering to his knees, he cupped my hips and held his lips against the wild beats between my breasts. I buried my fingers into his hair, fastening him to me. He kissed me there over and over, and my heartbeat slowed, relaxing to a soothing rhythm. Sliding his hands up my ribs, they came to rest on my breasts, kneading my nipples through the lacy material. He groaned, pulling it aside, and moved to clasp one perky bud between his lips. My head fell back as I pushed myself further into his mouth, my breathing picking up pace. In one swift motion, Blake was on his feet, sliding his hands under my arms and lifting my small frame off the floor, leaving my legs to drape down the front of his body.

Holding me at his eye level, he said, "You'll let me know if any of this is not okay with you." It wasn't a question.

I nodded, wrapping my legs around him, and his lips found mine once again as he lowered us onto the mattress.

He left me then, backing away to stand at the foot of the bed, and I felt cold and exposed in his absence. Instinctively, I wrapped my arms around my chest, covering myself.

Blake took in my discomfort. "I'm coming back, Angel." And then he took his top button between his fingers and slowly released each of them until he hit the last one at his waistline. He stood there for a moment in his suit pants, his shirt open and draped around him.

My arms fell to the sides, coming up behind me so I could prop myself for a better view. *Absolutely perfect.* Just as I'd remembered. It never failed to blow my mind how flawless he was. How deep each cut in his abs were, the perfectly smooth coloring of his skin.

He smirked then, enjoying how I ogled him. "I'm going to take you a number of different ways before the sun comes up. But we'll start out slow. When you leave here tomorrow morning, you'll have no doubt who you belong to."

My insides bunched in anticipation. I licked my lips knowing there'd be no turning back. Knowing I didn't want to. After living my life at the mercy of someone else's demands and control, I never imagined I'd feel this way, but I was so turned on by the possessiveness of his words. I wanted him to claim me. To do with me what he wished. To take away the need to think and calculate and plan. I wanted to give myself over to him. And it both shocked and confused me.

Before I could think too deeply, his fingers dug into the clasp of his belt. I swallowed long and hard as his pants fell effortlessly to the floor, leaving him standing there in an opened collared shirt and boxer briefs with an obvious steel line erected down the center. Then the shirt fell away and his socks were plucked off and tossed to the pile and all that was left was the strip of material covering what I wanted to see most. Blake hooked his thumbs into the elastic, toying with it and I bit my lip. Eyes on mine, he inched them down, one inch, then two, until they met the carpet as well.

There he stood, proudly before me. *Every* part of him standing proudly before me. I scrambled to my knees, anxious to get to him.

He held up a finger. "Ah, ah, ah. Not so fast." He smirked. "Lie back."

I reluctantly did as he asked, pushing my head back into the pillow and sending a wave of petals floating on a puff of air. He prowled up my body on all fours, dipping to nip and suck at me along the way, skimming velvety petals along my skin. I watched him over the panting landscape of my torso as he took his time, trailing kisses along every inch of me—down my neck, my arms, my legs, even my feet. I felt claimed, consumed.

Blake suckled the calf cupped in his hands when he looked up at me with hungry, eager eyes. He came to rest between my thighs, leaning onto one forearm as he brushed a curl from my forehead. "I need to be inside you. I want to make love to you, Angel. But it needs to be just you and me in this room. No pasts. No pain. Only pleasure. So you're going to stare into my eyes the whole time. You're going to see every bit of what I do to you." He trailed a finger along my lips. "Of what you do to me." Looking me square in the eyes, he commanded, "Understood?"

I merely nodded in response, the weight of his finger on my lips too much of a distraction. It was hard to believe only a few months ago I'd freaked out and told him never to do that again. But things were different now. *I* was different now.

I sucked it into my mouth and groaned, loving the taste of just that small piece of him. The sweet, saltiness of his skin.

With a grunt, Blake covered my lips with his, his tongue mingling with his finger inside my mouth, and then he broke the kiss, his breathing heavy.

"Touch me. Everywhere." Leaning up, I closed the small distance between our faces and swiped my tongue across his lips. "Please."

Wildness filled his eyes as if I'd given him a green light and unleashed something deep within him. Something he'd been holding back all this time, surely for my benefit. But right now, nothing would benefit me more than becoming one with him.

Blake flicked his fingers to the clasp between my breasts, and they spilled out for him. He dipped his head, sucking one hard tip into his mouth, and dragged his teeth along it. My body bucked at the sensation of it and then he moved, paying equal attention to the other. His mouth never left me as he kissed a line down my belly and across my navel, his hands slipping into the lace at my hips and pulling it down my legs. Sitting back on his heels, he crumpled them and discarded them onto the floor.

I realized how much preparing he'd actually done when he reached over to the nightstand, extracting a foil packet from its drawer. I covered his hand with my own. "Don't. I want to feel you."

He looked at me, a huge question in his eyes.

"I'm on birth control and have never, um . . . been unprotected. It's safe."

"You sure?"

"Positive. I don't want anything between us."

Blake tossed the packet aside. "You don't have to ask me twice. I've never been unprotected either, and the thought of feeling you bare . . ." He shuddered.

I wanted him so badly my body ached, every cell sensitized and waiting.

Straddling me at the knees, Blake stared at me. "You look amazing right now, naked and waiting. Your cheeks all flushed, breasts full." He placed a hand over my chest feeling the frenzied rhythm. "So gorgeous. I want to remember this moment forever. I wish I could take a picture."

I skidded my bare foot up his chest. "How about if I just look like this for you over and over and over—and over."

Something in him turned primal. He grabbed my calf and bit down. "Stop me if it's too much, but I can't hold back anymore." Blake dropped my ankle to his shoulder and leaned forward, letting his swollen erection lay on my belly.

I watched, breathless, as he teased me, dragging his cock back slowly, leaving a trail of pre-cum in its wake. He positioned himself at my entrance and I braced myself, fisting the comforter at my sides. He took himself in his hand and rubbed it over my sex, spreading my juices from my opening to my clit and back down again. "Already wet for me, baby. I love it. I love you."

"I love you, too."

Hearing him affirm it one more time before we took the last step was just what I needed. He pushed in slowly, testing my limits, and I relaxed even more, knowing he'd get in easier if I did.

I sucked in a ragged breath, tilting my hips, and he was able to slide in the rest of the way so his pelvis rested against my wet folds.

I felt full.

Complete.

My missing piece.

Blake trembled, using all of his willpower to remain still and be sure I was okay. I cupped the side of his face and nodded, and he dropped forward, surrounding me with his body and my leg fell into the crease of his elbow. He pulled back, only to push in more forcefully, and I dug my nails into his back, pushing my chest up to meet his, a hiss escaping my lips.

"Keep going," I whispered in his ear.

That little bit of encouragement was all he needed, and he began tapping into me at a quick, fluid rhythm. "God, you feel so good. So bare. I can feel every bit of you. Fucking amazing."

My own breathing picked up, the sound of flesh meeting flesh turning me on.

He slowed his pace, reaching deep inside me, pulling back, and then pushing deep within my core again. I moaned his name in total ecstasy. Each thrust made me feel more whole, our bodies slick with sweat sliding off one another.

Blake growled in my ear, "You're mine, Angel." Pushing deeper with each word, he repeated, "Mine. Say it."

"I'm yours," the words barely audible from my breathless mouth.

"Fucking scream it."

"I'm yours!"

"Yes!" He slowed his pace, dipping his tongue into my mouth. "I love you, Angel. More than I've ever loved anything."

"I love you, too," I breathed. "Come for me. I want to feel you inside my body."

With that, Blake lost all control. He dropped my leg, and I wrapped them around his waist, knowing what he liked. I used them to hoist myself up, allowing him to penetrate me as deep as possible. My body held tight to his erection as tension built until neither of us could hold on to it any longer. We came together, my channel clenching, milking his hot arousal deep within me. Somehow we never lost eye contact the whole time until he fell, burying his face in my hair and kissing a soft line up my neck.

We laid in silence for a few moments, trying to gain a hold of our breathing. Blake wrapped his arms around me and pulled me close, tucking me deep into his side, kissing the top of my head. I needed him that close, unable to see my face as a tear leaked out of the corner of my eye and rolled into my hairline.

Blake pulled back, looking at me. "Angel? You okay? Did I hurt you?"

"No, you were perfect. Everything about this day was perfect. I'm just happy. I never thought I'd be happy again, and I never thought something that was always so disgusting to me could feel so good and so beautiful."

"That's all it'll ever be, baby. I knew we would be that good together. In my gut. I just knew. Now you know, too." He tapped me on the
nose, the way he liked to do.

Complete contentment washed over me as the long day made itself
known and my eyelids weighted down. Blake traced small circles on my
shoulder blade with his thumb as I sank deeper into him. I blinked rapidly to stay awake, nervous my night terrors might find me, but eventually
I succumbed and sleep took hold.

Chapter 24

I FELT SOMETHING. EYES? A presence? Where was I? My eyes burst open and I sucked back a breath.

Blake's hand shot out, soothing down my arm. "Calm down, Angel. It's just me."

"Blake?"

I sat upright, holding the sheet protectively to my chest. I looked around the room as memories of last night came flooding back, and I finally relaxed back into the bed. Blake propped his head in his hand, the sheet draped low on his hip, showcasing his bare chest, and I bit down on my lip, soaking up the beauty of him.

I looked around, noting how dark it still was. "Did you sleep?"

"Nope. I couldn't." Blake looked down, worrying his lip.

"Why not? You feel okay?" I asked, immediately concerned he was having second thoughts.

"Yeah, I'm fine." He patted my hip. "I just . . . I was nervous is all. I didn't want to wake up and find you gone. That you had regrets or something and ran out on me." He shrugged, his gaze skirting away.

"So you stared at me all night?" I frowned at him in the moonlight.

"Something like that."

It was my turn to comfort him. "Blake, I told you I'm with you now. Sleep, crazy."

He sighed, knowing I was right. "Old habits I guess. But I'm glad I did. You're cute when you sleep." He smiled his adorable smile and kissed my nose. "You murmur and breathe heavy, and I'm pretty sure I heard my name once or twice and something about a cupcake."

That made my mouth water. Why'd he have to mention those damn cupcakes? I hadn't had one since . . .

Blake reached behind him, pulling something off the nightstand and setting it in front of me. "Do over?"

A cupcake sat majestically in its clear container. I scrambled to a sitting position and crossed my legs in front of me, nodding my head emphatically.

Blake popped the lid, and swiped his finger through the cream, leaving it raised in the air for me to do what I liked. "This time, you're getting the full experience."

I pushed up on my knees and took his finger, putting it to his lips to trail the icing there. His breath weighted, and I smiled before licking it off and sucking his lower lip into my mouth.

Blake growled. "So you're playing dirty, I see."

"Filthy," I panted.

"Well, then, let the games begin." Blake picked off a piece of the edge and popped the cake in my mouth. I giggled and then broke off a piece, doing the same to him. Blake's next slice was bigger. It was the whole length of the cupcake including the icing. He brought it to my lips and I widened my mouth, trying to accommodate it. When I couldn't, I decided to start nibbling from the bottom, sucking on Blake's fingers along the way.

Before I could finish, Blake's mouth came crashing into mine, trapping the oversized bite between us. His tongue mingled with bits of cake and icing in my mouth, creating the most delicious concoction I ever imagined. He pushed me back on the bed, both of us devouring each other. When he broke the kiss to retrieve another piece, our faces glistened with moistened chocolate.

He took the next bit of icing and brought it to my neck, trailing it down and then around my nipple before dragging his tongue along the same path. Blake sucked and nipped, eating the cream off me as all of my sexual parts awakened. My nipples pebbled, my breasts became fuller, and I was soaked again between my thighs.

I clamped my legs around his waist and flipped him beneath me so

I could reciprocate in kind. I spread the icing over his cock and drizzled crumbs up his six pack, first sucking him off, then dragging my tongue to pick up the scattered cake along his taut skin.

Blake's moans echoed throughout the room, fueling me further. With a growl, he tossed me on my back, hunger radiating from his eyes. He took what was left and smeared it over my belly, rubbing it onto my clit, and then his mouth was on me again, licking and nibbling me into oblivion. When he spread me open and found the sweet spot at the apex of my thighs, I cried out, the sensations too much to hold on to. Blake sucked up every last drop before holding my knees apart and pushing his glistening cock inside of me.

Our slick bodies moved with force and determination. Instead of the slow and tender love making we'd done a few hours ago, this was insatiable—fucking, needy, and ravenous. I didn't know who was more intent on proving they needed the other more, but with each push and pull, I suspected we were both on equal measure.

Blake leaned back on his heels, pulling me with him to settle over his lap. Fondling my breast in one hand, he guided my hip with the other, grinding and rolling while his tongue hungrily invaded my mouth. I followed his lead, moving how he liked, clenching the walls of my sex so it dragged along his steely erection. He penetrated so much deeper that way. Every time I lowered myself, he touched a new place, further inside me, closer to my heart, obliterating another piece of the wall that surrounded it.

Our panting breaths filled the room. The feel of his muscles wrapped securely around me, his tight core gliding against my belly as he sucked on the soft exposed skin of my neck, sent tingles racing over my flesh. The buildup consumed me until it was too much. I wrapped my arms tight around his neck, he did the same to my waist, and we came together, squeezing as though we wanted to mesh into one another and truly become one being.

My release pulsed around him, mingling with the hot flood of his. Then Blake took my mouth, hanging onto me tight, and scooped my breath into his lungs. We stayed like that, joined at the hips for a long time, kissing slow and steady as our breathing evened out.

Blake looked to the window and rolled onto his back, taking me with him. I giggled as he rolled again, sending us off the bed and to our feet. "Stay there." He ran to the bathroom, and I stared at his tight ass. He quickly reappeared covered in a fluffy white robe, and I couldn't help but be disappointed.

He smiled at my pout and held open the matching set. "Put this on. We'll wash up after. We need to hurry."

I slipped my arms through the soft sleeves, and he brought his arms around my middle to fasten the strap around my waist.

Back in the naughty elevator, we exited onto the roof once again as a rosy hue started to peek out from beneath the earth. Blake secured two mugs of coffee from the station, and we settled on a lounger with the perfect view of the sunrise.

I drew my knees up, and he straddled me from behind, allowing me to rest back on his chest as an array of vibrant colors poked out of the sky. During my sleepless nights, I'd seen many a sunrise, but none were as beautiful as this one. Usually, they left me feeling abnormal and helpless—highlighting the fact I was still awake while the world slept, watching different hues bleed together as I stared blankly through a veil of tears.

But this time was different.

Maybe it was the company or the change in circumstances or maybe the change in me. Whatever it was, I was grateful for it, and I was grateful for the man sitting behind me, staring off into the horizon.

Blake took a few pictures of the colorful sky and then turned the camera so it faced us. "Smile." He snapped. After a moment, he spoke from behind me, still looking past my shoulder. "Spend Thanksgiving with me, Eva. I'll take you to the parade, and then you can eat some turkey with my family."

I turned my head to look at him. "Yeah? You don't think it's too soon?" Truthfully, I was ecstatic at the prospect of not having to go home. But I didn't want to rush things.

Blake cocked his head, his eyebrows squishing together. "Too soon for what? You're not going anywhere, so we might as well just bite the bullet. Besides, I don't want to be away from you anymore."

A slow smile crept across my lips. "I don't want to be away from you anymore either."

"So you'll come?" He seemed as though he'd stopped breathing and was hanging by a thread waiting for my reaction.

I bit my lip, knowing how important holidays were to my family and how long it'd been since they'd seen me. "My parents won't be too happy about it, but sure, I'll come."

Blake tightened his arms around my waist and drew me closer, talking into my hair. "Thank you."

The next few minutes were spent in silence as the sun made its debut, signaling the start of a new day. I thought today would have been awkward, but it was the furthest thing from it. If anything I felt more secure than I had yesterday. I wondered if Blake felt the same way. After the roller coaster ride that had been "us", it felt good to finally stand still and just be with each other.

Be with him.

That's all he'd ever asked for in all of this and now that I was, I didn't know why I'd resisted for so long. Nothing ever felt as right as when I was wrapped up in his arms. I'd tried so hard to protect us both, thinking this would make me feel exposed and unguarded, but the truth was I'd never felt so safe and secure in all my life. Not even before . . .

No, I wouldn't go there.

Although it felt like a lifetime ago I'd walked away from all that, it was only a few short months and the "problem" still lingered. Though now a state away, at some point I would have to go home and face it. I just didn't know how it would play out this time. Things were different now. I was finally noticing the change in me, and I wasn't about to go backward.

I'd spent the night with a man, made love to him, and at no point did I freak out. That was huge. Monumental. Somehow in the short period of time I'd known Blake, he'd become my center. I wasn't sure how he did it, but I felt like he'd been chipping away at my outer layers, exposing me, and then covering me back up before anyone could notice. I owed a lot to him for that—my life. He'd given me one.

"Angel?" Blake's soft voice stirred me from my thoughts, and I jumped.

"Yes?"

"How 'bout that shower?" He pretended not to notice I'd slipped away, but his eyes told another story.

His chin was settled on my shoulder, and I stared at his plump lips. I spun to fold myself into his lap and caress his mouth with my own, anxious to rid my mind of the place it was headed. His tongue still tasted sweet like cupcake, laced with coffee. "On one condition. You have to clean every inch of me spotless. I'm a very dirty girl."

He growled into my mouth, slipping a hand into my robe to swirl around my nipple. "How about I lick you clean first, and then I scrub you down after? Just to make sure I don't miss any spots." He pinched my nipple and I gasped.

Jumping from the chair, I yanked him up and sprinted to the elevator, dragging a chuckling Blake behind me.

Chapter 25

MY FIRST TIME WITH BLAKE was over a week ago, and I still got chills thinking about it. Every time we'd been together since just deepened our connection further, making me wonder how I'd ever survived without him. With everything I'd been through, I never thought I could hand myself over to someone, but with Blake it just felt natural. Like it was what I was supposed to do.

Still, negative thoughts popped into my head randomly, but I was working on pushing them away as quickly as they came. And although they'd become less frequent, I still awoke with night terrors periodically. I knew I had a long road ahead, but I was proud of myself for standing on the road at all, instead of staring at it from behind a bush.

I swept a speck of lint from my neatly pressed dress pants and fixed the shoulders of my flowy, flowery top. "Are you sure this is okay to wear to meet your parents?"

Blake placed his chin on my shoulder, wrapped his arms around me, and spoke to my reflection in the full length mirror. "You could wear a potato sack, and you'd still be gorgeous."

I was still thawing out from the Macy's Thanksgiving Day Parade. We'd gotten up with the birds, dressed extra warm, and set up folding chairs right at the start in the front lines. We'd cuddled and laughed and drank hot cocoa. I couldn't help my excitement seeing Santa at the end. Seeing him for real, up close, made me forget he was just a childhood fantasy. Like a kid, eyes squeezed shut, I wished with all my might that

I'd get everything I wanted for Christmas. Though, I already had most of what I wanted in Blake.

I turned to the side, examining myself further. "Are you sure? It doesn't look like I'm trying too hard?"

Blake took my hands and turned me away from the mirror. "You're perfect. Now stop worrying."

I brushed my hands over his sweater, smoothing out any crinkles, and adjusted his cowlick collar. "Wanna just stay here and show me what I have to be thankful for all day?" I smiled a toothy grin, batting my eye-lashes.

"Tempting, but we can't." Blake laced his fingers with mine and walked me from the bedroom. "But I do promise to show you just how thankful *I* am later." He moved my hand to the hard bulge straining through his dark denim jeans.

I stroked its length and it got even harder, if that was possible. "Why don't you let me take care of that for you?"

"Oh, you will." He smirked. "Don't worry. But right now we have to go. My mom hates when the food gets cold." He kissed the tip of my nose, adjusted himself, and tugged me along.

WE STOOD OUTSIDE A DELUXE Brownstone on the upper east side of Manhattan and I stared up at its overwhelming clout.

"You ready?" Blake asked and I replied with a curt nod. He slipped an arm over my shoulder and guided me inside.

Blake rapped his knuckles on the door a couple of times before pushing it open. A girl with the same stunning features as him squealed and threw her arms around his neck, jerking him away from me.

"Lakey!"

Lakey?

"I couldn't wait for you to get here!" She turned her lips to his ear, lowering her voice. "These two are driving me insane."

Unraveling her arms, she looked down at me with friendly, sparkling blue eyes and a gleaming smile. She was blessed with the same height as Blake, as well as his beauty. "And you must be my new best friend." Her arms grabbed me in a choke hold, and I patted her back with one hand, looking at Blake questioningly. Just barely his junior, he'd said she was colorful, but I wasn't expecting full, crayon box colorful.

"N-Nice to meet you. Victoria, I'm guessing?"

"Tori, Tor-Tor, whatever you want. Come in." She looped her arm through mine.

Blake smirked, shoving his hands in his pockets, and kicked the door closed.

"Mom, Blake's home!" Victoria called as she pulled me through an enormous entryway. The black and white checkered tiles and spotless appearance were a cool contrast to the vibrant and lively souls Blake and his sister were. I had a hard time envisioning them growing up here.

We entered a beautifully designed kitchen, loaded with top-of-the-line appliances and granite countertops. A striking older woman turned and wiped her hands on her apron. Though shorter than her offspring, she had the same kind, piercing eyes and sharp features. Blake stood behind me, covering my shoulders with his hands, and I immediately relaxed, grateful for his support.

"Isn't she pretty, Mom? Look at that hair." Victoria swirled a golden lock in her fingers.

I blushed, stepping forward. "Nice to meet you, Mrs. Turner."

"Call me Elaine. Please." She gave me a chaste hug and then withdrew, folding her hands neatly in front of her.

"Elaine." I smiled. "I'm Eva."

Elaine chuckled. "My son is so enchanted, he never told us your real name. I just assumed it actually *was* Angel."

"It is," Blake retorted.

"Stop it." I nudged him with my elbow.

Elaine took in our banter, looking back and forth between us, seeming to size up our relationship, and then a warm smile spread across her face. "Finally, something makes my boy happy. I should thank you, Eva."

The heat of a blush warmed my cheeks. "Don't thank me. I've made him miserable for the last few months. He's the one making *me* happy." I pulled Blake to my side and circled my arms around his trim waist.

He kissed my temple. "Don't listen to her, Mom. She really is an angel, and I've never been happier."

A sharp clearing of a throat caused all heads to turn, and a large man filled the entire frame of the door. "Blake."

"Father." Blake's smile waned and he squared his shoulders, never removing his hand from the small of my back. "I'd like you to meet my girlfriend, Eva."

"Nice to meet you, Evangelina." He took a few steps and extended a stiff hand to me, holding a glass filled with amber liquid in the other.

I shook his hand, suddenly feeling meek and small. *How did he know my full name?* Blake and his mom had made it clear he'd never told them. How much had he found out about me? My heart thumped, but I kept my cool. "Nice to meet you too, sir. You have a lovely home."

"Yes, thank you." He brushed me off, looking past me to his wife. "Elaine, is the food almost ready? I've had enough waiting for these two. I'm starved."

"Daddy!" Victoria cried, her cheeks turning a pinkish hue.

Elaine shooed her husband away. "It's coming, Jack. Go wait in the dining room. It'll be right out."

He took one more judging look at Blake and my intertwined hands and walked out, the ice clinking in the glass.

I let out a big puff of air and looked to Blake who was stiff as nails, a visible tic in his jaw. I reached up and soothed a hand over his cheek and his eyes flicked to mine, bringing him back from wherever he was. I offered him a reassuring smile.

"Don't pay him any mind." Blake's mom grabbed each of our hands and moved us from the door. Handing all three of us different dishes, she went back to the refrigerator and extracted drinks. "Bring those to the dining room, and I'll be right in."

Blake bent so only I could hear him. "I'm sorry. If you're uncomfortable we can go. I didn't think he'd do this today, but I should've known better."

"I'm fine," I reassured him. I wasn't, but for him I would be.

Victoria flanked my other side. "Don't let him bully you. He eats the weak for breakfast. You need thick skin to survive in this house, and I want you to stick around."

Her words opened my heart to her even more. I had no intention of not "sticking around". Wearing a huge smile, I took a deep breath and entered the dining room with my head held high.

Mr. Turner looked up briefly. He pushed his drink in front of him and folded his hands, scrutinizing me like the common criminals he came across every day.

I knew Blake and his dad didn't have the best of relationships, but this was insane. My heart constricted for the man I'd grown to love, knowing how badly he yearned for this wretched man's approval. Suddenly, I was desperate to help any way I could.

I placed my tray in the center of the table, and Mr. Turner wasted no time scooping his portion. "So, Eva, no family looking to see you on Thanksgiving?"

I cleared my throat, impervious to his brashness. "Actually, they were pretty disappointed I wasn't coming home, but it was important to Blake that I meet his family, and we didn't want to be apart for the holidays."

"So you put the wishes of someone you just met ahead of your family?" Mr. Turner raised his eyebrows in a disapproving manner.

"Not at all," I countered but kept my tone friendly. "I'll see my family for Christmas, and I'd hardly classify Blake as someone I just met. We've grown quite close." I filled my dish with a heaping spoonful of stuffing and covered Blake's hand with my own.

Blake squeezed my fingers. "I'll be with Eva and her family for Christmas."

My eyes darted to his, then quickly away. I hoped my shock would go unnoticed. Blake just looked to me like his mind was made up and that would be that.

I unconsciously squirmed in my seat. I hadn't thought about it since he'd brought it up on our date.

"Does your mother know about that?" Jack asked.

"Do I know about what?" Elaine entered the room, carrying the turkey, and I hurried from my seat to make room on the table.

"Thank you, dear." She brushed her hands on her apron and then untied it, hanging it over the back of her chair before taking a seat. "So, fill me in. What don't I know?"

"I'll be spending Christmas with Angel, Mom. I'd like to meet her family, and we want to be together for the holidays."

Elaine tensed, clearly uncomfortable with the situation, but seemed to gauge her reaction carefully as I was sure she'd had to do over the years around her husband. "Well, that's disappointing. You know how I love to see your reaction Christmas morning. But I guess it's time for me to let that go now that you're not a little boy anymore." She smiled a small smile that didn't meet her eyes, and my heart broke a little for the woman trapped inside who probably hadn't shown her true face in years.

It dawned on me that Blake had lived his life the same way I had. A lost soul trapped in his own skin. Never able to be himself, even in his own home. We were more alike than I'd thought.

I suddenly associated Mr. Turner in the same category as the person who'd locked *me* away, and I grew cold. I calculated each word from that point on with venom on my tongue. I wanted him to know what a piece of shit he was for making me feel unwelcome in his home. For making his own *son* feel unwelcome in his home.

I plastered the biggest smile I'd ever worn across my face and laced my fingers with Blake's. "My mom will be ecstatic you're coming home with me. She loves to spoil new guests and anyone who I care about is family in her book. She'll love you."

"Sounds like fun. Can I come?" Victoria called from the opposite side of the table.

I grinned at her. "The more the merrier. Holidays are huge in my house. You'll have a blast."

Elaine gasped. "You're not serious, are you, Victoria? I need to have *one* of you here for Christmas."

"You're welcome to come too, Elaine." I smiled at her.

Elaine blushed, looking down at her napkin, and I hoped I hadn't taken it too far.

"Don't worry, Mom. I'll stay with you." Victoria put her arm around her mother's neck and squeezed.

Jack cleared his throat, switching from one uncomfortable topic to another. "So, Eva, what's your major?"

"Psychology," I answered, but I was sure he already knew.

"Psychology?" He held his fork in a fist, chewing on a lump of turkey as he scrutinized me. "So you plan to deal with tiddlywinks for the rest of your life?" He sliced another piece of meat.

I blinked. "Excuse me?"

He raised one condescending eyebrow. "Hardly seems like a stable career when your clients are one pill shy of a loony bin. Ever thought about law, young lady?"

My blood boiled beneath the surface. *Pompous fucking ass.* "Law? No. Excuse me if I'm being too bold, but that's just too drab for me. I want to help people."

He rested a forearm to the edge of the table and narrowed his eyes at me. "And you don't think representing those in need is helping?"

"I . . ." I gulped. "I didn't mean to imply what you do isn't important. I just—"

Blake cut in, rescuing me from my blunder. "Eva sings too, Dad. Very well. I'm thinking of making her famous." He smiled in an attempt to sway his father.

"Well, then maybe you *are* the perfect match for my son. He has his head in the clouds too, thinking an artist can be anything but nothing in this life."

I felt the air pouring heavier out of my nostrils, but I kept my cool. Barely. "There are plenty of people who make a decent living doing what they love."

"Yes, a rare few who make it. The rest don't have a pot to piss in, and I'm not about to let my idiotic son ruin his chance at a good life."

Okay, last straw. "Your *son* is quite talented, Mr. Turner. You'd know that if you knew who he was."

Blake stiffened beside me.

Mr. Turner's face reddened. "I'll let that pass since this is your first time in this house, but you'll keep in mind that this *is my* house." Dropping his napkin to the table, he gave me a look that should have slaughtered me.

I took a deep breath, steadying myself as I attempted to plead with a man who might have been the most unreasonable in the world. Though I was never able to do it for myself, I would be strong for him. I softened my voice. "Sorry, sir, but you really should see him for who he is. He's no stuffy suit. Those law classes you make him take make him miserable."

"Eva—" Blake tried to interject but was quickly cut off.

"Miserable? Success is what brings happiness, young lady. A struggling artist won't be happy at the end of a bread line when he's got mouths to feed." He pushed back from the table and stood. "Now, if you'll excuse me."

As he exited the room, I looked down in my lap, strangling my fingers, both ashamed and infuriated. I hadn't meant for things to get that heated and ruin their family's holiday, but I couldn't let him talk to us that way.

Blake put his hand on my thigh. "I told you not to go there. Why do you think I never do?"

"I'm so sorry. I ruined Thanksgiving for all of you." My eyes began to fill as the enormity of what I'd done hit me. I just couldn't bear to see Blake belittled that way.

"Now, there will be none of that," Elaine reassured me.

Victoria chimed in. "Yeah, babe, we're used to this. You're just new, that's all. Don't let him get the better of you."

I looked around at their understanding, compassionate faces in awe. They should be furious with me for ruining the small amount of time they got to spend together, yet somehow they looked like they felt just as bad as I did.

"Well, now I know where Blake gets his kindness from. You guys are amazing."

Blake kissed my cheek and then stood, straightening his back. His face was serious, his jaw tight. "I'm going to have a talk with my *father*."

I grabbed his arm, and he immediately flexed. "Wait, please. Maybe this isn't the best idea. You already have enough problems with him."

"Angel, we aren't having this discussion. I don't care what him or anyone else thinks. And it's time he knew that."

"Blake, I'll go." Elaine stood.

"Sit down, Mom. I'm a grown man. I can handle this. No one talks to my girl that way. I don't care who he is."

With a tight nod, Elaine reclaimed her seat, worry lines crinkling her forehead. When Blake left the room, she turned her focus to me. "I'd like to apologize for my husband's less than hospitable behavior."

"It's all right, really. I was forewarned." I gave her a small smile. "You've been more than welcoming."

"He does mean well." The corners of her mouth dipped. "He has a funny way of showing it, but he only wants what he believes is best for us."

I didn't have a kind word to say about that man, so I just nodded, my lips pursed in a tight line. "I'm going to find Blake and make sure he's okay."

I followed the sound of raised voices until I came upon a closed door. I hadn't meant to eavesdrop, but before I knew it, I found myself inching closer, trying to make out what they were saying.

"I don't think she's appropriate for you." Mr. Turner's stern voice held no room for discussion.

My heart sank. This was just another thing Blake felt strongly about that his father was knocking down as if what he wanted didn't matter.

"You don't even know her."

"I know enough. Your head is supposed to be focused on your career, not lounging in the clouds with some girl."

"I'm doing what I have to do, same as I always did. And she's not just some girl. Nothing you can say will ever make me feel differently about her, Dad. I'm sorry. You can't have your way this time."

"I only want what's best for you, son."

"She *is* what's best for me. I'm doing what you want. I'm pursuing a career in law that I can't stand, but I will not let you tell me who I should and shouldn't fall in love with. This girl means a lot to me, and I'd appreciate it if you'd apologize for the way you treated her."

There was a brief pause before he continued and my heart swelled with pride hearing him put his foot down, but broke at the same time for the pain he probably felt having to do it. "She's not like us, Dad. And she doesn't deserve it. If you want to see me, you'll have to accept her because she's with me now and that's it. I let you control enough aspects of my life." Blake's tone was hard and cold, but I heard the hurt laced in his words.

"Is that so? You'll watch how you talk to me, boy. I'm still your father. We'll finish this discussion another day. Right now it's Thanksgiving, and your mom went to a lot of trouble cooking for everyone."

"You finish it. I'm leaving."

Wow. He'd finally stood up for something—me. I was so proud of him.

There was a rustling, and I slowly backed away, not wanting to get caught. The door flew open, revealing a red-faced Blake. Anger rolled off him, but behind his eyes was a lost little boy and my heart ached for him. For how he must have been feeling. I knew he said what he needed to say, but I also knew it wasn't easy for him.

He stopped short, flexing his jaw, and then took my hand and pulled. "Come on. We're leaving."

"Wha—I," I stammered, trying my best to keep up with his rushed pace.

"Blake!" Mr. Turner's voice boomed from behind us, but Blake kept his course.

"Goodbye, Mom. Eva doesn't deserve to be treated this way. I'll call you later." He gave his mom a quick kiss on the cheek.

"No," she cried. "Please. Wait. I'll fix it."

"You can't. No one can fix him." Blake continued to drag me around the dining room. He kissed Victoria next, who just looked down at her lap, lost for words. For the first time, I saw the scared little girl in her as well.

Blake pulled me out of the house with such force I was tripping over myself. When we were finally on the sidewalk, I yanked my arm back, trying to stop my feet along the concrete. "Blake, wait! Just hold up a minute."

"No. I told you I'd protect you, and that includes from my father."

"Well, I don't think he likes me very much." I rushed alongside him again.

"I don't think he likes *himself* very much." Blake looked straight ahead, undeterred in his stride.

"Can you just stop for a second. I'm getting runner's cramp here."

Blake stopped short, and I collided into him. I cleared my throat and smoothed my hands down my jacket. "I think we should go back."

He frowned. "You're nuts. I'm not going back there."

"I'm serious, Blake. You don't get to see them, and your mom looked heartbroken. I'm sure she put a lot of work into today. I can handle him."

"You shouldn't have to handle him," he argued.

I nodded. "Well, I can deal with him then. For you."

Dropping his head, Blake fisted his hips.

I took his hands, ducking my head under his to reach his eyes. "Hey," I said softly.

Without lifting his head, he met my gaze, uncertain and questioning.

"I know you want to be there, and I want to be there with you." I squared my shoulders. "We'll be a united front. That's probably the biggest step you've ever taken with him, and you did it for me. That's huge and I appreciate it. I'm sure he got the message. Now let's be the bigger people. What do you say?"

Blake let out a huge puff of air. "I'm shaking, Angel. Look at me." He raised an unsteady hand.

I turned it over and kissed his palm. "You're strong and you have me. You'll be fine. Let's just go back. It'll make you feel better."

"How could you want to go back there?"

"Because I love you, and your mom and Victoria are awesome. Let's go make it right."

Blake studied me, considering my proposition. The corner of his mouth twitched. "Did it hurt?"

"Did what hurt?"

"When you fell from heaven?" He smirked.

I rolled my eyes. "Oh, please. I think we're past the cheesy one-liners, don't you? Come on, we can still make dessert."

Back in the hallway, we stood for a moment staring at the same brown metal door we'd entered a few hours prior. Blake took a fortifying inhale and creaked the door open, letting the sound of irate voices spill out.

Rounding the corner to the dining room, a red-faced Elaine wept as Victoria held her shoulders.

Mr. Turner was sitting stoic in his chair, rolling another full amber colored glass between his fingers.

Blake cleared his throat, and all eyes turned on us. I fidgeted at his side and squeezed his hand for support. "You have this girl to thank that we're back." Blake nodded in my direction.

I ducked my head and tucked a strand of hair behind my ear.

A frantic Elaine stepped forward. "He's sorry. Aren't you, Jack?" Her pointed stare landed on her husband.

Jack cleared his throat. "Yes, um, Eva. I behaved poorly. I'd like to get to know you better . . . if you'll stay."

"Of course." I raised my chin at that. It was a small victory, but a victory nonetheless. "And I'm sorry if I came off a bit snarky. I just care a great deal about your son."

"Yes. Well, that gives us something in common then." Although he seemed sincere, I could see something tucked behind his apology. I wasn't convinced he wasn't done with me.

For the first time, Blake relaxed at my side, gesturing for me to take my seat at the table while Elaine rushed to fill it with dessert.

The rest of the evening went smoother. Though I wouldn't call Blake's dad amicable, he wasn't outwardly rude. I guessed that counted for something. We said our goodbyes, and I exchanged numbers with my new best friend Tori.

I wrapped my hand around Blake's, keeping it warm as we began our walk back to my apartment. "See? Aren't you glad we went back?"

His eyes remained focused ahead, but the sexy smirk tipping his lips told me I was right.

I nudged his side with my elbow, and he finally looked over at me, a smile spreading across his face.

"Okay, Angel . . . I'm glad we went back."

With our hands intertwined, we continued our walk. The full moon stared back at me as I gazed up, wishing on the brightest star I could find. I wished everything would turn out okay for us. That we would always be this happy and nothing would come along and pop the bubble we were living in. But part of that bubble was a charade, and the burden of it was wearing on me. I didn't want there to be anything between us any-more, but how could I tell him? It would all be out then, and I'd not only chance losing him but my family as well.

A knot formed in my belly. I had to bring up the Christmas thing now that he'd blurted out he planned to come. Was I ready for him to meet my family? To be smack dab in the middle of my nightmare?

"Blake?" My voice was quiet, unlike the harsh beating in my chest.

His hand squeezed mine. "Yeah?"

"About Christmas . . ."

He stopped abruptly, his face stern as his body went rigid. "That's not a topic up for debate. I'm going with you. I may not know the whole story, but I know whatever happened to you happened there, and I'll be damned if I let you go back there without me."

Warring emotions pulled me in every direction. Though the thought of him finding out made me nauseous, a weird sense of calm washed over me knowing I'd be protected. That nothing would happen to me this time. So I'd figure it out. I always did.

I nodded and resolved to not let him know what I'd been thinking. "I was just going to say that you'll have to fight Jace to sit shotgun. He's not going to be happy about this."

Blake relaxed and tugged my arm. I slammed into his chest, wrapping my arms around him as he pushed his nose into my hair. "Well, that's a chance I'll have to take."

Seemed we'd both be taking a chance come the next holiday.

Chapter 26

I SPIT OUT THE PEN crammed into my mouth. "I can't study with you staring at me like that."

"Then stop looking so hot while you read. Biting that pen and shit . . . there's only so much a man can take, woman." Blake's eyebrows danced over his glittering irises.

I uncrossed my legs and pushed up off my belly, pulling them Indian style on Blake's bed. "This isn't gonna work. It's finals week. This is important and you're distracting me. I've finally pulled my grades out of the shitter and you're gonna make me fail if you keep looking at me like I'm dinner."

"Excuse me? I do believe I'm the reason your grades are where they are, thank you very little." Blake brushed his toes over mine, further distracting me.

"And now you're rubbing those sexy friggin' feet on me. Stop it! Focus! You're no help anymore."

"I'm sorry, but I can't help myself. Your hair all knotted up and popping out in seventy-five different directions is turning me the fuck on."

"Idiot." I laughed. "Ugh. I'm so stressed over this." I slammed my head back on the pillow.

"Let me relax you then." Blake crawled up my body, settling over me.

"No, thank you. I have to get this done. God, you're the worst." I turned my head to the side, unable to bear the weight of his heated gaze.

Two more seconds and I'd fold.

"The best. You meant the best," he corrected, dipping down to lick the soft exposed skin beneath my ear.

Tingles raged across my skin. "Yes. The best at being the worst." My head bent toward the warmth spreading on my neck.

Blake put his lips to my ear, whispering, "I want you."

My voice dipped low as I swore, "Fuck me . . ."

"Yes, please." He smiled against my neck and nibbled.

My head relaxed into the pillow and a soft moan escaped my lips, giving away my weakness. "Another hour. Just let me study one more hour."

"Okay, Angel. I'll let you study . . . *in* one more hour." Blake kicked the papers out of the way and pushed up on his arms, grinding into my pelvis.

I gave in.

Lord, did I give in.

I SPOTTED BLAKE ACROSS CAMPUS. Running full speed, I leaped and wrapped my legs around him. "I got a ninety-seven!"

Blake twirled me around. "Congrats, babe. I'll let you thank me later." His dimple greeted me whole-heartedly.

"Always taking all the credit," I scoffed. "It was my brain that took the test, ya know."

He gave me a naughty grin. "Yes, but it was my dick that pounded the information into you."

My cheeks flushed as memories of Blake's unorthodox teaching methods flooded my thoughts.

A hearty, sexy laugh rumbled in Blake's chest. "I want to take you somewhere to celebrate. You need to unwind."

"Where?"

"Just dress warm. I'll be by in twenty." Blake set me on my feet and slapped me on the ass, sending me scooting away, as I rubbed my sore bottom. He and Jace wouldn't quit with that.

To keep Bertha from getting lonely, we stopped there first before venturing out on Blake's little excursion. It'd been pretty cold and she was starting to look depressed, but she seemed happy to see us, so we didn't rush. By the time we left, her branches were extra perky.

A short train ride brought us to mid-town. Blake insisted on covering my eyes while we walked. My heel caught on his toe, and I tripped for the umpteenth time.

"This is awkward. Are we almost there?"

"Almost. Haven't you learned you need to have patience with me yet?" Blake stopped walking and turned me to the left. "Now you can look."

He dropped his hands, and my head fell back to take in the enormous tree before me.

Glittering lights lined every inch. It was so tall, it seemed to go up to the clouds. I stared at the golden statue of the Greek God Prometheus, contemplating the irony that I, myself, was standing next to my own God as well. I took in all of the beauty. I'd never come to see the tree at Rockefeller Center before.

Flash.

I blinked repeatedly, trying to focus on Blake.

"Sorry. I gotta take my moments." He moved his line of sight to the tree and snapped another photo.

I frowned. "You really do have to start warning me when you do that. You're going to blind me one of these days. I'm seeing spots now."

"Nonsense. Then it wouldn't be the spontaneous shot that I'm looking for." Blake laced his fingers with mine and tugged me alongside him. "So can you skate?"

I shrugged. "Kinda. I can't do anything fancy, but I liked to skate when I was little."

We approached the rental counter, and my mind drifted as Blake ordered our skates.

Giggles echoed in my ears, children playing, and I felt myself being swept away by a memory.

"Damon stop!" I laugh, trying to keep my newly developed body balanced on my skates.

"I am stopping. See?" He races at me full speed again and then twists to the side, sending a blanket of ice my way.

I cross my arms over my face to block the spray.

"Control your boyfriend!" I squeal at Abby.

Abby crosses her arms over her chest. "Leave her alone, Damon. Don't pick on people smaller than you. It's not flattering."

"Oh stop. She knows I love her. I'm just playing." He turns toward me. "Sorry, beautiful. You okay?"

"Now I'm all wet and cold," I pout.

"Here. Take my jacket. I'm sorry." Damon puts his coat over my shoulders and takes my sister's hand.

She offers a soft smile, forgiving him quickly, and they skate off together at a much slower pace.

Jace skates to my side. "For a cute boy, he can be a real jerk sometimes."

It's taken some getting used to, hearing him talk like that. I'm the only one he's been comfortable enough to 'come out' to. It's our little secret.

"I know, but he was just kidding around. He wouldn't actually hurt me. It's just annoying."

"Very. Come on. Pretend to be my date."

I nudge his shoulder. "I am your date."

Blake snapped his fingers in front of my face. "You left me again."

"Sorry." I shook my head, pulling myself back to the present.

There was a teasing glint in his eyes. "What did I say about that word? Now you owe me a kiss."

"That's my punishment? Sorry, sorry, sorry, sorry, sorry." I laughed as Blake leaned in, peppering me with short, sharp kisses.

"Sorry," I added for good measure, and he smiled against my lips.

"Keep it up and you will be."

"Uh-oh. Sounds serious. I better—sorry—watch what I say—sorry."

I bent to unzip my boot when a sharp pain stung my backside. I jolted upright, grabbing my rear and turned to see Blake rubbing his palm with his thumb and smiling wickedly.

"You fight dirty."

"I warned you. Do it again and later you get it without the clothes to protect you."

I swallowed hard. Was it weird that this turned me on? Every word this guy said seemed to shoot straight to my vagina.

Flash.

Mother—"I give up." I slapped my hands against my thighs and dropped myself onto the bench.

Blake inspected his latest picture. "Cute."

After lacing our skates, he came up behind me, placing his hands on my hips and steering me toward the ice at the foot of the tree.

I walked with my nose in the air, inspecting it while my head rested back on Blake's chest and I let out a soft, contented sigh. I couldn't remember a time when I'd felt so relaxed and free.

We stood face to face, holding hands. Blake swiveled his hips left to right in a backward motion as he pulled me straight legged. It'd been so long since I'd been on the ice; I hoped I didn't wind up like Bambi. But Blake was a pro. The fluid movements of his hips made the muscles in my belly dance, and my eyes couldn't help but follow the smooth figure eight they created.

"You're gonna fall if you don't pay attention," Blake warned with a playfully boyish face that told me he really didn't mind the attention at all.

"I can't help it. You're just so good at that." I couldn't tear my eyes away from his nether region.

"You like that, huh?"

He exaggerated his motions even more, incorporating little circles, and my nipples beaded against my bra. He pulled me to him and I almost fell, but he held on tight. Holding his pelvis flush against mine, he moved me along with him. It felt like a sexual dance. I wasn't quite sure how he was pulling it off, but somehow he kept us in motion and connected.

My chest expanded, my breathing quickening, and I moaned. I could feel our connection had the same effect on him, and I became conscious everyone else would see it as well. "We're going to cause a scene," I whispered in his ear, breathless.

"That's okay. I'm not shy. Let 'em stare." He ground into me.

"Women and children, Blake."

"Ugh, fine." He dropped his forehead to mine and let out a breath of air, moving to my side to take my hand. "But your ass is mine later."

"It better fucking be," I said under my breath, still looking straight ahead.

Blake cocked an eyebrow. "You're getting brazen lately. I *like* it."

I smiled. "For you. Only for you."

IT WAS MY NIGHT TO work again. I loved the bar, but lately I was enjoying just being alone with Blake. Finals were over and it was almost time to go home for Christmas. I didn't want to think about what that meant. I just wanted to stay in our own little world we'd created for ourselves where pasts and families didn't exist.

I'd called my mom earlier to let her know Blake would be accompanying me home but that I wasn't staying the week because I had to work. She missed me and wasn't happy about it, but the fact I was bringing a guy home made her ecstatic.

Blake took his regular seat at the bar. I pushed up onto my palms and leaned over to give him a kiss. "You're early."

"Couldn't stay away." His dimple dimpled.

Eric slid in the seat beside him. I placed a bar napkin in front him. "What's up? It's been a while."

"I stayed away so you didn't realize you made a huge mistake and chose the wrong boyfriend." He smiled briefly before wincing from the jab of Blake's elbow to his ribs.

"Watch it, buddy," I warned. "My boyfriend doesn't like to share."

"I see that." Eric rubbed his tender side. "Congrats, Blake. Seems you have it all, I guess." He played it off like he was joking, but I noticed a hint of jealousy laced behind his forlorn expression. It wasn't something I was used to seeing from the cocky womanizer, and I wondered if there was more to Eric than he let on.

"So what're you guys drinking?"

Blake's expression turned menacing, his mouth opening to answer with another dirty drink no doubt, so I placed my hand over his. "No, no. Don't tell me. Let me."

Blake cocked his eyebrow and I winked, my ponytail whipping over my shoulder as I spun on my heel to create my masterpieces.

I returned a moment later, balancing a blue drink in one hand and a white one in the other. Eric lifted a questioning brow to me at the blue glass I'd placed in front of him.

"Blue balls." I grinned.

Blake grabbed his stomach, falling back with a loud laugh. "Oh, that's priceless. Please tell me what mine is."

"Yours is . . ." I curled one finger at him, and he inched forward. I leaned over the bar. "Angel's tit." I breathed into his ear and then licked his lobe.

Blake froze, his head still turned to the side as he processed. He grabbed the glass zealously and downed its contents in one shot before licking the brim. "I'll take a pair of those, please." He slammed the empty glass in front of me.

"The pleasure would be mine."

He winked. "Count on it."

"Oh, I will." I turned, purposefully swaying my hips as I went to make him a second drink.

I smiled, adding a cherry to Blake's glass when my phone buzzed in my pocket. I extracted it and saw an incoming text with my sister's name displayed across the screen.

> *Abby: Look up.*

My face screwed in confusion. I lifted my line of sight to the other side of the bar, directly in front of me.

"Surprise!"

My mouth fell open as I looked into eyes the same shade of green as mine. "Holy shit, Abs. What're you doing here?" My heart bounced all over my chest, and my belly freefell to my knees. My eyes darted around, taking inventory of who she was with.

"I got tired of waiting for you to come visit me, and I wanted to check up on you. Plus, these guys wanted a girls' night." She thumbed toward a group of friends.

A girls' night. I scanned their familiar faces, my pulse slowing.

"Rick, cover for me a minute," I shouted as I ran out from behind the bar. I wrapped my arms around Abby's neck, then turned to her friends with a huge smile on my face. "Hi, guys! I haven't seen you in so long." I kissed each of them, and then laced my fingers with my sister's. "Come on. There's someone I want you to meet." I wanted to take full advantage of finally having Abby to myself without Damon. I missed her something fierce.

Blake's gaze followed me around to his side of the bar. Recognition showed on his face. He must have put the resemblance together.

"Abs, this is Blake. My boyfriend. Blake, this is my sister, Abby."

"Hot damn, girl. You can pick 'em." Abby offered Blake a toothy smile and stuck out her hand.

"What's with the hand? Give me a hug. We're practically family." Blake pulled her in for a tight squeeze.

"And this gentleman here is Eric. But don't get too close. He bites." I nudged his shoulder.

"Very funny." Eric stood to his full six-foot height and took my sister's hand, staring into her eyes. "Nice to meet you, Abby."

Her eyelashes fluttered as she looked away, her cheeks growing flush.

"Told you." I smirked.

Abby withdrew her hand and fiddled with the buttons on her chest. "Nice to meet you, too." Then she remembered her friends. "Um, this is Barbie, Jena, and Kelly. Ladies, meet Blake and Eric."

She looked down to the floor as they shook hands. I'd never seen Abby so flustered. She was always so controlled and put together. And she'd never once had eyes for anyone but Damon. Maybe there was trouble in paradise?

One could only hope.

"I have to get back to work. What're you girls drinking?"

"Long Island Iced Teas."

"Oh, that sounds delish. I'll take one, too. Gimme some sugar." Jace came up and wrapped his arm around Abby's neck.

"Jace!" she squealed.

"So he *is* alive." I scowled at him.

"Hush it. I've been getting my freak on." He looked at Blake and waggled his finger in a zig-zag motion. "And so have you, I might add."

"Touché. Gimme a kiss. Some of us have to work."

Jace leaned forward, dangling one calf behind him as he planted one on my lips. He turned to Blake. "Not a word. I'm allowed to do that."

Blake put his hands up defensively. "I wasn't going to say anything. Don't get catty now."

Jace smiled. "Good boy." He turned his sights on Eric. "And you. You ready to play with the big boys yet? I won't wait around forever, ya know."

Eric scoffed. "Psshh . . . I know I couldn't handle you. You're too much man for me."

So his flirting really *did* know no boundaries.

"Honey, you have no idea what you're missing. You'd love a ride on this disco stick." Jace pulsed his hips and turned dramatically, throwing a hand in the air. He palmed a stool and wrapped his legs around it, staring at Eric with his eyebrow raised and his tongue propped on the side of his mouth.

I nearly spit out my drink. "Okay, calm down, killer. There are no poles in this bar."

"Too bad." Jace fingered the straw in the glass I'd set in front of him, took a long hard pull, and then let out a shiver. "Whew. God, I love your heavy hand." We blew air kisses at each other.

Jace patted the stool next to him. "Abby, get your ass over here. We need to catch up. You bitches, too. It's been too long." He waved her friends over.

Abby, it seemed, still hadn't recovered from her encounter with Mr. Smooth. She nearly tripped, pulling her gaze from the side of Eric's head as she took the seat beside Jace.

"Pretty, isn't he?" Jace winked at Eric, who was caught staring at Abby.

"Are the girls coming?" I asked Jace.

"Yep. They'll be here in three . . . two . . . one . . ." He flicked his wrist toward the door and snapped. Sure enough, Sandra and Jessie came floating through its frame.

Thankfully, the break in Sandra's leg wasn't that severe and she didn't need the cast for too long. She still harbored a slight limp and a small scar beside her eye, but other than that, you'd never know anything had happened to her. Physical therapy three times a week had done wonders. Jeremy hardly ever let her out of his sight, which made me smile when he filed in behind her.

Jace did the honors of introducing everyone, and instantly my old crew was socializing with my new one. I took a moment, looking at my sister, boyfriend, and all of my friends lining the bar. My vision blurred, and I turned so no one would notice the mist covering my eyes. For someone who had spent so much time trying to push people away and remain alone, I sure was surrounded by a lot of love.

I busied myself for the next few hours as everyone took a turn at the mic for karaoke night.

Everyone but Blake.

And his fine ass was walking in that direction.

This should be entertaining. I propped my chin in my hand and leaned on the bar.

A quick, fun drumbeat started, and Blake threw his rocker fingers in the air, air banging his head to a cute little bop as the intro to Cheap Trick's, *I Want You To Want Me* played.

Blake circled his hands around the silver stand like a rock star and looked right at me, seductively purring the opening line into the mic.

I threw my head back and laughed, coming up to yell in Rick's ear, "Be right back."

Pouring a bottle from each hand, he shouted back, "Sure thing."

I scooted out from behind the bar, through the throngs of women who looked like they wanted to throw their bras at my boyfriend, and headed toward the awful voice crackling from the speakers.

But it was Blake's voice, and that made it beautiful.

Blake squinted his eyes, accentuating the inflection in his words with feeling and emotion. And then . . . he scrunched up his nose and wiggled his ass, telling me he'd come home early from work if I told him I loved him.

My eyes never wavered as I howled in encouragement and mouthed, 'I love you'.

He let out a rocker's yell, lost in the role. Wincing, I laughed, as I continued to stare in awe at the man of my dreams as he played the air guitar. Blake slammed to his knees as the tempo slowed again. He crawled toward me, finishing off the lyrics. When he reached my feet, he slithered up the length of my body, flushed and huffing, and then he claimed my lips.

"I don't think I've ever wanted you more," I spoke into his mouth.

Blake broke the kiss and yelled into the mic, "You hear that, guys? She wants me!"

The place erupted in a roar, and I wrapped my arms around his neck and jumped onto his waist. "Always. You fucking rock."

Blake laughed. "I told you I can't sing."

"No, but you were right. You make for a hell of a show trying." I winked.

We made our way back over to the group, who by now were sloshed and rowdy. Blake set me on my feet, and Abby slurred, "Oh my god, Eva. I love your boyfriend."

I laughed. "Thanks. He's pretty amazing, isn't he?" I smiled at Blake.

Abby smacked my arm. "Yes! He's so much fun. His friend's not too shabby, either." She bit her straw and moved her eyes to Eric, nudging me with her shoulder.

"Uh-oh. Still on that?"

"I wish I was." Her gaze roamed the length of him before she clapped a hand over her mouth, her eyes going wide. "Oh my God. What's wrong with me? What did you put in these drinks?" She squinted, inspecting her glass.

I put my hand on top of it and pushed down until it rested on the bar. "I think you've had enough of those."

"Yeah, maybe." She scratched her head and shrugged. "I'm gonna go potty. I'll be right back."

A while passed, and I noticed Abby still hadn't come back. I hoped she wasn't sick in the bathroom. "Hey, Rick, can I have another minute?"

"You got it."

My eyebrows knitted together as I searched the faces in the crowded bar. None of them belonged to my sister. Walking to the next room, I went up on my tippy toes, craning my neck when I spotted her. She was backed into a corner, her chest rising and falling heavily as Eric stood, enveloping her, with his head drawn down and slanted, obviously ready to go in for the kill. I had to think fast.

Did I want this to happen? This was my chance to get her away from Damon. But with Eric? The guy was a player who'd been with half the female population.

But she liked him, right? And I wanted her to have fun. I also wanted her the fuck away from that scumbag.

I ducked my head and moved to get closer and hear what was going on.

Eric was whispering something in Abby's ear, running his nose along the bridge of her jaw. Her face was flushed, her body arched toward his. She wanted this.

Eric's lips were only a breath away from Abby's. "I'm going to kiss you now. Is that okay?"

Abby nodded slowly, licking her lips and closing her eyes, her body drifting toward him like a magnet.

Eric lowered his head the rest of the way, cradling her face. His tongue flicked out to taste her lips, and then he tilted his head the opposite way and kissed her slowly like he was trying to memorize every inflection of her mouth. She wrapped her arms around his neck, pulling him closer. I felt funny intruding on their intimate moment though I couldn't help the smile that played on my lips.

Eric broke the kiss, resting his forehead against hers as they both panted in tandem. He dragged his thumb along her bottom lip. "Too bad these belong to someone else. They're fucking incredible."

Abby's eyes flew open. Her hand came up to cover her mouth as tears filled her eyes. "What've I done? I'm so sorry." She ducked out from under his arm, causing him to fall against the wall.

I hurried to catch up with her, but she sprinted past her friends, calling over her shoulder on the way out the door, "Come on, guys. We gotta go."

Disappointment washed over their faces, but it was probably for the best. They were all pretty toasted.

The cool air hit me as I bolted over the threshold, looking left and right. Abby was bent over, one hand resting on her knee and the other at her mouth.

"Abs!" I called after her.

She straightened. "Eva, what the hell did I do? I can't believe I just cheated on Damon!"

I swallowed the bitter taste of that. "You obviously felt something for him, Abby."

"We can't speak of this—ever. We have to pretend this never happened. Do you hear me? If Damon ever found out . . ."

"Wouldn't be such a bad thing," I muttered under my breath.

Abby blinked at me. "What did you just say?"

I squared my shoulders and leveled my voice. "Maybe Damon isn't as right for you as you think." There, I said it.

She narrowed her eyes and barked at me. "Do you hear yourself? Are you insane? He's all I know. We're meant for each other. You fucking know that!"

And here she was, defending him as usual. My blood boiled as I spoke through my teeth. "He's no prince charming, Abby. Stop acting like he's perfect." *Fuck.* I'd slipped up.

"I can't believe you're saying this to me right now," she spat at me. "What's your problem with him anyway? You act like such a cold bitch around him."

My spine stiffened. That was a slap in the face, but she was drunk and didn't know the truth. "I'm going to act like you didn't just say that because you've had too much to drink." Then I softened my voice. "I don't want to fight. I haven't seen you in months, and I love you." I tucked a strand of hair behind her ear. "All I'm saying is, maybe seeing what else is out there isn't the worst idea in the world. That way you know for sure you're making the right decision." Which would never be the right decision, but I couldn't find the words to tell her that. *Not yet.*

Abby fell back against the wall, the weight of everything taking a toll. "God, it felt so good. I *felt* it. I felt things I can't ever remember feeling before. I'm horrible, aren't I?" She put her face in her hands and sobbed.

I rubbed a soothing hand down her arm. "No, you aren't horrible. You're human and maybe Damon's not the one. And that's okay."

"I love him, Eva."

I winced hearing those words, but covered it up quickly. *That fuck's got her brainwashed.* I knew all too well his ability to do that. "Maybe you're not *in* love with him anymore."

She shook her head, rubbing her temples. "I can't think about this right now. My head's spinning."

"Hey, Abs . . ."

"Yeah?"

I almost told her her right then. My mouth hung open as I tried to find the right words. She should know what she was dealing with, that she wasn't a bad person for having feelings for someone else.

But then I looked into her glassy eyes and thought better of it. This wasn't the time or place for that bomb. "Never mind. Go sleep it off. You'll feel better tomorrow."

Blake emerged, winded. "You guys okay?"

"Yeah, we're fine," I said.

Abby offered Blake a strained smile as her friends joined her. All but Jena, the designated driver, were walking crooked.

"Well, it was nice to finally meet you." Blake gave her a lopsided smile. "I don't know what went on back there. I'm sorry if he crossed a line. If it's any consolation, my boy's tore up. You did a number on him. You Ricci girls are no joke." Blake winked and pulled her in for a hug. "You're sure you're okay? Do I have to give him a slap?"

"I'm fine, really." She sniffed. "Thanks for asking."

"No problem." Blake turned to me. "See you inside, Angel." I watched him jog back in with a grateful smile on my face.

Jace appeared, bracing his hands on either side of the doorframe. "You bitches are too much drama for me. One of you full time is enough to handle." He stumbled beside Abby and dropped a heavy arm over her shoulder, causing her to rock on her already unsteady feet. "Come on. Drop me off and you can tell Aunt Jace all about it."

I kissed Abby's cheek. "You guys better be careful. Call me when you're home."

I planted my hands on my hips and exhaled a deep breath, looking back to the door, not wanting to finish my shift. I was spent. Though I hoped I'd at least planted a seed for Abby to think about.

Eric sat at the bar with a scowl on his face, two shots in front of him and one empty glass. He looked up as I wiped a towel in front of him, clearing away the remnants of what he'd spilled in his haste. "I'm sorry, Eva. I don't know what got into me. I wanted her so damn bad, I couldn't stop myself. She told me she had a boyfriend—not that that's ever stopped me before, but I know she's your sister. I never would've disrespected you that way, even though I like to give you a hard time." He slung another shot down his throat and spun the last full glass between his fingers.

"Don't worry about it. You kind of did me a favor actually. I can't stand her boyfriend."

"Yeah, well, I didn't do *me* any fucking favors. I'm not getting her out of my head anytime soon."

I pulled back, studying him. "Whoa, I've never seen this side of you before. Don't you usually bang anything with a heartbeat? I always kind of thought you were incapable of feeling or something."

Eric snickered. "Gee, thanks. Tell me how you *really* feel."

"I'm sorry. That came out wrong." I covered his hand with my own in an attempt to apologize, but he quickly pulled it back, emptying the last shot down his throat.

"I don't wanna talk about it." Eric shoved away from the bar, unsteady on his feet. "I'm outta here, B." He gave Blake a pound and ran his fingers through his hair, bunching a fistful at the back.

I nodded to Blake. "Go with him. I don't like how he looks."

Blake frowned. "Yeah, you're right. Something's really got him going. I'll be back before you're done." He took off after him, and I looked on, concerned for the guy who, before tonight, I wasn't sure I even liked. The guy I was praying would change the course of my life.

Chapter 27

BLACK.

    That's all I saw. I hadn't realized how long I'd been sitting on the roof, staring off into space, faintly registering snowflakes falling around my tucked in knees. I'd dressed in sweatpants and a hoodie, and climbed up here because there was something about snow on Christmas that made me brush aside my hatred for all things precipitation.

That was hours ago.

At least I thought it was based on the fact my hair was crunchy and frozen, and my fingers were blue . . . or purple. In the dim light of dawn it was hard to tell. I clenched and unclenched my fists, trying to bring back circulation as I stared out into nothingness.

Blake had bought me an iPod and loaded it with songs for me to listen to when we were apart and I couldn't sleep. He spent most nights with me, but last night he'd stayed at his parents to celebrate the holiday early. That was probably a big factor of why I was up here right now. Thankfully, he helped to keep my night terrors away somehow. But in his absence, and with the weight of this day looming, it couldn't be avoided.

Steven Tyler's voice bled into my ears, singing about an angel coming to save him. The corner of my mouth turned up. I was numb, but that knock on my heart I felt. Like a little tickle, letting me know he was always there, tucked inside its beating walls.

Of course, Aerosmith's *Angel* would be on there. When he sang how loneliness took him for a ride, it brought my mind to a young Blake.

Living his life as his father's pawn. No one knowing what he was going through internally, drifting along in his stilted journey.

I smiled, hoping I was making a difference in his life somehow. Starting with today. The day he'd spend his first holiday away from his family. With me . . . and mine. I took a deep, jittery breath.

I was scared out of my mind.

Not knowing how this would pan out was eating me alive. But I would do it. For him. I'd bring him home. To a house that was no longer a home. I just hoped I wasn't making a huge mistake.

I'd have to stay on my tippy toes to make sure everything went smoothly. I was very different from the girl who'd left a few months ago, and I needed to be strong today. I'd left as Evangelina, but I was bringing *Angel* home. I wasn't perfect and I didn't know if I'd ever be, but I was slowly changing. My cracks were still visible, but they were superglued now. I'd put off going back long enough. It couldn't be avoided anymore.

Blank.

It was like being asleep while you were awake. I didn't even know where I went when I drifted away. Like my mind was giving me the reprieve it knew I needed against my knowledge.

I shook my head, trying to evoke life.

The sun was barely up. I tilted my head to the dusky gray sky and caught a snowflake on my tongue, scrunching my nose. That action brought me back to Blake once again. Seemed everything led to him these days.

Ironic, Phillip Phillips' *Home* was next on his playlist. As I contemplated the loss of a home, the song told me he was my home now. And he was. He was always with me even when he wasn't.

I smiled broadly, feeling my strength fortify. I'd never be alone again. Not if I could help it. I'd spent too many years trapped away with those demons.

I rubbed my hands together and hopped off the lounger. Even though I hadn't forgiven myself yet, it was time to move on. Blake needed a place to call home too, after all, and my walls needed to be sturdy for him.

A FEW HOURS AND A steamy shower later, Jace knocked on the door with a travel mug in his hand. "Ready to go, sugar lips?"

That smile was reserved for one thing, and it was barely noon. I looked at him questioningly. "Yeah, I guess so. It's gotta happen, right?"

"Do you know how you're going to handle all this?" He hopped up on my stool, and swung his legs, crossed at the ankles.

"Not yet. I'm hoping with everyone around and Blake with me, there'll be nothing to worry about. Fingers crossed." I held up two twisted fingers and made the sign of the cross.

"I'll come by later on and check up on you." He took another hard swallow, smacked his lips together and smiled with the grin that gave himself away.

"Jace, what're you drinking?"

He shrugged. "Eggnog. Why?"

I raised an eyebrow. "Plain eggnog?"

"Hell no. Go wash out your mouth." He crinkled his nose in disgust.

"You lush. You realize it's still morning, right?"

"Hey, I'm on vacation. This is what I do on vacation."

"Yes, in the Bahamas maybe."

"Hush it. It's five o'clock somewhere. It's all good."

"You have issues." I shook my head.

"I do. My best friend's a lunatic. I need this fuzz in my head to make it through a day with her."

"That's not nice," I pouted.

"Oh, I'm only kidding." He hopped down and put his arm around my shoulder, his mug landing right under my nostrils.

"Gimme a sip. That smells delicious."

"Oh, really? I thought I had *issues*."

"Well, we all know *I* have issues. No secret there." I rolled my eyes and took a sip. A coughing fit ensued. I should have known better than to taste anything in that boy's hand.

"How much rum did you put in there?" I wheezed.

"Mind your business." He snatched the cup out of my hand and cradled it to his chest. "Come on. Let's go get lover boy."

"Okay." I laced my fingers with his. "Jace?"

"Yeah, baby girl?"

"I'm scared." I looked up at him from the corner of my eye.

His features softened. "I know you are, but you're handling it very well. You'll be fine. You're fierce. Rawr." He nudged his shoulder into mine.

I smiled unconvincingly. "I hope you're right."

"Sweetie, I'm always right. Trust. Now come on. Let's do this."

BLAKE JOGGED TO THE CAR with Victoria on his heels. He leaned his forearm on Jace's window. "How's it fair that you ride shot gun with my girlfriend?"

Jace's face was smooth. "Don't make me bite that arm, honey. My name's been on this seat since she got this car. It's got the indent of my ass and everything. I only let you borrow it when I'm not around so she doesn't feel like a chauffeur."

I leaned over the inner console. "Told you you'd have a fight on your hands."

Blake frowned and lugged his bag in the backseat before following it and slamming the door. Victoria took his place at the passenger window, extending her hand to Jace.

"Hi, I'm Tori. You must be Jace."

"The one and only. Aren't you a pretty thing."

"Well, aren't you sweet?" she gushed.

Jace winked. "Like candy, baby."

Victoria laughed, but then her smile faded. "I wish I was coming with you guys."

I felt bad leaving her here. "Next time, I promise. Someone has to keep your mom company."

"Yeah, yeah. I know." She sighed, sweeping her long, dark hair over her shoulder. "Ugh, that man." She straightened. "Well, have fun. I just wanted company while I sulked. Love you guys." She tapped on the door and flitted off.

Blake scooted to the middle of the backseat with a smile in his eyes.

"What?" I asked, wondering what he was up to.

He brought his arm up to drape a familiar looking green leaf above my head and licked his lips, inching forward. "Merry Christmas, Angel."

He pressed his lips to mine, and I melted into them with a smile. He pulled back and kissed my nose before sticking the mistletoe in his pocket.

"Where's mine?" Jace looked longingly at Blake.

"Don't push your luck." Reaching through the opening, Blake adjusted the radio. "So, what're we jamming?"

Jace swatted Blake's hand away. "Don't even think about it, tight buns. That bitch is all mine. Music is my thang."

"Well, then thang already. I hate a quiet car."

Jace looked at me while he pushed the presets, searching the stations. "So demanding. How do you put up with him?"

"He's hot." I shrugged. "And he smells good." My eyes glittered as I licked my lips and looked at Blake in the rearview mirror. "And he tastes even better . . ."

"All right, shutty. You're making me lose my nog." Jace cranked the volume. "Yazzz, here's my jam!" Madonna's *Vogue* invaded the car, and Jace bounced up and down in his seat, bringing his hands around to frame his face in different poses.

I laughed as Blake slammed his back against the seat, huffing and crossing his arms across his chest. I mouthed, 'I love you'.

Blake sneered and nodded as if to say, 'Yeah, okay'.

I shook my head, smiling. I loved having my two men with me. I just had to concentrate on holding onto this feeling for the next two days.

THE WARM AND FUZZY FEELING was gone already. I had dropped off Jace and now stood, holding Blake's hand and staring at the white, custom colonial, two-story home that had housed both the best and worst memories of my life. Large windows overlooked the front lawn, and a quaint porch accentuated the large house.

Fuck.

"You okay, babe? You don't look so good." Blake put the back of his hand to my forehead.

"Huh? Yeah, I'm fine." I chugged a bottle of water and gave him a smile.

"If you say so."

He bent to retrieve our bags, then we started up the drive. I focused on the swing that held so many happy times. This was my home. *My* home. Not *his*. I squared my shoulders. I had my rock by my side. My boulder. I could do this.

Fuck. Him.

With a smile, I fisted the doorknob, hearing the Christmas music blasting on the other side. Knowing my trusting family would leave it unlocked, I twisted it and we waltzed right in. Garlic and clams and all things Christmas Eve curled through the air, and my heart constricted, missing the warmth of my family. An extreme homesick feeling slammed me in the chest like a bag of bricks.

My dad rested on the couch, his feet propped on the coffee table, catching flies as he snored. Smiling, I walked over and patted his arm, jolting him awake.

"Hey, ladybug." He jumped up and pulled me in for a bear hug.

"Hi, Daddy. I missed you." I squeezed back, enjoying the familiar scent of Old Spice.

"How's my baby girl? Let me look at you." He held both of my hands in his own and inspected me. "You're too thin. Your mother needs to put a little meat on your bones before you leave."

I waved him off. "Stop it, I am not."

My dad looked to my left. "So who's the mountain?"

Blake laughed and extended his hand. "Nice to meet you, Mr. Ricci. I'm Blake."

My dad shook Blake's hand. "One sec. Let me lower this." He turned the music down and then focused back on Blake. "So you're a lawyer, I hear?"

"No, not yet. That's the plan, though," he said on a nervous chuckle.

"Yeah, well, don't let 'em steal your soul. From what Eva tells us, you have a good one." He clapped Blake on the back.

Blake's smile faltered, no doubt realizing how different my dad's outlook was from his own. "No, sir, I wouldn't dream of it."

"Cut the 'sir' crap. This ain't England, and I'm not Paul. Although, I wish I was. Ba-da-ba." My dad made drum motions with his hands. "Just call me Joe so I don't twitch. My father was Mr. Ricci."

"Will do." Blake nodded, and my heart warmed at their easy exchange. I wondered what I'd been so nervous about and how I'd let myself go so long without seeing my family.

"Come on. You gotta meet the woman behind all the magic." I grabbed one of Blake's hands in both of mine and walked backward, pulling him into the kitchen.

My mom was standing in her bare feet, her blonde ponytail extending the full length of her back. All burners were on high alert, and steam climbed up to the ceiling as she stirred a pot, She looked over her shoulder.

"You made it!"

Putting the spoon in its rest, she rushed over to pull me close. "I missed you so much. I can't believe you didn't come home for Thanksgiving." She pulled back from me and frowned. "You're too skinny."

"Not you, too," I whined. "I'm just fine. No wonder I was never able to lose weight in this house." I popped a mini quiche into my mouth.

"Yeah, well, no diets today. I'm making your plate." She redirected her attention to Blake. "Whoa, get a load of you. Eva, did you bring a tree home for dinner? I think I better get more food started."

"Stop it, Mom." I laughed.

Blake blushed and stepped forward. "Nice to meet you, Mrs. Ricci. I'm Blake. Everything smells delicious but trust me, it's enough. I'll control myself."

"Please don't." She grinned. "No one holds back in my kitchen. I'll be insulted if you don't leave here rounder than when you came in, and with a doggy bag. And it's Connie, please. Now give me a hug. I can't believe my Eva's in love." She held her arms open.

"Don't make a spectacle, please," I spoke through my smile.

"How could I not? You're the first one. Did she tell you that?"

"Mom," I warned.

"Abby told me he was good looking, but man, you're like a model." She gleamed.

Blake's cheeks reddened even further.

"Okay, Mom. We're gonna go get settled while you calm yourself." I turned to Blake. "Hurry up before she makes a move on you or something. I think she's lost it." I chuckled at his rare loss for words.

I cracked open the door to my bedroom. It was just the way I'd left it, decorated in different hues of purple—my favorite color, with pictures lining the walls and dresser, displaying happy moments from my past. A small desk sat in the corner. I smiled as I looked at the knob I knew was loose on the drawer where I'd kept my journal all those years. Instinctively, my eyes drifted to Mary's vacant place next to the bed. I hadn't felt the need to bring her with me, knowing Blake would be here.

I dropped my bag on the comforter. "Told you they'd love you." I rocked to the side, nudging Blake's shoulder.

"They're awesome. This is like a real home. A real family." Blake placed his bag next to mine and looked away with a half-smile, seeming far away.

"Hey, don't do that. Your family's great and they love you. There are people who don't even have that. Besides, you're my family now, too." I smiled, tucking my head beneath his so he'd focus on me.

Blake wrapped his arms around my neck and put his lips to the top of my head, breathing into my hair. "I don't know what I'd do without you anymore."

"Thankfully you'll never have to find out." I poked the tickle spot on his side, and he jarred to the left.

"You think you're funny?" Blake hooked his forearm around my neck and gave me a noogie.

"Stop it, you bully!" I pushed against his ribs as he dragged me down the hall.

The front door flew open, and we stopped in our tracks as Abby and Damon hobbled in, balancing piles of gifts. My heart flatlined as a bundle of nerves slammed into my stomach, knocking the wind out of me.

Abby poked her head around her stack. "Hey, you guys. Merry Christmas Eve!"

Blake released his grip, and I straightened, smoothing my hair. "Hey, I didn't think you'd be back yet."

"Are you kidding? I never get to see you. We finished up at Damon's house as quick as we could."

With a huff, she dropped her pile and hurried to us, scooping me into her arms. "Hi. I missed you."

"Missed you more," I said, looking past her to Damon, who was placing his stack beside hers. My mom's hors d'oeuvres teetered at the back of my throat.

Abby hugged Blake. "Nice to see you again. I'm sober this time, I promise. Well, for now anyway."

"Nice to know." Blake winked.

While they chatted, Damon rolled up from the floor, his pointed glare nailing me to the ground. Prickles covered the back of my neck as he clenched and unclenched his jaw. He brought his hands together in a loud clap, and I jumped, the malice in his face seeping from every pore. I should have known he'd mess with me for bringing someone home. Rubbing his palms, his lip curled back over his teeth in disdain.

"Let's meet the guy Eva finally decided was good enough for her, shall we?" He dragged his condescending eyes away from mine. They widened as they landed on Blake. "Holy shit. Blake?"

"Hey, dude. What the hell?" Blake stepped in, giving him a pound.

Damon's eyes twinkled with delight. The corner of his mouth twitched into a smile. He looked like he'd just set up his checkmate pawn. "What a small world. You got the other sister, I see."

"You two kn-now each other?" My nervous tongue stuttered.

Damon turned his triumphant smile on me. "Sure do. We grew up in the Hamptons together. Our parents run in the same crowd."

Whatever kept my body functioning seemed to stop, except for the loud thumping of my heartbeat in my ears. *How can this be happening?*

"Wait, really?" Abby exclaimed. "How did I never meet you? Eva, this is like kismet." She beamed.

My insides rolled over and flopped again. A coolness raced up my lower spine and the room had begun a slow spin. *Air. I need air.*

Blake's voice sounded distant in the haze of my mind. "I can't believe this. You're going to have to tell me some Angel stories, man." His dimple sat deep in his cheek and he didn't seem to notice anything was amiss. He placed his hand on the small of my back, and I twisted my sweaty palms together.

"Angel?" Damon cocked his head to the side.

"Right. I always forget that's not her real name. Eva." Blake kissed my forehead, and I offered a weak smile.

"Oh, I have plenty to tell about *Angel*. Isn't that right, beautiful?"

Blake's fingers dug into my side, and he looked down at me for a reaction. He knew my trigger word, and I was scared he would put the pieces together.

The dryness in my mouth and buzzing in my head made it impossible to speak. A heat settled in my core as I struggled to find my voice. "Would you excuse me, please?"

I broke away from Blake. He looked to Damon, who still had a broad smile, and then back to me, his eyebrows knitted together.

"Can I get you a drink?" I asked Blake in the calmest voice I could find, giving myself a reason to leave the room.

"A glass of red is fine, thanks," Blake answered, but I could tell by his concentrated look that his mind was somewhere other than his response.

I turned to leave, and he caught my arm. "Hey, you okay, babe?"

"Me? Yeah, I'm fine. Why?" I pulled my arm away so he wouldn't feel my trembles.

"You're a little pale."

I waved him off. "Jace's eggnog caught up with me, I guess. That kid and his heavy hand." I smiled. "I just need some water."

I glanced over Blake's shoulder into dark brown eyes atop a sneer. At one time, I'd considered Damon a good looking guy. Brown spiky hair and a boyishly handsome face topped off a built upper body. You could tell he was a country club kid, born with a silver spoon in his mouth. Coming from the neighborhood we lived in, it was no secret we were all well off, but he wore it on his sleeve along with his designer emblems.

He'd been the sweet boy next door growing up. Always hanging around, flirting with Abby from the second puberty hit. I'd like to go back and smack myself for secretly being jealous at the time. I used to love to tag along and get in the middle of them, busting their chops. Even though I was sure it annoyed them, they were always cool with it and let me believe I was part of their clique. I trusted him—with everything.

But the eyes I saw now . . .

Those weren't the eyes of that boy. I hadn't seen *him* in years.

"I'll be right back." I took off for the bathroom.

You can't leave them alone. I know. Shh, let me think.

I closed my eyes, rubbing circles over my temples. *They fucking know each other. What kind of personal hell is this?*

I dug my nails into my palms, bull breathing. Shaking out my hands at my sides, I tried to pull it together. If Blake found out, I'd lose everything. No matter what he thought, he wouldn't be able to get past what I'd done. Kid or not, no one with decent morals would do that. And now, knowing the way Damon could manipulate the truth, I'd be done for if he ever got to his ear.

Slamming my back to the door, I fisted the hair at my temples and stared across the confined space into the mirror. *Own your decision.*

I stood up straighter.

Don't let him win again. He took enough. He can't take Blake, too. You decided to be with him, now go be with him. If he sees you falter, he'll know and Damon will be in control. Again.

I splashed water on my face and took ten deep breaths. I couldn't leave them alone too long, but I didn't think he'd risk saying anything in front of Abby. Still, I wasn't taking any chances. Bellowing laughter smacked me in the face when I opened the door.

My eye twitched.

They liked each other.

Another fissure down my heart, but I pushed on and ignored it. I filled a glass of wine for both Blake and myself, put on my big girl panties, and sauntered into the living room. I handed Blake his drink and tucked my hand into the rear pocket of his faded jeans. Damon stared at the action and swallowed visibly, no doubt choking on whatever snide remark he wanted to make.

"Ohhh." Blake wiggled his ass against my palm, and I squeezed playfully.

Abby whispered something in Damon's ear. He absentmindedly answered, "Sure, babe." Still staring in the area of my hand. "Don't you girls think you should be in the kitchen helping your mother?" he added.

Blake looked at him, evaluating his sexist remark, and then to me for my reaction. "I can give you guys a hand, too."

My dad walked in the room. "You're not going anywhere. I have a CD of the new band. Wanna hear it?"

"Sure," Blake replied. "How is it you're in a band, yet we have to twist Eva's arm out of its socket to get her to sing?"

"Don't get me started. That girl will only sing in her room, her car,

or the shower. I've been trying since she was eight years old. I gave up."
My dad knelt in front of the CD player and popped in the disc. He stood,
bopping his head as the harmony of the two front singers began.

Feeling more comfortable, I nodded to Abby. "C'mon." I went up on
my tip toes and kissed Blake's cheek. "We'll be back."

Before we reached the kitchen, Abby pulled me aside. "I need to talk
to you."

"What's up?"

She bit down on her lip and picked at her nails.

"Abby?"

"It's Eric."

"What about Eric?" I asked, confused.

She dropped her hands. "I can't stop thinking about him."

A smile tugged at my lips, but I cleared my throat and replaced it
with my 'concerned' face. "What're you going to do about it?"

Abby stared at me as though I had grown a second head. "Seriously?
I can't do anything about it. You know that. I just don't know how to
stop it. And seeing Blake just made it one hundred times worse," she said
in a harsh whisper.

I tried to tamp down the happy dance going on inside of me. "Well,
maybe there's a reason you don't know how to stop it."

"Not this again," she groaned, leaning against the wall outside the
kitchen.

"You wanted to talk about it. It's not my fault you don't like my
answer." I exhaled. "If you're not going to do anything about it, then
what's there to talk about?" I pressed gently, trying to plant the idea of a
different future in her head without being too conspicuous.

"I'm treating Damon differently, and I think he's noticing. It's not
good, and I'm scared I'll fold and tell him."

My heart raced. I knew a different side of Damon. I wasn't sure
what he'd do if he ever knew the truth, and I couldn't let Abby do anything that would jeopardize him hurting her. Any lightheartedness I was
feeling at the prospect of her leaving Damon washed out of me and I
suddenly became serious. "Try not to think about it. Maybe if you can
convince yourself it never happened, you'll believe it and not act different anymore. I mean, if you don't plan on doing anything about it,

what's the difference?" I shrugged.

"That's your advice? The guy's a freaking masterpiece, consuming my every thought, and you think I can just convince myself it never happened?"

"What other choice do you have?" I was agitated and just wanting to end the discussion. "It's that or break up with Damon and explore your options, but you can't let him know you cheated. Who knows what he'll do?" I couldn't hide the panic in my voice.

She blinked at me then, no doubt wondering why I just said that. "I'm not scared he'd do anything. He's not like that. I'm scared I'll be making the wrong decision, and then I'll be screwed."

He's not like that? She didn't even know him, and she'd been with him for years. A bitter pit formed in my stomach.

Abby's eyes flared. "What if I saw him one more time? To see if I still feel the same. Maybe it was just the alcohol. Then I can put my mind to rest."

My body stiffened. "I don't know, Abby." *Is she insane?*

"Well, what else am I gonna do?" she whined.

"For right this minute, you're going to ignore it," I ordered. "Go help Mom with the kitchen and then go spend Christmas with your *boy-friend.* Are you trying to give me anxiety? He's right. In. There." I shoved my pointer finger down the hall.

"Okay. Okay." She gave me a pointed look. "But we're not finished with this."

"Whatever. Come on, lunatic." I grabbed her hand and pulled her into the kitchen.

"There you two are. Could use a little help here." My mom balanced a tray between her potholder-clad hands. "Grab a hot plate, would you?"

I dropped the piece of ceramic in front of her as she lowered the dish and shook out her hands. "We're basically ready. Better bring this stuff out before your boyfriends run for the hills. Daddy loves when he has an audience."

We set the table and yelled to the guys to come eat. I stood behind my chair, my palms tight around the top of it as I waited for everyone to take their seats. The guys came through the archway, laughing as my dad snapped his fingers, still singing the newest song his band had learned.

"You guys are really good, Mr. Ric—I mean, Joe. I gotta come see you play one night," Blake said, sounding genuinely impressed.

My dad beamed. "That'd be great. Evangelina used to come, and now I can never get her there anymore. These two are there all the time, though." He thumbed toward Abby and Damon. "Maybe you guys could double date sometime."

I choked on my wine.

Blake patted my back. "You all right?"

My nose stung with the burn of the liquid trapped in my nostrils. "Fine," I said through the fire and teary eyes.

Damon wrapped his arm around Abby's hip. "You didn't make my dish yet?"

"No, I didn't get to. What do you want?" She grabbed his plate and a fork.

"Tsk, tsk, what kind of service is this?" He was pretending to joke but I could hear the menace in his tone.

I ground my teeth together and stared, waiting for her to put him in his place. I did this every time he spoke to her that way. But, like always, it never came. She continued to load up his dish, and Blake looked at me from the corner of his eye with his eyebrows raised. I merely shrugged and asked him what he'd like.

"I've got two hands, I can make it." Blake scooped large helpings into his dish and took his seat beside me.

Damon's cocky face seated across from me was enough to make me lose my appetite, but I was used to it. I'd spent many holidays this way— him licking his fork suggestively at me while his hand was on my sister's knee. Fucking disgusting.

"So how'd you guys meet?" Damon directed his question at Blake, his fork motioning between the two of us.

"I harassed her life until she said yes. This little girl's a tough cookie to tie down." Blake patted my hand, a roguish smile playing on his lips.

"She is a tease, isn't she?" And there was the menace again, seeping through his grin.

The hair on my arm prickled. Blake's smile dipped at the corners and my mouth went dry as my eyes darted across the table.

"Damon! That's not funny." Abby backhanded his chest.

He laughed, recoiling from the blow. "What? She is."

"I don't find it funny either, Damon." My usually unaffected father raised a brow.

Suddenly anxious, my knee began to bob up and down feverishly. Blake's jaw tightened, but he didn't lose his gentlemanly stature. He curled his fingers over the top of mine and squeezed, quelling my jitters.

"I'd hardly call her a tease." He shrugged. "She just has high standards." Then he lowered his voice and added, "You're also lucky we're at a dinner table, and that I'm meeting her parents for the first time."

Wow. My cheeks grew warm hearing someone finally stick up for me to him. My dad's gaze flicked to Blake and he opened and closed his mouth, seeming unsure of how he wanted to react to that statement.

Like a dog salivating over a bone, Damon was undeterred. His smile turned cocky at the challenge. "Bro, you have no idea how many guys she's led on, making them think they had a shot with her. And she went out with not-a-one. Trust me. She's a tease." He popped a forkful in his mouth, chewing with a smirk.

At that my mother's head snapped up.

I could tell Blake's patience was waning but he was trying hard to keep it together in the presence of my family. He leaned forward as if to assert but also restrain himself. "*You* have no idea how well I know her, *bro*. I'm not intimidated by a girl who knows what she wants." He brought my knuckles to his lips and kissed them. His expression softening as his eyes found mine. "I would've waited till I was old and gray if she wasn't ready."

My mom dabbed the corner of her mouth with a napkin and placed it back on her lap. "I don't like this talk. We're at the dinner table. Find your manners, Damon."

Damon ignored her statement, which surprised me. He usually did a better job of looking like the golden child. His demeanor turned venomous as he squirmed to the edge of his seat. "Well, look at Blake being a regular Casanova." He smiled, sarcasm oozing from each syllable.

My palms were growing sweaty at their exchange.

"I'm no Casanova. I'm a gentleman. I know how a lady is supposed to be treated. I could give you a few pointers some time when you're ready, *bro*." A twisted grin flashed across his face, and I tried my best to stifle a laugh. Blake forked a large bite of eggplant rollatini and stuffed it into his mouth.

Damon leaned back. "Don't get your panties in a bunch, Blake. I was only kidding."

Blake shook his head nonchalantly, swallowing. "They're not in a bunch. I'm just clearing up whatever misconceptions you might have. Think of it as a formal education. Chivalry one-oh-one." He stabbed his string beans and rested his forearms on the table. "And just so *we're* clear, if you ever talk that way about Angel again, bunched up panties will be the least of your problems."

Blake and Damon had a staring stand off and all hopes I'd had of enjoying Christmas Eve dinner went out the window. I was uncomfortable, but at the same time, my subconscious had her pom poms held high. *Give me a B!*

My dad's voice boomed from the head of the table. "Okay, guys. That's enough. Damon, you'll watch your mouth. That's my baby girl you're talking about."

"Yeah and I thought you two were supposed to be friends. What's gotten into you?" Abby questioned Damon.

Damon shrugged, now radiating his famous charm. Too bad it was fake as the day was long. "We are friends. I'm just making sure he's good enough for our kid sister. Sorry, Mr. R. I was just testing him, that's all. I didn't mean to come off disrespectful. Eva knows I love her. "

Testing? Loves me? I might puke at the dinner table.

Blake leaned back, resting his arm behind my chair. "Well, you can relax. No one will protect her better than me. I'd never let anyone hurt her."

I didn't miss the curl in Damon's lip at Blake's last statement. I cleared my throat. "So, Daddy, when are you playing again?" It was all I could think of to get the focus off me and loosen things up.

"This Saturday. Wanna come?"

"I can't, I have to work. Hey, what if I ask my boss if you could play at the bar one night?"

A smile slid across his face. "I never thought of that. Sure thing, ladybug. This old man can show you youngins how it's really done."

I grinned, still uncomfortable with the giant elephant in the room.

"I'll set it up when I get back."

Mom clapped her hands together. "Time for presents. You know it's my favorite part. Family room. Stat."

There was only room to walk single file as gifts seemed to come from every corner. "Ma, we're not babies anymore. This is crazy." I talked a good game, but really, I loved presents. Christmas just wouldn't be Christmas without the ginormous stacks we always got.

"Says who? You'll always be my babies." Her eyes practically glistened as she took us in.

"Blake and I are going to exchange tomorrow. His tradition is Christmas morning," I said.

"Us too," Abby added. "Damon said he got me the best gift ever this year, so I think he's trying to torture me." She pushed her lip out in a pout, shoving Damon's shoulder.

Time got away from us and, before we knew it, it was ten o'clock and we were still peeling paper off our gifts with no end in sight.

"Abby, I'm ahead of you. I gotta use the bathroom. Catch up while I'm gone." I hopped off Blake's lap, ignoring Damon's eyes on me as I left the room. I didn't remember how much wine I'd consumed sitting there for so many hours, but my bladder was reminding me it hadn't been a little. After a while, Abby had set a bottle in front of each of us and we'd gotten rid of our glasses. Now my head was light and airy, and I finally felt relaxed.

Having Blake here made me feel safe. I replayed how he'd put Damon in his place during dinner and smiled, picturing the flush on Damon's cheeks when there was nothing left for him to say.

I washed my hands, reapplied my lip gloss, and then tightened my ponytail, draping it over my shoulder. In a rush to return to Blake, I threw back the door and ran straight into a brick wall.

A gasp caught in my throat when he covered my mouth with his hand and pushed me back inside the small half bath with his chest. "You think you're safe hiding behind your little boyfriend, letting him make a fool out of me, beautiful? You'll pay for that one, I guarantee it."

I shook my head in denial, my eyes darting behind him as terror coursed through me.

Damon's purple-red, wine-stained teeth pushed into my face. The smell of stale alcohol on his breath made my stomach lurch into my throat. "I'll always own you, you little bitch. You better find a way to tone him down. What would he think if he found out our little secret?"

He released my mouth, and I sucked in a large gulp of air. He dragged his finger down my jaw to the top of my breast, and I turned my head, squeezing my eyes shut. "You owe me one now. I don't like to share, and your little attitude just ensured you're not going to enjoy it next time."

Bile rose in my throat, and I bit down my cry as he squeezed my breast, twisting my nipple. Everything flashed before my eyes.

What he was doing . . .

Blake in the other room . . .

Blake.

In the other room.

I pulled from somewhere deep within me, and my eyes snapped open as I grabbed his finger, twisting it in my fist. Staring him straight in the eye, I spit out through clenched teeth, "You'll do no such thing. You're never going to touch me again. Do you understand? It's over." I threw his hand away from me in disgust.

Damon laughed. "Feisty, too. I think I like this even better." He moved in closer to my face, backing me against the wall. "I say when it's over. Get out of fucking fairyland. You're mine." He dug his fingers into the tops of my arms.

Those words enraged me. They belonged to someone else. I pushed against him, whispering harshly through gritted teeth, "Damon, I fucking swear. Keep your hands off me, or I'll tell them. I swear to God, I'll tell them how you like to touch little girls. How you tricked me." I wasn't kidding. I'd open up my shame to the world if it meant I never had to deal with him again. I was done with this. "Now back. The fuck. Off me."

He laughed again, and my blood boiled. Finally he released me and crossed his arms over his chest, a confident smirk on his face. "They won't believe you. They love me."

And there was the truth we both knew. The reason why this had gone on as long as it had.

Another slice to my heart.

But, true or not, I needed to move on from this. I couldn't wash the last few months down the drain. "I don't care what they believe. It's over. Now get the fuck out of my way before someone comes looking for us, you asshole." I shoved past him, my hands visibly shaking, and took the stairs to my bedroom two at a time.

I sent a quick text to Jace.

Come here. Now.

I opened my window and stuck my head out into the freezing, snowy air, dragging giant gulps into my lungs. I needed to compose myself or Blake would know. My family was oblivious, but he'd be able to see right through me.

When my breathing returned to slow, even beats, I descended the stairs, smoothing back my hair, reveling in the fact that I'd just stood up for myself for the first time in my life. I felt invigorated and empowered.

Feeling saucy, I winked at Abby who was talking to Blake. I grabbed the wine bottle from the floor and threw my head back, pouring a good amount down my throat, then I pushed Blake back on the couch and straddled his lap. "I'm so glad you're here with me."

Blake held me by my shoulders and pushed back, his cheekbones tinged a rosy pink. "Whoa, Angel. I'm glad too, but time and place. Remember?"

"I know. I just wanted to tell you how much I love you."

His face softened. "I love you too, babe."

My parents walked back in the room. My dad's eyes went wide over the platter of cookies he was carrying. "Okay, ladybug. Put the bottle down. I don't need any grandchildren just yet."

I blushed, scooting next to Blake and throwing my legs over his lap.

Damon returned with a scowl on his face as he sat next to Abby, who hadn't taken her eyes off of me and Blake. She stared straight ahead as if she were somewhere else.

Suddenly, the front door bounced off the wall, and Jace stumbled across the threshold. "Merry Christmas Eve, bitches." He wore a huge smile as he sashayed over to my parents, kissing each of them and then Abby. He put his finger to his chin. "Damon, have you gained weight?" He slapped the back of his hand across Damon's gut. "Got a little pudge in the tub?"

"Nice to see you too, Jace," Damon ground out.

"I know it is." He squinted his eyes at him before spinning on his heel to face me. "Eva, come get me some alcohol. My throat's dry." He curled his hand around mine and tugged, dragging me alongside him. In the kitchen, he opened the freezer and dug around the bottom, revealing a half-filled bottle of Grey Goose.

"Hey. How'd you know that was there? I've been drinking crappy wine."

"Sweetie, I always know where to find the vodka. Now spill. What happened?"

I let out a big breath. "He cornered me in the hall and told me I'm his and that I'd pay for bringing Blake here with me, but I told him where to shove it. I did it, Jace!" I quietly squealed.

"That fuck!" He looked back toward the other room and then lowered his voice. "Good girl. I'm proud of you. You okay?"

I expelled a trembling breath, not realizing my nerves were still bunched somewhere in my tonsils. "I am now, but that's not something I want to do again any time soon."

"Yeah, well, I'm sleeping here. He won't get close enough again."

"It's okay. Blake's sleeping with me." Thankfully, since Damon and Jace had been around so many years, my parents were cool with them staying in our rooms. It was a blessing *and* a curse.

"Yes, I know. I've been dying for that sandwich and now I finally have an excuse, so back off the goods, bitch."

I wrapped my arms around his waist and squeezed. "Thank you."

Jace laced his fingers with mine and walked us back. I reclaimed Blake's lap as my seat, snuggling into his neck.

"Mother effer!"

My head snapped up as Damon sprang to his feet, wiping down the front of his slacks.

"Oopsie. I'm so clumsy sometimes." Jace licked the vodka that'd spilled over onto his fingers, a lopsided smirk adorning his face. "Well, now I need another drink. I just wasted that one on some tacky pants."

"Don't you think you've had enough, freak?" Damon asked, wadding up bits of napkin and dabbing at his crotch.

Abby was finally thrown from her trance. She narrowed her eyes at him. "Hey, it was an accident. Don't talk to him like that."

"Go get me a change of pants," Damon barked back at her.

"Watch yourself, Damon." My dad's voice was stern for a rare moment. "Jace is just as much a part of this family as you are."

Jace flicked his wrist at Damon. "It's not my fault there's not much there to absorb it. And go get your own pants. Your legs are wet, not broken." He brushed past him, knocking him on the shoulder before bouncing onto the loveseat. He crossed one leg over the other and stared him down, daring him to counter.

A tic broke out on Damon's flushed jaw and his nostrils flared. I had to fight a laugh when I noticed the smile tug at the corner of Blake's lips. Something told me he wasn't as fond of Damon as he'd originally let on.

"Now, now. I think everyone's had enough to drink for tonight. Go to bed all of you." My mom stood, picking up discarded wrapping paper. When no one moved, she repeated a little more forcefully, "Now."

"*Fine.*" I turned to Blake. "We inherited Jace for tonight. I hope you're not shy."

Although I knew he loved Jace, Blake's hard swallow told me he was a little worried. I patted his bicep. "It's fine. I'll sleep in the middle."

"Be flattered, hot stuff. Not everyone gets to share a bed with all this." Jace did a wiggle, dragging his hands over his body.

I snorted out a laugh. "Come on, trouble maker."

After the three of us changed and washed for bed, I peeled back the purple duvet and crawled up toward the pillows, thankful my parents had handed down their queen size when they'd upgraded to king. It'd still be a tight fit, but we'd manage.

Left in only his boxers, Jace skipped over and hopped onto the bed on his knees. Blake still hadn't budged. Knowing he usually slept just about naked, I laughed at the thick sweatpants and long sleeved shirt he wore as he stood at the foot of the bed.

"Blake, get your ass in here. I'm not diseased." Jace slammed himself back on the pillows and wiggled onto his side.

Blake rounded the opposite corner and kissed my forehead. "It's after twelve. Merry Christmas, Angel."

"Merry Christmas." I bit my smiling lip and scooted back, flipping the sheet open to invite him in.

Blake slid beneath the covers and took me in his arms, tugging me close to his chest. He wrapped his legs around mine and kissed my nose. I delighted in the fact that tonight I was sandwiched between the two guys I loved the most, and that I finally felt safe in my home. In my bed. It would be the first peaceful rest I'd had here in what felt like forever. I kissed the divot at the base of Blake's neck and buried my face in his chest, inhaling his scent.

Blake's body tensed beneath my touch. "Angel?"

"Mmhmm."

"Any chance you grew a third hand?"

"Wha . . . uh . . . Jace?" I twisted my neck to look at my traitorous best friend.

"I'm sorry." Jace definitely didn't sound sorry. "I might never get this opportunity again. I needed to feel those rock hard buns for myself and woohoo does it feel as good as it looks. Congrats, doll."

"That's it!" Blake threw the covers off, about to spring from the bed. I jumped up, silencing him with my lips and pressing into him while trying to stifle a giggle.

After a moment, he relaxed and I whispered into his ear, "Let it go. He got his free feel. He'll be satisfied now."

"I'm just nervous. I kinda liked it." Blake's voice squeaked as he shivered.

I laughed, reaching behind me to lace my fingers with Jace's. "Go to sleep, boys."

"Merry Christmas, Blakey," Jace called over my shoulder.

Chapter 28

WARM LIPS PRESSED AGAINST MY temple. My eyes blinked open, taking in the dusky light. I panicked for a moment when I realized I was in my old bed, and then I felt Blake's warm body snaked around mine. I looked up at Jace's soft cocoa eyes.

"Morning, baby girl," he whispered. "Merry Christmas. I'm gonna head home before my mom sends out the troops. You good?"

"Yes. Thanks for coming. You always save me."

"And I always will. See you tonight. Text me if you need anything. Love."

"Love."

I closed my eyes and burrowed deeper into Blake, drinking in his scent. He stirred and, without opening his eyes, tugged me even closer. The rhythmic beating of his heart and smooth rise and fall of his chest lulled me. My body felt light as a feather, as if it were floating on a cloud.

Thump. Thump. Thump. Hisssss . . . . . .

I faintly registered the bed dipping down behind me.

Fingertips dug into my ribcage, dragging me back and slamming me against a chest. A chill replaced the warmth I felt seconds before. An erection poked me in the back while a hand snaked around my neck, covering my mouth. I cringed as warm breath touched my earlobe, and I tried to tuck my ear into my shoulder to shield it.

"You belong to me, beautiful. Don't ever forget that. I don't know what gave you the balls to fuck with me and think you could get away with it." Damon's hand left my mouth, and I gasped, staring at Blake sleeping peacefully on the opposite end of the mattress.

He pushed his erection into my backside while squeezing my breast to the point of pain. "You feel that?" he whispered harshly. When I didn't respond, he pushed into me harder. "Do you?"

"Yes," I replied, barely audible, scared Blake would wake up and see what was happening.

"You're going to feel it. Trust me." He turned me to my back and settled his full weight on top of me.

"Don't do this," I cried, frantically turning my head to look at Blake. I stared at his even breathing, not understanding how he was sleeping through this.

"Help me." I don't even know if the words left my mouth as a tear escaped the corner of my eye and fell into my hairline.

Damon jerked my tank up, exposing my breasts. There was a crazed look in his eyes as he lowered his head and bit down on my nipple.

My back bowed, and I screamed, "No!" Slapping him on the head. "Get the fuck off me!"

"Angel? Angel!" Blake's voice broke through my cries, but his body still lay beside me calm and motionless.

Damon's hand grabbed my chin and pulled my focus back to him. "Look at me! Look at me!" But the voice wasn't his. It was Blake's.

I pushed against him, trying to get up. He grabbed me by the shoulders, shaking me. "Angel, wake up! Open your eyes!"

Breaking free of his hold, I scooted haphazardly on the bed, slamming my back to the headboard and drawing my knees in. My eyes darted around, trying to focus.

The lamp on the bedside table clicked and Blake's concerned face illuminated as he squatted over me and cupped my face in his hands. "Do you see me? It's just me." His eyes were wild as they bore into mine.

My head bobbed up and down quickly. I did see him, but I was still so confused. I looked around the room trying to force reality to sink in. Dusk was peeking through the blinds and the day was about to make itself known. Jace was gone, so that really happened, but everything else was still intact. The rest was just a dream. We were alone.

Oh no. I sunk my head between my knees and wept, mortified Blake had seen this.

"It's me, baby. Look at me." He tilted my head back to focus on him. "There you are." He scooped me onto his lap. "I couldn't get you to come back to me. Jesus Christ, where were you? How often does this happen?" Blake rocked me in his arms, smoothing his hands down my back. He pulled my hair over my shoulder and searched my eyes. "Angel?"

I shook out my hands and rubbed my temples. "Give me a second." I sucked in a ragged breath through my nose and blew it out my mouth slowly, counting to ten. "I'm so embarrassed."

"Hey, don't you dare." He put his finger under my chin and lifted my gaze. "It's me. Don't ever hide from me. Tell me what that was. Does this happen all the time?"

"It used to." I looked away. "It hasn't happened since . . ." I looked back into his icy blue pools. "Since you." I shrugged and looked away again, tucking my hair behind my ear. "I should've known . . . being here . . . I shouldn't have let you see that. I'm sorry."

"Are you kidding me? Evangelina, I need to know these things." A territorial fierceness coated his eyes. "I don't want you sleeping without me anymore. What if I wasn't with you?"

I scoffed. "I'm used to this, Blake. Why do you think I live alone? Why I spent all my time before you alone? I told you. What I live with isn't pretty."

Recognition of the deep-rootedness of my issues shown in his eyes. I secretly prayed he'd have the sense not to press. Not here. Not now.

His jaw clenched with determination. "We're going to fix it."

I pushed out a condescending snort of a laugh. "There's no fixing me, Blake."

"Bullshit, Eva. I am going to fix it. Do you trust me?"

The million dollar question. Of course I trusted him, but this was out of the realm of his control and he needed to accept that. Knowing how relentless he was when he was determined, I knew I had to agree or he wouldn't let up.

"I do trust you."

"When we get home, you need to open up to me. I want to know exactly what's happened so I can help you. No more secrets. Okay?"

I found myself agreeing before I could think better of it. "Okay."

His hold loosened as he relaxed a little. "Good. You're sleeping with me from now on. No exceptions."

"I don't need a babysitter, Blake," I muttered. "I'll be fine once we're home."

"I'm not babysitting. I'm protecting my investment." He winked, lightening the mood.

I couldn't help but smile. I didn't know what I'd done in my life to deserve someone like him. Always so loving and nurturing, putting my needs above all else. Some sick part of me was happy he'd witnessed that. As strong as I was, and as independent as I'd become, a small piece of me still yearned to be taken care of. To know I wasn't alone. It was exhausting keeping up the appearance of someone who was strong and unaffected.

Though, sticking up for myself for the first time last night had to count for something. Maybe my strong façade was being replaced by true strength and determination to move past this. I didn't know when this transformation had taken place, but I had to believe the man sitting before me had everything to do with it.

I couldn't view this night terror as a setback. I wouldn't. It would only thwart my progress. I owed it to Blake and to myself to try. To see the good in this. The truth of how I suffered was out and it felt liberating. And it put me one step closer to being one hundred percent open with Blake. To accepting what'd happened in my life. I didn't want to hash it out yet, though. I wanted to enjoy Christmas with my first boyfriend. That asshole didn't deserve to continue consuming every aspect of my existence.

I cupped Blake's face in my hands and kissed the tip of his nose. "You're an amazing man, Blake Turner."

A broad smile spread across his face. "Thank you, Evangelina Angel Ricci. You rock pretty hard yourself."

I wrapped my arms around the back of his head and moved onto my knees, kissing him deeply. Then I drank in his scent, pushing my chest into his, wanting to get as close as I could.

Blake broke the kiss and pressed his forehead to mine. "Time and place, Angel. I don't like to start things I can't finish."

I exhaled, bringing myself back down. "Okay." I raised an eyebrow. "Want your Christmas gift?"

"Here? Now?"

"Looks like morning to me." I smirked.

"You know I love surprises." Blake sat back on his heels as I scrambled off the bed. I rummaged through my bag until I found the bundle discreetly rolled into my jeans.

"Sneaky, sneaky." Blake smirked.

"I try." I hopped on the bed, tucking my feet beneath me and handed him the shiny gold package.

He turned it over, examining it and raised his eyebrows at me.

"Just open it," I said.

Blake slipped a finger under the tape. He peeled the paper back, revealing a silver corner, then pulled slowly, ripping a line down the center until my gift was fully exposed. His eyebrows drew together while he studied the picture frame in his hands. The crease pinched between his eyes began to slacken as he looked up to meet my hopeful gaze.

"Is this for real?"

"For really real." I smiled a toothy grin, proud of my well thought out gift.

Blake ran his fingers over the engraved scroll at the top.

Laughter is Timeless, Imagination has no Age, Dreams are Forever
~With Love, Angel

The Walt Disney quote stood out to me, perfect for Blake and all he believed in, but I knew the most important part of the gift was tucked beneath the glass.

"How did you afford this? I . . . I can't accept this." Blake's eyes glistened as he stared down with bowed shoulders.

"You can and you will. What's done is done. You're registered and you start next month. Now say thank you and give me a kiss."

"Angel, you can't afford professional photography classes. We'll get a refund and put it toward your tuition. Thank you. It was the most thoughtful gift I've ever received in my life. But I just can't." He placed the registrar's paid bill down beside him and my eyes fell on it.

I'd saved every possible penny to afford those classes. He would have been able to take them for free at Columbia, but I couldn't chance his dad finding out, so I'd bought him a semester at the New York Institute of Photography instead. The fact he was refusing my gift made me irate. I walked on my knees until I met him on the bed. "Blake Turner, I love you and I put a lot of thought into this gift. Now, you will accept it, or I will not even open your gift. You feel me?"

Blake let out a small laugh, swiping his forearm under his nose and sniffling. "Look at you all forceful and shit. You're scaring me again. It's not Tuesday, is it?"

"Hardy har har. You done ruining my gift now? I was happy a moment ago." I narrowed my eyes, pretending to pout. A smile split Blake's gorgeous face.

"Well, if you insist."

"I double insist." I threw my arms around his neck and squeezed. "Are you excited?"

"Honestly, I'm numb right now. I can't feel my toes. This is right up there with sex."

"Hey, now don't talk crazy."

"You're right." He shook his head. "I don't know what I was thinking. C'mere." Blake tugged on my arm, and I fell into him. He wrapped his arms around my back and dipped me, kissing me softly through smiling lips.

I lost myself in the sweet moisture, his soft tongue gliding in and out of my mouth.

Then he sat me up so quickly; my eyes lingered closed and my lips remained pursed as though I was still kissing him. "Your turn." His grin turned wicked as he reached under the bed and stopped. "Put out your hands and close your eyes."

I squished my eyes tight and reached my hands out in a grabby motion. He wasn't the only one who liked surprises. "Gimme, gimme."

Something smooth met my palm.

"Open." Blake's voice sounded full of anticipation and excitement.

I opened my eyes with a huge smile on my face and looked down at a leather bound book, wrapped in a red bow. My eyebrows knitted together as I peeled the bow open with two fingers.

The leather was soft as butter in a rich chocolate color. I opened the cover and my hand came up to my mouth. Inscribed on the front was Blake's handwritten scribe:

A place for all your Forget-Me-Nots

A dried out flower was fastened below it, along with the selfie we'd taken our first date on the rooftop.

"I want you to make happy memories. I don't want our moments mixed with all the bad memories in your old journal. A new journal for a new life. Nothing should taint what we have, and I never want you to confuse the two."

A tear fell, wetting the petal. "Better and better. God, I love you, Blake. Nothing could be more perfect than this."

Blake smirked. "Come on now. Give me some credit. You're not done yet." He swiped the moisture from my bottom lashes with the pad of his thumb. "Turn the page."

I bit my lip and turned. The next few pages were all the words Blake ever wrote me. I laughed through tears, seeing his candid photos of me, his forget-me-not poem, and each note he'd left me the day of our date. He'd even written out the playlist he'd downloaded on my iPod. I turned one more page, and my breath caught in my throat.

A delicate gold chain was draped down the page. Different charms hung from scattered points. With a shaky hand, I examined each one. The first was a tree, and I smiled, thinking of Bertha. Next was a camera, followed by a microphone, a rose, a horse and carriage, angel wings, a music note, a unicorn, and a feather pen. My fingers grazed the gold back and forth, amazed at the thought he'd put into this gift.

"Blake, I'm speechless."

"Your face said enough. I'm happy you like it." He plucked the chain from the page and sat behind me. I lifted my hair, and he clasped it around my neck. Putting his hands on my shoulders, he kissed the soft skin, letting his lips linger there as he breathed me in. His nose traveled up my jaw, toward my ear, and his whispered breath sent a chill down my spine. "I love you so much, Angel. So much it hurts sometimes. I hope you know how important you are to me. You're my life now. Nothing makes sense without you anymore."

"I love you, too. More than I think you realize. You gave me my life back, and I could never repay you for that." I turned and placed each leg around his hips. "I feel like I've been with you forever. It's weird it's only been a couple of months. You're a piece of me now. I almost feel like you always were."

Blake knotted his fingers in my hair and brushed his nose against mine. I breathed in a slow breath, dragging in his scent, closing my eyes. He pressed a soft kiss to my lips before licking the seam. I parted them, inviting him in. My head buzzed with the overwhelming sense of what could only be classified as Blake racing through my system. It couldn't be confused with anything else. I wanted to pull him inside my skin but at the same time I already felt him there, living inside me.

I looked into his eyes that were full of so much love. "Can we make this quick today? I want to go back to your place and cuddle. Alone."

"Sounds perfect." Blake fingered the necklace so it sat just right, a soft smile on his lips as he admired it. "I plan on filling this with memories for the rest of your life."

I smiled. "I'm sure you do."

A loud knock sounded at the door, and I hurried off Blake's lap, smoothing down my hair. "Come in."

Abby stuck her head in. "Breakfast is ready. Come eat. I want my gift." She bounced from the door, excited, and Blake and I followed.

The smell of fresh brewed coffee floated up the stairs. Breakfast Christmas morning was enough to make anyone's mouth water. Bacon, eggs, French toast and, of course, leftover Christmas cookies were laid out buffet-style on the dining room table. Damon was practically perched on the edge of his seat as though he was waiting for something, and I wondered faintly what that could be. Though I was used to ignoring him at my mother's table, that night terror was enough to bring back the vilest of memories, making me acutely aware of his presence. I choked them down and focused on the delicious assortment before me, so not to tip anyone off.

After shoveling abnormal amounts of food into my face, I leaned back, holding my belly. "This is my favorite part, but now I want a nap."

"No shot," Abby argued. "I waited long enough for my gift. Pony up, Da—" Abby's words trapped in her throat as she turned to face her boyfriend. Damon was down on one knee, a black velvet box propped open with a shiny diamond sitting in the plush center.

I shot forward in my chair, my mouth hanging open and instantly dry as the desert. "Holy shit."

Abby clamped a hand over her mouth, her eyes dancing in a watery shimmer.

He looked up at my sister with adoration and I thought for the briefest of moments that his love might have been real. "Abigail Tracy Ricci, I've loved you since before I knew what love was. You're my best friend and my soul mate. I want to spend the rest of my life making you happy. Would you do me the honor of becoming my wife?"

I looked back and forth from her to him, emotions warring inside me. Part of me was ashamed I felt relief this might end my constant torture. That maybe he'd finally leave me alone. The other part was sick knowing if she said yes, I'd have to live with this scumbag for the rest of my life, and my sister, who I loved more than anything, would unknowingly be taking a rapist as a husband. I played my part in all of this, and carried around my own lot of guilt, but I was smart enough to know that that's what he was.

I was freaking out inside, my heart racing a mile a minute. Was I supposed to finally tell her? Chance losing her? Or was I supposed to swallow it down for good as though it never happened and let her be happy? I watched her own question bounce back and forth behind her eyes as her lack of response started to make it uncomfortable.

"Abby?" Damon's pasted grin faltered just a smidge. "Are you going to answer, sweets? I want you to be my wife."

Her eyes left the ring and met his. Recognition of her decision showed on her face. I knew what was coming, and I hung my head, closing my eyes.

"Yes," she said low, at first, and then it seemed to hit her. "Oh my god, yes, Damon!"

I looked up as a smile split his face. I wanted to see the old Damon behind it, but I didn't. He slipped the ring onto her shaking finger and hugged her. Then his eyes found mine as he glanced at me over her shoulder and for the first time I thought he actually did look happy.

"Congrats, bro. That's awesome! I'm glad I was here for it," Blake boomed, hopping to his feet to rush to their side of the table. I sat, shocked, feeling as though I was in a bubble outside the room.

Abby examined her finger and squealed. "Mommy!"

"Baby!" My mom held her arms open. "Do you have any idea how hard it was for me to keep a secret?" They ran to each other, wrapping their arms around one another. "Oh my god, this means grandbabies!"

Grandbabies. What if they're girls?

I swallowed hard. I couldn't let that happen. It was time to break the news somehow. Abby's well being was more important than anything else, more important than my betrayal, more important than the shame and guilt I've been carrying all these years.

But Christmas morning wasn't the time.

My stomach caved inward, and I suddenly felt like I was about to lose my breakfast. I had to save face. I wet my napkin in my water and quickly dabbed it on the back of my neck while everyone bestowed their congratulations on the lucky couple. Finally able to string a few words together, I forced a smile. "Congrats, you two."

Abby waved her hands in the air. "Eva, you have to be my maid of honor! Say yes!"

I rubbed my palms on my thighs and let out a shaky, nervous laugh. "Yes, of course."

My dad clapped Damon on the back. "Congrats, son. I always knew you'd officially be part of the family one day."

Family. He'd be an actual part of my family soon.

I'm living my worst nightmare.

Chapter 29

"ARE WE ALMOST DONE? MY eyes are blurry." I scrubbed my palms over my lids and blinked, then opened my eyes wide to focus back on Blake's laptop.

"I think so. I just have to figure out where I'm sticking the law class." Dressed in only a pair of boxers, Blake pulled the computer onto his lap. The chiseled lines of his abs were something I'd never tire of seeing.

I huffed. "Who cares? You don't want to take it anyway. We've been registering for hours already. Just skip it this semester."

Blake put the back of his hand to my forehead. "You feeling okay? I think you've lost your mind."

I scowled at him, and he smiled, shaking his head. "Why do you have to give me a hard time? You know I have no choice." He clicked the mouse and squinted at the screen.

"*That.* That sentence right there is why I give you a hard time. There's always a choice. It's your life. That man doesn't deserve the respect you give him."

"Back off, short stack. He's my father." Though his words were teasing, Blake's eyes were stern.

"Well, that doesn't make it right." I stood, placing pressure on my lower back while leaning backward to stretch, causing my pink satin undies to peek out from the bottom of Blake's T-shirt.

Blake's gaze settled on the curve of my ass before he peeled it away to look me in the face. "Can't you just support me?"

I stopped moving and put my hands on my hips, staring down at him. "That's exactly what I *am* doing."

He sighed. "Angel, I'll make a good living for us when I'm done. You'll be able to have anything you want."

I bent so we were eye level. "I already have all I want. I'm not superficial. I chose my major so I could make a good living *without* the help of a man. And I don't need to have a miserable husband so I can be dripping in diamonds."

"I know you're not—Hey . . ." Blake caught my wrist when I turned to walk away.

I looked down at him. "Do what you want. I'm done trying to help."

In the kitchen, I filled a glass and went to the balcony to water Blake's forget-me-nots. I stood with the cup, staring at the wilted box, and then decided to dump it in anyway before returning inside. Rubbing the cold from my arms, I stood before Blake with a frown. "Your babies are dead."

He remained focused on the screen, a smirk playing on his lips. "They'll be fine. Have some faith."

I nudged his knee. "Are you done wasting your time?"

Blake scrambled to grab the computer before it fell from his lap. He huffed. "You're taking all those psych classes. That can't be what you want to do, but you're doing it so you can be successful, yes?"

"Of course that's what I want to do." I frowned at him. "It interests me. I can't make a living writing poems, and I'm not going to be a famous singer either."

"You could make a decent living doing either of those things. You're really good at both. But instead, you take those boring-ass psych classes to become something you're not, trying to prove something to . . ." He cocked his head. "Who *are* you trying to prove something to?"

I dug my fingertips into my hips and lifted my chin. "No one . . . myself . . . this isn't about me." I turned and marched down the hall.

He followed close on my heels. "It's as much about you as it is me."

"No, it's not." I turned, pointing a finger. "I made my *own* decision to become a psychiatrist. You're just a puppet." I clapped my hand over my mouth, sorry the instant the words left my lips.

Blake squared his shoulders, hurt shadowing his eyes. "Is that what you think of me?"

"No . . . Yes . . . No . . . Blake! Come on. Think about how you're wasting your time. I hate watching you do this. I only say it because I love you. You deserve to be happy."

"I am happy." Suddenly, the disappointment in his eyes vanished and he stepped closer. He trailed his fingers down the crevice between my breasts.

"I'm not talking about that," I stuttered, feeling lightheaded already. "Don't distract me. Sex won't make you happy when you're working eighty hours a week and you never get to see me."

"Sex will always make me happy, Angel." He forced my back against the wall.

"You're not taking me seriously," I huffed.

His heated gaze bore into mine. "Oh, I'm taking you. Seriously." Without notice, Blake bent, scooping me behind the knees, and wrapped my legs around his waist as he pressed into me. He nibbled my collarbone and licked a trail up the side of my neck, nipping the edge of my jaw.

"Blake . . ." *Damn him!*

"Oh, say my name, baby. Just like that. Scream it." He scrunched his nose, biting down on his bottom lip, and ground into me.

I whimpered against his neck.

He yanked my shirt up and over my head and then his warm breath teased my ear as he fingered the strip of silk at my core. "You insulted me," he whispered.

I closed my eyes and let the sensation engulf me. "I'm sorry. I love you. You know that."

"Show me how much." Blake slipped his finger under the material and dragged it across the seam of my wet silken folds. "I'm gonna make this pussy sing." He pushed his boxers down, and I felt the roundness of his ass under my calves. Moving my panties aside, he snaked his arms up my back and cupped my shoulders. Then he pushed upward, impaling me in one swift motion.

I gasped, feeling so full so quick, but Blake didn't move. He applied pressure to my shoulders, still pushing up with his groin until he was in me to the hilt. He shoved his tongue in my mouth, and I clawed at his back, dragging my nails up to fist his hair.

Breaking the kiss, he bit down on my bottom lip and dragged his teeth along it before sucking it back into his mouth. "We'll see who the puppet is. You're going to do exactly what I say. Understood?" Without waiting for a response, Blake grabbed a fistful of my hair and tilted my head back, biting and sucking his way down to draw a pebbled nipple into his mouth.

I let out a whimpered moan as his hips started to move. "You like that?"

"Mm hmm." *Fuck, did I ever.*

"Come for me."

His ass hardened with each thrust, slamming my spine into the wall as he picked up the pace. He covered my mouth with his again, and then dragged his teeth along my jaw. "Come on. I want to feel you explode around me." Blake moved quicker. His eyebrows pinched together in ecstasy as my climax heightened. "Whose pussy is this?" He licked his thumb and pressed it to my clit, rubbing circles.

"Yours," I breathed into his neck.

"I didn't hear that. Whose. Pussy. Is. This?" Blake drove into me with every word.

"Yours!" I screamed.

"Come for me, baby. Show me. Now."

Instantly, my world split in two as my release tore through me. He cupped his hands around my shoulders and pushed himself deeper as he emptied into me. His release hit a spot inside, bringing a fresh wave of jolts, and I vibrated against him, before falling limp in his arms.

"Puppet *master* is what I am. See how I just did that?" He pushed into me once more for emphasis.

I nodded into his neck, too weak and euphoric to rebut him.

Still joined at the hip, Blake walked us back to his bedroom. As he laid me down, his still hard cock twitched inside me, hitting a spot that made me squirm beneath him. I cupped his ass and held him to me. "Don't pull out yet."

"I'm not going anywhere." Blake rocked into me slowly. "I'm gonna make love to you now. I just needed to show you who was boss first." He slipped his tongue inside my mouth, caressing mine. Then he took his time, gliding in and out of my core, moving so slow I could feel his mushroomed tip sliding along my walls.

I kept my legs tight around his waist, using my heels to urge him on, but he kept his slow pace. My body let out random jolts and twitches, searching for its release. Blake circled his hips, sucking the rosy peak of my breast into his mouth.

"Blake . . ." I begged, my climax teetering on the edge. I clamped my walls around his shaft, massaging its length with each glide and eliciting a moan from him. Gripping the hair at the back of his head, I bore down, hoping he'd give me what I craved. "You like that?"

His eyes pinched shut as he dropped his forehead to mine. "You know I do."

"Then fuck me. Make me come again."

Blake growled. Cupping my ass, he squeezed to the point of pain and lifted me off the bed. His speed quickened, and I twisted the sheet at my sides. My lower back arched in the air, my shoulder blades pushing into the mattress. His thumb was back on my clit as he applied just the right amount of pressure to bring me to release.

He dragged his fingers up my back and pulled me to him so we were sitting up and my legs were wrapped around his hips. The hot spurts of his arousal poured into me while his mouth muffled the cry of his name on my lips. He lapped up each of my moans, and then buried his face in my neck, and bit down on my shoulder. I jumped at the prick to my sensitive flesh.

We stayed that way, sweaty and panting, silently petting and sucking each other until our breathing evened out.

Blake put both hands to the side of my face and kissed me softly, his fingers brushing the hair at my temples. "Mine."

I smiled against his lips. "Yours."

He wrapped his arms around my waist and laid us down on our sides, scooping me in. Nestling back as far as my body would allow, I smiled as his wet hardness pressed at the back of my thighs, knowing he was drenched with me. "I don't think I'm done. It still hurts." His cock twitched against my legs. I pushed back on it, and he moaned. "Fuck." He dragged his palm up my torso and cupped my breast, toying with my hardened nipple. I leaned my head into his shoulder, exposing my neck for him, and he sucked at the soft skin. His hard, round head pressed into my backside, and I hooked my leg behind me, over his hip, opening myself to him. Blake let out a hiss, pushing up and pulling my breast as he slid into my core. "God, you feel so fucking good. You're still so wet and tight."

I mewed softly in response, unable to speak at the fullness I felt having him that way. I rolled my ass, teasing his cock, and he clamped his hand on my hip and ground into me. His breath at my ear sent tingles down my spine. He growled as his hand skidded up the front of my body and he cupped my jaw, bringing my lips to his. His tongue danced with mine, dipping in and out of my mouth, stealing my breath. Still gliding in and out of me, he licked his way down my jaw, twisting me so he could suckle my tightened bud. He sucked on it hard, biting down, and I moaned in ecstasy.

Blake cupped my breast in his hand and pushed his hard chest into my back, searching for his climax. "I'm gonna come. Come with me, baby. One more time." He pushed further inside me, his hand coming around my belly to find my sweet spot. He flicked it between his fingers, and my body convulsed around his, bucking and shaking as he screamed my name with his release.

Still on our sides, we both melted into the mattress. My body lay limp in his arms, drained of everything. Blake ran his sexy feet up and down my calves, nuzzling into my neck. "Sleep. I want you in my arms all day."

"Trust me, I'm not going anywhere. Ever. I love you, Blake Turner."

"I love you more, Evangelina Ricci." He kissed the top of my head, and his breathing became slow and even.

I prayed for the millionth time that it would always be this way.

"CHECK, ONE-TWO-THREE."

I smiled at my dad as he and the band set up. Walking to the register, I leaned my hip against the back counter, popping some bar nuts into my mouth. "Thanks again for letting them play here. I really appreciate it."

Rick smiled over the stack of bills in his hand. "Anytime, munchkin. You know I'd do anything for you." He kissed my forehead. "Would you go grab the Coronas from the back? We're kinda light up here."

"Sure." I stopped at the corner of the bar. "Ma, take a walk with me."

My mom never missed my dad play. Thirty years later and she was still his biggest fan. They'd met when he'd been playing at a club in her neighborhood one night. She'd followed him home like a groupie and had been trailing him ever since. It was kind of cute when I thought about it.

"Grab a box, would ya?" The bottles clanked inside the heavy confines as I hoisted the load to my hip. "Got it?"

"Yeah." My mom grunted as she lifted, struggling with the weight.

"You sure?"

Her green eyes gave me a pointed look. "Eva, I carried you around inside my body for a full nine months. I can carry some beer to the front."

"Touché."

Laden with clamoring boxes, we waddled by the band and a sharp whistle sounded through the speaker. My mom shook her head and blushed, acting as though she wasn't used to my dad by now. I dropped my burden behind the bar and stood, blowing air up toward my forehead to rid loose strands of hair from my face.

"You almost ready, Big Joe? We're about to open the doors," Rick yelled over the bar.

"We're good to go. Let them in," my dad called into the mic.

He clapped his drumsticks together and began their rendition of *A Hard Day's Night* by the Beatles. My dad played hard like a rock star. He lived for this stuff, and I always had a blast watching him. It never got old for me. He didn't let his day job as an international banker 'steal his soul' as he liked to say. He always provided well for his family, while still holding onto his spirit, and I admired that.

Lately, things were slowly returning to normal, and I couldn't have been happier. I was seeing my family more, relaxing around my friends, and the night terrors seemed to have stopped again. I had Blake to thank for it. He'd helped me to feel again. Live again. Be in the world instead of gliding in and out of each day with my head buried in the sand. I owed everything to him.

A few hours later, I needed a breather. I wiped the back of my arm across my forehead and took a sip of water, proud of how receptive everyone was to my father's band. It always amazed me how young people enjoyed them just as much as the more suitable, older crowds. The place was packed with wall to wall bopping heads and dancing figures. Their cover of well-known, older rock like The Beatles was always a crowd pleaser.

I positioned a row of glasses, then shook the metal container between my hands and poured shots of snakebite in a single line. Setting the container down, I glanced to my right. Blake and Eric were laughing, joking the way they always did. Blake looked so relaxed with his hair gelled back, away from his face, a rosy hue to his high cheekbones. He seemed so carefree in his white V-neck, leaning one forearm on the bar. I pictured his black jeans perched on top of the barstool and got warm inside.

"I'm ready for another one, beautiful." An empty Miller Lite bottle slid and hit the side of my hand.

A cool chill raced down the back of my neck, and my hand snapped back as I met the eyes I despised most. Gathering the pieces of my newly empowered fierceness, I straightened my spine, swiped the bottle, and threw it into the cardboard box under the bar. "Abby, too?"

"Nah, not just yet. She might have to get a slap if she has another. She keeps staring at your boy's pretty little friend over there." His eyes dripped with malice as he nodded in Eric's direction.

The inside of my skin grew hot. Damon was progressing. He'd gone from the nice boy next door, to someone who connived to get his way, to a rapist, and was now making physical threats. Watching it unfold was frightening, and the thought of my sister spending the rest of her life with him made me nauseous.

I leaned over the bar and stared him in the eye, swallowing down the bitter taste at the back of my throat. "You better not mean that, asshole."

Damon cocked his head to the side, analyzing me, no doubt surprised by my newfound strength. He expelled an appraising *humph* and leaned closer to me. He had to raise his voice because of the noise around us, but because of our proximity, it was done in a way only I could hear. "I'm not sure I'm digging the way you're acting lately. We might have to have a chat about that next time we're alone."

I refused to back down from his glower. "We're not going to be alone."

"Right, I forgot."

His narrowed eyes glittered with an unkind amusement, and I could tell my words held no weight with him. He reached across the bar and covered my hand with his. My fingertips hardened into the wood, but despite my racing heart I didn't move them, not wanting it to seem unnatural. His smile turned bright so he wouldn't attract attention, and I matched it with my own.

"I'm not going to say it again, Angel, is it? Watch your fucking mouth." Then he straightened, releasing my hand, and I took in a large gulp of air, not realizing I'd been holding my breath. "And I don't plan on touching your sister. It was a figure of speech. Just make sure your boy keeps to himself."

"Aren't you all 'boys'?" I air quoted, still trying to act surly despite the race in my heart.

His eyes narrowed and his face dropped its smile. "Not when my girl's drooling over one of them, we aren't."

"She's just having a good time. Stop acting like you're a saint." I tried to drive my hidden meaning into his brain through my eyes.

"What'd you say?" He cocked a brow.

"Nothing." Losing a bit of my nerve, I shook my head, twisting the cap off the fresh drink and sliding it toward him.

Pushing back off the bar, he watched me over his bottle as he took a swig. "Don't forget to mind your manners now, beautiful. We wouldn't want anything unfortunate to happen."

I swallowed hard as he walked away. Glancing to my right, I caught Blake's cool eyes. I gave him a small smile, waving my fingers, trying to hide my unease, but something seemed off in his stare. His eyebrows were pulled inward, and his back was straight as a tack. He curled a finger, calling me over.

Oh man. I fumbled with my fingers, hoping I hadn't given anything away, and tried to think of a cover-up. "What's up?"

"What'd that asshole say to you? You look upset." His hand was fisted on the bar as his eyes bore into mine, daring me not to tell him the truth.

"Asshole? I thought you liked him."

"I don't like him. I was being polite. Now tell me."

I toyed with my nail beds for a second, and then dropped them, knowing it was a tell of mine. "I didn't get upset. He was just being a dick because my dumbass sister can't keep her eyes off your friend here." I fought a smile as I motioned to Eric.

With a grin, Eric's chest swelled. "She knows where it's at, that's all." Then, in a rare moment, Eric grew serious. "Come on, Eva, admit it, I'm so much better than that douche bag. Tell her to move on. And what's with the ring? She's seriously going to marry him? That guy's trouble." He looked longingly in their direction.

Damon turned, catching Eric's eyes once again. He shook his head and slid a possessive arm around Abby's shoulders. She laid her cheek on his chest, then his lips curled in a cocky smile, and he kissed the top of her hair, still staring at Eric.

I pulled his attention back to me. "Trust me, I have. But that douche bag's a thorn in my side, so do me a favor and hold your horses while he's around. And what do you mean he's trouble?"

"We've known him a long time," Eric explained. "Let's just say if I had a sister, that's not who I'd let her marry. He's not exactly the monogamous type." He relaxed back in his chair and spread his legs.

My body stiffened and I swallowed hard. Of course, *I* knew that. But what did Eric know? Unease settled deep inside and I clutched the rolls in my stomach trying to tamp them down. *How many more were there?* I never thought of the prospect of *more* until this moment. I'd always assumed I was the only one. I pressed harder into the nerves coiling in my belly as I thought of Abby. What else had he done behind her back?

Blake scowled in Damon's direction. "I still don't like the way you looked. I'm ready to put him in his place already."

I so wish you could, Blake.

Unfortunately, he couldn't.

I shook my head. "Oh no, you're not. Time and place, remember? I'm working and my whole family is here. Cool your jets. You can't go all caveman every time someone gets under my skin."

"Like hell, I can't." His eyes were cool, his tone impermeable.

"What happened to polite?"

"Polite goes out the window the second someone disrespects you."

I had to change the mood. I could see this going down a bad road if I didn't. "Well, he didn't. So come on, let's do a shot. On me."

Blake rolled his shoulders in an obvious attempt to rein himself in. He dragged his eyes back to mine and slowly moved them down my body, licking his lips. "Which part?"

My cheeks flushed. "Such a naughty boy. What am I gonna do with you?"

He winked. "Anything you'd like. Twice if I'm lucky."

Eric waved his hands back and forth. "Hello, I'm still here!"

I stayed and did two rounds of shots with them to be sure Blake's mind was far from Damon, and then answered the calls of the rest of the bar for the next couple hours. When things calmed down a little, I left Jasmine to tend bar and went in search of my sister. My dad was between sets and she, Damon, and my mom were talking to him over his drums.

"Good job, Daddy." I placed a peck on his sweaty cheek, then turned to Abby. "Come to the bathroom with me." I didn't give her a chance to respond as I took her hand and dragged her away. I was scared for her and needed to find a way to tell her the truth, but now was not the time and the way she was acting was only going to create more of a problem.

I pushed open the door and leaned into the mirror, wiping the mess accumulating under my lower lashes as I waited impatiently for the other occupant to exit the stall. She washed quickly, then scooted out.

Once the door closed behind her, I narrowed my eyes at my sister. "What're you trying to do, Abby? Your boyfriend's getting all territorial watching you stare at Eric." Logically, I knew I had no right to be mad at her, but I couldn't help it. The fucker had me shaking and Blake was moments away from figuring it all out.

She pulled her hair over her shoulder. "I'm trying, all right? It's not easy. This is the first time I've seen him since that night, and I keep feeling his eyes on me. I can't help myself. I want to talk to him so bad."

"Well, help yourself. You just got engaged, you nutcase. He'll go crazy if he finds out you have feelings for someone else. I just can't understand why the hell you would say yes to him?"

Her posture slackened. "Because I know this is what I want."

Sadness filled her eyes, and they drifted from her fingers straight to the floor. "He's what's best for me."

Gag. *Fucking hell.*

I touched her shoulders. "Look, I have no idea what's best for you. I just know tonight's not the night to figure it out. Capisce?"

She shook her head in agreement, but I could tell her mind was miles away.

My eyebrows knitted together and any selfish thought I harbored flitted from my mind. This was my sister. All I was concerned about was making her feel better. Fixing the mess she'd found herself in. The words fell out of my mouth without thought. "I'm worried about you, Abby and there's so much to say, but not now. Not here." I smoothed a comforting hand down her arm. "I'll come by tomorrow and we can talk. Deal?" *Wait. What?*

She picked at the label on her beer. "Yeah, you're right. I just . . . forget it." The somber look on her face broke my heart. I didn't understand why she didn't see the writing on the wall. She wasn't happy. Probably realizing the same thing, she changed the topic. "Hey, when are you singing? You do it every shift, right?"

I exhaled, pushing all thoughts of this conversation and the one I had in store for me as far from my mind as I could. "I have no clue how Rick maneuvered it, but yes, I do. It'll be the first time I'm singing with Daddy in public, too. Speaking of which, I'm gonna need another shot. Liquid courage all the way." I winked, trying to lighten the mood. "Want one?"

"Sure do. Can we invite Eric to join?" A teasing smile split her face.

"Abby," I moaned.

"I know, I know. Come on. Let's make Mom do one, too." She looped her arm through mine.

A little while later, the sound of my dad's voice in the mic sent butterflies knocking around my stomach. "This night will go down in history for me, ladies and gentlemen. For years, I've been trying to get my daughter to sing with me and, thanks to that fine gentleman behind the bar, it's finally going to happen." He pointed his drumstick at Rick who smiled and nodded back at him. "So, Eva, get your butt up here and sing with your daddy." The catch of emotion in his voice couldn't be ignored.

Everyone shouted my name. I blew out a puff of air and looked at Blake. "Here goes nothing."

"You'll do great. You always do." He stood and came to meet me in front of the bar, lacing his fingers with mine. Then he kissed my forehead and handed me off to my dad, stepping back to watch me the way he always did.

"Okay, Dad. You got me here." I smiled over his cymbals. "I hope you know Demi Lovato because it's somewhat of a ritual for me."

He beamed. "Eva, I'll play whatever you want. I'm just so damn excited you're actually doing this."

I was only kidding. I'd already pre-picked *Warrior*. There wasn't much background to the song, so it wasn't hard for them to learn. There was no way I was singing The Rolling Stones. Mick Jagger, I wasn't. That song choice was a big step for me, and I selected it knowing the chance I was taking.

The keyboard player softly stroked the keys in a solemn tune. I dipped my head and curled my fingers around the mic stand, closing my eyes and letting the enormity behind the song sink into my veins.

In a soft, low voice, I began telling the story I had never told, letting the words pour from my soul. I used the lyrics to get it off of my chest and let it go. Taking back the light Damon had stolen from me. With my lips bowed, eyes still downcast, I told the story of the pain and the truth I wore like a battle wound, liberation fortifying my voice with each word.

When the chorus came, I looked up with a fierceness in my eyes, a stronger voice leaving my throat to exclaim I was a warrior. I pounded my fist at my side, growing sturdier each passing second.

Blake's arms were slack at his side, his eyes glistening with unshed tears, but I didn't let that deter me. I needed to get this out. My voice cracked as I sang about the shame and the scars I would never show. Emotions that had been locked inside me for so long burned leaving my throat, but it felt amazing. I needed Blake to know I was a survivor and because of him I would move past this.

The second chorus came around, and the bar was quiet but for the sound of the keyboard and my voice echoing through the speakers. I straightened my spine and looked past Blake, seeking out the eyes I really needed to find. Damon stood in the corner, his eyes wide and a look of horror on his face. He fisted the bottle in his hand and met my gaze. Undeterred, I stared straight at him as I sang about a little girl who had grown up too fast, telling him I was taking back my life. My lips curled over my teeth in disgust as I bit out every word, squeezing the mic stand so tight my knuckles turned white.

He grabbed Abby by her arm and spoke into her ear. My voice was still ringing from the speakers when they kissed my mother goodbye and he dragged Abby from the bar. I was glad he'd gotten the message. He could never hurt me again. I was sure of it. And, after tomorrow, whether I lost my sister or not, I would make sure he'd never hurt her either.

With my newfound thicker skin, a lone tear rolled down my cheek as I said goodbye to the frightened little girl I'd held onto for far too long.

The ending of the song was met with screaming applause and teary eyes, everyone oblivious to the truth behind my performance.

Everyone but Blake.

My dad came out from behind the drums to hug me, drowning me in praise, but I didn't hear a word he said. Over his shoulder, I watched Blake. His head was cocked to the side as he studied me with a puzzled look on his face. He turned to look at the door Damon had just exited and then back to me. Then he straightened, his eyes widening as if he was putting together the pieces of my tragic puzzle. He took three long strides and stood before me. He took me by my arm as the band started playing again.

"Come with me."

He pulled me outside the bar, and I wrapped my arms around myself, shielding the cold. Grabbing my shoulders, he bent to my eye level. "What was that?"

I recoiled. "What was what?"

"Were you singing that to him? Is it him?" His eyes implored mine as he squeezed my upper arms to the point of pain.

"What're you talking about?" I tried to break his hold, but he tightened his grip.

"Tell me, Angel. If it's him, so help me God I'll end his life right now. Fucking tell me!" He shook me.

"Blake stop it. You're scaring me." I yanked my arms from his grasp and took a step back. "What's gotten into you? It was just a song." My voice broke with fear. I'd never seen him this way.

He stepped toward me, and I backed up again. The vein in his neck was pounding as he bit down tight on his jaw. "You'd tell me right? If it was him? You'd tell me?" His eyes pleaded with me. Begging for the truth I'd never given him.

My voice sounded meek in my ears. "I would," I lied, amazed I could get the words out. I hated deceiving him, but I had no choice. "It was just a song. Please stop before you cause a scene." My eyes filled with tears. I was slowly losing the strength I'd had only minutes ago.

He closed the gap between us and took me in his arms. "I'm sorry. Fuck, I'm so sorry. It's just . . . the way you were looking at him . . . I was sure . . ." He blew out a breath into my hair. "All I saw was red. I'd kill him, you know. You'd never have to be afraid again."

For the first time, I felt like a shell as he held me in his arms. I was used to feeling protected and safe, warm and secure. Right now I just felt empty and hollow. My arms hung limp at my sides, and all I wanted was for him to let go of me so I could leave.

It was hard for me to let that out tonight, and I couldn't process Blake's reaction with the buzz in my head. I backed up from him. "I think you should stay at your place tonight. I need to sleep."

"Don't do that, Angel. I said I was sorry. What'd you want me to think?" His voice raised an octave.

"It's fine. I'm not mad. I just need to sleep it off."

Another lie.

I was confused and hurt and scared, and even though I knew he was only looking out for me, I had to do this my way. On my terms. Once this came out, I could potentially lose everything. I was scared shitless. This truth, this ugly fucking truth had the power to make me lose everyone I loved in my life.

Blake's voice caressed my fraying nerve endings. "I would never hurt you. You know that right? I was only trying to protect you."

I knew he was trying to fight for me, to protect me. But what he didn't understand was I was trying to do the same thing.

"I know." I nodded, on the verge of tears. "I'm just going to finish up and go home. I'll have my parents drop me off. I'll talk to you tomorrow, okay?"

His eyes gave away his uncertainty, but I could tell he didn't want to push me any further. He smoothed his hand down my arm. "Okay, baby. Text me when you get home, please?"

I half-smiled. "Sure."

Another lie.

Chapter 30

POUND. POUND. POUND

Drawing in a breath, I turned my swollen eyes to the clock. Five A.M. I'd just gotten in at four and crashed. I stumbled out from under the sheets. "I'm coming!"

Blake stood at the door, resting an arm on either side of its frame, looking a mess with crumpled clothes and hair in the same state. "You never texted me when you got home."

"I'm sorry, I passed out. I told you I needed sleep." I rubbed my palms into my eyes. "Why are you still up?"

"I feel shitty about the way we left things. Can I come in?"

I stepped back, holding the door open.

Blake barged in, raking a hand through his hair. "Angel, I'm trying really hard to be patient with all this, but I need to know the whole truth. I can't be in the dark anymore. It's driving me crazy and draining me, the constant fucking wondering. Look at me!" I hadn't noticed before how deep the worry lines between his eyes had become or how purple the bags below them were. Maybe I was in denial thinking we could go on like this forever, him never knowing the whole story.

But he was right. He needed to know. I couldn't risk him freaking out again the way he had tonight. "Sit down."

His eyes widened, and he took a deep swallow, slowly dropping to my couch.

I breathed in deep, scrubbing my palms together and focused on the tread in the carpet. "I thought it was okay. I was young and inexperienced and Damon was just . . . there. He was *always* there. But the way he watched me after I hit puberty was different. He looked at me like a woman when everyone else still looked at me like a child, and I . . . liked it." I looked up at Blake's confused eyes. He sat perched at the edge of the couch, waiting for the blow.

"I could tell right away it was wrong. I felt it in my bones the second he touched me, and I barely made it through. I tried to stop him after that first time, but he wouldn't. It went on for years behind my sister's back, and it's my fault. That's why getting over it's so hard. I . . . agreed to it." A tear slipped from my eyes and, though I felt small and ashamed, I forced myself not to look away.

Blake processed my words, his eyes pinched together, and then a swarm of coldness blanketed them. He stood, his hands fisted at his sides and his jaw tight. "You lied to me."

I stepped back, not expecting his anger to be directed at me. "I didn't lie to you."

"How could you make me think all this time you were forced? You're nothing but a slut and you made me think you were a victim?"

I pushed my fist into my crumbling heart. My worst fear was coming true. He was disgusted with me, and now I'd lose him. I couldn't. "Blake, please. I can explain better."

"Save it. I've heard enough." He walked away from me and turned back abruptly, stabbing his finger at me. "You had me ready to kill a guy who did nothing wrong. Girls like you make me sick. It's so easy for you to point a finger. *This* is the reason why I'm taking those law classes. To try and put a stop to manipulators like you." Blake ripped open my door and spoke with his back to me. "Don't bother calling me. We're done."

The sound of the door slamming ricocheted off the walls, and I dropped to my knees a sobbing heap of flesh. I rocked back and forth. "What have I done? What have I done? No!"

My cries rang in my ears, and suddenly my body flew up. The sheet bucked with the sharp movement of my chest as I tried to gain oxygen. Then my eyes focused on the blackened room, searching back and forth, frantic for reason.

The clock next to me read five A.M. My cheeks were soaked with tears, and I dropped my head into my knees.

It felt so real. My fears confirmed. He'd be gone the second he found out.

This was my mortal sin. My living nightmare. My doing. Damon had engrained that in my brain since day one. Etched it onto my veins. My choice. It was always my choice.

Until it wasn't.

I couldn't bear the disgusted look on Blake's face stuck behind my eyelids each time I closed them, attempting to wash away the memory.

It wasn't real. It wasn't real.

Wake up!

I threw off the covers and paced, pressing my fingertips into my temples. "Get out of my head!"

I flipped the switch, illuminating the room, and searched frantically for something to erase the horrible look on his face when my eyes zeroed in on the journal he'd given me sitting on top of my desk. I took long rushed strides to get to it, throwing open the cover to see a picture of his gorgeous happy face, smiling in the break of dawn, and me tucked happily beneath his chin.

My fingers lingered over the print, scared to touch it as I cried through a tortured smile. I loved him so much. I couldn't lose him. He was only trying to protect me, and I had pushed him away. Again.

I grabbed my phone and saw eight missed text messages. All from Blake. All asking if I'd made it home all right and if I was mad at him.

I typed out a quick response so he didn't worry.

Me: I'm okay. I'm home. Going to bed. XO.

My phone quickly pinged back.

Blake: Good. Text me when you wake up. I love you.

Me: Love you.

I responded, then threw my phone into the sheets.

I turned on every light in the apartment so I wouldn't fall back asleep, and drew open the blinds to the balcony. I made a cup of tea, and curled up on my couch with my new journal.

After I read through all of Blake's words five times, I convinced myself it wasn't real and I was being silly. Tomorrow I'd apologize for pushing him away, and I'd tell him the truth. The whole truth. It was time he knew. And at least it wouldn't be between us anymore. I'd set his mind free and hopefully my own as well.

I moved to the first fresh page.

He's the One
Air in my lungs
Light in my eyes
He came out of nowhere
A blessing in disguise

I never knew what I wanted
Never believed I'd be worth someone's time
Though I tried to push him away
He stole my heart like the perfect crime

He's the one
The one in my dreams
The one I can fall apart with
Who keeps me together at the seams

He's the one
The one I want by my side
Through thick and thin, for better or worse
Tossing all of my fears aside.

My heart is so swollen

Anything else doesn't matter
It races and lives
Soaring with each pitter patter

He lives in me
And I in him
And once I can set us both free
Our lives can truly begin

He's the one
My breath, my air
My light, my freedom
Who broke my walls and stripped me bare

To the edge of the earth
Till judgment day comes
I'll follow him endlessly
Because he's the one

By the time I wrote the last word, the sun was coming up and I was yawning. I put my cup in the sink and crawled back under the covers.

It felt like five minutes later when a never-ending ringing buzzed in my ears. I groaned into the pillow.

"Go away."

When it finally stopped only to start again, I fished around for my cell and swiped the screen with my eyes closed.

"What."

"Eva? Oh, thank God. Why weren't you answering?" Abby's voice was thick with alarm, sobering me up quick.

I rolled over and looked at the clock. It was already noon.

"I didn't get home till four, and then I couldn't sleep. What's wrong?"

"It's Damon. He's been acting all crazy since last night. We got into a huge fight the whole way home over Eric, and he doesn't believe I don't have feelings for him. You know I can't lie for shit." She started sobbing.

I sat up. "Hey, calm down. I'm sure it'll be fine."

"You didn't see his face. I've never seen him like this, Eva. He said if I wanted Eric then he's done with me."

God, I wish. "Well, do you want him?" I pinched the bridge of my nose, squishing my eyes shut.

"I don't fucking know! I don't even know him. I mean, I said I didn't, but I could tell he didn't believe me." She tried to catch her breath through her sobs. "Please, Eva. I've never asked you for anything, but I need you. I can't talk to anyone else about this."

Silence ballooned on the line as I chewed my lips, contemplating whether or not I could go through with this in the sober light of day. I swallowed, pushing down on the lump in my belly as my stomach churned over, wrought with anxiety that my long held secret would finally be revealed. That bastard weaseled himself into me like a debilitating fucking disease and, even if I purged it from my system, I wasn't sure I could ever really be rid of it.

But she needed to know. It was time. Whether she believed me or not, I'd deal with the consequences. I couldn't live with myself if I just let her marry him and never told her.

"I'll be there as soon as I can. There's something I need to talk to you about, too."

"Thank you. I love you."

"Love you." I pushed end and a bunch of missed texts from Blake popped up. I texted him back.

Me: Hey. I love you. Everything's fine with us, but I need to go see Abby. We'll talk later. XO

I combed my fingers through my hair and pulled it back in a messy ponytail, washed my face, and brushed on a few coats of mascara, not bothering to put in the customary amount of effort. I needed to get to her so I could get back here and explain everything to Blake.

Abby, I have something to tell you. No, that wasn't right. *Abby, Damon . . . he . . .* No. Fuck, how was I going to do this? Straight out. I'd come straight out.

Abby, I slept with Damon.

God she was going to hate me. I fucking hate me.

It was a long time ago, and I was young. Naïve. Please, let me explain before you freak out.

I tapped my foot impatiently as I waited to get my car from the lot. I slipped a tip into the attendant's hand, tossed my bag across the seat, and pealed out.

Less than an hour later, I parked in front of my parents' house. The driveway was empty. Abby's car was probably in the garage, but I left the driveway open in case my parents came home early. I skipped steps, jogging up the porch, and flung the door open.

"Abby," I called out. "See, I came as fast as I could. Where are you?"

I tossed my keys in the bowl by the door and took a few steps toward the kitchen when I froze.

Damon was standing in the way.

I'd never seen him so disheveled. He looked strung out, his shirt hanging from one side. Hair stuck up every which way as if he'd spent the night pulling on it, and his red-rimmed eyes were trained on me with a seething hatred.

I backed up a step, fear encroaching on my being like a smothering blanket. My limbs prickled to the point I thought them useless. "Where's Abby?"

"Where's Abby. Where's Abby," he mocked in an almost child-like manner. "Always with the where's fucking Abby. I should be asking you that question, you little fucking slut." Stumbling, he took a swig from a half-filled beer bottle hooked in his pointer finger.

I hadn't noticed that before.

Who is this? This isn't Damon. It was as though he was unraveled and shredded. It almost looked like the state he was in was scaring *him*. I put my hands up defensively, still backing up as he made his way toward me. Feigning the composure I wished I had, I attempted to reason with whoever it was he'd morphed into.

"Damon, it's the middle of the afternoon. Have you even slept?"

He cocked his head to the side and placed the bottle on the end table with the faintest of taps. Almost calm.

That scared me more.

Bloodshot eyes met mine. "Slept? For real? My fiancé is fucking some other guy, and it's all because of you and your little fucking boyfriend. You think I can sleep?" I flinched at the lashing his tone dished out.

Swallowing my fear, I straightened my spine. "Abby isn't sleeping with anyone. She'd never do that to you. You need to sleep this off and calm down." I reached for my keys.

But he was quicker.

In two large strides, his shadow cast over me. "Don't tell me what I need to do." My head flung to the side as the loud smack of his backhand filled the room.

I recoiled from the blow, sheltering my cheek. My eyes filled with water at the sting it left behind.

"Damon . . ."

"Shut the fuck up!" He grabbed my ponytail, twisting my neck at a painful angle. I screeched, clutching my head as he dragged me to the couch. He threw me down and my body bounced like a flimsy doll onto the cushions.

This can't be happening. Not like this.

My hands and feet stammered to gain traction, scooting until my back hit the armrest. "Damon! Think about what you're doing right now. She can come home!" It was all I could think of that might stop his assault. Reason with the logical person who must have still been buried in there somewhere.

"I—don't—give a fuck!" he shouted in my face. A burn smacked against my already numb cheek as he delivered his second blow to the tender skin, sending my face into the stiff plush.

Each morsel of me was shutting down, frantically searching for its hidey hole. But I pushed deeper, trying my best to ignore it while I gathered my pieces. *No fucking more!*

I ground down on my molars. "You can't touch me anymore. Get off me! GET OFF ME!" I pounded my fists against his chest in a fury, desperate to get him to stop. *God, I can't breathe.*

His face contorted into a calm, twisted smile, and I froze in terror, realization hitting me that my efforts would bear no fruit. He was determined and too far gone. He used my moment of weakness to hook his arms under my knees and yank me flat on my back.

Grabbing my wrists, he pinned my arms above my head. His hot breath coated the skin around my ear, his voice a low growl. "I told you, you wouldn't like it this time."

He pressed his lips to mine, and I pursed them together, squeezing my eyes shut. The wretched stench of booze and sticky wetness of his lips churned my stomach.

"I know this is all your fault. She hasn't been the same since she came to visit you that night."

I searched my frazzled mind for a way out of this. Blake's eyes and soft smile flashed before my eyes and tears pooled, swelling my bottom lids. *This can't happen. I can't do this to him.*

I needed him off me.

Turning cold, I looked right at the person I hated most, and fastened on a cocky smile, determined not to let him break me this time. I'd had enough.

"It is not. Maybe she just realizes what a piece of shit you are." I spit the words in his face.

Damon sneered, unaffected, and the air was sucked out of my heart like the whoosh of a vacuum, deflating any hope I'd had. "You think you're slick? Well, you're going to make it up to me. You're gonna to pay for ruining the one good thing in my life. She's mine! You hear me?" He paused briefly before determinedly adding. "And so are you. You just need to be reminded." He clamped both my tiny wrists in his fist, and I yelped as his weight bore down and he tore off my leggings.

"Stop!" I yelled, but the monster on top of me didn't flinch. Horrified, I was immobile to do anything as he maneuvered himself between the slit of his zipper. My back bowed with a dry heave, and I swallowed down its bitterness.

"You think you can hide behind that pussy boyfriend of yours? Well, think again, sweetheart." He took himself in his hand and rubbed his palm over his hardened tip, salivating over what he was about to do. The lesson he was about to teach me. "What's he gonna say when he finds out I was inside his precious *Angel*?" The hiss of my favorite name from his lips curdled the contents in my stomach.

"No!" I cried, trying to push my weight against his chest. He slammed me down again and ripped my shirt and bra up in one swift motion. "Don't do this. They can come home at any minute!"

"Good. Then they'll realize what a WHORE their little goody two-shoes is!"

He clasped my nipple between his teeth, and bit down. I cried out in pain. He usually wasn't forceful about it, but he was pissed and unwavering in his efforts to make me suffer. To prove his point. Any attempt I could make would be futile.

So I did the only thing I could think of—I shut off.

Turning my head to the side, I let thoughts of Blake and his loving face invade my mind as I blocked out what was about to happen. A tear leaked out of my catatonic eyes, seeping into the cushion. Nothing else would matter after this.

A sense of serenity washed over me. A calm as I detached myself from my body. With a soft smile on my face, I imagined a future that would never be as tears slipped from my eyes. My body bucked with Damon's movements, but I didn't respond. I stayed inside my soul. Out of my skin. I felt his hands all over me but imagined they were different hands. Warm, loving hands. Hands that were supposed to cradle the babies I'd never know. That were supposed to hold me when I was old and sick. Hands I'd never feel again.

The sound of my underwear ripping tore through me. He'd take the last piece of me this time. Pluck the final shard of glass and flick it in the air. Into nowhere. There was nothing left for me. Nothing left *of* me. All that mattered would never be anymore.

I screeched as he shoved two fingers inside me, my ribs jerking at the abrupt intrusion. With a disgusting smile on his face, he worked his fingers in and out of me, spreading me painfully wide.

"Tell me you want this."

I remained silent.

He shoved a third finger inside me, and I winced at the pain, but I wouldn't give him the satisfaction of hearing me say those words. This time he'd know it was rape, even if his sick demented mind was convinced I was a willing participant.

"Say it! Tell me you want it!"

I dug through whatever was left of me and forced a triumphant smile. If I was going out, I was going out with some dignity. "Fuck. You." I spit out. "This is rape. It was *always* rape. I. Don't. Want. This!" I howled, finally saying that horrible word out loud. Even though I was pinned down, I felt liberated.

His enraged eyebrows pulled low in the center. He took himself in his hand and rubbed the head of his cock along the slim line of my sex. As he paused at my opening, I held my breath, waiting for the blow. "Have it your way then."

Suddenly, the sound of a car door shutting and the beep of an alarm crashed over me like an ice cold bucket of water.

I was saved.

But my relief was short lived and replaced by fear. *Oh God, don't let them see this!*

I pulled my arms free and slammed my fists on Damon's chest. "Someone's here! Get off me!"

He jumped, pulling the blinds down.

I scrambled upright in time to see Abby fixing her purse on her shoulder and walking up the drive. I kicked him in the chest and leapt off the couch, frantically pulling up my pants and securing my shirt.

Damon stood nonchalantly, closing his zipper with a smug look on his face, and smoothed a hand through his hair.

Footfalls clanked on the stairs, and I pulled the elastic band out of my hair, letting it cascade over my bruised cheek. Then I grabbed my keys just as Abby opened the door.

"Eva?" She paused. "Sorry, I ran out. I . . ." She did a double take, thankfully not taking note of my state, and narrowed her eyes at Damon. "Why are you still here?"

Not sticking around for his answer, I blew past her. Jogging to my car, I squeezed the burn invading my throat.

I slammed myself onto the leather seat and skidded away from the curb. My knuckles were bright white, strangling the wheel as I took the turns at a speed that made my car fishtail. When I pulled onto the highway, lights from passing cars bled together through my tears. I couldn't make out the lines or one object to the next as I sucked in ragged breaths. I punched the wheel and the dashboard, screaming, and then cried harder.

I wanted to die. Plain and simple. I couldn't do it anymore.

He'd won.

He'd ruined me.

Everything was so blurry through my tears, I didn't see it coming. And then my head snapped up at the blaring sound of a horn, and I stared wide-eyed at two bright headlights barreling toward me.

Chapter 31

A FEW CARS SWERVED, NARROWLY missing me as I yanked the wheel to the right, sending my car spiraling to a stop. I put my head between my hands on the wheel and let sobs wrack through me. I wiped the back of my arm across my nose and took a few deep breaths, then put the car back in gear and drove a few more blocks to The Backdoor.

I stared at the familiar burgundy awning that had become somewhat of a home, wishing I could go back to last night. To the strong Eva who was sure she owned her own life. Who was ready to take on the world and the man who had destroyed her.

I fished around in my bag for the spare key Rick had given me and rolled it around in my fingers. Sniffling, I fixed my face as best I could in the rearview mirror before going inside and locking the door behind me.

I flipped a switch, sending a flickering buzz to the room before the lights came to life. I could have texted Jace to come help me, but I was beyond that. No one could help me anymore. I wanted it all to be over. No more do-overs or second chances. They didn't exist, and I had been a fool to entertain the notion.

I snatched the bottle of Grey Goose from the back bar and pulled the cork from the top, taking one of the rock glasses and filling it half-way.

Dropping my head back, I squeezed my eyes shut as the liquid fire poured down my throat. Rumbling surrounded the sloshing in my belly, and my head snapped up. The abrupt harshness of its intrusion was too much to hold on to. I lurched over the sink, throwing up what little contents remained in my stomach. Out of breath, I clutched at the basin, breathing in and out furiously, my eyes soaked with tears as I choked.

I dragged my arm across my mouth and looked to the right. Blake's seat sat bare, mocking me. The bottle of Grey Goose pronounced itself in the hazy setting of my periphery and I made up my mind.

This was the end.

With determination I stalked back over, poured another half a glass, and dumped it into my mouth, holding it there before letting it slide down my throat.

Then I poured another.

And another.

Another.

Feeling a lightness surrounding me, I snickered out a laugh, twirling with my arms open as I let the numbness take hold. The bottles blurred together in a whirl, eliciting another bout of strangled giggles. My feet moved in a criss-cross pattern as I tried to walk a straight line to the register. I popped the drawer and retrieved a handful of quarters. They scattered on the floor as I stumbled out from behind the bar, then I collapsed against the jukebox and pushed in an undetermined amount of coins.

I stabbed my fingers into the square button, watching the plastic tabs flap across until I found what I was searching for. I had no clue why Rick had this song in his bar and could only imagine it was for my benefit. Demi Lovato's voice rang out loud singing, *Let It Go*.

Childish? Maybe, but the words resounded so deeply. I scream-sang along and I let it all go, emotion tearing through me and flying from my lungs. Exploding from my soul. Finally setting it all free.

Setting young Eva free.

I pounded my chest and ripped at my hair, hugging myself tight and ridding myself of everything I'd held on to for far too long.

When it ended, my chest ached with the effort it took to breathe. I bounced off the stools lining the bar, making my way behind it when a glimpse of my swollen, bruised face stopped me. I cocked my head to the side as I brushed my fingertips along my cheekbones.

What have I become?

I smoothed down my shirt and swiped my fingers under my eyes, as if that would make me look presentable. Then I placed a hundred dollar bill in the drawer for all the alcohol I had consumed, tossed the glass aside, and chugged from the half-empty bottle. I slammed it down and my head followed, my forehead bouncing off the bar rail. If I could feel, it probably would have hurt. My heart rate sped up, an overwhelming need to throw up engulfing me. I leaned over the sink, relieving myself again.

When I was able to stand upright, I squinted, trying to focus. I closed one eye, then the other. Still, all I saw was a blur of melded bottles and wood.

I put my hand to the bar rail and used it for support as I climbed out from behind it. Though my body was buzzing and numb, the pain still sat deep within its confines. I wanted to erase it, but no matter how hard I tried it was settled into my heart and glued to my insides.

Somehow, I managed to lock the door behind me. The sun was just setting and Rick would be here soon. I couldn't chance him seeing me like this.

Stumbling to the driver's side, my fingers unsuccessfully fumbled with my keys. They clanked as they hit the ground and bounced beneath the door.

Fuck.

Holding onto the hood, I tried to bend, but a wave slammed into my head and rolled through my belly. Somewhere in my clouded state, logic told me I shouldn't be on the road, so I wrapped my jacket tighter around me, shamefully ducking my head to not draw attention, and bared down against the cold.

One . . . two . . . three . . . I counted each step that took me closer to my apartment. A little further and I'd be there.

My building was in sight, I was pretty sure of it, but brick, stone, and glass were all meshing together. I fought hard against the power pulling inside me to give in and collapse, and dragged my body up the short staircase that led to isolation.

But it wasn't home anymore. Blake had assumed that position, and now he would be just another home I had lost. That had been ripped from my hooked fingers and taken away from me.

Draping my hair over my face, I waved to the doorman so he wouldn't think anything was wrong and moved as stealthily as my legs would allow. By the time the elevator reached the top floor, my eyes were blinking drowsily. The saliva in my mouth had dried up to nothing, and a cold heat was racing up the back of my neck, prickling my sweat-soaked skin. I held onto the wall, squinting and dragging my legs, searching my bag for my keys when I remembered I'd stupidly dropped them in the street.

Defeated, all I wanted was to give in to the overwhelming need to lie down. To let the darkness closing in from the outside points of my periphery have its way and take me over. Drown out my line of vision completely and give way to the nagging numbness.

My shoulders hunched, and I watched my toes pull across the carpet, slowing me further. I looked up at my door at the end of the hall, wishing it would come to me, the fight against my own body too much to bring me there. Then I tripped, wobbling, and banged my head off the wall, which sent me spiraling to the ground.

I watched her then, young Eva, as I lay crumpled on the floor. She dislodged herself from somewhere within my body, floated up and turned back to me with a smile, then blew me a kiss and disappeared into thin air.

An angel.

She looked like an angel.

I reached one hand out, then the other because, as luck would have it, my legs were no longer attached to my body. Or so it seemed.

Just a little further . . .

Just a little . . .

Just a . . .

Chapter 32

BLAKE

THE ARCHES OF MY FEET ached from treading the carpet all day. Pain was starting to spread to my lower back, but I couldn't sit. I wouldn't. Not when she wasn't answering any of my texts or calls. She'd messaged me earlier saying everything was fine, but I had a bad feeling. A really bad fucking feeling.

I raked an unsteady hand through my hair, and then stopped the incessant walking and put my hands to my hips, dropping my shoulders. Something wasn't right.

Come on, Angel. Where are you?

> *Me: You're really making me nervous now, babe. I wish you would just answer me.*

Minutes later—nothing.

"Fuck!" I punched the wall and flinched, shaking out my hand. I hadn't expected the wood to be so unforgiving. I cradled my bruised knuckles and shook them out once more.

I can't sit here anymore.

I swiped my keys from the counter, each stride exuding my determination, and slammed the door behind me. The few city blocks to her apartment felt like full states as I jogged the short distance.

Please be there . . .

Please be there . . .

Please . . .

"Hey, James." I waved to her doorman, breathless as I scooted past him.

I jammed my finger into the up arrow and stuck my hands in my pockets, pacing the small space. When the elevator dinged, I stood with my nose pressed against it, waiting for it to open. I wrapped my fingers around the rail as I watched the numbers tick by, taking me to the top floor.

Be here . . .

Be here . . .

Be fucking here . . .

The silver slats glided open, revealing a blonde heap on the floor. My legs felt like lead as I slipped between the doors before they closed on me. It was her. *It can't be her.*

"Angel!" The strangled voice in my ears didn't sound like my own. She looked broken and discarded—one arm straight out on the floor, her matted head slouched on top of it. I dropped to my knees and brushed the hair from her face, revealing a purple swell over her cheekbone. The eyes I loved so much were poking out from thin slits in her lids, but they held no sign of life, and her lips looked dry and chafed. The stench of vomit and alcohol burned in my nostrils.

"Angel," I whispered, not knowing where to touch her as my fingers roamed, looking for a spot I wouldn't hurt her more.

"Eva?" My voice found some muster.

"Evangelina!"

Nothing.

I grabbed her chin between two fingers and shook her. "Angel!"

I scooped up the top half of her body and rocked with her. "Oh, baby, what did you do? Talk to me, Angel. What did you do?"

I moved her wet hair aside, realizing I was crying. I swiped the back of my forearm under my nose and placed two fingers to the edge of her throat, begging to find a pulse.

A faint brush at my fingers gave me hope. "Oh, thank God." I slid my arms beneath her and pushed to my feet. "Please, God, let her be okay." Her head fell back over my arm and her mouth hung open. She looked so small. So helpless.

I began to sob. "Hold on, baby. Hold on to me. I'm getting help. Do

NOT leave me, do you hear me?"

Running, I fisted Jace's door on the way to the elevator. "Jace!"

His door flung open just as the elevator doors were beginning to close.

Through the narrowing slats, I shouted, "Meet me at the hospital!"

His face contorted in horror as he stood there, unmoving.

"Come on . . . Come on . . . Come on . . ." I shook, waiting to shoot like a cannon when the doors reopened.

"James, call the hospital and tell them to expect us. She's unconscious." I ran past him, barreling out the door and took the stairs two at a time. I hoisted her higher, tucking her head under my neck as I ran. "Hold on, baby. Please. Fuck!"

My legs burned at the hips, and my arms felt ready to give way, but I wouldn't slow down. I burst through the doors to the emergency room, unable to breathe or call for help when a gurney slid in front of me.

"Put her down," a lady in a white coat with kind yet urgent eyes instructed.

I kissed the top of Eva's head before lowering her onto the hard tabletop. *Be okay. You have to be okay.*

A male doctor joined in my nightmare. "What do we have here?"

"I found her this way. I don't know what happened but the smell of alcohol is so strong." I bit back the burn that made my voice crack and grabbed her fingers as I walked beside them rolling her swiftly down the hall.

"Sir, you have to stay here."

Are they fucking insane? "No way. I won't leave her."

The female pushed her palm into my chest. "Please, sir. You have no choice. Let us tend to her."

They rushed off with the most important piece of me. All that was left was the short breeze of the swinging door they'd swept through. I fell to my knees on the cold, unyielding green tile and dropped my head into my hands. It felt like my chest was cracking open and pieces of me were spilling out.

I heard panting behind me, and a firm grip squeezed my shoulder. "What happened? Where is she?" Jace was hunched over, winded.

I used my knee as leverage as I pushed up from the floor and hung my head. "They took her. I have no idea what happened. She wasn't answering my calls or texts all day, so I went to check on her and found her in the hall that way. She reeks of alcohol, has vomit in her hair, and I could barely feel her pulse."

Jace's shoulders bobbed as tears fell from his eyes. "I've been so preoccupied with Shay, I haven't even talked to her in a few days."

I looked up, surprised. "Shay? Shay Goldie?"

Jace waved his hand, dismissing my inquiry. "I can't believe she was laying outside my door dying, and I didn't even know. Why the hell didn't she come to me for help?" He looked hurt and . . . confused?

"Has she ever done this before? She texted me this morning and said she had to go see Abby. Do you think something happened?"

Jace's eyes widened, and a look of something close to recognition took over his face. He looked back to the door they'd just wheeled Angel through and stared, seeming far away.

"Jace? Do you know something? What're you thinking, man?" *Tell me what the fuck happened to my girl.*

"Hmmm? No. I just . . . I hope . . ." He hung his head and cried even harder. "My poor baby girl. I'm so sorry," he said on a whisper.

"Sorry for what?" I craned my neck, trying to get him to look me in the eye. When he wouldn't, I grabbed his shoulders and shook. "Jace! Talk to me! Sorry about what? What do you think happened to her?" I searched his face for an answer.

"Blake, I love that broken little girl more than anything, and I love how much you love her. Trust me, I want nothing more than for you guys to work out." He paused. "But I can't tell you. It's not my story to tell." He hung his shoulders and slouched into a nearby hard plastic chair.

I started pacing in front of him. "Jace. Come on, man, you have to tell me. She almost killed herself tonight. Hell, I don't even know if . . ." I let my thoughts linger there. I couldn't speak the words out loud. If anything happened to her, I wouldn't survive it. That girl lived in me. She pumped through my veins. I couldn't be without her anymore.

I dropped into the chair next to Jace and hung my head in my hands. "I'll die without her, Jace. I can't even think . . ."

Jace sniffed. "Eva's a strong girl. Don't doubt her. She'll pull through this. She always does. The girl's got amazing will." He said it as though he was trying to convince himself, too. He put a hand on my knee. "She loves you, you know. She'll tell you in her own time. Just don't pressure her. She's bottled up so tight, I'm afraid she might explode. Let her come to you. When she's ready."

I met his concerned eyes and pondered what he was asking of me. I just couldn't. "Jace, she almost died. If I hadn't found her . . . I can't even think about what they're doing to her in there."

Glancing back at the door they'd wheeled her through, I pictured her body contorting as they tried to rid her of whatever toxins she'd harmed herself with, and I felt sick. The burn of tears were back in my throat, and I buried my head in my hands again as I anxiously rocked.

Jace rubbed circles on my back. It was easy to see why Eva loved him so much. "You have to trust me, lover. She's going to be extremely fragile after this. It's going to be like walking around with tempered glass. One false move and she'll crack. Do you understand?"

When I didn't answer, he jerked my chin in his direction. "I'm gonna need a yes or a no on that one. This is too important to fuck around. Do you understand?"

"Yeah, Jace. I got you. But I can't help her if I don't know how. You're asking a lot from me."

"It's not for me. It's for *her*." He pushed that last word into me with his eyes.

I understood.

Something in my face must have given that away because Jace relaxed against his seat. "You've already helped her more than you'll ever know. I have confidence in you. You'll know what to do."

Chapter 33

GASTRIC LAVAGE—OR GASTRIC SUCTION, WAS the medical term the doctor gave me when he told me they'd pumped my stomach. That was after I'd spent twenty minutes retching and dry heaving.

I drew my arm around my tender belly and curled on my side into a ball. I didn't know what they were observing anymore. There was nothing left of me to see. I felt as though I could disappear into the sheets and it wouldn't make a difference. I was already dead. The fact that I'd tried to make it official today was the nail in the coffin.

I dragged a shaky hand to my throat and squeezed as I swallowed what felt like nails. My fingers brushed the necklace Blake had given me for Christmas, and the burn in my throat crept up higher as I fought to keep my eyes free of tears.

Losing the battle, I let one tear leak from its duct, and I looked up, blinking rapidly. I wouldn't let myself feel this anymore. I made a fist around the delicate gold and tugged, breaking the clasp which held it together. Taking each charm between my fingers, I committed them to memory—the tiny specks in the top of the microphone, the intricate lines in the angel's wings, the small shimmer that acted as a flash in the lens of the camera. So detailed.

"Where is she? I want to see her!" Blake's voice didn't sound far, and I couldn't face him yet. My voice was hoarse, and I didn't have the strength I'd need. I let the chain fall from my fingers next to the container of melting ice chips and the pink puke pail on the small brown table they'd set beside me.

Wincing, I removed the blanket and held my stomach as I pushed from the bed. The pain in my abdomen radiated through me, and I could barely stand upright. I searched the room for my clothes and moved as quickly as possible, pulling them on with shaky hands. My heart pounded in my chest all the while hearing Blake arguing down the hall, praying I wouldn't be caught.

Flipping the switch in the bathroom, I avoided looking in the mirror. My hair felt thick with substance and caked together, and there was a deep ache in my cheekbone. I laid my palm over that spot and buried the memory.

Cupping my hands under a stream of cold water, I took a gulp before splashing it over my face and neck.

Without making a sound, I tucked my hair behind my ear and peeked through the door leading to the hall. Blake looked distraught as his arms flailed, pointing in the direction of my room. I pulled my hood over my head and tried to blend into the bustle of people. Moving in the opposite direction, I squeezed myself as small as possible. The ache in my stomach throbbed as I straightened, attempting to appear like a regular passerby.

A commotion ensued behind me, and I peeked over my shoulder just as Blake pushed past a guard and barreled into my empty room. "Where is she?" His voice was faint in the distance, but the weight it held was heard all the same. I worked through the pain and quickened my steps.

Once outside, I used the concrete wall as support and any sturdy structure that could aid me. Searching the streets, my heart sank. I felt so lost. The first place Blake would look for me would be my apartment.

As they had so many times before, my legs took me where I needed to be, and a few minutes later, I dropped to my knees at Bertha's feet and stared up at her. The break of day had just started poking through the bleak sky, and she looked solemn as she peered down at me.

I quirked the side of my mouth, drew my coat tighter, and resumed the fetal position, curling in as small as my skin would allow. I wanted to melt into her bark.

I hadn't realized I'd dozed off until the sound of a twig snapping jarred me awake. The sun was only slightly more pronounced so it couldn't have been long.

Blake.

My eyes trailed from the sad orbs of his, past his heaving chest, down to the flicker of gold dangling from his loose fingers.

I closed my eyes and picked through all of the people inside me, looking for one who could handle this, but I came up empty. Seems they'd all fallen for this man as hard as I had.

When my eyes reopened, they were blank, not really meeting any part of him.

"Running again?"

When I didn't answer, he continued, "You want to tell me what happened?" His voice was calm but the crack in it exposed his desperation.

I rolled my body to a sitting position and shrugged. "I had too much to drink. I guess I didn't eat enough today." I focused on the grass beside his foot, not wanting him to see the lie in my eyes.

"Bullshit."

My head snapped up at his abruptness. His jaw was tense as his eyes bore into mine. I pulled from deep inside myself, calling each piece to the forefront to gather my strength, and I stood to face him. Setting my chin in defiance, I crossed my arms over my chest.

"I'm going to ask you again. What. Happened. To. You? I can't help you if you hide from me." His tone was firm, but I knew him well enough to hear the melancholy laced through each word.

"Help me?" I scoffed. "We've been through this, Blake. You can't *help* me. I thought for a while maybe you could, but you just can't. So do yourself a favor and cut your losses now. Walk away. I told you, I'm no good for you."

Blake narrowed his eyes at me, acting as though I hadn't spoken. "Who hurt you?"

Damon's gritted teeth flashed in front of me, and I shook my head. "No one. You're being ridiculous."

"There's a fucking bruise on your face, Eva. Do you think I'm stupid? Stop shutting me out!"

Caught off guard, I reached the tips of my fingers to the sore spot.

My voice lost its muster. "I fell. You found me on the floor, remember?"

"I'll never forget." Blake looked far away for a moment and then brought himself back to reality. He lifted his fist. "You lost something."

My eyes fell on my necklace. "No. I *left* something."

I took a deep breath, bit down on the pieces of me screaming to stop, and made the statement that would change the rest of my life. "We're over, Blake. I was acting like a silly schoolgirl leading you on and it was selfish of me. I'm sorry, but you need to go. Just forget me."

His body stiffened, but he didn't move. I saw him clamp down on his resolve to see this through, and I admired his fortitude, though it snuck some extra sadness into my heart.

Maybe this didn't have to end . . .

My mind started weaving a tale in my head. Then I remembered what a life by my side would entail for him. I had to save him from that.

I found a new piece of me, one that clearly didn't belong, and I tugged on her and begged her to take this burden.

Blake's eyes softened. "I can't forget you, Angel. I told you that a long time ago. Second chances, remember? I won't let you forget, either. What happened to you was terrible. It's fucking horrible. But you have a choice. It's up to you now. You can throw away what we have and remain a slave to your past, or you can move forward. With me. What do you choose?"

Feeling my walls slam down around me, I lifted my chin, my face a sheet of stone. Through gritted teeth, I bit out, "I never had a choice. Now go. The fuck. Away."

He shook his head slowly, determined. "I know you don't really want that."

I laughed, my insides balling up in frustration. "What don't you get? I don't want you anymore! We're done!" I screamed through the slicing pain in my throat.

Never one to give up, Blake pushed further. His tone was strong, conveying his unrelenting pursuit. "Do your worst, Angel. But I'm not going anywhere. I know you're only trying to break me. It's not working. You're gonna talk to me and let me in and that's it."

I slapped him across the face.

His head barely flinched but for the tightening of his jaw.

I punched him in the chest.

Still no movement.

Heat bubbled up my neck as every emotion poured out through my fists, tears exploding from my eyes as I let it all go, bashing at him as if he was the one who had wrecked me.

And he stood, stoic, unaffected and unmoving, despite my efforts to hurt him. Harming him was the last thing I wanted to do, but I couldn't control my rage. I hurt so much. On my insides. I needed the poison out.

"Just go away! Leave me alone! I was fine before you. I was numb! I don't want to feel. What're you trying to do to me?" I cried so hard, the violent jolts were hurting my recently pumped insides.

He grabbed my wrists, stopping the assault. In a voice so calm I almost didn't hear it, Blake said, "Love you. That's all, Angel. I just want to love you. Every piece of you. Even the broken ones."

I crumpled into him then, my legs unable to hold the weight anymore, and I sobbed and sobbed, feeling wetness pool on his jacket beneath my cheeks.

He grabbed my upper arms and peeled me back. "You just don't get it, do you? I don't just love you. I'm *living* you! My heart *beats* you. My lungs *breathe* you. You're in my fucking veins!" He released me and raked his nails up his forearm.

"You're here." He jabbed two fingers into his temples. "And here." He scaled his neck with his nails. "And here." He pounded his fist against his chest. "You're everywhere! I feel you there. Like a whisper on my fucking soul." He lowered his voice and looked away from me. "I never knew a whisper could be so loud."

With more gumption, he turned back to me. "But you're always there. And you always will be. You're part of my makeup now. My me. Let me be your you." He took my face between his hands, searching my eyes. "I'll be strong for you. Live *me*, baby. Live *for* me. Please." His voice broke with that final plea, setting free a fresh stream of tears.

I covered his hands with mine and pressed my lips to his, committing their feel to memory. Tasted the sweet, wet saltiness resting between them, unsure if it was mine or his. Savoring all of him, I inhaled the smell of his skin. Of my Blake. I needed to keep this forever. I spoke with closed eyes. "I can't even live for me, Blake. You can't expect me to live for you."

Cool air replaced the soft feel of his mouth, and I opened my eyes.

"Angel, please." The crack in his voice did the same to my heart, but I swallowed down the ache and backed away from him, forcing his arms to drop to his sides.

"You said whatever I need, right?"

"Whatever you need. Just tell me and I'll do it."

Knowing it was the only way he'd listen, I took whatever strength I had left and turned cold, rigid. "Right now . . . I need you to leave."

"Angel, I'm begging you. Don't do this. Do you realize what you're doing? This is number three. There's no coming back from this."

Bug out strike three. I'd reached my quota with him.

When I didn't answer, he continued, "You're really gonna turn your back on me? Throw me away like I meant nothing to you?"

The hurt in his eyes stung deep in my heart, but I was done. Done pretending I was something I wasn't. Done trying to be something I couldn't. I stood up straighter. "I already have. Go away, Blake. I have nothing left to give you."

Something in him changed then, and I watched Blake's own gates come down, shielding him from me. From my demons. He tucked the necklace into his pocket and put his hands in the air, backing away one step at a time, his eyes never straying from mine. There was a small glimmer of hope showing through those gates, but mine held none.

A few yards away, he dropped his hands. His eyes emptied when he realized I wasn't going to stop him. He shook his head before letting a disapproving, clipped laugh escape those beautiful lips. "Fine, Angel. Whatever you need."

He turned and never looked back.

Reaching up and around my neck, the demons came to demand their right to me then, groping every inch of my being.

Claiming me.

Consuming me.

Tormented and grunting they pawed at my flesh, dragging me into the deepest, darkest depths of my soul. To join them as a fallen angel.

And I didn't fight them. Couldn't. It was where I was meant to be all along, Blake's name for me a sarcastic irony.

Every pore in my body opened, each nerve ending flailing in a fit of fire. Pieces of me crumbled as each cell shut down, breaking apart as if they were riddled with a virus. Whether or not it would result in death was irrelevant—I was dying. My heart gone. There was no more gray area. No more bubble. Only blackness.

My knees hit the dirt, and the world turned into a veil of darkness.

And everywhere that Mary went that lamb was sure to go . . .

The End . . .
For now

APPROXIMATELY 4 OUT OF 5 of assaults are committed by someone known to the victim. 68% of sexual assaults are not reported to the police. 44% of the victims are under the age of 18.

82% of sexual assaults are perpetrated by a non-stranger

47% of rapists are a friend or acquaintance.

25% are an intimate.

5% are a relative.

Source: *www.rainn.org/statistics*, U.S. Department of Justice, *National Crime Victimization Study: 2009–2013.*

Sexual abuse can happen behind closed doors or in plain sight and can start from the littlest of children to the oldest of adults. It's debilitating and degrading and can cause the most helpless of feelings in the strongest of people.

There is help.

If you are being abused, or suspect someone you know is being abused, please seek help:

Rape, Abuse, and Incest National Network

National Sexual Assault Hotline ~ 1–800–656-HOPE

National Sexual Assault Online Hotline ~ *www.ohl.rainn.org/online/*

Visit *www.rainn.org* to find more information and resources.

Acknowledgments

I BLED YEARS OF MYSELF into this book. Years. This was not a quick write by any means. So much time away from my family, not being present while my body was. A house left to self-destruct and family members that felt neglected. I know at times you didn't understand, but hopefully after reading this you do. These characters swarmed my brain, consuming it until I had every last bit of their story on paper. They wanted out. Needed to be heard. I love you all so much. For your constant support even when you didn't know what was going on.

So many will see pieces of themselves in this book. You all mean so much to me and I tried to incorporate as much of each of you as possible.

I need to begin these where this journey truly started. With a phone call. My friend Jessica on the other end who said, "I've been dying to tell you something. I wrote a book!" To which I told her, "Oh my God, I've always wanted to write a book. But how?" She took my hand in guidance and has been dragging me along ever since. She since has put out six books in less than two years and you now know her as the remarkable Faith Andrews.

I love you, Jes. For real. NONE of this would be happening if it weren't for you. I will forever be grateful you gave me the outlet to express myself and explore this side of me. In your words, "Stop making love to it (the book) and just fuck it hard!" LOL. Wise words, my friend. I tried. Thank you for brainstorming with me and helping me birth Blake and Eva and then patting me on the bottom and saying, "Now, go!" A million thank yous.

Since that phone call, I've raised a newborn turned toddler while continuing to work as a Certified Public Accountant and running my own accounting business, all the while keeping my story and my new friends on the front burner. It's consumed me. In my wildest dreams, I never would've thought this possible. During the last year, I added pregnancy and the birth of another child to the mix. So, it's been a whirlwind of events for sure.

Back story is, when I was younger, a street palm reader once called out to me as an afterthought, "Oh, and you're going to write a book." Interesting, I thought. I wonder what kind.

Enter a second psychic (this one after I began writing) who told me that this was my calling and that I should in no way be shoved into a cubicle with a boring job all day long. That I needed to be doing something creative. He said "I want you to hate it (my job) so much that you make the writer happy." He was hell bent on it and brought it up repeatedly during our one hour session.

He died exactly a week later.

I was sure there was a reason I got to see that insightful man and I will forever be grateful for his encouragement and his push. Many New Yorkers know him as Raymond Pero and he truly had a talent. I really feel he delivered a message I was meant to hear, as my appointment with him was moved up due to a cancellation. Had it not been, I never would have had the privilege. So my determination grew further. I was getting this book out if it killed me.

And it almost did.

Three years. Yes, you heard me right. Where most get a book out in three months, I bled every word of this book from my veins. I really hope you connected with my babies and enjoyed them. Which brings be to my next round of thank yous. You. If you are reading these words, then I am grateful to you. If it wasn't for you, Blake and Eva would be talking to themselves. Trapped souls in Neverland. I'm grateful for every one of you.

Now, on to my superstars.

To my loving husband, Fred and son, Christian. I can't even tell you how much I appreciate your part in all this. What part you ask? You let me do it. So many do not have that privilege. Instead of being met by a brick wall, I was given the freedom to work on what I had to work on whenever and as often as needed. I was encouraged and left to be. That is more priceless than you know. Thank you for always having my back.

For loving me when I'm "not there", and managing to not take it personal. So much of this comes from having a strong support system and you have made mine rock solid. I love you more than I can ever sum up in a little paragraph.

To the reason I am. My parents. From day one (literally) you've supported me. Always. You truly believed I could be anything and do anything I wanted , and here it is. The proof. I think you always knew I had something inside. Thank you for always taking any idea I had seriously. For never crushing my dreams and goals and standing by my side as I saw them through. No matter what they were. I'm a stronger person because of that.

And to ALL of you (my immediate family), stop holding us all in New York and let's move already so I have more time to write these! (Ahem, Alli). Alli and Tracy, thanks for always having my back. You're always the first to hold up your pom poms and push me along, believing in me as much as mommy and daddy. I love you guys and I hope that after reading this, you finally "get it". "Chance made us sisters, hearts made us friends."

To Joseph Anthony Crecco (E), (yes, I needed the world to know where Jace's name came from). Though he's not an exact replica, there would be no Jace without you. I know you're not his biggest fan, wanting me to change a lot of him because you couldn't see yourself, but he's PERFECT and the FIRST person anyone who reads this book says they love. So hush, lol. He's amazing. You're the Will to my Grace and I love you in my guts. Thank you for you. (And for him.)

Daniel Dash-Montera, "Yazzzz!" There's a little bit of you in Jace, too. Perhaps a whole lot. I mean the boy is fabulous. Without you, there'd be no yazzz. Thank you, my amazingly talented friend.

Kelly Siskind! Girl! My sister CP. They say you never forget your first. You've secured a piece of my heart, love. From your brutal truths to your unrelenting willingness to help me in my time of need and talk me off a ledge, your friendship means everything to me. And can I just say I'm so proud of you! Look at us!! What you've become from the time we met to now amazes me. I am grateful for you and humbled by you.

Faith Andrews, though you didn't make it to the end, your CP work with Live Me was priceless. You taught me the rules and the ropes and weeded through my garbage. I'm a time consuming, slow, wordy bitch (the opposite of you) so I commend you, lol. Thank you for molding me.

Barbara Wolfe. I said, "What would Live Me be without you?" Your response, "What would *I* be without Live Me? I shudder at the thought." And, there it is. To my editing buddy. No one knows that you saw almost as many edits as me with this book. You wore so many different hats in creating this, I don't know what to call you. CP? Beta? Editor? Connoisseur? Whatever your title, you're fabulous and my lifeline and lifesaver. What you mean to me can't be put into words. #pound.

Jena Mason Campbell. Oh, Jena. My cheerleader. You have fought for this book with some heavy gloves, girl. God puts people in your life for a reason and I truly believe you're meant to be in mine. Who would've thought one random day I decided I needed more betas and threw a post up on a forum I didn't even know how to work, I'd get an "I'm willing" email from someone who would become so important in my life and in shaping my baby? I treasure you and can't wait to keep working with you.

Heather Carver, what would Live Me be without Heather? Not sure since you helped me plot so much of it. You lived and breathed these characters almost as much as I did and could see their next moves sometimes more clearly than me, their creator. I'm so happy to have found you. You're irreplaceable and passionate and I wouldn't want to do this without you. Now on to book two! Expect a phone call.

To Heather Carver, Roxie Madar, Jena Campbell, Danielle Renee, Danielle Plane, Jennifer Diaz, Cassie Baker Fite, and Trisha Rai, my beta chicks, Thank you for reading and for your help and words of encouragement. I loved how you loved Live Me and how eager you were to help even with small changes. I can't wait for you to read book two! Love you, ladies.

A special thanks to my firsts, Heather, Roxie, and Jena. You're with me for life now. "Now, you can't leave." I love you girls. Thank you for loving Blake and Eva even when you didn't love pieces of them or things that they did. They love you right back.

Megan Hand, you complete me. And my sentences. Live Me would have been more hollow without your skilled eye and attention to the little things. In so many ways, we are so much alike. Thank you for going back and forth with me and finding the right story for Blake and Eva, and for your finishing touches.

Jennifer Roberts-Hall, foot-to-toot? What does that mean? I'm still not sure, lol. You're a gem. Your ability to slice and slash and dice is unsurpassed. You took this wordy bitch and attacked it with your samurai sword and I truly believe the finished product is a lot cleaner and easier to read because of you. Thank you for looking at the same thing seventy-five times and never complaining.

I need to pause because just writing this is making me realize how many people made Live Me their own and truly did love these characters. From texting or calling or emailing me asking for this to happen (or not to happen) to these characters. To random messages about ideas, these characters are not only real to me, but to so many of you. To that I am just amazed and humbled and a million thank yous.

Gail McHugh, Thank you for taking the time to talk to a scared nobody and for prettying my words at times. Your encouragement and guidance means more than you'll ever know. Five hours on Christmas Eve is no joke to an Italian! I bow to you. And Live Me is especially grateful that because of you she kept her beautiful name. I truly feel what started as a fan-girl moment has blossomed into a friendship, and I am forever grateful for that.

To my Indie Chicks Rock girls. You know you do. Your daily messages and words of inspiration are what keep me going most days. I can't say you don't know what it means, because you do. You all do. We are solid. Each one holding up the other at different points and to different degrees. You are all sister souls of mine and I can't wait to see where we go with this. (Cue Gold Girls song).

Barbara, Eleanor, Elisabeth, Faith, Livia, Niecey, Ruthie. "We started from the bottom now we're here!" Besides the fact that you rock, you girls have *been* my rock. If anyone ever saw those conversations, eh? Though it stinks they've dwindled, I hold all of you near and dear to my heart. You're each special to me and the bond we've created can never be replaced. Till we meet on a beach somewhere. Floppy hats for life!

Niecey Roy, my "Go-to girl". How many times have you tried to save my ass even though you're busy as hell? I love your willingness to help and your selflessness. You're going to find your zen one day and when you do . . . take me with you, lol. I love you, girl.

Najla Quamber of Najla Quamber Designs, your patience is unsurpassed. Thank you the beautiful original Live Me cover, and for sticking by what is the indecisive ridiculousness of me. And for working with me last minute on a new cover. You're a true gem and an artist and incredible at what you do. This cover is amazing because of you.

Lorie Rebecca of Lorie Rebecca Photography, you've saved my ass and restored my faith in humanity. You, my dear, are true to your word and a dying breed. Your willingness to do anything you had to has me floored. You're a beautiful person and you're passionate about your work and the images you create. Thank you. From the bottom of my heart, thank you. And thank you for giving Live Me a chance and connecting on a deeper level.

To Kristianna DeBlasio and Harlee Tanner Bartlett, thank you for being the gorgeous faces of Eva and Blake on the original cover. You guys were amazing especially so last minute making the effort to get together for me for this amazing shoot.

To Lauren Perry of Perrywinkle Photography, your work is amazing. When I saw this couple I just knew they were meant to be Blake and Eva. The beauty of your work takes my breath away. I can't wait for future projects with you.

Sommer Stein of Perfect Pear Creative Covers, oh Sommer how I tortured you. Thank you from the bottom of my heart for sticking it out with me and sending me countless possibilities. You're incredible with your gift and the new branding of Live Me is incredibly beautiful.

So many have stepped in to calm the beast when I hit panic mode. Reading pieces, commenting or just giving general "that's normal" advice. My biggest, BA Wolfe, Jena Campbell, Heather Carver, Niecey Roy, Gia Riley, Faith Andrews, and Gail McHugh. Love you girls.

Julie Deaton, thank you for using your keen eye to find all of my leftover boo-boos and for making my first born book baby prettier. And thank you for your patience when I held you off ten times because I just couldn't get her finished!

To my formatter, Christine of Type A Formatting, thank you for accommodating my timeline and for making my baby so pretty. The final product surpassed what I ever thought it could and it's beautiful.

To Xpresso Blog Tours, thank you for making my cover reveal, blog tour, and release day blitz phenomenal! You're awesome at what you do and I look forward to working with you on future projects.

To all of the blogs and bloggers and Facebook groups out there who pimped my page, shared my links and teasers, you have no idea how grateful I am for all of your support. For helping this newbie any way you could and taking a chance on me. Thank you! I owe a multitude of thanks to each and every one of you who post, share, like and promote me and authors like me. We wouldn't be where we are if it weren't for your help and kindness. Kisses to each and every one of you.

Lastly, to all of the readers, friends, family and random strangers who offered support and shared excitement, thank you. None of you went unnoticed.

Cupcakes for everyone!

XO

C

LiveMe Playlist

Angel ~ Sarah McLachlan

Heart Attack ~ Demi Lovato

Eye of the Tiger ~ Survivor

Lightweight ~ Demi Lovato

Blackbird ~ Sarah McLachlan

Possession ~ Sarah McLachlan

Kryptonite ~ Three Doors Down

Happy ~ Pharrell Williams

My Own Worst Enemy ~ Lit

Livin on a Prayer ~ Bon Jovi

All of Me ~ John Legend

I Want You to Want Me ~ Cheap Trick

Angel ~ Aerosmith

Home ~ Phillip Phillips

Vogue ~ Madonna

A Hard Day's Night ~ The Beatles

Warrior ~ Demi Lovato

Let It Go ~ Demi Lovato

About the Author

CELESTE GRANDE GREW UP LOVING words. From an early age, it was easy for her to open her heart through pen and paper and come away with something poetic. She never thought anything more than releasing her emotions would come of it though. A workaholic that can't keep still, in her 'real' life, she's a Certified Public Accountant who dreams of writing sexy books all day long. When she isn't working, she's reading, writing, mommying and being a wifey to the love of her life. She lives in New York, and is still putting pen to paper. Live Me, a new adult romance, is her debut novel.

www.celestegrande.com
authorcelestegrande@gmail.com
Facebook
Twitter
Instagram

Celeste Grande is a proud member of the Indie Chick's Rock group. If you haven't found them yet, you can find them here: www.facebook.com/groups/rockinreadersgroup/ AND www.indiechicksrock.com
#IndieChicksRock #FollowTheMovement

Thank you for purchasing Live Me ~ a Pieces of Broken Novel. Please consider leaving an honest review.

Made in the USA
Las Vegas, NV
24 August 2021